DEATH TRIP

Lee Weeks left school at sixteen and, armed with a notebook and very little cash, spent seven years working her way around Europe and Southeast Asia. She returned to settle in London, marry and raise two children. She has worked as a cocktail waitress, chef, model, English teacher and personal fitness trainer. She now lives in Devon. Her debut novel, *The Trophy Taker*, was a *Sunday Times* bestseller as was her next, *The Trafficked*.

Please go to www.leeweeks.co.uk for more information on Lee.

By the same author:

The Trophy Taker
The Trafficked

LEE WEEKS

Death Trip

AVON

A division of HarperCollins*Publishers*
77–85 Fulham Palace Road,
London W6 8JB

www.harpercollins.co.uk

A Paperback Original 2009

First published in Great Britain by
HarperCollins*Publishers* 2009

Copyright © Lee Weeks 2009

Lee Weeks asserts the moral right to
be identified as the author of this work

A catalogue record for this book is
available from the British Library

ISBN-13: 978-1-84756-126-8

Set in Minion by Palimpsest Book Production Limited,
Grangemouth, Stirlingshire

Printed and bound in Great Britain by
Clays Ltd, St Ives Plc

Mixed Sources
Product group from well-managed
forests and other controlled sources
www.fsc.org Cert no. SW-COC-1806
© 1996 Forest Stewardship Council

FSC is a non-profit international organisation established to promote the
responsible management of the world's forests. Products carrying the FSC
label are independently certified to assure consumers that they come
from forests that are managed to meet the social, economic and
ecological needs of present and future generations.

Find out more about HarperCollins and the environment at
www.harpercollins.co.uk/green

Thanks to my agent Darley Anderson for your support and friendship and to Maxine Hitchcock, a great editor who knows how to bring out the best in me. Thanks as always to my family and friends and to all the people who read my books.

For my children Ginny and Robert who have given me so much more then I've given them.

1

Mae Klaw Refugee Camp, Thai/Burma border, April 3rd 2006

'Down on your knees!'

Saw Wah Say forced Anna to kneel as he pulled her head back by her blonde ponytail and held a knife to her throat. All around them, bamboo houses burst into flames, sending plumes of sparks up into the night sky.

Saw's bare chest rose and fell, wet from blood and sweat, glistening in the hellish glare of the napalm. He stood over Anna and twisted her hair in his hand. He watched it fall like liquid gold through his gnarled fingers as he stretched her neck up.

Anna squeezed her eyes shut and held her breath as he ran the blade along her throat. Saw grinned at the other four young volunteers, dragged out from their hiding place and now held at gunpoint. All around them people ran screaming, trapped within the barbed wire walls of the refugee camp, whilst Saw's men picked them off.

'What do you want from us?' Jake cried out. 'We have no money.'

Saw grinned at Jake; his teeth were stained dark red from betel berries; his eyes were black as a rattlesnake's. Saw's head was shaved like a monk's but Saw was no priest. His soul had long since dropped into some place dark. Anna gasped and a trickle of blood ran down her neck.

'Stop, you bastard.' Jake lashed out. But Saw's deputy Ditaka was strong and he held Jake's face down in the dirt. Jake could smell the napalm gasoline on his hands. Saw tilted his head to the side to look at Jake. He grinned.

'You came into my kingdom. I did not invite you. Here I am God.' Ditaka pushed Jake's face further into the dirt. Saw's men began closing in on the five like hungry wolves. Saw threw his head back and howled to the burning sky as Anna whimpered and the blade cut deeper into her neck. Then his black eyes came back to stare coldly at Jake. 'Your parents will pay, or you will die. The world will know the name . . . Saw Wah Say.'

2

Johnny Mann was bathed in the pink warm glow of Casa Roso before he got anywhere near it. Two-metre-high photos of flushed-faced couples threw off an oozy glow.

'With drinks,' Mann said as he collected his tokens before taking a left and climbing the illuminated stairwell into the bar and small upper viewing area.

In exchange for one of his tokens he got a large vodka on the rocks from the golden-haired cherub behind the bar. Mann looked around. The place was empty except for a handful of bored-looking American lads who occupied the front two rows.

He took his seat and sat back to watch the show. On the stage below, a pink circular bed was beginning its slow rotation and a man, a woman and a bottle of baby oil were in position.

Mann suddenly felt the full weight of tiredness hit him. He'd just come off a thirteen-hour KLM flight from Hong Kong to Schiphol airport, Amsterdam. It was a long way to come for the weekend and he hadn't been able to sleep. His mind was a jumble of questions but no answers. Now, he needed sleep badly, or he needed a hard, punishing workout. But he wasn't going to get either. Instead he was sitting in Casa Roso watching one of the eight shows an hour, audience participation welcomed, and he was waiting to meet the person who had asked him to come all this way.

He rolled the iced vodka glass around in his hands and took a good slug of it whilst he watched the couple dispense with the oil and move into position. He glanced over at the American lads. They were trying to make conversation and ignore the act. Mann smiled to himself. He knew that if there was one sure way of spoiling their evening it was seeing a big black guy with a huge cock showing them how it's done to a white girl.

From his seat on the left side of the auditorium, back against the side wall, Mann watched two men emerge from the top of the stairs. They were short, dark-skinned Asians, wearing black puffer jackets. They bypassed the bar and sat down on the opposite side to Mann and stared at him. Either, thought Mann, they had been in the Casa Roso too often and had seen the same eight shows an hour too many times, or they found Mann more interesting. He stared back. Nestled against the underside of his forearm Mann felt the reassuring coldness of his favourite shuriken, Delilah. Shuriken meant 'sword hidden in the hand'. He had several such throwing stars: some were no bigger than a coin, individually scored along the edges and made razor sharp. Mann had firsthand knowledge of what

4

they could do. It had been such a coin that had turned his boy's face into a man's as it sliced a crescent moon into his high cheekbone; a scar which now always stayed a few shades lighter than his tanned face.

Mann looked across at the men in puffer jackets. One of them was texting; the other was now pretending to watch the show. The black guy was getting a well-deserved round of applause from a stag party in the main auditorium below as he managed to do the splits whilst still continuing to thrust. The Asians hadn't bought drinks, which struck Mann as odd. The bar was the only reason for coming up to the smaller viewing area.

Just as the act on stage was reaching its truly acrobatic climax, Mann saw a woman emerge from the top of the stairwell. She had long brown hair. She was wearing jeans and a T-shirt under a cream-coloured fleece. Mann looked and then looked away. It couldn't be her – the woman on the stairs was too young, only a few years older than him, forty, he reckoned. But, as he turned back to find her staring at him, he knew it must be her. She went straight for the bar. Leaning across, she kissed the golden-haired cherub on the cheek as he knocked the top off a beer and handed it to her. Mann watched her move; she was solid, armyish – she could have doubled for a policewoman the way she held herself, filling up the space around her with her no-nonsense presence. She picked up the bottle and walked straight over to Mann. The Asians in the puffer jackets got up and left.

'Thank you for coming.' Her English was good with only a slight Dutch accent. 'I am Magda.'

She sat down in the seat next to him. In the gloom of the auditorium the one thing he was sure of was that her eyes were the colour of bleached denim, beautiful but hard.

From the stage came different music. The curtains rolled back. The black guy had been replaced by an equally muscly white guy who was shagging so fast and furiously to the loud techno beat, it was as if the continuation of the human race depended on him, and he only had ten seconds to save the earth.

'Is it okay to meet here?' Magda asked as she looked down at the antics below. 'Have you been to Amsterdam before?'

'First time here. But . . .' He shrugged and then smiled. '. . . I didn't come to see a sex show. I can see plenty of those at home. Your email said you needed to see me?'

The email had come to him via 'customer relations' in Police Headquarters. It had said just as much as it needed to to get him on a plane: no more, no less. It said that Magda had been his father's mistress and that she needed to speak to him in person.

'It must have been a shock, finding out about me.'

'It was,' Mann replied. 'Why did you choose to tell me now and why did you need to see me urgently? What is it about?'

'Can I ask you . . . have you ever been to Thailand?'

Mann looked perplexed. 'I have, a few times, why?'

'Did you hear about the five Dutch kids who were kidnapped recently from a refugee camp there?'

Mann nodded. 'It was a couple of weeks ago, wasn't it? They were working on a volunteer programme on the Burma border.' He shook his head. 'The world is full of teenage kids travelling the globe like it's just one big Disney ride. It was bound to happen sooner or later. But something like that is every parent's nightmare.'

'Yes, it is.' Her eyes fixed on his, the strain showed on her face as she fought back tears. 'One of them was my son. Your brother.'

3

Despite himself, Mann felt a pang of something new twist his stomach. No one had ever said 'your brother' to him.

Mann looked down towards the stage. A female dancer had come on in stockings and suspenders and was laying out her props: a riding whip, a bunch of bananas and a large pink dildo. She moved energetically between and around the poles at either end of the stage, stripping as she went. The Americans leant over the balcony, they had fallen predictably quiet.

'Jake is eighteen. He and the other four kids were helping to build a school when the camp was attacked and they were taken across the border to the Burmese jungle. We have not been able to raise a ransom and we have heard nothing for over a week now. Please help us.'

Mann was reeling. To find his father had a mistress on the other side of the world was one thing, but to find he had a whole family was quite another.

'Believe me, I am deeply sorry for your situation but I am not sure I can help,' Mann said.

Magda looked away and stared down towards the stage. But Magda didn't see the dancer. Downstairs the audience was rowdy – the stag party was queuing up to take part in the audience participation slot. Magda's eyes were watery when she turned back to him.

'Someone has to do *something*,' she said, desperation in her voice as she fought to stop herself from crying. 'We are going out there, my partner Alfie and I, he is a policeman like you. We will do everything we can, but . . . but . . .' She looked at him as she shook her head in despair and a tear broke free. 'We have no idea what we are doing.' She wiped her eyes, angrily.

He waited for her to compose herself. 'What do you think I can do?'

She turned sharply back to him, steeliness in her eyes. 'You do not know me, but I know you. Alfie and I have followed your career. We have seen that you are a man who takes risks.' She hesitated. 'I know that you are not afraid to cross the line. I know that you were involved in a case where western women died in snuff movies.' Magda searched his face. 'I know that one of those women was someone you loved. I am sorry, Johnny. I understand your pain. That is why I asked you to come here. That is why I think you are the only one who can help me. We share some of the same pain. We both lost your father.'

It had been nineteen years since he had witnessed his father's execution and two years since his girlfriend Helen's lifeless body had been found. She had been tortured to death. The more Mann tried to make sense of his life, the more hollow he felt inside. He was haunted by memories. Sometimes he felt buried with the dead.

'That might be so . . .' Mann shook his head '. . . but I don't know anything about jungle warfare. If you have the Dutch government negotiating there's little else you can do.'

'The whole region is politically unstable, who knows what deals they are making? You have contacts all over Asia. You can find out what has happened to Jake – I *know* you can. You can get my son back. There is no one else who cares. He is just a boy and he is your brother.' Magda looked close to breaking. She shook her head miserably. 'I'm sorry. I would not have troubled you if I did not have to. Believe me.' She looked up at him, her eyes imploring. He did believe her. She was a mother who would do anything for her child and Mann was her last hope. And he knew she was right. Now he knew about Jake, there was nothing left for him to do. He had to help.

He smiled and nodded his acceptance.

'Thank you.' The tears in her eyes spilled over and she wiped them quickly. 'He looks like you,' she said as she pulled out a tissue and blew her nose. The Americans turned at the noise, but just as quickly turned their attention back to the stage where a group of lads was lining up to eat a banana from the dancer's vagina. Mann stood and picked up his coat.

'Let's go somewhere else to talk.'

They were greeted outside by a blast of icy wind. Flanked by the tall houses that leant over as if magnetically drawn towards the water, the canals acted as wind tunnels. Magda steered Mann left. It was Saturday night and De Wallen was busy. People and bikes were filling pavements and spilling onto the roads. Bikini-clad prostitutes smiled and pouted from behind their windows, their bodies softened by neon. They chatted to one another and drummed their nails on the glass to attract passersby that they liked the look of, and then they stopped to take up negotiations at the door. Mann looked around for the men in the puffer jackets. There were enough suspicious-looking types hanging about doorways to warrant paranoia but those particular two were not amongst them.

He caught Magda watching him as they walked alongside each other past the Granny and the Tranny quarters, where young men and old could indulge their confused fantasies.

'You're taller than I thought you'd be,' she said.

'And you're younger.' He smiled. 'The height's from my mum's side.'

Magda pulled up her fleece around her neck. 'Did she tell you about me?' she asked, not looking at him.

Mann shook his head. 'No.'

Magda nodded as if it was what she had expected.

The will had been read a few weeks after his father had died. Mann had been eighteen. He remembered his mother being led into a private room and emerging some time later, ashen faced. She had never told him what had gone on in there but that's when she must have found out about Deming's indiscretions. It must have broken her heart. She never spoke about his father again. She sold the house, got rid of many of their belongings and she never touched the money he left behind. If Magda hadn't got in touch it was unlikely Mann would ever have known about the existence of a brother. What hurt him now was the knowledge that his father was so evidently

11

missing something in his life that he had to travel to the other side of the world to find it. It left Mann feeling insecure, unsettled. His world had turned on its head.

'What about Jake, is he tall?'

'A bit taller than me. But I think he is still growing. He's just eighteen.' Magda's voice softened as she talked about him – he was clearly the light of her life.

They stopped outside one of the prostitutes' windows and Magda waved at the occupant who was dressed in a black rubber corset and stockings, and sitting on a stool in the window.

The woman grinned back and gave a small wave of the hand.

'That's Carla – she has been working this window for a few months. She does the evening shift from eight until two, or until she's had enough.'

Carla mouthed something and pointed to Mann and began drumming her long nails on the window. Magda turned to him, amused.

'She says special rate for you – suck and fuck, thirty euros.'

Mann pretended that he was giving it serious consideration and then tapped his watch and mouthed that he was sorry, he didn't have the time. Carla shrugged and winked back at him.

'She a friend?' he asked as they walked away.

'Carla? Yes. Sort of. The girls come and go but the window stays the same. I wanted to show you this window because . . .' Mann looked at her. Her eyes were burning in the reflected light from the street lamps, watering from the icy wind. 'This is where I met your father.'

4

Burma

Saw Wah Say ran on ahead and then stopped at the edge of the ravine. He shielded his eyes from the afternoon sun as he studied the horizon and craned his head to listen to the sounds in the air. He looked strong and fresh after the seven-hour march. He carried no extra fat. His body was stripped down to its finest components. He was born to fight and to run.

He looked down towards the teak forest below; there was no sign of a disturbance. No monkeys screeching or birds squawking in alarm. It had been a good plan to take this route. The jungle was a friend to Saw and to his men – it had hidden them well for many years.

He looked at his line of hostages as they passed him. Their wrists were tied together in front of them. Ditaka, his second-in-command, held the girl Anna by a rope around her neck. Saw knew that the others would not try and escape and leave her behind. They looked like adults but they were children. The girls were the ones that Saw admired. They had beauty and strength. He was fascinated by their blonde hair, their white skin, and strong bodies. He looked beneath their thin tops, he smelt their fresh sweat and he growled inwardly. Saw knew his men were dribbling after the girls and they would have them, but not now. Anna was his favourite. She always looked him straight in the eye. Anna would give him the greatest pleasure. Saw looked across to the distant hills, woolly and green as they rose in sharp peaks towards the north. They had another two hours' march before they could afford to stop for the night. He looked at the boys and felt nothing but contempt for them; they were babies. Saw had become a man as soon as he could carry a rifle. By the time Saw was their age he had already killed a dozen men. He stared at Jake. Saw had witnessed the affection between Anna and Jake. Saw had never touched a woman with a soft hand. Saw took his women when he wanted them. He never waited for their consent. When the time came, Saw would take these girls too. They would be his prize. He would make Jake watch as he raped Anna.

Saw looked back along the path they had come and he saw the setting sun set fire to the Thaungyin river that separated Burma and Thailand. Tonight he would leave his hostages and head towards the town of Mae Sot. Tonight someone was waiting for him and tonight would decide the fate of the five. In the morning he would hand them over. If not, they would be dead by nightfall.

5

'It's not my business, Magda . . .' Mann hurriedly stepped out of the way of a passing bike.

'Yes, it is.' Magda stopped walking and refused to move until Mann faced her. 'I used to work the same shift as Carla does. I need to tell you because I am asking you to become involved in my life, in my son's life. Now that you know about us – everything is changed. Besides . . .' She gave him a sidelong smile. 'I know all about you, Detective Inspector Johnny Mann. You will want to know everything.'

Mann smiled. She was right, of course. He was a detective; everything had to be exposed, every layer had to be peeled away for him to examine underneath it.

'I will answer any questions that you have. I have nothing to hide; all I want is my son back.'

They crossed over the bridge. Lights from the bars reflected in the black water of the canal. The wind picked up again and Magda dug her hands into her jeans pockets. They pushed on at a pace and turned west away from the canal onto a small side road flanked by high-sided narrow canal houses.

'How often did you see him?'

'About once a month. He would stay for a few days, sometimes a week.' She carried on walking and pulled the fleece further up around her ears.

'Do you want my coat, Magda?' Mann asked.

She stopped, looked over at him and smiled.

'Thank you, but no, I never mind the cold and the rain. I wouldn't live here in Holland if I did.'

'What business was my father doing here in Amsterdam?' Mann asked as they crossed the road. She looked over at him and shrugged.

'He never said what, exactly. There is a strong Chinese community here. Twenty years ago it was even bigger. There were many Chinese-owned businesses then.'

'In De Wallen?'

'Yes, some sex clubs, shops. But I am not sure what brought your father here in the beginning. In the end, I think we were the reason he kept coming back. He was a good man. I don't want you to think badly of him.'

Mann looked across at her; she was striding ahead. He could see what his father saw in her: she was strong, sassy. Just the sort of woman Mann usually went for. Maybe Mann had more of his father in him than he realised. That thought sat uneasily with his conscience. Was he like his father, unable to commit to anyone, always searching, never content? Mann didn't know the answer, but he knew that his world was too dangerous to bring love into it; people died when they loved him, people got murdered. He knew that only too well.

'You must have been very young when you met him.'

'Yes. I was eighteen when I started working as a window prostitute. I met your father about six months after I started. I didn't feel young. I was a kid with problems. At that time heroin became very big here. It took Amsterdam over for a while and I was hooked. I grew up fast after that. And – despite the way it sounds – I liked being a prostitute. I liked the honesty in it. The window prostitutes are self-employed. No one tells them to work if they don't want to. They look after each other. If there is any trouble they just press the panic button that's in every window and the whole street will come running. For me, it was a good life and I earned good money.' Her eyes were shining in the dark cold night as she stared at him – the streets were less busy now as they got further from De Wallen, only the odd inviting bar tempted Mann in as the chill seeped into his bones. 'I would have been happy to stay working but your father wanted me to stop; he wanted to look after me.'

'So what you're saying is, you gave up a promising career in prostitution for my father?'

Magda looked shocked for a moment, then saw he was teasing her and she laughed, embarrassed as she held up her hands in surrender.

'Sorry . . . sorry . . . It's so hard for some people to understand, especially when they come from conservative backgrounds. They think prostitute . . . must be a bad person.'

'My world is not in the least conservative, Magda. In Hong Kong it doesn't matter how you get your

17

money as long as you get it. It doesn't matter whether your father was a peanut seller or a king, as long as you make your millions – everyone is equal in money. What do you do now?'

'I work behind the bar at the Casa Roso and I help run the PIC – the Prostitute Information Centre. I give tours of De Wallen, show people what it's like in the girls' world, plus I go into schools and talk about sexual health, that kind of thing.'

'Whereabouts is your apartment?' asked Mann.

'Not far, the end of the next street.'

'Okay, I'll catch you up.'

Magda looked at him curiously.

'I have to see to something. I'll be a few minutes. Take a detour; go round the block again.'

'Okay.' Magda understood the urgency in his voice. She lived with a policeman, after all; she understood that they thought in ways and at levels that no one else did. She walked across the street, took a left turn at the end. Mann continued on towards Magda's road but the footsteps which had been following now disappeared. Mann stopped, looked back, then turned to hunt down the men who were following Magda.

6

Mann caught up with Magda, approaching her from the opposite direction. She was standing outside a block of flats that looked like it had been built in the fifties. Its yellow balconies jutted out over the street. Beside the metal-framed front door was a notice:

DON'T PISS HERE – PISS OFF

She looked relieved to see him and punched in the code and pushed the door open. Mann followed her in along with a noisy black cat with a pink collar around its neck. The hall light came on automatically as they made their way up the concrete flight of stairs.

They stopped on the third-floor landing. There were four flats in all. As he watched her find her keys he took the chance to study her in the light. Her ice-blue eyes were piercingly harsh and her square face broad, almost Tahitian-looking. Her toughness, her bare-faced attractiveness, was handsome but not pretty. But, no matter whether she was beautiful or not, Magda had meant enough to his father to keep him flying halfway across the world.

She unlocked the door at the end of the landing;

19

the smell of weed being smoked drifted out. The cat walked straight in.

'Alfie?' she called out and looked down at the cat which was meowing and looking up at her expectantly. 'It's always hungry and it's not even my cat. Jake always fed it,' she said as she pushed the door wide.

'Here!' came the heavily accented reply.

A large man appeared in the lounge doorway. He had blond, collar-length tight curls. His face was so scarred by acne it looked like fermenting pizza dough. His eyes were set close together and the colour of burnt caramel, fringed with lashes the colour of straw. There was softness, a kindness and honesty about his big face, Mann thought. He had on sloppy jeans and a large eighties-style, big-shouldered black leather jacket with a shirt that was patterned with indiscriminate blue and cream splodges. In his left hand he held a fat joint. With his right hand he took Mann's hand, shook it and he looked deep into his eyes the way that policemen always did – always looking beyond, below, never quite believing what they were seeing. He was older than Magda by a few years – Mann guessed mid forties.

'Was nice?' He grinned at Mann.

Magda stood between them, hands back in her pockets, looking a little embarrassed.

'He means the show at Casa Roso. He didn't think I should meet you there. I told him I knew you would appreciate it – anyway, I had just finished my shift.'

Alfie chortled and nodded his head as he dragged on the joint.

'Was good?'

'Was great.' Mann smiled. There was something instantly likeable about Alfie.

'Stop smoking that shit.' Magda scowled at Alfie. 'We need to talk . . .'

They walked into the L-shaped lounge, which looked like someone had hidden the mess rather than found a home for it. Alfie walked across the lounge and opened the balcony door. He took a few hard drags before blowing the smoke outwards and flicking the joint out over the side of the railing. Magda rolled her eyes.

'You could hit someone on the head when you do that.'

Alfie chortled. 'They expect that kind of behaviour from this house. We are the trashy end of the street, remember?' Alfie disappeared onto the balcony for a few minutes. He came back in and looked curiously at Mann. 'The street was busy when you came tonight?'

Mann nodded. Alfie studied him for a minute and then took off his jacket to reveal a still strong-looking man, but one who looked like he was on the cusp of loading on middle-age spread.

Alfie was about to throw his leather jacket over the sofa until a glance from Magda told him that he should hang it up in the hall where it belonged.

'We will sit in the kitchen. I need to show you some maps.' She gestured towards the door that led off from the lounge.

Alfie caught them up. The kitchen was organised clutter. Spider plants and saucepans on hooks. A collection of fifties cocoa tins. Kids' drawings. There was no wall space left. Above the sink was a signed photo of Bob Marley – that had to be Alfie's, smiled Mann.

The kitchen table itself was covered with maps dotted with sticky notes. On the wall above the table there were photos. 'Is that Jake?' Mann asked, pointing to a picture of two lads, one obviously Oriental looking, and the other tall, blond.

'Yes. Jake and Lucas have been friends forever. They have known one another since kindergarten. They are like brothers. Lucas's dad is a single parent. He's had mental health problems, depression. Lucas lives here most of the time.'

Mann tried to make out what the boys were pointing to in the photos. 'What's that on their T-shirts?'

'It's a joke. When they were younger they loved to play the Super Mario game with the Budweiser advert in it. They say it to one another all the time – "Wassup". We got some T-shirts done for them to take on the trip, just a joke, just something silly.'

Magda turned away, her face collapsing as she struggled to keep a hold on her emotions. Below the picture of the boys was an article about the kidnap that had been cut from a newspaper, and there were photos of the five kitted out and ready to set off. Mann looked at Jake standing with his friends. They were all smiles. He had his backpack on, jeans, 'Wassup' T-shirt – all ready for his journey of a lifetime. Mann moved in closer to study his face – Magda was right, he did look like him. He had the same high cheekbones and Chinese eyes. He looked very young, thought Mann. Too young to die.

Magda excused herself and seconds later Mann could

hear her crying in another room. Alfie whispered across to Mann:

'You had trouble? You left one man wounded on the street below? I saw his friend helping him.'

'We were followed. Two sets of men. I would say unconnected. The two in Casa Roso were dressed in puffer jackets and jeans and the two who followed us back here wore dark suits, expensive coats. They were all Asian. I took this from one of the smart ones.' Mann handed Alfie a business card.

Alfie studied it. 'This is from a shop in the Chinese district. I will check it out.'

'Magda must have something they want, Alfie.' Alfie shook his head and drew up his shoulders. 'It's got to be something that has to do with Jake's kidnap.'

'You lost me.' Alfie shrugged again.

'Was this flat Deming's?'

'He bought it for Magda.'

'He used to stay here, right?'

Alfie nodded.

'When he died, he didn't exactly have time to tie up loose ends. He was a man with lots of business concerns. Perhaps there's something here of his. Have someone watch Magda at a distance. We have to find out what they want. And . . . Alfie, you have to trust me on this . . . I will go alone to find the kids.'

Alfie nodded, resigned. 'I understand. Magda wouldn't make it anyway.'

'What do you mean?'

'Magda has terminal cancer. We are living on borrowed time.'

7

Jake tried to make out Anna, but she was hidden in the dusky light and the dense forest ahead. Jake hated not being able to see her. She was being led by Toad. Saw had nineteen men altogether but three of them were his deputies. They had given them nicknames. Ditaka was the oldest. He was short and broad shouldered, battle-scarred. His skin was sagged and wrinkled like old leather. He was always muttering under his breath, always bad tempered. He was the one Saw turned to for advice – he was the wise one. The five had named him Toad because he had a wide, downturned mouth and boggle eyes.

Anna looked behind her, as if she knew he was thinking of her, and she smiled. Her face was dirty, she was hot and tired, they were in a living hell, but she still smiled for him. Jake had realised in this last two weeks that he had always been in love with Anna. He had known her a long time but he had never realised what that feeling was in the pit of his stomach, every time he saw her. One morning, in the refugee camp, he watched her walk towards him, her laugh as clear as church bells – he realised *that* feeling was love.

Behind him he could hear Thomas wheezing as he struggled to keep up. He was the youngest: he had just had his eighteenth birthday. Silke, his sister, was the oldest at twenty. With his goatee beard and his big limbs, Thomas always looked like the baby amongst them. He was a sci-fi enthusiast, always on the PC playing games when he was at home; he was a DJ in his spare time. That's what he wanted to be when he finished college. Jake didn't really know what career he wanted yet. He would be going back to study history and economics at university. He thought he wanted to be a businessman of some description, the next Bill Gates. He wanted to make a lot of money and travel and he wanted to marry Anna. She was his first love and he hoped she'd be his last. That thought sent a pain that shot through his heart and caught in his stomach, making him catch his breath as he realised that it might be the only love he would ever know if they were to die in this jungle. If so, he hoped he could die in Anna's arms.

Jake looked behind.

'Come on, Thomas.' Thomas was lagging behind again.

Weasel was making pig noises at him. Weasel's real name was Jao. He was stupid, cruel and warped. He was tall and thin and laughed like a girl. His teeth were spikes. In the evenings, when they stopped and the drink came out, he was the one who tortured the porters and insti- gated the trouble. On drunken nights he wrapped himself in the women's sarongs and danced for the others. The other deputy and the most worrying of them all was Kanda or Handsome. He was vain and cruel. He looked at himself in the mirror that he wore on his belt. He was the one Jake feared most after Saw. He was always after the girls. He loved to watch them squirm.

'Ignore him, Thomas,' Jake called back. 'He'll keep doing it unless you pretend it doesn't hurt.'

Weasel often tormented Thomas as they trudged along. Now Weasel was alongside him, hitting him with a stick. The more Thomas cried out, the more Weasel did it. Jake had learned to pretend it didn't hurt, not to flinch. Weasel enjoyed watching pain. If Jake ignored him he usually went away. But Thomas couldn't do it. He had to cry out. Jake could hear it now. He turned to see Thomas stumbling as Weasel hit him every time he tried to get up.

'I'm trying.' Jake could hear that Thomas was close to tears, breathless from the effort. Now Jake heard the whir of Weasel's bamboo cane coming down harder, faster, and more viciously. The men laughed as Thomas screamed out in pain.

'Stop it,' Jake shouted back. Thomas couldn't hide his distress. He was crying and yelping with the pain and fear and Weasel's demonic giggling grew more manic and shriller as he chased him with the stick and its movement became harder and quicker as it sang in the air.

Handsome came alongside and Jake said, 'Make him stop.'

But Handsome only grinned at Jake as the noise of

Weasel's cane and the sound of Thomas's crying suddenly stopped, only the grunting of the men continued. Jake turned to see if Thomas was all right. But he was gone and so was Weasel.

8

Magda sat with her head in her hands, scanning the table as if she was too scared to keep looking at it but too scared to look away. She had taken off her long wig and now had a silk scarf wrapped around her bald head. She leant forward, resting her elbows on the table as she thought.

'But we want to help,' she said as she looked from Alfie to Mann.

'You will be more help to me here,' said Mann. 'You have to trust me on this, Magda. I will do everything that is humanly possible to get Jake home.'

Magda looked spent, overwhelmed by the hundreds of sticky notes, maps and other pieces of paper scattered around.

Alfie thought hard and then nodded. 'I understand what you are saying, Johnny. We each have a part to play. We must work as a team.' He got up, opened the fridge, and pulled out three beers. 'First we need to tell Johnny what we know, before we get all these maps out.' He came back over and gently moved the maps to one side.

Magda took a deep breath and rubbed her eyes and spoke quietly.

'It was supposed to be a fantastic trip for Jake. He has had a hard time in the last year, with my illness and everything. I didn't want it to stop him going. I was in remission when he left. This week I found out I have secondary and I can't have any more chemotherapy. I just have weeks left.'

Alfie took the tops off the beers and set them on the table, careful not to touch the map; then he placed his hand on Magda's shoulder and gave her a supportive squeeze before sitting back down.

'We live for today and today you are still here and Jake is still in the jungle. And today we have new help. We have Johnny Mann. We have hope.'

'Tell me from the beginning, Magda. How did it all come about?' asked Mann.

Magda looked down at her hands, gripping the edge of the table without realising she was doing it. 'They wanted to do something fantastic together before going to university.'

'Why did they choose a volunteer project inland? Usually the kids head to a beach somewhere like Koh Samui, just lie around and smoke weed for a few months.'

Alfie answered for her. 'Jake didn't want to go to the usual places, to the south, the beaches. They all agreed that they wanted to help someone. We researched it – found out about the Karen people who have been displaced from Burma. There's been a civil war going on there for sixty years. The hill tribes are forced out of their villages, they end up in refugee camps along the Thai/Burma border . . . They were going to help build a school there. We thought it would be a great opportunity for him.'

Magda held up her hand. Alfie paused.

'*I* thought it best to go there.' Magda closed her eyes and clenched her hands in mid-air as she shook her head emphatically. 'It was my idea. I was so wrong.'

'It's not your fault, Magda.' Alfie placed his hand over hers. 'You are not the one to blame.' Magda smiled gratefully at him and sighed deeply.

'So, what have you been told?' asked Mann.

'We got a phone call from the people at NAP to tell us that the camp had been attacked.'

'Is that the company that sent them out?'

'Yes. Netherlands Adventure Project. We got a call from Katrien – I call her the Bitch – who runs it. She told us there was likely to be a ransom demand. She didn't know how much then. But she said we should get our homes on the market, look at taking out loans, anything we could, as the Dutch government were definitely not going to pay.' Alfie gave a grunt of disgust as he swigged his beer. 'I tell you.' He shook his head with disbelief. 'She is the coldest bitch on the earth.' He slammed his beer down. 'She talks to us as if Jake being kidnapped is a trivial matter. They are supposed to look after the kids – they take big money from them to send them into *this*. She is a lying little bitch.'

'Alfie, please . . .' Magda held up her hand.

'Sorry . . . sorry . . . just makes me so mad,' Alfie said and went back to drinking his beer.

'What did you tell her?' Mann asked Magda.

'I said we did not have any money. All the parents said the same. We are all doing everything we can; we have our homes up for sale, but people are not buying at the moment. We don't have any savings – even if we did, it would never be enough.'

'She came to see us,' added Alfie. 'She walked in here, dressed all in black as if she was coming to a funeral. She looked around the place as if she was trying to see how much we were worth. Then she said they were asking two million US.' Alfie shook his head. 'It may as well be fifty million. We don't have it.'

'Did she say where the ransom demand came from?'

'She said it was from a breakaway group of Karen freedom fighters.'

'Did you talk to anyone in the government?'

'Yes, some stuffed shirt. They say only that the Burmese are doing everything they can to help. There is a Commander Boon Nam from the Burmese army who is leading the rescue mission. This is him . . .' Magda pointed to a photo on the board of a stocky-looking man with a moustache in full military uniform. He looked smug, vain, thought Mann. His eyes looked coldly back into the lens. '. . . but when it's Burma, who knows?'

'And then the political situation kicked off,' said Alfie. 'Suddenly we stop getting any news. There's trouble in Thailand, a military coup about to happen, there's trouble in Burma, it's politically unstable and they're killing the monks. Laos has fighting on the borders.'

The room fell silent as the fridge hummed away and the cat ate its food. Laughter drifted up from the street below. Magda held her face in her hands and closed her eyes as she said: 'We can't wait any longer. We don't have the time. *I* don't have the time. I must have him home now. Please God, before I die, let me know he is safe. They say we have to be patient. They tell us – it will be all right. They will survive. They will come home. No one will die.' She shook her head as if suddenly it was all too much, all hope had left her. She stared at her hands for a few seconds before lifting her head and looking straight into Mann's eyes. Her eyes were glassy like cloudy sapphires. 'It doesn't matter what they say. I am so close to my son. We dream the same dreams sometimes.' She gave a sad smile. Tears fell freely now and landed on the map. 'Now, every bone in my body, every beat of my heart, tells me my boy needs me, and every day takes him further from me and takes us both closer to death.'

9

Jake knew how much his mum would be missing him right now. He managed to slip his hand into his pocket and pull out the piece of paper. It was a photograph of them together on the beach. He unfolded its corner just enough to glimpse Magda's smiling face looking back at him. Jake didn't know what had made him print out the photo when they stopped at an internet café on the way up to Chiang Mai but he was so grateful that he had. Now the photo gave him hope that he would see his mother again. He knew that she would be thinking of him at that exact moment because they were so alike. Silently he told her that he loved her. He folded it back up and eased it into his pocket; he would not be able to open it again many more times; it was deeply creased where it had been folded too many times. From where they lay on a rough mattress of ferns and forest debris Jake could see the distant lights of a town. Across from them, the five porters, four women and an old man, huddled together forlornly. Saw had forced them to come with them from the last village they had stayed in. Jake hadn't seen them eat anything for days. They were being worked to death, carrying the heavy loads and never allowed to stop for a rest. He looked around at Saw's men, they were drinking heavily and fights were breaking out. It was always the same when Saw left them.

He had disappeared as soon as they made camp for the evening. From his place by the fire Weasel was watching Jake and the others. Jake looked across at Thomas. He felt terrible for him. He felt frightened for them all. Until today the attacks had just been threats: now they were real.

'If he comes near me again – I will fucking kill him.' It was the first time Thomas had spoken all evening.

'It's all right, Thomas. It's all right . . .' Silke wrapped her arms around him as Thomas buried his head in his knees and continued rocking. Eventually he went quiet as he lay on his side. Jake could see that his eyes were wide open. Jake wanted to say something to help Thomas but he didn't know what. Jake had never felt more helpless in all his life as he did now. He looked over at Weasel watching them.

'Silke, sit up . . .' said Jake.

'But Thomas is my brother. He needs me.' Silke held Thomas and hugged him.

'You will make it worse for him. They think we're all pathetic enough,' whispered Jake.

'I don't care . . .'

'No, Silke, Jake is right. Please . . .' Thomas gently pushed her away and drew his knees back into his chest. 'Don't worry. I'm okay.'

'Walk in the middle of us tomorrow, Thomas,' said

Jake. 'Don't give Weasel a chance to . . .' Jake stopped mid-sentence as Thomas rocked violently back and forth and moaned and cried. Silke went to hold him again but he turned away from her.

'You don't know what he tried to do to me . . . If Saw hadn't stopped him because he was in such a hurry to keep moving, he would have done more.' In the moonlight Jake could see Thomas's eyes were full of tears, his face stretched tight and terrified. 'You don't know what he did to me, Silke.' Silke put her hand on his arm. 'No. Don't, please, Silke, don't touch me.'

'You couldn't have done anything, Thomas,' Jake whispered as he looked across at Weasel, still with his eyes fixed on the group. 'That bastard Weasel is a psycho.'

'None of us could have done anything, Thomas,' said Lucas and he looked across at Jake. Both of them seemed to hit on the same thought at the same time.

'We need to escape.' Jake looked across to Lucas. He nodded. Thomas said nothing. Anna smiled and nodded but Silke looked worried. 'Saw's gone somewhere tonight. I saw him leave. If he's still gone tomorrow, then that's our chance.'

'How?' whispered Thomas.

'When one of the girls is tied to Toad,' said Jake.

'Yes, when it's steep and he has to hold on to the branches, then he lets go of the rope around our neck,' explained Anna.

'Then that's what we aim for,' said Jake. 'It's getting steeper every day. We stay close and wait for our chance. We take our time, then hang back. Saw's men will go ahead.'

'Weasel's always running on. He hates going slow,' said Anna.

'Yes, then we'll be left with just Toad,' agreed Lucas.

'We keep an eye on Toad, make sure Handsome and Weasel are at the front, and we jump Toad at the back. We jump him, cut our ties, take his weapons and run.'

'We will have to kill him,' said Anna.

'Who's going to do it?' asked Silke.

They looked at one another. There was silence.

'I will,' replied Jake.

10

As Mann left the hotel the icy wind hit him full in the face. He pulled the collar of his navy cashmere coat up around his neck and he dug his hands into his pockets as the bitter chill made his eyes water. It had been a long time since he was this cold – probably not since he ran around a freezing rugby field in England when he was at school. He had left behind a beautiful thirty-degree day in Hong Kong to come to windchill factor six below in Amsterdam. Spring looked like coming late to the tulip fields that year.

There was a lull on the streets as the rush to work was over and the tourists were not yet out in force. Mann cut a smart figure striding athletically across the cobbles, his eyes always fixed on the horizon. In the melting pot of Amsterdam society his Eurasian ethnicity, his mix of Chinese and English, didn't look out of place, though his tanned face stuck out amongst the pasty look of people emerging from a European winter.

The place he was looking for was situated on a side street in a five-storey merchant house that had once been a beautiful eighteenth-century building and was now carved up into at least thirty companies. Mann found the right intercom. He pressed the buzzer. There was a loud click as the heavy door lock was released and he was buzzed up. Standing in the hallway, he looked at the board of company names in the hall. NAP was on the second floor.

There was the sound of clacking keyboards and muted telephone conversations as he emerged onto the second floor. NAP was one of three companies that had their offices there. The NAP office door was open. There were six desks that Mann could see, laid out in a herringbone fashion behind a long, modern, wood and chrome reception desk. There were two men and four women busy on PCs and phones. On the walls were posters of exotic faraway places.

It was a plush office. So far as Mann could tell, it looked like the expedition industry was booming.

Mann went inside and stood in front of the reception desk and waited for the young receptionist to remember that, when the buzzer sounded downstairs, it usually meant someone was on their way up. Her black metallic fingernails drummed away on the desktop whilst she rocked slightly in her seat and giggled into the phone. She had last night's heavy makeup smudged under her eyes and her hair was flattened at the back of her head. It looked like she'd been lying on her back for most of the night but probably not sleeping. Her glitzy top revealed more than it covered up and she had the aura of stale wine, stale cigarettes and something else around her. When she finally looked up from her desk and saw Mann, she blinked, grinned and slammed the handset back on its base.

'Can I help you, sir?' she asked in Dutch, tilting her head slightly to one side and then the other as she leant forward over the desk to show him some more cleavage.

'You can if you speak English.'

She giggled. 'Of course, sir. What can I do for you?' She played with her hair. It looked like she could do a lot, thought Mann, except he liked his women washed and at least ten years older.

Mann placed his hands flat on the desk in front of her as he leant across. He gave a lingering look down her top and then he slid his eyes upwards towards hers as he gave her a big smile. She looked up at him, her eyes wide with surprise and delight. He could practically hear her panting. She was as excitable as a kitten with a new ball of string.

'I am here to talk about the five volunteers who have been kidnapped,' he said, a little too loudly, whilst keeping the smile. All other activity in the office stopped as all heads turned his way.

'I'm sorry . . .' The receptionist blinked at him a few times. She lowered her voice instinctively as she lost her smile; just when she was beginning to think it was her lucky day. 'We are not allowed to speak about *that*.' She looked over her shoulder and smiled nervously at an older woman who had been watching and listening. She had a nameplate that said 'Dorothy Jansen' on her desk.

Mann kept his hands on the desk as he gave a sweeping look around the room, before he stood up to his full height and brought his police badge out of his inside pocket. And, just in case anyone in the room was hard of hearing or had trouble with English, he pronounced the words slowly and precisely as he flashed his badge.

'Hong Kong Police.'

It wasn't worth a damn here but he knew she didn't know that.

The receptionist looked over at her colleagues for support but they looked away nervously and tried to act like it wasn't their problem. Only Dorothy continued to watch the situation.

'One moment, please.' The receptionist stood, wriggling her micro black skirt down from where it was lodged at the top of her thighs, revealing a hole in her tights, before tottering away on her skinny legs and oversized platforms. She disappeared through the door at the back of the office. Whilst she was gone Mann looked around at the rest of the team. Only Dorothy was smiling back. She looked like she was in her late fifties. Probably come back to work after the divorce. She looked like she had something she wanted to say but wasn't sure how to begin. She also had a look that said it couldn't be said in front of everyone.

The receptionist returned. Two minutes later a chic-looking woman in her late thirties appeared. She was olive-skinned. There was something Oriental about her appearance. She was five foot two at the most, size zero, short boyish hair with auburn lights in it. The way she was marching towards him as fast as her pencil skirt allowed, she reminded Mann of an angry wind-up doll in one of those horror movies. Her eyes were glued on him, beautiful but cold, hard and calculating: all black kohl eyeliner. Her full lips were perfectly painted in burgundy. In an otherwise casual capital like Amsterdam, this woman was a power dresser: a black, tiny-waisted jacket and a pewter-grey silk camisole tucked into the waistband of a black pencil skirt. Mann looked at her feet – Victorian-style black ankle boots with aubergine-coloured straps lacing them, plus stiletto heels – she was a brave woman, given that the whole of Amsterdam's centre was cobbled. She studied him as a female spider eyes a potential mate.

'This is our manageress, Katrien.' The receptionist smiled at him apologetically.

The woman's face remained stony as she said: 'Follow me.' This must be the Bitch that Alfie referred to. There would only ever be one woman in one office. Otherwise, like territorial rats, one would definitely have eaten the other.

Mann did as he was told and followed her through the office past the two rows of desks. Only Dorothy dared to look up as they passed. She smiled at Mann sympathetically. Mann winked back.

'Nice offices,' he said as they passed two open doors, one with a long hardwood conference table in it, and the other a lounge and informal meeting room with black leather armchairs and a wall of expensive artwork.

The fact that he was taking his time to have a good look around as he went seemed to annoy Katrien greatly. She glanced back irritably a few times to see why he wasn't coming to heel. At the end of the corridor they came into a chrome and leather office, glass on two sides with a window overlooking the medieval part of town. Mann could see the old church where sailors had come to pray for hundreds of years, after they'd used the local whores and got blind drunk in the taverns; their sin and their salvation neatly contained less than a few feet from one another. Belle – Amsterdam's brass statue in honour of sex workers – stood waiting to have the bike removed from its base.

The room had a hint of expensive perfume, under-tones of jasmine. There was an orchid growing in the corner but little else – no photos, no personal effects. Katrien's laptop lay closed but blinking on the desk. The room was devoid of character, thought Mann. Either it wasn't a place she spent much time in, or she wasn't a woman who liked to leave a trace. She closed the door behind them and snapped the louvre blind closed to block out the mid-morning sun as it cut a swathe across the black fossil-inlaid desktop. Then she sat down behind her desk and waited for him to sit.

He didn't take his coat off – there was definite chill in the air – but sat and immediately pushed the chair away from the desk and eyeballed her as he rested his forearms on the chair's leather arms. She didn't flinch. He could see that Katrien didn't intimidate easily. He could see she liked to be in charge.

'Nice orchid. Never seen a golden one before.' He smiled. She didn't smile back. 'Does it remind you of home?'

She looked startled by his suggestion.

'No.'

'But you are Asian, aren't you?' Her English was impressive but she had hardly any intonation; all her words ended and began flat – which was an Oriental trait, maybe Thai, thought Mann. But if she was Thai, she was from a region he had never been to.

Her eyes took on a new light, a mix of fire and ice, as she stared at him intently.

'I was born in Burma. I was brought over here when my village was destroyed. A Dutch couple adopted me. I am nationalised Dutch.'

'Whereabouts in Burma?'

'The mountains in the north.'

'You're from one of the hill tribes?'

'Very good.' For a second he saw a hint of a proposition in her eyes. This could get interesting, he thought.

'The Karen?'

'No. I am a member of the Lisu tribe.' They went cold again.

'Sorry. I only know the Karen.'

'Everyone only knows the Karen but there are five others: Akha, Hmong, Lisu, Lahu and Yao, each with its own culture, religion, language. Not all of us want the same things as the Karen.'

'What about the civil war? Doesn't that affect you?'

'My tribe is a farming tribe. The Burmese junta leave us alone; we leave them alone.'

'Magda Cremer isn't being left alone, is she? What's she got that you want?'

'Excuse me?' She fixed him with a stare that could have cut diamonds.

'Why are you having her followed?'

43

11

'You expecting a demand for ransom to come directly to them and you want to be able to handle it, maybe? Take your cut? Or perhaps you just don't trust them, is that it? Look, I'm impartial here,' he lied. 'I am just one of the people trying to help free the kids. Do you think they are hiding something from you?'

'That is ridiculous.' She studied his card. 'I don't know what you want, Inspector . . .' she placed it on the desk '. . . Mann. But we are already cooperating fully with the Dutch and Thai authorities. I am not sure how we can be of help,' she said, looking him straight in the eye.

'It doesn't seem to be getting the kids freed though, does it? It's been two weeks since they were last seen, since you sent them into a war zone.' She blinked; otherwise her facial expression didn't change.

'It is unfortunate – an unforeseeable turn of events. We are doing everything we can. I can tell you that they were going to work for five months in an established long-standing refugee camp set up to help the Karen. It is on the River Mae, west of Bangkok. Their job was to help build a new school and to teach the children basic woodwork, literacy, that kind of thing.'

'You send people all over Asia?'

'Only to Thailand.'

'Why only Thailand?'

'We specialise. We are a small charity. We prefer to build up relations with the local people where we go. We like to keep it personal.'

Mann resisted his urge to smile. God help anyone who got the personal touch from her, he thought.

'What happened this time?'

'They were kidnapped after a wave of unrest. Karen freedom fighters. Their ringleader has been identified as a man named Alak. He is responsible for the attack.' She didn't hesitate with the answer. She didn't fluster, she was reciting rather than reasoning, thought Mann. She had learnt her lines well. She watched and waited for a response from him, which he didn't give. She was definitely an ice maiden. 'I don't know whether you are aware of the problems the Burmese and Thai authorities have with these rebels?' she said with a flicker of scepticism in her eyes and a curl of cynicism on her burgundy mouth. Mann looked suitably perplexed. 'They have used the unrest to attack the Burmese government.'

'Why is that, do you think?'

'I can't answer that. The Thai government has been very supportive to the displaced Karen villagers for many years; they have housed them in refugee camps. The Thai government is not wealthy – it is a great burden for them – but they are magnanimous and kind to these people. But the people in the refugee camps still support the rebel freedom fighters.'

'So you think they want the money to use for arms to carry on the civil war and fight the Burmese junta?'

'I think it's likely.'

'What is the latest?'

'They have disappeared into the hills. The Burmese army are doing all they can to track them.'

'Captain Boon Nam?'

'Yes.'

'What does Captain Boon Nam think is going on?'

'He thinks that, as no ransom was raised by the government or the parents, they are headed north.'

'To where?'

'He thinks they will be handed over to a second group of rebels who have a foothold in the mountains of northern Burma.'

'On the border with Laos and Thailand?'

She nodded.

Mann looked at her coldly.

'You know as well as I do, if they go into the Golden Triangle, they won't come out alive.'

12

'The Golden Triangle is merely a name for an area that spans four countries: Burma, Laos, Vietnam and Thailand.' Katrien's facial expression didn't change.

'Tell that to the heroin addicts of the world. Next to Afghanistan, it's the world's largest supplier of illicit opium.'

'The Burmese government have done what they can to eradicate it.'

'Bullshit. It's their biggest export. The money from it is laundered into hotels, utilities, banks. The whole of the Burmese army is funded by it.'

She rose from her chair. She was clearly agitated. 'I cannot answer any more of your questions. I simply don't have the answers. We are cooperating all we can. We hope it will be resolved soon.' Mann guessed that meant his time was up. He stayed where he was.

'Okay.' He eyeballed her. 'Let's understand one another. I want an exact – an *exact* – printout of their itinerary before I leave these offices. I want to know where they were going at every stage of their journey and who they were going to meet. I want

47

numbers, addresses – everything you have. And I mean *everything*.'

She stared back at him, her eyes getting colder by the second.

'Is that understood?'

He knew she would have loved to lean over the desk and roar in his face. He was intrigued to see if she would snap. For a few seconds he watched her – he could see her contemplating whether to tell him to fuck off, but instead she picked up the phone and asked the receptionist to print off the itinerary. When she put the phone down she picked up Mann's card from the desk. She held it in her square-edged acrylic talons and studied it. Then she looked up. She could scoop out a lot of flesh with those claws, thought Mann.

'Of course, Inspector. We are very keen to cooperate with the police . . .' She held his card in the air and gave a one-sided, sarcastic smile. '. . . Even those who are not directly involved . . . The itinerary you require will be ready now. I am sorry I can be of no more help.'

Mann took his time getting to his feet. He was still trying to see how much it would take to make her snap. As she click-clacked ahead along the corridor he dawdled, stopping to get a good look at some of the expedition photos up on the walls. There was one of a group of children crowded round a family of volunteers.

'You in any of these photos?' he called to her as she marched ahead. 'What about this one?'

He read the title: *Orphans of the conflict*. She turned sharply on her heels, her patience exhausted.

'Were you ever a volunteer? You ever part of an expedition?'

'No. I am not in the photos and, no, I have never been on an expedition. Follow me, please.'

They walked back through the line of desks and the receptionist handed him the file in a kittenish fashion. Mann noticed that she'd reapplied her makeup and brushed her hair. He gave her an appreciative smile.

Katrien walked him to the door. Mann stopped just short of it. A group of eager-faced teenagers and their nervous-looking parents were waiting in the lobby.

'Are you still planning to send kids on expeditions?'

'Yes, of course. We have commitments. We believe the crisis will be over soon.'

'Do you? Let's hope you're right.' He looked around him at the plush office – the latest Macs, the freshly brewing coffee. 'You're a charity, right?' She nodded. 'You must charge a lot to send kids into war zones.'

'We do not send any of our volunteers into an area which is . . .'

'So you said – but that's exactly what you did. And – by the way – you keep people in camps, policed and without citizenship, dignity, work or proper respect, you are creating a problem – the exact problem that we have now. There are always people willing to die for a cause.'

He was about to leave when Dorothy appeared in front of them.

'Excuse me, sir. Mrs Cremer – Magda – is she okay?' Dorothy kept her eyes fixed on Mann. She wasn't going to risk looking at Katrien stood next to him. He could imagine she'd be glaring at Dorothy right now with those beady black eyes set to stun.

'Just about.'

'Please tell her that we are all praying for Jake . . .'

'Thank you. I will pass that on.' Mann was about to walk away but Dorothy still hovered.

'It must be especially hard, coming so soon after the last time . . .'

'The last time?' Mann could feel Katrien breathing down his neck. Something was making his stomach churn; he felt a terrible weight in the pit of it. 'What do you mean?'

'It's barely a year since her other son was killed.'

13

Mann found himself a sunny spot in a café on Dam Square, sat back and sipped his double espresso as he studied the world through his sunglasses and waited for Magda. He had an early evening flight booked back home, it left in a few hours. He needed to talk with her alone. He saw her coming from way off. He watched her walk across the square towards him. He still didn't get it. He could not understand his father having an affair for all those years and on such a scale . . . He knew that it was how it was with Chinese men in the old days, but Mann had never thought of his father in that way. Maybe if Mann hadn't been educated in England he would see things differently. To find out his father had conformed to the old Chinese ways of keeping a concubine made Mann feel at best disappointed, at worst betrayed. Infidelity just didn't sit right with Mann.

Sure, he'd had his fair share of one-night stands, some mistakes, plus a lot of good times. It wasn't that Mann had never known love. Helen had been a good kind of love, solid, sweet and dependable. He had never felt the need to look elsewhere. They were well matched in every way. She kept him on his toes. If she thought he was ignoring her she made sure he knew it. He had loved her as much as he could but it wasn't enough. She'd wanted kids, commitment. He was married to his work; he was committed to finding his father's killer and a part of him was too scared to love and lose. She knew that but it didn't stop her wanting more from him. Now he could see that she'd deserved more. He wished he had not let her leave that day. He had driven up just as the taxi driver was putting her case in the boot. Helen was looking at him through the back window with love in her eyes and still he hadn't stopped her. He wished he'd known then that the taxi driver was taking her to a place to be tortured and killed.

Watching Magda cross the square now, Mann saw the other side of being a mistress. He realised how much of Magda's life must have been on hold; how much of it must have been destroyed by his father's death. As she neared the café she caught sight of him, waved and walked over.

'Are you okay sitting outside?' he asked.

'Of course. It actually feels like spring today.' She smiled but her eyes were full of sadness at the irony of the world coming to life. She was wearing the same jeans, the same fleece that she'd had on the previous evening. She had a beanie pulled over her head. She ordered a hot chocolate and sat down opposite him. There was some softness in her pale face today, thought Mann. It was almost serene. She caught him looking at her.

'Sorry. I am on strong painkillers. It makes me drift away. Sometimes I find it hard to come back and sometimes I don't want to.'

Mann smiled. 'I understand, Magda.'

He waited until the waitress brought her drink. Magda cradled her mug of chocolate and closed her eyes for a few seconds as she enjoyed a brief respite from the turmoil and savoured the sun on her face.

'I went to the NAP offices this morning. I found the manageress, Katrien – the one Alfie calls "the Bitch". I can see what he means.' Mann set his cup down. Magda spooned the frothy cream from her chocolate into her mouth. 'I think she's not telling us anywhere near as much as she could,' Mann continued. 'I want Alfie to follow her. I want to know all about her. I want you to keep the pressure up on her every day, Magda, you and the other parents. You need to get more vocal. You need to stamp your foot in the government departments. Don't let them ease off.'

'I can do that.' Magda stirred her chocolate vigorously, her spirit returning.

'I also want you both to look into NAP's business. Find out what projects they have completed. There is a woman in the office called Dorothy Jansen.'

'I know her. She's a nice lady.'

'Get her on your side and get her to pry into Katrien's life, personal and professional. Who is she? I want to know everything about her and NAP. Find out everything you can about what they do. There is nothing like having an insider, Magda. Get Dorothy to help, discreetly.'

'Thank you, Johnny.' She smiled gratefully at him over her chocolate. 'I feel so much better knowing that you are helping.'

It was a nice smile, thought Mann. But he didn't know how long it would be there. He hated to make her life any worse right now but he had something to ask her – something that had been bugging him since this morning. He set his cup down and looked at her.

'Magda, who is Daniel?'

She looked at him, shocked for a few seconds as her eyes searched his face in a panic. Then they softened and the pained, numb look returned as her face drained of all colour. She stared down at the hot chocolate.

'Daniel was my eldest son.'

'He was also my father's?'

'Yes.'

'What happened to him?'

Magda kept her eyes on the table as she spoke.

'Daniel was twenty-one when he decided to go off on his travels. He also wanted an adventure and he signed up for a volunteer programme at NAP. He spent three months moving around Thailand, working on various programmes until it was nearly time for him to come home. He had one week left. It was Christmas. Jake and I arranged to join him to spend it together. Alfie couldn't come; he was working on a case. I didn't mind, I thought it might be the last time my sons would want to holiday with me.' She looked fleetingly up at Mann, as if seeking reassurance. He smiled at her and leant closer across the table so he could hear her voice, which had gone quiet.

'Afterwards we were all going to come home together. Daniel was going to go to university later that year. I booked for us to stay in a place on the beach. Patong Beach in Phuket. I thought it would be a good place for all of us – not too quiet for the boys, a nice pool for me. It was a lovely Christmas. It had been a great evening – lots of carols on the beach, lots of hugs. So many things to look forward to, with Daniel going to university, Jake doing well in his exams, learning to drive, playing his sports; we were really happy. We talked of everything, about when they were boys, about their father. We even talked about finding you. Both of the boys wanted to.'

She looked up at Mann. 'I am glad we had that time. The next morning we met up just before eight and went for a morning walk on the beach to get some appetite for breakfast. The minute we walked out there we looked at each other – everything looked strange. The beach was so big and bare. It looked like mud and there were so many fish left in pools. Children started playing in the new pools. Everyone on the beach was saying, "Isn't it strange?" Then we heard some people shouting. Some locals were running and screaming and pointing to the horizon. When I looked up I saw that the horizon was not as it should be. It was tall, raised, a blue wall, coming so fast towards us. People started to scream and to run. We didn't understand. Daniel said, "I think we should go quick, Mum, something isn't right." Suddenly our feet were submerged, the beach was covered in water up to our knees. We started running. It was so hard to run in the water which was rising so fast. Children were screaming, everything from the beach was lifting up, tables, chairs, all rushing forward. I didn't dare look back, I knew something terrible was coming. I heard the noise of the water, it roared in my ears, and the sound of screaming. We climbed over our hotel wall. The water had already come over to fill the swimming pool. People were just pointing and screaming from the windows above us. Screaming to us to run, to get up, to hurry. I knew it was coming. The water was so loud. It was close behind me. Then I was picked up into the air. The wave picked me up like I was nothing and it carried me up and over the hotel pool. People were swallowed, furniture crashed into us. My boys were close to me. I could see Jake so frightened. I could hear Daniel shouting to him to try and grab on to something. And then the wave pushed us up onto a balcony on the first floor of the hotel. We managed to climb into a room. The water was in there up to our knees. There were other people in there, a family. We waited huddled together as we looked down, out onto the street where the restaurants and shops had been. We saw people drowning, desperately trying to hang on to anything. Dogs yelping, children and people screaming, crying for each other. People shouting. People screaming in pain. So many people were hurt, glass broken everywhere – people bleeding, people dead in the water, people desperately clinging to anything to stop from being washed away, the wave was so powerful. Then people started to shout: "It's coming! The water's coming again!"' Magda jolted the cup in her fear as her hand shot out, reliving the memory. Her face was flushed, her eyes wide. She was breathing hard.

'We knew we had to get out.' She looked up at Mann, experiencing the terror all over again. 'The water in the room was starting to rise. We were already waist deep in it. Daniel led us outside to the landing and there were the steps to the roof. We looked up – we could see that there were others there. One girl was crying below us. Her mother was trapped. We were running up the stairs. I looked at Daniel and I knew he was not going to come with us. I knew he was turning back, looking at the water rushing in at the base of the stairs, it surged so fast and strong and . . . I knew that he was going to go and help her and I knew that . . .' She stopped and her voice broke as a sob caught her breath. She clasped her hand to her mouth to stop it from escaping and she squeezed her eyes shut to try and hold back the wrenching sorrow that was about to erupt from her throat. She took a few deep breaths and stared out at the passersby, the tourists and the backpackers, the pigeons and the children playing, and then she turned back, her eyes swimming with tears.

'I would have given my life for his but I could not stop him. He said to me, "I love you, Mum", and he was gone, swallowed by the water. We found his body four days later.'

She stared at Mann, stony pale now. 'I had to identify him. He was lying in a row of hundreds of bodies. I saw him from the far end. I knew it was him right away. I recognised his big feet.' Her face strained as she smiled. She caught her breath for a few seconds. 'Ever since he was a baby he had very big feet.' She looked at Mann, her eyes now blue icebergs swimming in an ocean of sorrow. 'It's been sixteen months and twenty-three days since your brother, Daniel, died.' She turned back. 'Please, I cannot lose both my sons.'

Mann looked at her and he felt something he never thought he would – loss for a brother he had never met. He felt the hollowness inside him fill. He knew Magda was right. He had to save Jake.

14

Burma

The next morning Saw had not returned and the five set off under the leadership of the three deputies. Toad was leading Anna by the neck. Thomas and Silke were near her at the back and Jake was just behind Lucas at the front.

'This is it, Lucas. This is our chance.' Jake spoke to Lucas's back as they pulled themselves up the steep hill. Lucas didn't answer; he seemed to be finding it tough going. Jake looked back at Anna. She fixed her eyes on his and he knew she agreed; this was the time. Silke looked at the same time and she moved closer to Anna.

Handsome came alongside and ordered Jake and Lucas to walk quicker. Jake pretended to have a burst of speed but Lucas couldn't manage anything. He had been walking slowly all morning and he'd been quiet. Jake waited till Handsome passed before he spoke to Lucas.

'Hey, Lucas . . . Wassup, dude? You all right?' He seemed to be stumbling more than walking.

Lucas answered but he didn't turn around.

'Just so fucking tired. I'll be all right.'

Jake looked over at the distant hills that were catching the first pink rays of the sun. 'We need to go for it now. Saw isn't here.'

'Yes. We'll do it now.' Lucas still didn't look at Jake.

'What is it, Lucas?'

'My stomach kills.'

Either side of them, Saw's men fanned out into the forest. The mule, laden with bags, plodded on, snorting as it went. The five porters were bent double beneath the weight of their heavy packs.

Jake looked back at Anna. He wished she wasn't the one tied to Toad but he could see that Toad's hold on her was slackening. He was finding it hard work, winding his way upwards through the trees. Jake could see he was ready to let go and so could Anna. She fixed him with a look that said, 'It's time.'

Jake whispered to Lucas, 'It's now, Lucas. Let's fall back a bit more.'

Lucas didn't answer but his feet slowed to almost a stop.

Jake looked behind; Anna and Toad had nearly caught up with them. Toad was distracted; he was looking at his feet. He had let go of the rope. Jake looked at Thomas; he nodded back. Jake bent down and picked up a stout piece of branch and kept it hidden against his body. He looked back at Thomas. He had done the same. Thomas had a look in his eye that told Jake he wasn't going to back down. They would hit him, one from the back, one from the front. Silke

60

slipped in behind Anna. The others slowed until they were just in front of Toad and Anna. Jake turned the branch in his hands and gripped the end with both hands. Thomas stood behind Toad's shoulder – Thomas was ready. Jake looked up at Lucas.

'You ready, Lucas?'

Lucas didn't answer.

'NOW!'

But Lucas wasn't looking at Jake, he was stumbling. Lucas grabbed at a branch to try and steady himself; it snapped off in his hand and he smashed his shoulder into the tree trunk and slipped to the ground. He lay there panting and Jake looked up to see Saw was looking straight at him.

15

After Mann had left for the airport, Alfie followed Katrien out of the NAP offices and watched her get into a cab. He got on his bike and followed. An expensive-looking woman like her wasn't going to live far out of town. He was right: she lived the other side of the Jordaan. She had an apartment overlooking a wide cobbled avenue in the rich part of town. He stayed out of sight, watched her get out of the taxi and then waited outside. He saw the light go on on the top floor. He saw her reflection in the window as she drew the curtains. Now he was sure of where she lived he would come back the next morning.

Katrien finished fixing her makeup in the bathroom. She chopped up a fat line of coke on a mirror and snorted it through a five-hundred-euro note. She never got over the thrill of snorting coke using big money: the smell of the money and the high from the coke went together. She closed her eyes and screwed up her face as the pain hit the top of her nose, between her eyes. She sniffed hard and set herself out another line for later. When she'd finished checking her makeup, she rested her foot on the side of the bath and twisted around to fasten her stocking. She smiled at her reflection in the mirror. It didn't get much better than this – coke and money and sex. She congratulated herself: Katrien was a clever girl and she wasn't going to let anyone fuck it up for her. Things might not have gone to plan but she would still come out of this a winner. She finished putting on her stockings, her lacy black thong and her peephole bra, before slipping on her black six-inch stilettos. She walked out of the bathroom but then doubled back to snort the other line. Back in the bedroom she poured herself a glass of Bollinger and sat down to wait for her PC to start up.

'Hello, darling.' She pouted into the camera, dipped her finger into the cold glass of Bollinger and ran it beneath the lace of her bra cup as she played with her nipples. 'Have you been a good boy? Because I've got something nice for you – you're going to like it. Are you ready?'

There was a pause as she read the typed reply.

Katrien gave a stamp of her stiletto.

'Don't ask me that now – you'll spoil the mood. No, I didn't find it yet . . . I have told you, I will get it. We will have revenge one way or another. Remember, it wasn't just your life that was ruined. Now, stay calm. Move them north. Hand them over and we will get what is rightfully ours. It will all be over soon, my darling. Anyway . . .' She rolled her eyes and smiled. 'I know you care about *that*, don't you, my darling? But this is also something you care about, isn't it? I have a surprise for you that you are going to like very much.' She stood and played with the tie sides to her panties. 'Are you ready?' She undid the sides of her panties and let them fall. She adjusted the chair so that the webcam could see her and she sat down and opened her legs wide, leaned into the webcam and whispered, 'I have seen him. The game has started.'

16

The next morning Alfie waited until Katrien went to work, then he parked outside her apartment and buzzed all of the flats until someone kindly released the front door catch. He headed up the stone staircase to the top floor. He walked to the door and took out his handy breaking-in kit, which he had used when he was a wayward youngster and which still served him today as a cop.

He was a little out of practice and it took him a few minutes, but soon enough he was in. The alarm started beeping. Alfie slipped a small tin from his pocket, flipped it open and pulled out what looked like a woman's makeup brush with a powder canister attached. He brushed the keypad, leaving a trace of charcoal on three numbers on the pad. The alarm beeped faster, louder. Alfie looked at the four dark squares: one, nine and six. Now, what was the order? He tried them numerically. 'Error' came up on the pad; he pressed clear and thought about it. She was forty. He knew that much. He pressed one, nine, six and six, the year she was born – and the alarm stopped beeping. Alfie held his breath – was it about to go ballistic? He waited, ready to run, but no. Alfie stepped inside. He raised his eyebrows and looked around appreciatively. She had good taste. It was the opposite of his and Magda's place. This was chic and minimal – and very expensive. It was gadget world. He had no idea how she afforded this kind of luxury on her salary. The kitchen was black marble, as was the bathroom. Alfie looked at the mirror beside the bath; he wet his finger and dabbed it on the white trail, then he tasted it.

He walked into her bedroom, animal fur, teak furniture, black walnut floor. For a minute he thought it doubled as an office because it had a PC, until he saw the biggest webcam he had ever seen. She was big into Skype, thought Alfie. He jogged the table as he passed and the screen lit up.

She had left herself signed in. Big mistake, thought Alfie. He sat down at her desk and opened her contacts. She had ten new emails. He guessed this was a personal account. Not many people called themselves katcream69, not at work anyway. He opened her emails. Most of them were from different men. They appeared to be clients, lovers. That must be how she afforded this apartment, thought Alfie; either Katrien was a highly paid call girl or she dealt in some heavy-duty drugs. One of them was an appointment for the following day, Friday, at the Erotica Museum. Alfie tried to access her other accounts. Two others came up when prompted. Alfie pressed the link for 'forgotten password'. He was presented with two questions. The place she was born and her favourite colour. He wrote down the email addresses and shut the PC down.

Alfie got outside and called his friend in surveillance – he would need a concealed camera. He smiled to himself. Now Alfie was about to uncover a lot more about Katrien than she would willingly show him. He might not fancy her but the Bitch performing sex acts on the webcam, that was too good to miss; and now he knew she had deep dark dirty secrets she really didn't want anyone finding out.

That night katcream69 signed in again.

Yes . . . Show me.

'What do I get, Big Man?'

You know what you get. You get my undivided attention. You get my devotion.

Katrien laughed. 'What else? Say it. It makes me excited to hear it.'

You will be richer than you've ever imagined.

'I have a rich imagination.' She giggled. 'But you're right. I can't wait to be able to cut out the middle men and grow my own opium, and then we'll all be rich. But, for now, we're still reliant on those greedy drug baron friends of yours. Is the next shipment ready to come over?'

They want to wait. They're getting nervous.

'No waiting, this is the time to act. We need all the funds we can get hold of if we are. Are they ready for him in the hills?'

Everything is in place, as long as he doesn't fuck it up.

'He won't. This means everything to him.'

The only thing that means anything to him is revenge.

'And I have seen to that. We will all have what we want from this. Each one of us will come out a winner.'

Show me.

She slipped the bra straps off her shoulders and rolled her hard nipples between her fingers.

17

Hong Kong

Mann came off the night flight from Amsterdam, took the first high speed train of the morning into Hong Kong, followed by the MTR link to Central, and then went on to his flat in Tai Koo Shing. He was glad to be back. He was always glad to return; Hong Kong was always in Mann's heart, she always drew him back home. But he didn't like getting back to his empty flat. It held nothing but memories for him.

He punched in his door code, said hello to the doorman and took the lift up to his floor. Stepping out onto his landing should have felt good but it didn't. Every time he came back he realised he should sell the place, but the same memories that made it hard to live there made it impossible to leave.

He opened the door and the smell of floor cleaner and window polish greeted him. His cleaner had to work overtime to find something to clean. He looked around: same plasma TV, same two chairs and same rattan elephant table with a glass top. Same everything, except him.

He took his bag into the bedroom and unpacked it on the bed. He tried to ignore the look of the crisp white cotton and the thought of the last woman to have slept in this bed. Two years after Helen had left in the taxi, Georgina showed up. He remembered the first time he'd seen her in Club Mercedes. His eyes had started at the feet and worked their way up. And his heart had stopped more than once. She had made him feel alive again, but that was when Helen's body had turned up and all hell broke loose. He took his eyes away from the sheets and the memory of Georgina wrapped in them and knew he had to acclimatise and to think things over. His head was in turmoil. The gym helped him think. His body was designed to be used. If he didn't, it got tetchy. He saw his body as his tool, his weapon and his protection – it was vital to keep it strong and supple. He stood six foot and two inches and weighed fourteen stone. Mann worked out most days. His body was firm and lithe, naturally muscled without being bulky. He had studied weight training schedules and alternated high reps and light weights days with maximum power days and he ran ten kilometres every other day. He liked being powerful but he didn't like it showing. He liked to be light on his feet – he needed to be. He went to the gym on the top floor and spent an hour running through everything in his head. Magda had opened up new roads to emotions he had either buried or didn't even recognise. The feelings he had towards Jake had unlocked his memories of his father. Jake was the same age Mann had been when Deming was murdered. At the time when Mann was pinned down and made to watch his father's execution, Magda must have been nursing a newborn, Jake. That summer had changed Mann forever. And this one would change Jake. If he survived this he would never be the same. He would be strong, resilient but also vulnerable. He would always have an Achilles' heel, just like Mann. Mann hadn't got the answers to his questions about his father's death and that was one of the reasons he had accepted Magda's invitation. He wouldn't rest until he knew everything he could about his father. Maybe Magda held one big piece of the puzzle over his execution. There were few coincidences in life: Deming died at the same time as he had a secret family on the other side of the world. If there was a connection, Mann would find it.

18

Saw ran past, distracted, and stopped to talk to Toad. He was agitated and preoccupied.

'Shit! Lucas, get up, quick.' Thomas and Jake looked at one another and both knew that the moment had gone. Toad had looked up just as Lucas fell at his feet and called ahead to Weasel.

'Watch it, Lucas, Weasel is coming,' Jake said as Weasel's tall, lanky frame trotted back, his pin head swivelling round to watch them and his small shifty eyes always looking for someone to inflict pain on.

Lucas didn't answer. His hands were tied and he struggled to lift himself from the ground.

Weasel was over him in a flash. He grinned and tilted his head from side to side as he looked at Lucas struggling. He picked up a stick and jabbed Lucas with the point of it. Lucas flinched and groaned as the stick found its mark. Weasel giggled manically. He jabbed at Lucas like a cat toying with a mouse. Jake stepped forward between them and knelt down to help Lucas. He managed to get his hand under Lucas's shoulder and started to help him to his feet but Weasel put his foot against Jake's back and pushed him down on top of Lucas. He held his foot against Jake's back as he kept him squashed on top of him. Lucas groaned in pain. Toad appeared beside them. At first the tone of his voice was jokey, then it became serious and Weasel reluctantly released his foot. Jake got another hold of Lucas and helped him up.

'You okay?' He examined Lucas's face. It looked grey. The blood had left his face and he had messed himself. There was a foul sulphuric smell. 'Lucas?' Lucas stood but his legs were buckling. He looked in a lot of pain as he clutched his stomach and turned away to vomit. It was bright with blood.

Weasel picked up another stick and started poking Lucas in his back as he was bent double. When he finished there was blood smeared across his hand as he wiped his mouth. Jake grabbed the end of the stick and wrenched it out of Weasel's hand. Weasel's face contorted in anger as he took one long stride to reach Jake and he began to shout, his words a torrent of rage. He spat into Jake's face as he took hold of his throat and squeezed it, and began whimpering softly like an excited puppy. The expression on his face turned to desire as, with his left hand, he reached down and cradled Jake's testicles before he began to twist and squeeze and pant like a rabid dog.

Toad finished talking to Saw, then he pushed Weasel away from Jake and stepped between them as he looked down at Lucas. He stared at him and then he said something that made Weasel laugh as he pointed to Lucas. He shouted something to one of the men and the bags

73

were pulled off the mule's back and it was led forward, its back shining with sweat.

Toad picked Lucas up as if he weighed nothing, although Lucas was a foot taller than him, and he dumped him onto the animal's back. It stood patiently waiting, taking the opportunity to eat the young shoots that sprung from the forest floor.

Saw was coming up behind them. Jake felt his fingers tingle with adrenalin and his guts twist. Saw stopped at Anna. Anna stared back. Jake admired her for her courage. She was always defiant. Saw walked past Silke and Jake's breath caught in his throat as he watched Saw pull at her clothing. He saw Thomas twisting the piece of wood in his hand. He hadn't been able to drop it without attracting attention. Jake looked at him. Thomas glared back as if begging Jake to let him try. Jake shook his head and his eyes dropped to the piece of wood in Thomas's hand. Thomas let it fall.

Silke flinched away from him and Saw's eyes rested on Jake. For a minute Jake thought he knew everything. He knew about the failed escape attempt.

Saw spoke to Toad before turning to Jake.

'Friend?' Saw gave his men a sidelong glance as he sneered and pointed towards Lucas. 'Friend?' He repeated it and pointed again towards Lucas as if the word conjured up a ridiculous image.

Jake nodded. Saw turned to Weasel and grinned. Weasel giggled and mimicked Jake. 'Friend. Friend.' He wiggled his hips like a woman.

'Friend sick – maybe fall from mule, huh?' Jake didn't answer. He knew that it was best to keep quiet. Saw wasn't looking for conversation. Saw jabbed him to make Jake look at him again. 'Soon, come Steep Pass – only room for one person.' Saw looked back at his men; he was speaking to the audience, not to Jake. 'Your friend fall, I think?' He called to Handsome to pass him some rope. As the mule looked at him incuriously, Saw tied the rope around Jake's waist and looped the other end around Lucas; pinning Lucas's arms around the mule's neck, he secured them together. Jake's side was pressed against the mule and he would struggle both to keep up and to avoid catching his legs in the mule's hooves. His body would get in the way on the narrow path. Beside him the steep ravine plummeted and, below, the tops of the teak trees seemed a long way off.

'He fall – you fall. He friend? You keep him alive.'

Saw laughed and his men whooped and seemed to walk with a new energy as they dragged their captives onward.

Saw stopped by Anna and looked back at Jake and grinned – his mouth dark red, he spat phlegm into Jake's path. He looked Anna up and down and nodded knowingly in Jake's direction as if he knew that they were lovers. Saw did know. His animal senses detected every weakness, every failing. His perception of the world was animalistic. He smelt her body on Jake. He smelt her sex. Saw walked back past Jake, fixed him with his black eyes as he grinned, leaned towards Jake as if about to strike him, then slapped the mule hard on its rump.

19

Mann waited whilst Ng ticked off his preferences from the dim sum menu. Bamboo baskets full of steamed dumplings were already arriving before he'd finished his order in the small side street café in Western District.

'Thanks for meeting me, Ng.'

'What is it you need, Genghis?' Ng and Mann had known one another for so many years that Mann had come to regard Ng as his friend, not just his colleague. Ng named him Genghis because in his youth he had looked like a wild man. Nowadays Mann was more groomed but inside he was the same lost soul. Ng was full of wisdom, both street and ancient. He knew the world and its failings. Ng saw the broad picture. He didn't have Mann's hot-headed temper. Ng was calm – a deliberator and negotiator. They had seen one another through difficult times. When Mann's world collapsed after Helen was murdered, Ng was the one who Mann leant on, and when Ng needed back-up Mann was the first to risk his life for his friend. Mann trusted his opinion. Ng looked at him now with his puppy dog eyes. 'It looks like you haven't slept recently. You should cut down on the gym and eat more.'

'I'm all right. I went away for a couple of days. I've got jetlag, that's all.'

'No, it isn't. You haven't been all right for a long time now, Genghis. It is five years since I saw you happy. You need to get yourself a woman. Did you ever get back in contact with that Eurasian girl?'

'Georgina?'

'Yes! That's the girl. She was just right for you.'

'She went back to England, as you know. She wanted to go home; she'd been through a lot.'

'You could have stopped her.'

'Wrong time, wrong place, Ng. Anyway . . .' Mann shook his head. 'That's what it always comes down to for you – food and females. The last thing I need is someone who needs me, Ng. I can't give it the time or the dedication. I'm strictly a single man, in love with his work.' Mann smiled.

'Huh . . . I thought being single was supposed to be fun. You don't look like you're having fun. You haven't taken any time off since that investigation in the Philippines, that's over a year now. Take some time off, go lie in the sun, go wave riding – what's it called, surfing?'

'Yeah, maybe you're right . . .' Mann smiled and rolled his eyes in defeat. 'I've had a lot on my mind. Actually, I have put in for some leave starting tomorrow, but it's unpaid.'

Ng lifted the tops from the dim sum baskets and began piling dumplings onto Mann's plate. Mann put his hand up to stop him.

'Eat,' Ng said, as he filled his own plate. 'Where are you going? Back to the Philippines?'

'Thailand.'

Ng looked at him and almost choked. 'You mad? No one is going to Thailand at the moment. Those kids were kidnapped, they haven't been released. It's not safe.'

'*Those* kids are why I'm going. I found out something about my father. I got an email from a Dutch woman, Magda. She told me she and my father were . . . lovers. Not just lovers, they had kids together. One of them is one of the kids who's been kidnapped. I am telling you this, Ng, because I trust you to keep it to yourself. Mum would hate the whole world knowing.'

Ng looked confused. 'Did your mother know all this?'

Mann nodded. 'She found out after my father was murdered, when Deming's will was read.'

Ng stopped eating, placed his chopsticks on their holder and thought for a few minutes.

'That's very sad, Genghis. Sad for everyone. But what does the Dutch woman expect you to do, exactly? Things are kicking off in Thailand and Burma. It's not a safe place to go right now.'

'If I go soon, I will be okay. I will always be able to get out overland and by boat.'

'I read the latest on the kids – they say they are almost certain to have crossed into Laos. It's a mess out there.'

'I can at least investigate what actually happened. The parents are being told nothing. I am going to take a day here to get all I need and then I fly to Chiang Mai tomorrow and follow their footsteps until I get to the jungle and then we'll see.'

'What do you know about tracking kids through jungles?' Ng stuffed a dumpling into his mouth.

'Thanks for the vote of confidence, Ng.' Mann grinned at his old friend. 'Don't hold back.'

Ng gulped down some water.

'I am just concerned, that's all.'

'I know, and you're right; it's new territory for me – all of it – but I am hoping to buy myself some help along the way.' Mann looked across at Ng. He knew by the look on Ng's face that, although he would always support Mann, he didn't think Mann should go. 'In reality, I have no choice. The fact that he is my brother makes this a situation I cannot ignore. I am glad she came to me. It makes me feel somehow good. I can't explain it – I feel as if I have some purpose to my life again. I might be able to uncover more about my father and I might fill up some of the emptiness I feel inside.' He smiled, embarrassed. Although he was close to Ng, he wasn't one for sharing confidences or pouring out his heart. 'Anyway, I can go out there and talk to people, suss out what happened. I might not be an expert at trekking through jungles but I am sure I can find someone who is.'

'This is totally out of your depth, Genghis, but okay. You will need help and you will have it. I will get Shrimp working on it.'

'Thanks, Ng. I knew I could count on you. I need you to do something else for me . . . I need you to investigate my father. I need to know what he was doing in Amsterdam. I need some closure on all of this, Ng. This has made me realise that I don't want to spend the rest of my life searching for answers. I want to move on.'

'You may never know the truth, Mann. Sometimes we have to accept and leave it there.' Ng shook his head. 'Life isn't that black or white. People are not just parents, they are flesh and blood. Men are built to sow their seed.'

'Maybe, or maybe it was love. The last summer I spent with my father was great. It was the happiest I had ever seen him. He seemed different, quick to laugh. He seemed like he wanted to get close to me. The night when I came back to the house and found him being tortured, when I saw him executed, I accepted that he was a brave man who had died because he wouldn't pay money to triads. But, do you know what, Ng? I don't even know who he was. Everything I believed in is gone.'

20

Magda had gone to bed ages before and Alfie was still waiting for Katrien to sign on to her messenger account. He was getting stir crazy staring at the screen. The camera wasn't a tracker. He only got to see her when she was sitting at the monitor; he was hoping that would be enough. He had sound, he had visual; now all he needed was for her to log on.

At midnight katcream69 was online and typing. She was sitting in her bra and pants. The webcam box was too small for him to see who she was looking at. He couldn't log in at the same time as her. It would cut her off if he did that. She seemed to be waiting and then she leant forward and looked into the webcam.

'Have you missed me?' Her voice was childlike, soft. There was no audible reply. Someone was typing. 'I know, it won't be long now, my love, and we will be together, just you and me and everything we have ever dreamed of . . . nothing will separate us then. No, there isn't enough money. We need to do this. It has to be this way, believe me, it will be worth it. We all have our part to play in it. You know what yours is, my love. He is coming out to you soon. Watch him, stay with him. Keep in touch. I need to know where he is all the time.'

'If you have to, yes. You've killed before and you can do it again. I was right then, wasn't I? I am right now too. Remember, you can't trust anyone but me. I've always been there for you. Of course I love you, baby. I love the way you kiss me. I love the way you taste.'

Alfie watched her shoulders rise and fall. She was playing with herself. He couldn't help feeling that she probably gave herself more satisfaction than any man could. 'Remember, baby, they're all against you, it's just you and me till the end.' She was getting excited now; Alfie listened to her moaning as she writhed in the chair and brought herself to orgasm. Then she blew a kiss into the webcam.

'Remember, baby. it's just you and me against the world, like it always has been, since we were kids.'

As she signed off, Alfie heard her talking to someone else; she was now out of camera range. He heard another voice in the room – it was a woman's.

21

'I just want to know, that's all.'

Mann was waiting for his mother to answer. He made her sit whilst they talked. It was all too easy for her to avoid it otherwise. She sat opposite him in the lounge on the white, French furniture, ornate, never meant to be comfortable. It was nothing like they used to have. She had got rid of all of that. Behind her were photos of Mann with his father on the sideboard in silver frames. Molly had moved into the small flat after Deming died and the furniture from the big house had been culled, but still the room seemed overcrowded and the furniture out of keeping in its new surroundings. Then, Mann hadn't understood why she had to downscale quite so much; now he did. The whole area had an air of 'seen better times' about it. As much as Mann kept nagging her, Molly never once spent the money she had sitting in the bank. Now he knew why.

She did not look at her son. He didn't mind waiting. He was used to waiting for her to say what it was that was bothering her. He knew this was her least favourite scenario, being forced into talking about a subject she'd rather never mention.

Mann sipped his tea and watched her. Her shoulders were narrow and stiff. Her hair was wound in a silver and pewter coil, and secured with an antique tortoiseshell clasp. She was getting thinner in her old age, but still upright as she sat perched on the edge of the chaise longue, as if there was a rod up her back, but the flesh on her arms was thinned and freckled with the sun damage. Her hands were long and graceful but papery thin. Mann put his cup down on the lace doily on one of a set of three mahogany side tables, and he sat back in the narrow, tall-backed armchair. Ginger, the cat, came to sit in front of Molly, waiting for a sign that it was allowed to jump onto her lap, waiting for her to sit back and make space. Molly put her cup down and gave an exaggerated sigh.

'I don't see what the point is in unearthing all these things about your father. He was a man like any other. He had his faults and his virtues. Why do we have to do it now?'

Mann looked at her; he could see she was trembling. He felt sorry for her and he spoke gently. 'Because it affects us *now*. Because, if they are not dealt with, secrets have a habit of reappearing, don't they? Nothing stays hidden forever.'

'It should have done. Why did *we* have to know about it? What business is it of *ours*? Your father made a mistake.' She was getting prickly. Ginger sensed it and backed off. 'We shouldn't let it ruin our lives. He has been dead for nineteen years. You spend too much time thinking about things like how he died. Who ordered his death? You waste your energy on things that cannot be answered and, even if they could, it would make no difference, it would not bring him back. You should stop thinking about these things, son, and move on. Put them behind you.'

'I won't give up the search for Dad's killer, Mum, I can't do that. I live with the image of his death cemented in my brain. But I realise now that I hardly even knew him. Now it turns out that he had secrets that affect us all and they might explain his death. I need to know them. I have a right to know them – everything, good and bad.'

Mann paused for a minute. He knew he was on tricky ground. If he pushed his mother too hard he would never get her to cooperate. She was better at building walls than any construction worker. She had turned her attention out towards the balcony where a bird had come to feed from the bird table. 'Mum, I know it's hard for you but it's too late to undo what's done. I don't know about you but I would rather not sit around and wait for that to unfold. I'm not too keen on surprises.' He saw her shoulders rise and fall and he knew she was trying hard to be calm. 'There was a time, not so long ago, that you wanted to talk about things. You mentioned that your relationship, your marriage wasn't so good.'

'That was before all this came up.' She snapped back. 'I don't see why she had to contact us. The children are nothing to do with us.' There was no anger in her voice, just exasperation and sadness. Mann could see she was upset. She started fiddling with the hem of her beige Marks and Spencer's cardigan that he had bought her last Christmas.

'You had no idea that he had someone else?'

She shook her head.

'You want to know my secrets? Then I will tell you . . . I was unlucky in love.' She smiled sadly. 'I picked the wrong man.'

She got up and went to watch the bird feeding on the crumbs she had left on the bird table.

'I was pretty. I was wealthy. I was educated. I had grown up with an idea of marrying well. When I was nineteen I got engaged to someone but he jilted me. He never loved me. He broke my heart. He took my father for a lot of money. There was a lot of shame also because I was pregnant. I lost the child. But it was still a huge disgrace and my parents sent me to Hong Kong to stay with a cousin out here to recover.' She gave a quiet, cynical laugh. 'They had no idea how the colonials lived out here or what kind of girl my cousin was. They thought she had a decent job out here; in reality, she hardly worked. She spent most of her time partying. She was racy for that time. She smoked, she drank. She was part of the "in set". I experienced a new type of people and I was introduced to your father. He seemed so quiet and respectful. We courted. I had known him for two months when he proposed and I accepted. I hardly knew him. I certainly did not know what life I would have here. I did not belong to Eleanor's party set. I was married to a Chinese. It was not right for either of us, not in those days of snobbery and racism; even in Hong Kong both sides kept their distance. It was an insult to be mixed race. I had no idea that my life would be so lonely. When you were born I was so happy, I didn't care what anyone thought any more. But, so soon, it came to be time to send you to school and your father insisted you went to England.' Molly sighed heavily. 'But a part of me died. I felt as if I'd lost you forever. I wanted to go back with you, to England, but Deming wouldn't allow it. My place was with my husband. My heart broke to let you go. My life was intolerable without you in it. Oh, he was kind enough to me but I was just a trophy wife to him. I had settled for respect, thinking it would become love but it never did. It must have been the same for him. That's why he looked for love elsewhere, I suppose.'

'What about you? Did you ever love anyone else?'

For a moment she turned back and looked fleetingly at him.

'A friendship, nothing more.'

'I am sorry, Mum. Really sorry. I can imagine how difficult it must have been. But the past is done with. We have all made decisions that we wish we'd reconsidered at the time, but Mum . . . Magda—' Molly tutted with annoyance at the mention of her name. Mann persevered. 'Magda didn't *want* to ask for help, Mum. She did it because she had no choice. She has already lost a son last year in the tsunami.'

Molly turned sharply round to look at him and he could see she was shocked. She lowered her eyes as she listened to what he had to say. 'She doesn't want to lose another. And I don't want to lose another brother.'

'Half brother,' she said, a wounded look in her eyes.

He smiled to himself. He could hear that she was relenting. Her voice had lost the panic, now only the sadness remained.

'Yes, half brother,' he said, kindly. 'But unless there are any more likely to come out of the woodwork then this young boy is my only sibling and I want the chance to get to know him. Things are always better out in the open, Mum.'

She shot him a look that stung. 'You're mad if you think that, Johnny. Hong Kong is built on secret handshakes and unspoken deals. There are things you don't ask about.'

'Hong Kong may be based on secrecy, but we need to trust each other. I need to know things about my father that affect me. If they don't, then by all means keep them secret, but something as important as him having other children, I need to know.'

'I had no reason to tell you at the time. You were eighteen. You had suffered enough. My main concern was you. You had gone through a terrible ordeal.' Her voice dropped off. She watched the bird pecking at the peanuts on the table. 'That night when your father died I was out with Eleanor. I became a novelty to her in the end and this was one of those nights when she was showing me off. We played bridge. I lost. I got a call from the servants. The amah was crying down the phone. She only told me that some terrible accident had happened. I remember asking her: is Johnny all right? She didn't answer me, she couldn't. I didn't wait for a taxi. I ran all the way from Eleanor's, my heart thumping, my lungs burning. I dreaded finding you dead. When I saw you standing there I was so relieved. But, as I walked forward, I saw Deming lying in front of the house, his head split open. And I remember my legs gave way and I crawled towards him. I tried to scream but I couldn't. I was frozen on my hands and knees, and then I was staring at his head, his skull was smashed, his brain bulging from a massive gap and his face gone. I remember looking at the blood seeping onto the driveway and I remember thinking: we'll never get that out; it will stain.'

The bird flew away from the bird table.

Mann stood and went over to rest his hands on her bony shoulders.

The sun hadn't reached that side of the building yet, soon it would come in so strong that she would need the blind down. Already the aircon was humming away. Mann knew she wasn't looking at anything.

'I'm sorry, Mum. It must have been terrible for you.'

She reached a hand back and covered Mann's that rested on her shoulder.

'I am sorry I did not tell you sooner. I am sorry that the other boy died in such terrible circumstances. I would not wish that on any mother. I never want to meet her – Magda – but . . .' She turned back from the window. 'Go and find your brother, Johnny.'

22

It was five by the time Mann alighted at Admiralty station. He bought himself a bun from the French bakery before emerging into the late afternoon sunshine. It was the perfect temperature: Hong Kong was enjoying its best season, low humidity and cloudless skies. But it didn't matter what season it was, Hong Kong was his home; he was born there and he would die there – hopefully not any time soon.

Mann's office in the OCTB was in Headquarters, Central Police Station, just a short walk from the station through Harcourt Gardens. Mann had worked in the department for the last year. He was trying not to blow it. It was the kind of job he had joined the police force for sixteen years before, straight out of school. After the death of his father he had had personal issues to resolve: he wanted to make a difference and he had a serious hatred of triads. They had long since lost sight of their lofty aims to serve the people – now they were drug runners and people traffickers like every other scumbag gangster the world over. But they were far from easy prey. They hid themselves within the business community like chameleons. They were more subtle than other mafia around the world. They had friends in high places and had nearly cost him his career and his life once or twice. But he had become an expert in their ways and now the police force needed him as much as he needed to work for it. His methods were unconventional and he trod on toes but Mann delivered. The OCTB needed him as much as he needed it – and it was what he lived for.

He turned into the entrance, through the electronic gates, and sprinted up the elevator and into a waiting empty lift. He stopped to show his warrant card before taking the elevator up to the twenty-third floor. There were four wings to each floor. The OCTB was spread over two floors. Mann's office was in the West Wing, along the semi-circular corridor.

Mann passed interview rooms. They were having trouble with gangs in the Mong Kok area and they had hauled in twenty for questioning. Pam, the new female detective, was interrogating a suspect. Lucky bugger, thought Mann – it would be nice to be interrogated by a woman in a white, crisp cotton blouse and a tight pencil skirt. It was a pity she was busy – this would have been a perfect chance to introduce himself properly. He walked into his office and was met by the fantastic view of Hong Kong. Headquarters had been designed so that all the boring stuff took place in the central sections of the building – it was where suspects were held, identity parades carried out and the Incidents and Communications room was located – whilst all the offices had massive windows.

Even though the paint on Headquarters was barely

dry, there was already an air of scruffiness to it. The offices were crammed with files and the corridor had become a dumping ground for unwanted items of furniture.

Most of the senior inspectors had their own office. The rest shared with three or four others. Mann shared his with Sergeant Ng and Detective Li. Detective Li, a young detective otherwise known as Shrimp, was waiting for him.

Mann had worked with Shrimp for almost two years. During that time he had seen him evolve from boy to man but he still hadn't lost that freshly scrubbed look to his face. He was an experimental dresser who normally favoured the vintage look. He swivelled his chair around as Mann entered.

'Hello, boss. Ng's on his way up, he had to go, but he filled me on the situation. Been busy looking at stuff for you. Discreetly, of course.'

Shrimp turned back round to his PC in the middle of his messy workstation, more tubes of hair gel than anything else, and he tapped on the keyboard, clicking various links until he found what he was looking for.

'Thanks, Shrimp. I've put in a request for leave but it's been refused. The Super wants to see me. I'll catch up with you when I'm done.'

Mann walked down the corridor and knocked on the Superintendent's door.

'You wanted to see me, ma'am?'

The slender figure of Mia Tan seemed lost behind the massive desk. She hadn't been in the post for long and she hadn't had time to change things. The walls still bore the outlines of the last occupant's photos. There was a stunning view down towards the harbour. As Mann came in, an eagle flew alongside her window.

'Sit down, Johnny.'

She might have looked small in stature but Mia was anything but diminutive. She was tough and clever and very ambitious. With her short hair and her oversized eyes, she had a quirky but striking look. She had a dancer's physique, slim but strong. She trained hard at the gym. She wasn't one of those women who wore full makeup to the gym and hated sweating. Whatever she did, she did well and with enthusiasm.

They had known each other since cadet school and had helped one another with some extracurricular night-time revision now and again, but Mia was too ambitious to put up with Mann's wild streak for long. Now she had been promoted over him and she was his boss.

'Can't let you take off to Thailand. There'll be questions asked about why a Hong Kong policeman is going into a politically unstable area. If you get caught in any trouble it could start a major standoff between us and the rest of Asia. You know the top brass is looking for any chance they can to discipline you. I can't stick my neck too far out for you, Johnny.'

'You don't have to, Mia.'

'Yes, I do.' She gave a small smile and lowered her eyes. 'We go back a long way. If you had toed the line a bit more you would have been sat behind this desk. We trained together. You've had more experience of high profile cases than me. You deserved the promotion. But you are never going to get it unless you play ball.'

'Mia. I need to do this. There are personal reasons why I have no choice. I have to go.'

She sighed. Outside the window the eagle lifted on the air currents and dipped its six-foot wings as it turned away from the window and flew off to find its mate.

'I hope it's worth it, Johnny. Whatever it is. If you get caught out there, none of us will be able to help you.' She turned back from the window. 'Just understand one thing, Johnny. You don't have many lives left. There are so many people in this building who hate you. You're really good at pissing people off.'

'Well, I have to be good at something.' He grinned.

'You're good at a lot of things, Johnny, that's what pisses them off. If they didn't need you, you'd be gone. You're a loner, I know, but don't spend too long out on a limb, Johnny. You may never be able to come back.'

23

Alfie kissed Magda goodbye and left for work. On the way out he looked up the street and saw the surveillance car. He thought it best not to tell Magda that she was being followed. She was bound to look around out of curiosity and Mann was right, neither Magda nor Jake had the luxury of time. They had to throw everything they had at it and chase any leads no matter how remote.

After Alfie had left Magda sat in her kitchen and dialled NAP's number. She had plenty to do now, which was good. She had to try and get all the information she could out of Dorothy and ask for her help.

'Can I speak to Dorothy, please?'

'Who's calling?'

'Her niece; it's urgent,' Magda lied.

'Hello?' A nervous voice came on the phone.

'Hi, Dorothy, I'm sorry. It's Magda Cremer here. I didn't want anyone to know who it was calling. Can you meet me for a coffee? There's a Brazilian place at the end of your street.'

'I know it. It's my break in twenty minutes. I can come then.'

'Thanks – I'm on my way.'

Magda was dressed and out the door in two minutes. She texted Alfie to tell him where she was. He texted his man outside to tell him she was on the move.

Magda sat in the small terracotta-tiled café and waited by the window. She waved as Dorothy appeared. Dorothy was always smart, today wearing a purple pashmina over a mauve jumper and a tweed skirt that ended mid-calf.

'Thank you so much for coming, Dorothy.'

'Please . . .' Dorothy took off her pashmina and hung her coat on the back of the chair as she ordered a coffee. 'I am so glad you called.'

She sat down, and looked hard at Magda before smiling kindly.

'I know you have been ill and what with losing Daniel last year and now this . . . I thought it best to keep out of your way. But I have wanted to get in touch to tell you how sorry I am and, of course, whatever I can do to help, I will. Sorry . . .' Dorothy reached over and put her hand onto Magda's. '. . . I didn't mean to upset you.'

Magda shook her head, trying to shake off her tears. She hated the fact that she could no longer get through five minutes without crying. She couldn't bear people to mention her sons. She had almost lost hope of ever seeing Jake again and she missed Daniel more than ever.

'Deming would have been so proud of you and the boys. You did a great job raising them.'

Magda looked shocked. 'You knew Deming?'

Dorothy nodded. 'Yes, in my youth. I was working as a bookkeeper and I was asked if I would like to do some secretarial work for a Chinese businessman. And the businessman turned out to be Deming. Those days we didn't have emails and laptops, we did it all on a typewriter. The secretary was a vital part of the businessman's life. I liked Deming. He was very generous. He made several large donations to charities.'

'Did you know about me?'

Dorothy nodded. 'Not from Deming, of course, I was his secretary, not his close friend. But I saw you together many times. I thought you made a lovely couple. You both seemed happy. Of course, I knew he had a family back in Hong Kong. I knew there was another son: I was responsible for typing letters to lawyers, making arrangements that concerned the will. Johnny Mann, he is called, isn't he? I recognised him when he came to the office the other day. It was lovely looking at him – he's such a big tall man, isn't he? I think he looks most like Daniel.'

Magda smiled and nodded but her eyes filled up straightaway and she bent her head to dig for a tissue in her fleece pocket.

'Sorry . . . sorry. I've upset you again.' Dorothy laid her hand over Magda's. 'Tell me, what do you want me to do?' she said in a business-like tone, and Magda knew if Dorothy agreed to do something she would do it well.

But Magda hesitated. It suddenly struck her that, as she was asking Dorothy, a woman she hardly knew, to supply personal information about her boss, she had better choose her words carefully. She didn't want to blow it. Not only was Dorothy kind, she was also lonely, and Magda knew Dorothy could be a goldmine of information if handled the right way. But she needn't have worried; it was as if Dorothy had kept it bottled for so long that once she started to talk, she couldn't get it out fast enough.

'I am leaving my job next month,' she started. 'Retiring. Although I could stay on, I'm not going to. This last eighteen months have been so terrible – I don't want to work for a company like NAP. It's changed so much since that awful woman Katrien took over two years ago.'

Magda leaned forward and whispered: 'Alfie calls her the Bitch.'

Dorothy put her cup down and whispered back, 'I know exactly what he means.' She nodded, her eyes wide. 'It's a good name for her. She has got well above her station. I don't know how she's ended up with so much authority. She shouldn't be allowed in charge of any of it.'

'What do you know about her?'

'She takes drugs. I caught her once when I went in to her office; she was snorting cocaine. She seems to have plenty of money coming in – she wears designer *everything* and that's not cheap, although why she bothers, I don't know; she always wears black, it could be any make. And she's always taking time off to go away.'

'Where does she get her money from, do you think?' Magda sipped her coffee and listened hard.

Dorothy raised her eyebrows and rolled her eyes.

'Men. That's where from. She plays her little games

with all of them. I've seen her out in town. She's always with a different one. Ugly, dishonest – but always wealthy looking. She's passed me in the street before now, in some top of the range flash car. She knows all the wrong people if you ask me. But I don't think she's planning to stay here much longer. She's been going to Thailand at least three or four times a year the last two years. I think she'll go and live there. And good riddance to her . . . I tell you something, though.' Dorothy beamed. 'She was riled the other day when Johnny Mann came in.' She chuckled. 'You should have seen her face!'

'Did she know who he was?' Magda asked, surprised.

'I don't know that but I do know that she cancelled the rest of the day's appointments and left the office. Oh . . . look at the time!' She panicked as she looked at her watch. 'I have to go. *She's* probably back in the office by now and that nasty little receptionist will be quick to tell her that I had a longer break than I should. But . . .' Dorothy stood and put on her coat and scarf. '. . . I will start doing some serious digging for you and I will call you.'

She hugged Magda.

'You can rely on me,' she said as she disappeared.

Magda watched her go and was left with the feeling that she could trust and rely on her. She was happy with the way the meeting had gone. Alfie would be pleased when she told him everything she'd learned. It confirmed his suspicions about Katrien – that she was a nasty piece of work, capable of anything.

Magda arrived back at the apartment and punched in her door code. No cat this time. She walked up the stairs, and it was as she took the last few steps onto her landing that she had a sudden sense that something wasn't right. As she turned the corner at the top of the stairs, she saw something that chilled her to the bone. Her legs buckled and she clasped her hand to her mouth in horror. Someone had nailed the cat to her door.

24

Mann drew up a chair and sat beside Shrimp as he drank his coffee. 'What have you got for me?'

'This.' Shrimp picked up a glossy printout next to the PC and unfolded it. Mann recognised some of the photos on it. They were of Patong Beach. He'd seen them on the wall at NAP. There were before and after photos of the tsunami, and photos of projects that were being worked on. As Mann studied them, he thought of Daniel and of Magda's account of that Boxing Day. Never again would he be able to look over the beach at the horizon in the same way.

His thoughts were disturbed as, from outside in the corridor, came the sound of a familiar male voice flirting with Pam. Ng came around the corner, his briefcase under his arm, smiling to himself. He was holding a piece of paper. He winked at Mann and fluttered the paper triumphantly in the air.

'The old dog's still got it – new girl, white blouse, tight skirt.' He looked very pleased with himself.

Mann shook his head bewildered.

'You must be fucking joking . . . How did you get her number?'

Ng always looked as if he'd just got out of bed. But the dishevelled look suited him and his sideways grin and puppy dog eyes brought him more than his fair share of female attention. He stopped mid-step when he saw Shrimp and feigned massive surprise.

'What's wrong with you? Why are you dressed like a normal person?'

'This is my "project manager's outfit". I'm just trying it out for size. Buff-coloured trousers show that I am a professional used to working on sites, plus . . .' Shrimp pulled the leg of his trouser to reveal sturdy lace-ups. 'I have hard-topped boots – always safety first on the site. The vacancy just popped up. I couldn't turn it down. I am going off to help rebuild a children's nursery on Patong Beach that was destroyed by the tsunami and which they are halfway through completing.'

'Huh?' Ng tried to follow Shrimp's quickfire dialogue. He always spoke too fast for him. Ng looked from Mann back to Shrimp and shook his head, confused. 'I told you to look into it, not get yourself hired.'

'No way, Shrimp,' said Mann, shaking his head. 'I appreciate it, but there's no way I want you getting involved. You would get in serious trouble if the boss found out you were helping me. I thought you were studying for your law degree? You can't afford to take time off.'

'Forget it, boss, the law degree is in its final stages.

I just need to find a case to show off my skills. Plus, I live for the adrenalin, you know that.'

Ng shook his head as if he couldn't believe what he was hearing. 'You might make a good lawyer – in the end – but, God, haven't those children suffered enough? What do you know about building walls and laying floors?'

Shrimp thought for a couple of seconds and then shrugged. 'I will pick up a book on it at the airport. I got Ting in Anti-Fraud to fix me up some credentials and references and they hired me subject to interview, which I did via webcam. I pretended I was from New York. To be honest, *I* would have hired me, Ting made me look so good. Plus they're desperate.'

'Ha.' Ng shook his head, stupefied. 'Good luck . . .' He slapped Shrimp hard on the back. 'You'll need it.'

Ng sat down at his desk. As untidy as Ng was in his person, his desk was immensely organised: papers were gathered in neat piles, sharpened pencils lay in tidy rows.

'Who interviewed you?' asked Mann.

'Versace suit, black – this season – grey silk Dior chemise underneath: understated chic.'

'That'll be Katrien – classy but as cold as ice. Okay, Shrimp. I do appreciate it but keep a low profile. Remember you have no jurisdiction there. Neither of us do. We get into trouble, we're on our own. If the governments aren't able to help the five missing kids, they sure as hell aren't going to help us.'

Mann had been through many scrapes with Shrimp and Shrimp had always put himself on the line for Mann.

'No sweat. I am just there for back-up for you. I want to do it and . . . I think you'll need me out there.

Besides, I'm owed a lot of leave so figured it could almost count as a vacation.'

'He's as bad as you. He never takes a vacation,' grumbled Ng. 'I wish I was owed leave. Let him go, Genghis. I will cover for him here.'

'Okay,' said Mann, reluctantly. 'I guess there's nothing I can say to change your mind. Thank you. I will pick up the bill for it all, Shrimp. When do you leave?'

'Tomorrow evening.'

Shrimp scrolled through the pages on his screen and clicked on a link to YouTube at the bottom. Devastating images of the tsunami came up: the empty beach, the massive wave on the horizon, and the muffled voices of people in the background, screaming for help. Mann wanted to turn away but couldn't. The tsunami had become personal to him now.

'You prepared, Genghis?' Ng turned his chair around to look at Shrimp's screen. Mann was still staring at the screen.

'Some things you can never prepare for.'

25

Burma

For three long days Saw marched the five north to the mountains of the Golden Triangle. They crossed the muddy Meekong river and trekked ever upwards until the air became cooler every day. Now they were passing through poppy fields that stretched over hill tops and swayed with the gentle breeze in a wave of red. In the fields the peasants stopped and watched as the strange band of pale hostages and wild men passed by.

On the third evening they marched up a track and passed a field where the poppy heads stood erect, grey and fat. They were dried now and ready for harvesting. A woman was working in the field, cutting fine vertical slashes into the poppy head and releasing the white latex. Her children were harvesting the opium they had left to dry twelve hours before, scraping off the brown gum from the poppy heads. As they passed the woman, she stopped her work to watch them. Saw beckoned to her. She looked nervously around and at her children, then back at Saw and she nodded. She handed her tools to one of her children and followed them.

The sun came down fast and the five sat on an elevated platform outside the woman's opium farm to watch it setting. The sky dipped from deep turquoise to charcoal.

'How long has it been, Anna?' asked Thomas.

'It's been sixteen days,' said Anna without hesitating.

'Do you think anyone knows we are alive?' he asked. None of the five answered him. 'Do you think someone will come looking for us?'

Jake lay on his back and looked at the stars above and wondered which one his mother was looking at right now.

Lucas managed to sit up. He smiled at Jake. 'Wassup?' He was shivering.

'You cold?' asked Jake, pleased to see his friend awake and smiling, although he could see he was being brave rather than feeling better.

'Freezing.'

Jake's feet and hands were tied, but he shuffled on his bottom over towards Lucas and looped his arms around him.

'What's happening, Jake?' Lucas whispered.

'I don't know. I don't think we were meant to still be here. Whatever it is, it doesn't look good.'

Saw seemed to be brooding and waiting. He rested whilst his men stood guard. The woman and her children prepared food for them all. Pots of rice boiled furiously and the children were sent to get food from neighbours. They returned with parcels wrapped in banana leaf. As the woman was busy cooking she cast a nervous eye over Saw and his men, the rest of the time she stared at the five. She had never seen westerners before. She looked at them all with a mixture of bewilderment and concern. She could see they were in a bad state and that Lucas was very ill. When she thought she wasn't being watched she brought them over some water. Squatting beside them, she washed Lucas's face with a cool damp cloth and fed him some herbal tea. When she went back to her cooking, Jake watched her cautiously push a small knife out of her own reach, towards the five. She pushed it behind one of the pots, then she looked at Jake, down to his tied wrists and finally to the knife. He thanked her with a smile.

26

Alfie raced back to the flat. It looked as if a tornado had passed through; the place was turned upside down, pictures smashed, sofas slashed, plant pots tipped upside down. Magda stood in the middle of it, holding the dead cat in her arms. She turned as Alfie came in and his heart broke as he looked at her face.

'I found it nailed to the door. Who would do that?' She bowed her head and started sobbing.

He stepped over the debris, glass crunching beneath his feet.

'Come here, Magda. Come.' He held on to her and the cat.

He could feel her bones. Every time he held her she felt thinner. He didn't like it. She had never felt small in his arms before. It didn't feel like his Magda. She was dying and in so much pain; she missed her sons so much, and now she had all of this too. Alfie was so angry he knew that he would happily kill the person who had done it.

'It's all right, Magda, these are only things. We can

buy new things. It will give us the chance to get rid of some of this clutter.'

She leaned back to look at Alfie. 'I can't find any of my precious things, the mementoes from when the children were small – it's all gone. They went into the boys' rooms and wrecked them. They tore Daniel's surfing posters off the wall. Why did they do that?'

Alfie swallowed hard and held her tightly. She sank into his chest and hid her face as she sobbed. His shirt was soon wet from her tears.

'You cry as much as you need to, Magda.' He soothed her and patted her back. 'We can buy the same poster again. I will put it back as it was.'

'The poor cat. Jake will be so sad.'

'We will tell him it stopped coming and we don't know what happened to it.'

She pulled away and looked at him. 'We can't do that, Alfie. I want him to know it never forgot him. I am going to take a photo for Jake. He'll want proof.' Magda handed Alfie the cat whilst she went off to look for the radiator sling that Jake had bought for the cat. She returned, picked the cat up and put it in the sling.

'It just looks as if it's sleeping now,' she said as she disappeared again to look for the camera.

Alfie smiled at her. Once she was out of earshot, he phoned in to work.

'Double the surveillance, but keep it covert – someone broke into the flat. They turned the place upside down but didn't take things like an expensive camera.'

Magda came back in the room, sniffing and wiping her eyes with her hanky.

'I tell you how this makes me feel, Alfie.'

Her face was blotchy from crying. Alfie's heart sank. He didn't know how much more of this either of them could take. He knew Magda was so afraid of dying, but she didn't know how terrified he was of losing her. Every day she slipped further from him. He felt powerless.

'It makes me feel like fighting harder than I ever fought in my life. I am damned if I'm dying till I get my son back and till I put a stop to all this, Alfie. I won't do it.'

Alfie's eyes filled with tears for the first time since Daniel's death.

Magda stared at him. 'Alfie, I'm sorry. I didn't realise how much it was all getting to you.' He put up a hand to stop her.

'No, Magda, it's not that. You just made me so happy. I have got my Magda back.'

27

Sometime after they had eaten, Jake saw headlights on the approach to the farm. Saw stood and watched the jeeps approach. He nodded towards Toad who turned and slipped out of sight. Jake and the others sat blinking in the glare of the headlights. The jeeps came to a stop and cut the engines. Four bodyguards jumped out from the first vehicle and then a short bald man in his early sixties stepped out with a younger man from the second.

'Welcome, Saw. It's been a long time.' The older man spoke. Saw nodded.

'Welcome, Kasem.'

The whole time Saw's eyes scanned the newcomers.

'You remember my son, Tai?' Kasem gestured towards the younger man who stood beside him grinning, his gold teeth flashing and his slicked black hair shining in the glare of the headlights.

'Turn off the headlights,' said Saw.

Kasem nodded towards the bodyguards. They killed the lights and now just the full moon and the firelight illuminated the meeting. The woman and her children edged away and hid around the side of the house. Saw's men moved stealthily around in the shadows until they surrounded the newcomers. The four bodyguards formed a ring around Kasem and his son. One of them held a 9mm Sterling sub machine gun, the others semi-automatics. Their weapons shone in the firelight.

'I have brought the westerners. We have a deal. Now the land is mine.'

'Let me see them.'

Saw signalled to Handsome to fetch the five. Handsome cut the ties around their feet and pulled them up by their bound wrists. He dragged them over and made them stand in front of Kasem and Tai. Kasem looked them over one by one and Tai stood nodding and grinning as he stared at the girls. He tried to kiss Silke. She squirmed out of his reach. Tai stepped back, laughing.

'Please excuse my son,' said Kasem. 'He is short of company up here in the mountains. But . . .' He turned to Saw. 'The deal has changed. We take the girls in exchange for a shipment of opium. That is all.'

Saw's eyes were bright and menacing as he answered.

'You take them all. You give me the land; I can grow my own opium.'

Kasem shrugged. 'Take it or leave it. The buyers I had lined up for them are no longer interested. They can't afford to hold on to them until things quieten down. They are not worth anything to me any more. I will take the girls and do you the favour of shooting the boys.' Tai nodded in agreement with his father as he grinned at Silke and grabbed at her breasts. Jake looked around.

He could still see the knife, its blade just visible behind the cooking pot. He looked back to Saw and the discussions going on. He did not understand their words but he sensed trouble in the air. Saw's men were becoming jittery. There was movement in the shadows.

Kasem's bodyguards edged forward.

'The girls will provide a few weeks' sport for my men, nothing more. Then I will kill them.' Kasem turned his head left and right. He too knew the signs.

'No deal.' Saw looked across at Handsome. Toad was nowhere to be seen.

'Then you've wasted your journey. That is all I can offer you.' Kasem held up his hand in a gesture of dismissal and turned back towards the car, anxious to leave.

'Let's go,' he said to Tai.

But Tai was used to getting what he wanted and he didn't understand why they didn't just take the girls. He hadn't the experience of his father. He didn't know how to judge the situation and he didn't know Saw. Instead, he glared at his father. Kasem glared back and his tone changed even though he maintained his frozen grin. He edged backwards towards the jeep.

'Get back in the car.' There was an understated urgency in it that Tai didn't pick up on until he saw that the bodyguard with the Sterling was waiting for him to get safely out of the way before he opened fire.

But he waited too long. He never had a chance to hone his intuition skills, Toad had already stabbed him in the back and through the heart.

28

Mann was waiting at the airport when he got the text from Alfie to tell him about the burglary. Mann was about to phone him back, but he decided to call his mother first. He took a deep breath.

'I understand that you must feel bitter about things.'

Mann waited on the other end of the line. There was no response.

'Maybe that's why you haven't used the money Deming left you. But I want you to use it now. I want you to give me the money to put up a ransom.' He could hear the silence and an intake of breath. He waited; she wouldn't be rushed.

Then, 'Yes,' came the answer, strong, decisive. It was as if Mann had offered her some way to move on and to forgive.

'I'll see you when I get back, Mum.'

'Take care of yourself, son.'

Mann phoned Alfie. He filled him in on the burglary.

'How is Magda?'

'She is mad, that's a good thing.'

'Do you think they got what they wanted, Alfie?'

'I don't know.'

'We can't afford to wait and see. Let's make it interesting. Contact Katrien and say you have a chance of getting hold of two million US to put up for their safe return.'

'Yeah, but we haven't.'

'Yes, you have. My mother has put up the money from Deming's estate. But don't let's give it to her on a plate. She has to prove to us she can deliver. I'm still going out there.'

There was a pause; Mann could hear Alfie dragging on a joint. 'Good. That is a good thing she does. Please thank her from us.'

'It's the right thing, Alfie – for everyone. Two million should prove tempting for anyone. Plus it's enough to make someone careless. Katrien would cut herself into a slice of that, and she'd come out of it looking really good. Now we get to see what kind of a negotiator she really is.'

'Oh, I already know what kind of negotiator she is. It takes a lot to afford this girl. She does deals with high-earning businessmen. Check this out – the Bitch is either a highly-paid call girl, or a dealer, or both.'

'Who are her clients?'

'I am in the process of trying to tap into her emails. She has contacts far afield, they cross many countries. Put it this way, I've seen the video footage – she doesn't have boundaries.'

29

Jake grabbed the knife from behind the cooking pot and the five ran for the cover of the poppy fields, frantic to get away as the fight turned into a bloodbath and automatic gunfire rattled above their heads, leaving their trace in the night sky just metres away. They used the knife to cut their bonds and then they crawled on their hands and knees across the dried stony earth of the poppy field and headed towards the track at the far side. They crouched in the cover of the poppies.

'We have to run for it,' Jake whispered as the gunfire stopped. 'Head diagonally across to the track and into the woods at the other side. We might have a chance in the dark. Thomas, you go the other side of Lucas, we'll run together. Anna, hold Silke's hand. Stay together. Ready?' They all nodded. 'GO!'

Lucas staggered to his feet and under the shadow of darkness they galloped and smashed through the poppy heads. Jake looked behind them. He could see the jeeps coming, their headlights searching across the field, heading straight towards them. In the darkness he dropped the knife.

'Keep running,' he shouted. The darkness made it impossible to see where the poppy field ended. The yelps and howls of Saw's men went up around the field. Then, ahead, Jake saw the trees rising black and blocking out the stars.

'We're nearly there! Quick!' They ran on.

The forest was half cleared at its edges: sawn trunks and discarded branches tripped them as they ran. They could hear the sound of Saw's men howling to each other and the jeeps' engines chewing up the poppy field. Jake looked across – for a second he couldn't see Silke, and then he saw Anna helping her up. She had fallen.

'Run, run . . .' Jake shouted across to the girls. Silke looked behind and gave a small cry of fear. Weasel was within ten metres of them. His long legs were flying over the fallen trunks and the sawn stumps, his head held high like a cheetah, intent on its prey.

'Thomas, take Lucas,' said Jake. Thomas held on to Lucas. Jake turned back to the girls and he picked up a thick branch. The girls ran past him and he didn't wait for Weasel to get to him – he sprang at him as he was running full pelt and smashed the wood in to Weasel's skull. Weasel staggered under the blow and crashed noisily to the ground. Jake threw down the piece of wood and turned to catch up the others but he was blinded by car headlights. The others were on their knees, guns to their heads. Saw was standing over them, laughing. The next thing Jake saw was a flash of light that accompanied the sharp pain in the side of his head as Weasel knocked him out.

30

Thailand

Nothing was moving out of Bangkok airport: the place was overrun by anti-government protesters. The prime minister was in hiding up near the old capital of Thailand, Chiang Rai, just a few hours north of Chiang Mai. Mann knew he was likely to remain there for a while until his safety could be guaranteed. The Thai military would have to do their best to see to it that the northern airports remain open the longest.

Mann flew direct to Chiang Mai. For one nasty moment, he was kept waiting for his luggage by airport security and he thought they had discovered his shuriken concealed in the lining of his case. He didn't dare risk losing his entire armoury to a nervous customs officer so this time he had hidden it. He also didn't want them to look him up and thus announce that he was coming. He was lucky, it was just a random security check and they let him through without a thorough search. The whole airport had turned into a protest centre with people camping everywhere. Their eyes were not focused on foreign threats, they were on the brink of civil war.

'First time in Thailand, sir?'

The taxi driver turned and grinned at Mann. He handed Mann a mock leather folder full of glossy photos: elephant treks, river rafting, snake farms – details of unmissable trips. Mann idly flipped the pages as they drove away from the airport and then set the book down beside him on the battered leather seat of the old Saab.

'No, it isn't.' Mann settled back to survey the scenery. There were no seatbelts but he was used to that. Hong Kong taxis never had them either. Mann would have said that he'd been there before, even if it had been his first time. He'd learned a long time ago never to tell taxi drivers this was your first time anywhere unless you wanted to see how long they could take to drive you the shortest distance and charge you double for it. But he wasn't lying, in any case. It was seven years since Mann had visited Thailand. Last time he came it was on vacation with Helen. It was there she had cured him of his fear of talking and had undone the legacy of a childhood spent in a boarding school.

'You here on business, sir? You come far?'

'Yes, business. I came from Hong Kong.'

'Ah ... Hong Kong ... great place, lovely city. No time for relax here, sir, take a trip? Buy umbrella to take home?'

Mann shook his head wordlessly.

'Please, take a card, sir,' the taxi driver said when they reached the hotel. He fumbled in the dashboard and extracted a business card. 'Maybe you find time for a trip. Relax.' He turned and presented the card by holding it between the tips of his fingers and giving a small bow as if it were made of gold. Mann thanked him and took it with both hands – just the way he would have done in Hong Kong.

'See the orchids. Touch the sleeping tigers, I will take you.'

'I don't need a trip, but I might need to take a taxi to Mae Sot.'

'Mae Sot, Tak province, sir?' He studied Mann in the mirror. 'Very far, sir, over mountains. Take maybe six hours. I cannot go there. This car is too old for those roads. What you make there? That place not for tourists. Mae Sot very dangerous place right now.' He looked at Mann; he wasn't smiling. 'All bad things come to Mae Sot, sir.'

'How much would it cost?' Mann asked but the taxi driver was already out of the car, Mann's luggage in his hand, bowing low.

'To get to Mae Sot? Many miles to Mae Sot. Cannot go. Apologies. Mae Sot is not good place for me.'

Mann walked inside the hotel and across the expansive airy foyer, which was decorated with tropical planters and now eerily quiet. He was checked in by three bowing receptionists wearing matching cheongsams, all very eager to make themselves indispensable as they floated gracefully back and forth behind the desk. Nice room, he thought, as he tipped the porter. He left his case locked for now, whilst he studied the five's itinerary.

The first thing on their list was to meet up with an American, Louis King, the official tour guide:

> ...*where they will get acquainted with the spiritual aspects of their trip and spend an afternoon at the Enlightenment Centre, meeting the monks and learning about Buddhism, one of the three main religions in the camps.*

Mann had already emailed Louis and he was going to be waiting for him inside the yoga centre where he worked.

Mann checked his email. One from Ng updating him on the situation.

Your father seems to have documents scattered all over Hong Kong. He had more than one accountant, and what appears to be several solicitors, still holding personal and business documents. It's not going to be possible for me to access those, you will have to do that when you come home. I will pursue the Amsterdam connection and hope it will be more transparent. Good luck, Genghis.

He had another from Shrimp to say that he had been on the last flight allowed into Phuket before it was shut down and that he'd get back to Mann in a couple of days once he had the situation sussed. Now the shut-down had begun in the south. They were all marooned until it was settled one way or another. He left his room and went out in search of a tuk-tuk. He didn't have to look far, there were several parked at the entrance to the hotel.

'Drop me off near the temple . . . and the Enlightenment Centre.'

The tuk-tuk belched smoke and shot off into the traffic. The pollution snatched at the back of Mann's throat. Tuk-tuks weren't equipped with suspensions: they bumped and grated and jolted their passengers and the fumes choked them as they sat in the traffic. They were the biggest death traps imaginable. If they were hit it would be like squishing a pea between fingers, but it was the fastest way to get up any alley or down busy main roads and, besides, it provided a few thrills. It wasn't long before they pulled up at the side of the high wall of the temple.

The tuk-tuk driver dropped him off and Mann walked through the crumbling entrance. Inside the courtyard everything was gold and beautifully ornate. What was referred to as 'the temple' was actually three temples of various designs, a small park, and a golden obelisk pointing towards the azure blue sky. At the far end of the park was the Enlightenment Centre where he was due to meet Louis in ten minutes.

Mann stopped outside the first temple and took off his shoes. He placed them on the steps next to a flailing Buddha who was being eaten by a goggle-eyed dragon. Mann had been brought up with the teachings of Buddha. His mum was a Catholic, his Dad a Taoist. Often in Hong Kong, Taoist and Buddhist worshipped at the same temple. Sometimes he had accompanied his father to the temple. Mann had never found comfort in religion, though it was a fascinating obsession for others. But he loved the peace, the tranquillity and the beauty of religious buildings. Ahead, the altar gleamed golden and red and around the walls were carvings and tablets and open, glassless windows. The stone floor was cool underfoot. Mann approached the altar.

An old monk was sitting to his right, his legs tucked beneath him on a bench. He was writing in a note-book. His head was shaved. His orange robes were wrapped around him and caught over one shoulder, then tucked between the legs to give him trousers. He looked up and studied Mann as he entered. The monk remained still as Mann went to the altar and stood in reflective contemplation.

'What is it you are seeking?' The monk spoke in good English.

Mann turned towards him and inclined his head in deference as he answered: 'Five young people came to this temple six weeks ago. They came to learn about Buddhism, to learn about the culture.'

The old monk did not answer for a few minutes; he remained passively staring out and Mann turned back to the opulent altar with its young-faced, slim Buddha smiling almost smugly back at him. Then came the noise of a shower of sticks falling onto the stone floor. Mann turned back to see the monk studying the formation of the fortune sticks that he had dropped.

'The five volunteers who have been kidnapped?' the monk asked, as he bent over the sticks to examine them. 'It was I who taught them about the writings of Lord Buddha, here at the temple. I spent two days with them. They were willing students.' He looked up and smiled.

123

'I learned a lot from them also. I pray for them every day.'

Mann walked over to the monk and sat on the mat beneath the bench. It was customary to keep your head below that of the monk's out of respect. The old monk was looking at the sticks, lifting them each individually.

'Did anything happen here that could explain why they were taken from the refugee camp?' asked Mann.

'Even before they came here, their fate was decided. Where there is cause there is effect. It is the Buddhist belief. Some bad deeds have been done in the past. Now these young people must pay.'

'What do you mean?'

The monk opened his palm and showed Mann the sticks. 'I read it in their fortune. I saw it in their fortune sticks. Bad deeds were done, not in their life but in another's. Those deeds have come back to be paid now.'

'What were the deeds?'

He shook his head slowly, deliberately. 'I know only that they are joined on a path that has no end and it was not of their construction. I knew you were coming, the sticks spoke of it. And now I see them again.' He looked at the sticks and nodded his head as if he had seen something crystal clear. 'I see that your death is joined to theirs.' He looked at Mann and his eyes seemed to stare into Mann's soul. 'Where is your faith?'

'I lost it a long time ago. I trust no man or god. I believe in people and their power to do good if they choose. There is no heaven and no hell, only the mark we choose to leave on others.'

'Neither fire, nor wind, birth or death can erase our good deeds.'

'What about bad ones?'

'Do not dwell on the past; do not dream of the future, concentrate the mind on the present moment. Where the circle begins, so shall it end in the place where all life and death is represented. In the place where men buy and sell each other's souls. I see you standing in the centre of your circle, surrounded by Death. I see you surrounded by the five young people. If they die, so will you.'

31

'Johnny Mann?'

Mann turned at the sound of a New York accent and saw a tall, curly-haired man entering the temple. He was wearing a faded sarong around his lower half and a bleached-out cotton shirt on the top. He greeted the monk with a low bow.

'Louis?' The man came over to shake Mann's hand.

Louis had a strong handshake and the frame of a man once large and muscled, now devoid of all fat. But still the outline of the strength could be seen under his summer clothes. Mann looked at his arms. Where his sleeves were rolled up there were the faded scars of blue tattoos that had been removed.

'I thought you might get here early so I've been looking out for you.' His hair was a frizzy mass of curls that moved as if on springs as he talked. His blue-grey eyes, rimmed with dark blond lashes, held Mann's gaze. His face was tanned and handsome, but weathered.

'Please follow me.'

Louis seemed anxious to leave the temple. But Thailand was not a country that encouraged haste of any kind. It was too hot to hurry, and Buddha's teachings did not allow for impatience.

When Mann stopped to bow his head towards the altar and pay his respects to the old monk, the monk raised his eyes from his notebook and held up his palms towards Mann, as if to communicate a message via his hands.

'When you lose your way, go back to the beginning. Go to where all men are equal and there is no one religion. The circle is not yet complete. You can break it. But you must hurry; you are very near to death. You will be faced with a mirror and you will not know yourself in it.'

Then he picked up his notebook and continued with his writing.

Mann followed Louis out of the temple. An orange-robed monk was sweeping up outside the temple as they left. In the shade of the golden obelisk a dog lay panting on its side. Louis walked purposefully as he strode in front of Mann and they crossed the open courtyard and passed the two smaller temples. A tan-coloured feral dog roamed hungrily. All the dogs had the same look about them here, Mann thought, like short-haired, short-legged dingos.

Louis gestured back towards the temple and the monk.

'Crazy, huh? It's a crazy world. Are you a Buddhist?'

'I've had a taster of most religions. I tend to take the bits I like and leave the rest. I haven't found one that offered me the whole package yet.'

'I converted to Buddhism but I don't go for the fortune-telling side of it. I try and live by the code of respect for others.'

They walked back towards the rear of the courtyard, past the sweeping monk and two young monks who were playing tag amongst a washing line full of sheets. They reached the Enlightenment Centre's doorway at the far end of the courtyard. Just outside the doorway a small altar sat, at eye level, and a sumo-sized Buddha smiled out from a garland of pink plastic flowers.

'Buddhism is the main religion here?'

'Not amongst the hill tribes. They are mainly animists. They make noises about being Christians or Buddhists but they sprinkle it with a liberal dose of their animist beliefs.'

'Animists believe in what – nature?'

'Yes. Everything has a spirit: the river, the mountain, men, and animals. All spirits must be appeased. It is a religion based on fear. They make blood sacrifices, go in for taboos, charms, that kind of thing. The dead worry them more than the living.'

Louis stopped at the entrance and was about to step back to allow Mann to enter first when he held up his arm to stop him.

'Like this mirror here . . .' In the entrance to the centre was a circular mirror. 'It has been left by an animist who is worried about the dead returning to this place. It is supposed to shock the spirit when it sees its own reflection and make him go away.'

'Was it left here because someone thinks the five volunteers are dead?'

Louis snatched the mirror away from the door.

'Maybe.' They entered the cool shade and musty darkness.

'Do you know why they were taken?'

'Wrong place, wrong time. That's the only explanation.'

'The old monk seemed to think someone else caused the trouble.' Mann followed Louis into a gloomy corridor with that unmistakable smell of the tropics and no aircon – a mildly fizzing, sweetly unpleasant smell of things rotting in the heat.

'He would say that. It's what all Buddhism is founded on – cause and effect.' Louis stopped in his tracks and looked across at Mann. 'What are you getting at?'

'You met them here that first day?'

'Yes, I did.'

'It was your job to look after them for their first week, wasn't it?'

'Yes. It was my job to shepherd them to the various people and places needed. That was all. My role was to give them an understanding of what the situation is with the hill tribes and their refugee status. I briefed them on what their specific job here would be at the camps – they were going to be helping to build a school. On a practical level, they needed to learn how to use the materials and what skills were involved in the actual building.'

'Where did you go to teach them that?'

'I took them up into the hills north of here. There is a centre for the tribes up there. We stayed there for three nights and they learned how to thatch, learned how to build. We had some fun. We trekked through the jungle and stayed with a remote tribe. They saw the problems, met the people, that kind of thing. The rest of the time they were here, they met monks and social workers and other non-government organisations – NGOs. I'll show you their classroom.'

He led Mann down a corridor. On the right were official portraits of the King of Thailand when he was a young prince. His hair stood straight up on his head in a boxy style that made him look more like the Fresh Prince of Bel-Air rather than the future king of Thailand. There was a second photo of him in his orange robes.

'Was the prince a monk?' asked Mann.

'Briefly. It is customary for most boys to enter the monastery for a few months, to learn about Buddhism. But here in Chiang Mai, where people are poor and education difficult to afford, there are many young boys studying to be monks – it means a free education for them and the added bonus that their parents are guaranteed a place in heaven.'

'Good selling point,' commented Mann, wryly.

The classroom was on the left, the whiteboard still up. The room had a couple of basic foldaway tables and a dozen plastic chairs – that was it. It echoed with their footsteps as they stepped onto the linoleum floor. The walls were decorated with acupuncture charts and drawings of human anatomy interspersed with posters of people on mats in various yoga positions. There was an appeal poster for the tsunami relief fund, with 'NAP' printed prominently across the top.

'Do you work exclusively for NAP?' Mann said, looking closely at a poster of smashed houses and fishing boats on roofs.

'Not exclusively. I do whatever I can. You acquire skills along life's road, don't you?'

'Like what?'

'I help out in a hospital in Mae Sot as a medic and I go into the Burmese hills as a backpack medic, to help the hill tribes.'

'Very worthy job. You're a trained doctor?'

'Somewhere between a doctor and a nurse. I am qualified to do certain emergency procedures.'

'More of a field doctor?'

Louis was busy tidying the chairs.

'I suppose so.'

'One of those skills you acquired along the way?'

'I suppose so.'

'What are you doing here now?'

'You emailed me, remember? I have things to do here, personal stuff.' He turned to stare at Mann. 'I have gone out of my way to be helpful. I feel like I'm being cross-examined. What is it you need – my name, rank and serial number?' He spoke half-jokingly, but Mann could see he was beginning to get pissed off.

'Look . . .' Mann turned around to face him. 'I'll be honest – I don't give a fuck about you or your life. I care about why five kids have gone missing. You can opt out of everything as far as I am concerned. You can spend your life saluting the sun and sticking incense cones up your arse, I couldn't give a damn. But, yes, when it comes to my job, even where you had those tattoos on your forearms done and why you had them removed – even these details matter to me right now.'

Louis looked uneasy but apologetic.

'Okay, okay.' He smiled. 'I'm not used to getting the third degree. Lots of people live here because they would rather not live somewhere else. This is a paradise where you can start again. I had the tattoos removed because I no longer believed in what they stood for.'

'Which was?'

He had lost the smile now. 'When I was young I belonged to the White Terror group. It's a racist group in New York—'

'I know what it is. The name kind of speaks for itself, doesn't it? You were in the forces though, weren't you? Which was it, the army, the navy, special?'

'No, you're wrong. Look, I have told you enough. I don't see why I have to tell you jack shit. Who the fuck are you anyway?'

'I am a rare thing around here: someone who gives a damn what happens to those five kids. I intend to find out why they were taken and who has them. If there's any dirty dark secret in your past that's put these kids in danger in the present, I want to know.'

Louis sat down on one of the plastic chairs and rested his elbows on his knees. He shook his head and, as his hair parted, Mann caught the glimpse of blue on his scalp. He had racist slogans tattooed on his scalp as well as everywhere else. The White Terror group wore them on their heads as a badge of honour.

'I came out here for some headspace. I never expected to stay but the people, the way of life here, made me rethink mine. My dirty secrets don't go beyond 1986. The kids going missing has nothing to do with me.' He stood and stacked the chairs and made ready to leave.

'When someone offered me the NAP work I jumped at it. It means I can hang about up here for a few days, relax. Things can get tense down in Mae Sot.'

'Did the kids say what they thought about NAP?'

'They thought they were lucky. They *were* lucky – small group, individual attention.'

They walked back along the corridor towards the rectangle of bright sunshine waiting for them at the end.

'How did they leave here?'

'By airconditioned minibus.'

'How did they seem?'

'Seem?'

'Happy, sad, worried? What?'

Louis thought about his answer. They stopped by the poster of the prince.

'Young. They just seemed young. They made me feel so old. Fuck! It seems like yesterday I came here but I've lived here for fifteen years. Time means nothing to me now. There's a slight change in the seasons but it always looks the same. It's all crazy shit, huh? You were young and then one day you wake up old.' He shrugged. 'How did that happen?'

'I've often wondered the same thing myself,' Mann replied as he walked away and left Louis standing in the entrance to the yoga centre.

Mann went to look for his tuk-tuk driver. The young monks had vanished between the drying sheets. The other monk had finished sweeping and was sat watching the dog feeding her young. But there was also someone new in the courtyard. From beneath the obelisk at the entrance to the park an old woman stepped into Mann's path as he made his way across the dusty square. She was carrying a small wicker basket in the shape of a ball. It contained a bird, barely more than a fledgling, startlingly ugly in the surrounds of so much gold and red and finery. This bird was grey, big eyed, and it beat its wings to try and maintain its balance as the woman turned the basket in her hands. Its dusty feathers flew from the ball. She grinned up into Mann's face.

'Free bird – free soul. One thousand baht.' Mann tried to sidestep her but she was small and nimble and determined. 'Free bird – free your soul,' she repeated, undeterred.

Mann looked into her eyes. She was ancient. How on earth had she caught this bird? He looked over to where she was pointing. There were four other cages, each with the same type of bird, a generic and ugly type of sparrow that could be found anywhere in the world.

She wagged her finger back and forth from her basket to the other remaining cages on the floor at the side of the temple.

'Family.' She grinned, brown stumps for teeth, still blocking Mann's path as he tried to go around her.

The old monk from the temple appeared behind Mann.

'Buddhists believe to set something free is to free yourself.'

Mann looked from the monk to the woman.

'But you have to trap it first?'

The monk and the old woman nodded in unison.

32

Alfie left Magda resting. He had cleared the mess up and had made her take a break. She was so exhausted but he was so proud of her. She had her fighting spirit back. Whilst she was sleeping he cycled over to Katrien's. He tucked his bike around the back of her building and sauntered casually to the entrance, carrying a box; it was his usual trick of pretending to be a delivery man. With the information that Magda had got from Dorothy he could now have a crack at getting Katrien's codes. He also needed to get back into her apartment to access her email accounts. Using his mobile, he rang NAP and asked to speak to her, making sure she was safely out of the flat, then hung up before she came to the phone.

Within minutes he was back in her flat. Nothing had changed. Everything was in the same immaculate state. Bed made, silk knickers left on the top. Maybe she was expecting company, thought Alfie. It would take more than silk knickers to make her attractive to him. He touched the mouse and the screen sprang into life. He clicked on the other accounts on the screen and saw that she was offline. He followed the 'forgotten password' link and prepared to answer the questions.

Place of birth? He typed in 'Burma'.

Favourite colour? He typed in 'black'.

A new message came up for katcream69. It was her password reminder: *bitch.*

Now Alfie knew her password and he had access to all her accounts.

33

Mann spent the rest of the day chasing up anyone who had had contact with the five but found out very little he didn't already know. He was ready to head south to Mae Sot the following morning, making this his one and only night in Chiang Mai. Now he was sitting at a portable bar in the centre of town. It reminded him of the burger vans outside a football match in the UK. It was parked up on a broad piece of pavement, just a few feet away from the busy main road and the River Ping. It was almost like Europe, with pavement cafés on cobbled streets, except it was as hot as a furnace: at forty degrees, the evening was no cooler than the day had been. He cradled his ice-cold glass and waited for cooler air from the circulating fan to reach him as it came by every thirty seconds on its rotation. It was plugged into a series of extension leads that disappeared out of sight around the corner of a building.

In the middle of the mobile bar was a pretty woman in her fifties. She looked like Imelda Marcos. She had dyed black hair and a puffy, pretty, made-up face. Her chubby hands moved at a measured pace across the bottles as she made the drinks slowly, deliberately. She did not have the luxury of space and one wild swing of her arm would have taken out most of her stock. Outside the kiosk, there were the other three members of staff – two men and Imelda's beautiful, quirky-looking daughter.

Mann looked up to see Louis walking towards him. He was dressed in jeans this time but he had on the same cotton shirt.

Louis sat down opposite Mann and waited for Imelda's daughter to acknowledge his existence. She didn't. She picked up the dirty glasses, refreshed the bowls of peanuts and kept up a constant conversation on her mobile, making sure that she made as little contact with the customers as possible. One of the others took his order. Imelda inclined her head in a slow Geisha bow and Louis returned it. She giggled; her teeth were tiny pins. 'How did you get on today? Did you talk to everyone you needed to?'

'I think so. I leave for Mae Sot tomorrow.'

'How are you getting there?'

'Don't know yet. Are you headed that way?'

'No, but I know a man – Gee. He goes back and forth. I'll ring him and tell him to pick you up outside your hotel. Don't give him more than five thousand baht and don't pay him till you get there. He's a like-able rogue but you can't trust him.'

'Thought you might consider helping; I could use a handy guy with a gun.'

Louis rested his keys on the table and pulled out a pack of Marlboro Lights. He slouched over the table and tapped a cigarette out of the pack. Imelda's daughter appeared from nowhere, lit it for him, and disappeared again. He turned his head and grinned at Mann.

'You had me checked out?' He sat back in his chair and studied Mann.

'I had you checked before I came. Although there wasn't a lot to uncover in the last fifteen years. Except . . . you are an ex-marine and you never mentioned you were once a mercenary and that you fought on the side of the Karen National Liberation Army.'

Louis took a drag of his cigarette and nodded.

'Well done, big respect, man. That took some digging.'

'Actually, I didn't know that last bit. I presumed you were out here for that long you probably got paid when the Opium King was handing out big money to foreign mercenaries, right?'

Louis realised he had walked straight into Mann's trap. He smiled and then shook his head sadly. 'That was when the KNLA had a chance of winning. Now they are screwed.' Imelda's daughter brought their drinks over. 'Now there are twenty thousand KNLA with little or no equipment against five hundred thousand fully armed Burmese. The villagers don't stand a chance. No one does in Burma. The kids are as good as dead. The Burmese do whatever the fuck they like and no one stops them – it's the teak, the resources. The world might be appalled but it's also a consumer. It still does business with Burma. The villagers won't be able to help the kids, they won't just face the Burmese army, they will face organised paid gangs of murderers. They're called Shwit. It's the sound of a throat being

139

cut. They kill anyone with links to the KNLA, past or present.' Louis looked up from his beer and gave a faint smile. 'Now, I'm a man who likes a cause but I also like to feel I can win.'

'So, will you help me?'

Louis laughed gently. 'You don't give up do you? Mercenaries are ten a penny in this part of the world. Some of them don't even want any money – they do it to get target practice. The hills have at least more than one crazy white mercenary in them at any one time. Seems Rambo is alive and well and living in the Shan State.' He shrugged and shook his head. 'They always go mad in the end, or they get killed. Sometimes they find God. Mercenaries and missionaries seem to go together. Mae Sot is everything a good border town on the edge of hell should be; it exists for darkness and misery and blood and fear, where the wealthy and the poor meet across the poker tables of life and bet on one another's souls.'

'Is that what you did?'

'Yes. But not any more. I am hoping the Buddhism will save my soul, but, if not, it's been a calming influence – one I needed. Us crazy whites can have a lust for blood once we kill; we cannot forgive ourselves and we cannot stop.'

Mann smiled ruefully. 'Yes, it warps the brain.'

'That's because we don't have a cause like they do. The Karen kill only to defend. They don't take a life unnecessarily because they are all on the same side really. They are all fighting the Burmese military junta, whether they are Karen or poor Burmese farmers. They should fight together, but they don't, of course. Buddhist Karen kill Christian Karen and so on. They are splintered. What's that old saying – "divided we fall"?'

'Yes. Something like that. So you're not interested in the reward money?'

'How much?'

'Two million US.'

'Jesus! Who put that up?'

'Anonymous. You interested now?'

Louis shook his head. 'I turned over a new leaf, remember?'

Mann smiled. 'I have to meet up with a man named Riley, he's the NAP contact at Mae Klaw. You know him?'

'I know him well. He's a good guy. He runs the whole NGO side of things at Mae Sot. Go to King's bar. He's there every evening. You can trust Riley,' said Louis before drinking the dregs of his beer.

'Trust means something different to everyone,' Mann said. 'It depends on what's important to you. Some people you could trust with your life but not with your wallet or your wife. Everyone has their Achilles' heel. I trust no one, it's easier that way.'

34

Alfie had spent the day looking at Katrien's emails. She had been in charge of setting up the volunteers' programme and questions were being asked as to where exactly the money had gone. One question was leading to another by the look of it, and she was finding herself in hot water – she was now being asked to account for the money raised for the tsunami and told to submit detailed reports on all the projects she had managed in the last eighteen months. She was fending them off with demands for more time to compile them.

She was very careful with her emails. She deleted all private ones immediately. Now he knew a lot about Katrien, Alfie was becoming a full-time voyeur. He watched her when she was sitting at the PC. She preferred live chat. Clients didn't have to have a webcam, messenger was fine, but she liked them to see her. It was a fetish she had: being watched, them watching her take off her clothes, performing solo sex acts.

But Alfie had realised it wasn't always solo. Sometimes there was a man with her, other times a woman. Sometimes Katrien would even stop her lengthy sex sessions to come and chat on the messenger when someone signed in that she wanted to speak to. Then Alfie would be able to see her. She liked to wear bondage gear. She liked to wear a dildo strapped around her waist that she used to penetrate people. Not just other women – Alfie had heard a few men taking it from her up the arse. He listened to her drunken antics, her drug-fuelled, all-night sessions. Every night she partied. Alfie had quickly come to the conclusion she was out of control.

He watched her now, walking past the screen. She was constantly checking who was online. She seemed to be waiting for someone. *Buzzz*. Her messenger reminder alerted her that someone wanted to speak to her. She sat down, drew her chair close to the screen and began to type.

'Hello, Big Man.'

Alfie had got used to the way she talked to different people. She had four people she liked to talk to on the webcam. He had realised there was one amongst them that she really felt affection for, the rest she was manipulating. The one she called 'Big Man' was a business arrangement.

'The two million is back on. That will buy us whatever we need . . . Nothing's changed . . . We are just expanding . . . We don't just sell it, we grow it and refine it and we ship it . . . You will have your share . . .' As Katrien signed off she saw something unfamiliar on the screen – she saw the reflection of something small, a light in the top left-hand corner; she saw the camera watching her.

35

Jake looked at Anna. She was walking just ahead of them, her head was down. He knew she was exhausted but she said nothing. Now that the mule had to carry Lucas, they all had to share out its load. It was heavy and it cut into her shoulders. Jake thought about calling to her but decided it was not a good idea; the less attention drawn to the girls the better. Saw's men were in the woods all around, calling to one another in their growls and barks. The woods were full of the rustlings of their feet and the stench of their bodies. The night was still hours away. They had been walking since dawn and they seemed to be walking faster than usual. Jake wondered where they were headed; all he knew was that it was getting warmer as they left behind the higher mountain peaks and headed back towards the lowlands. He took out his water bottle and hurried to catch up with Lucas. The mule was plodding on, its head down, as its small hooves picked their way carefully over the difficult ground. Jake held the water bottle to Lucas's mouth and helped him drink. Lucas's eyes rolled in his head. Jake held on to him as he lurched forward on the steep pass. Jake looked behind.

'Come on, Thomas, keep up,' he shouted quietly back to a flagging Thomas. 'We'll be stopping soon.'

Toad and Weasel overtook Jake now as they ran ahead, their bare feet sending up showers of fine dust and stone. They were coming to the remnants of a road.

Saw appeared beside Jake and, with a wave of his hand, he ordered them all to stay where they were. Saw's men crept forward through the forest and a shout went up, answered by others, and Toad called them on. They came cautiously out of the forest and hit what must have once been a well-used track. It was wide, fit for vehicles, but it hadn't seen much traffic for many years now – there was a green snake of grass up its spine and the jungle was beginning to encroach across it.

For a minute Saw stood, his chest rising and falling with the exertion of the run. Then, reassured that all was well, he ran and caught up with his men, over-taking them on the road.

At the edge of the road, a wild she-dog lay panting in the shade of the overhanging vines, feeding her puppies. Her skinny ribcage rose and fell as her puppies suckled. She lifted her head as the group came up the road. Saw approached her first and she snarled. Saw kicked out as he passed. One of the puppies flew into the air and landed with its neck broken, still twitching on the side of the road. The she-dog snatched up her remaining puppies in her mouth and scampered off.

Jake and the others followed Toad along the road. Small houses began appearing, dilapidated and deserted.

Then, further on, two long tall barns and several small single-storey buildings came into view and, below them, what looked like a manmade lake. Whatever had been made here, it had been a big operation, thought Jake. It wasn't exactly easy to find. Although Jake hadn't read the guide books, Anna had, and he remembered her telling him about the old heroin refineries. Jake was pretty sure he was looking at one now.

Jake held on to Lucas and the mule whilst they stood still and watched as the porters' packs were laid down and they were made to walk on along the road and into the old buildings to check for booby traps and mines. Saw and his men walked afterwards into the ruins. They were trackers, hunters, more at home in the forest than in a house. Here they crawled and crept along the outside of the buildings, they felt their way around its walls. They signalled to one another with animal calls as they swept through each building.

Toad led Jake and the others down and they joined Saw under the ramshackle roof of a large open-sided barn. All around them were the remnants of the building's former life: the vats used to distil the heroin, lengths of plastic tube, old sacks of sugar, everything lying discarded and rusted, frayed at the edges. It looked like it had been many years since it had been operational.

Saw was standing above them on a raised platform. Jake could see that Saw looked elated, his feet planted wide, hands on his hips. He seemed to be smelling the air as he looked all around and shouted to the grey, shredded, fragile leaves that made the roof. Jake watched the birds rise unsettled from the rafters, and it struck

Jake that this was home for Saw. He had brought them to his home. They were going to be able to rest, which was good, but it would not be without its downside. The more Jake spent time with Saw, the more he understood what made him tick. He seemed to be able to tell when he was about to kick off, even before his deputies could. Jake felt it in the air. He saw it in Saw's expressions. Every day Saw looked more demonic than the last.

This place felt more like a lair than a place of comfort and Saw looked empowered; he was the man in charge.

Saw stood on the platform remembering what it had been like to stand on that very spot many years before. It was where the heroin was stored ready for transportation. He had had his first taste of wealth and power and dominance on this platform, in this camp. Here he had raped his first woman on this *very* floor. Here in front of the others he had beaten her unconscious and left her for others to finish. This place had made Saw what he was. He had given his youth to working for the good of the Opium King. Here he made massive wealth for his master and he had been promised much. He looked across and saw Jake watching him.

Saw had been betrayed then.

He would not be betrayed again.

36

Mann waited at the front of the hotel. He looked at his watch. Bang on five, a black Nissan Navara grunted up to the front of the hotel and a small dark-skinned man in his early sixties, wearing a red Nike baseball cap and a gold chain around his neck, hopped out of the driver's seat and came around to shake Mann's hand. Outside the hotel, some anti-government protesters were setting up a blockade.

'Welcome to Thailand.'

'You must be Gee.'

'Please . . .' He held the passenger door open. Mann stashed his bag behind his seat.

'I appreciate the lift.'

'It is no problem for me. I have business there. Louis is an old friend.'

They turned out of the hotel, took a right past the night markets now quiet and deserted, and onto the highway heading south.

'What kind of business?'

'Import, export.'

'Right.' Mann left it there. It seemed like import,

export was the profession of everyone and anyone in Asia.

'And you, sir?' Mann could see he was being scrutinised.

'I am here about the missing volunteers.'

'The five young people?'

'Yes, that's right. I am going to try and find them if I can.'

'Ah ha . . . I see. That is why you go to Mae Sot? Ah ha . . . I see. It is a very important thing you do. The world is watching. Thailand depends on the world to make economic growth, you understand?'

'I understand.'

'You been to Burma, Mr Mann? Beautiful place. But so many troubles.'

'No, I haven't been, not yet.'

'Ah ha . . . Maybe you will see Burma when you look for the five?'

It was still early – the earth had a pink post-dawn blush to it. Mann dozed. They stopped for fuel and for Gee to stretch his legs. There was an air of suspicion and suspense on the troubled streets. Anti-government protesters gathered in packs and lurked in shadows as the government troops passed in displays of authority.

Three hours down the highway, Mann opened his eyes as the car slowed then stopped at a police checkpoint. One of the two officers looked first at Gee, then peered in at Mann. Armoured vehicles were nose to tail waiting for deployment as soldiers smoked cheroots and sipped coffee. The men stared in at Mann, as did their commander, leaning on his vehicle, arms crossed.

One of the policemen ordered Gee out of the car. Gee did as he was told, nodding and smiling in the direction of the commander. They walked a few feet away from the car with one of the officers whilst the other came around to the passenger side to talk to Mann.

'What is your business here?'

Mann smiled. 'Tourist. I'll be going home soon.'

The officer continued staring at Mann but he had no idea how good Mann was at staring back and eventually he gave up. The military commander was still watching Mann. Mann watched the police officer saunter back to his colleague who was shaking Gee's hand. Money passed between them.

'What are they looking for?' asked Mann as Gee got back into the car, started it up and drove away, leaving the policemen standing in the middle of the road watching them go.

'They look for refugees from camps. They look for people with drugs and now they are looking for trouble-makers. Sometimes they just want money, otherwise they will put something in your car for the next road block to find and then it will cost you double. Better pay when they ask. Less trouble.'

'Why did he want you out of the car?'

'You're a foreigner. It made him nervous.'

'Nervous, but still greedy.'

'Ah ha . . . you understand the way things work,' Gee laughed.

The distant mountain range grew closer. There was an ancient, Jurassic Park feel to the place The cloud settled in the depths of dense forest and the spiky mountains rose above. There was a suffocating stillness, a claustrophobic feel. Ivy smothered the trees. As they reached the mountains, the road swallowed them and plunged like a rollercoaster ride.

Gee sounded the horn three times as they made their tricky descent of the treacherous road, wet from the morning cloud. On the other side of the road a lorry driver beeped three times back.

'Why do you do that?'

'Many people die here,' he answered. 'We must make . . .' he banged his hand against the middle of the steering wheel '. . . three times. Spirits on road, dead people, we must say to get out of the way.'

Two more road blocks and another half an hour's driving and the hills levelled as they approached the outskirts of a town. Roadside vendors appeared and without warning they were stuck in the mayhem of a spice and livestock market.

'This is Mae Sot, sir,' Gee laughed. 'Always the same. Always madness here. Every colour of persons, every religion and no religion. We have every type here.'

They were stuck next to an open-air spice market where women slept, curled between the mountains of red chillies, dried fish and tamarind pods, camouflaged by the henna prints on their skin and intricate patterns on their bright sarongs and saris. They looked like part of the goods for sale. If the stories were true then perhaps they were – human trafficking was apparently big business in Mae Sot.

They inched past the tangle of tuk-tuks and crept forward with the cart pullers and the bicycles. They reached one of the main junctions in Mae Sot centre before taking a right and heading straight along a dusty pot-holed road. On one side there was a large temple, its gold shimmering in the noon sun, on the other, open-fronted shops selling replica goods alongside rubies and emeralds. They eventually pulled up outside a small guesthouse.

'We are here, sir. Here is the hotel.'

Mann peered out of the car. The name Mary's was hanging from a large board outside.

This was the last place the five had slept before they were taken. Maybe this place held the answers to where they were now.

37

'Lucas, you okay?'

Lucas murmured something and tried to smile, but his mouth was parched and his lips cracked. He had not been properly conscious all day. He had only just managed to swallow some water. He shivered as if he was cold and yet he sweated at the same time, his face was blotched crimson and white with fever, and he shook violently. Jake knew whatever illness it was that Lucas had, it was getting worse. Jake pulled a piece of discarded sacking near to him and lifted Lucas's head a little as he placed it underneath. It was all that Jake could offer to his friend for comfort. Jake touched him. He was burning up. He was obviously in pain as he brought his knees up to his stomach and groaned. There was nothing for Jake to wipe his face with, no water to cool his head. Jake knew he had to get more water for him.

Jake and the others lay on one side of the platform in the large open-sided barn. The ragged group of exhausted porters sat on the other.

Anna and Silke were curled up, lying on their sides,

both of them sound asleep. Jake was resting with his back against one of the many struts that held up the old roof. He was keeping watch. There was an air of nervous excitement amongst the men tonight. They were back on familiar territory. It wasn't a pleasant feeling for the five. They seemed to Jake to be electrically charged. They were fighting, drinking, running wild amongst the old ruins.

Handsome jumped up onto the platform, his body swaying from the rum he held in his hand. He had come to watch the porters. He stood over them shouting at them to hurry up as they emptied the sacks, found the rice, and dragged out the pots for cooking. Jake felt so sorry for them. They had been with them a week now, no food, hardly any rest. They looked so frightened. The women were constantly goaded and harassed, their shoulders raw from carrying the heavy packs. Every day they seemed to get thinner and weaker. Every day they grew more like the walking dead. Jake looked over at Thomas. Thomas was lying on his back, knees up, feet on the floor. His eyes were wide. He looked as if he were staring at the roof but he wasn't really looking at anything.

'You all right, Thomas?'

Thomas didn't answer; instead he shook his head and kept staring skyward.

'Thomas?' Jake repeated.

'Today, for the first time, I feel like we are not going to get out of this,' Thomas answered softly.

Jake looked at Thomas more closely. His eyes were red-rimmed and so dark and tired that they seemed as if they had been drawn in charcoal and then smudged.

154

His words hit Jake in the pit of his stomach. Thomas was the baby in the group and yet he was also the one who usually kept them all focused and gave them hope. Each of the five played a vital role for the others. Jake was the leader. If Lucas had been well, they would have made all the decisions together, the way they always did. They argued about stuff, then they laughed about it, but in the end they always agreed on a scheme. Anna was the strong one who never lost her fight. She also always knew what time it was back home. She knew exactly how many days they had travelled and she could detail the landscape in every hill they had crossed. Silke was kind and compassionate. She saw the best in people and she was always the first to offer sympathy. She was always the one who knew how the others were feeling. Silke carried the weight of everyone's problems on her shoulders. Thomas made them laugh. He lived in a world of dragons and extra-terrestrials. He could mimic the robots from *Star Wars*, he could make them laugh with his impressions of Toad and Weasel. But not today. Today Thomas had turned a horrible corner and had fallen into a void of despair.

'We will, Thomas, as long as Saw hasn't got what he wants, we have a hope.'

'But how long will he keep waiting? We have been moving for – what did Anna say – nineteen days?' He looked across at Jake. 'If anyone was going to help us, they would have done so by now. I think he will kill us soon.'

'We have to keep strong, Thomas. We can't give up hope now.'

Thomas turned his head and looked at his sister and Anna and at Lucas in turn. Then he turned back to stare at the ceiling.

'Whilst you were unconscious in the poppy field, Saw tortured and executed that man and his son and shot the bodyguards. He put them in a pile, poured petrol on them and set them alight and then he raped the woman and her children and threw them onto the fire. They were running around on fire, screaming. Saw just laughed. He doesn't care, Jake. He doesn't care about life, about death or anything. He's a devil. I don't want to watch Silke being raped, killed. I don't want to see you get murdered.' He turned to look at Lucas. 'Lucas is dying. I envy him. I would rather go first.'

'Thomas, don't say that! Don't give up now. The girls rely on you. We all need each other, Thomas. For fuck's sake – we all need each other.'

Lucas had started moaning again. His lips were cracked and dry. His body shook and sweated.

'Thomas, have you got any water left?' Jake asked him. Thomas shook his head. Anna and Silke were still sleeping. Handsome was nearest to them, harassing the porters whilst they prepared the food. As much as he didn't want to ask Handsome for anything, Jake could see that Lucas desperately needed water.

'He needs water,' Jake called out. In the still of the barn, his voice sounded flat. The porters turned to stare at him, as if he were mad. 'He needs water,' repeated Jake, louder this time. Anna stirred.

Handsome strode towards them and stood over Jake, looking disdainfully down at him.

'My friend is very sick. He needs water.' Handsome looked at Lucas but his eyes wandered to Silke and Anna and stayed there.

Thomas looked from him to his sister.

'Water! We need water.' He added his voice to Jake's to try and distract Handsome's thoughts away from the girls.

Handsome answered with a grunt and he strode back over to where the porters were and began to kick the old man. The female porters screamed as they tried to get out of the way but couldn't. The old man covered his head with his hands. Handsome started shouting at the women. They scrabbled onto their knees and began frantically searching in their packs. Handsome stood over them, pulling at their clothes, laughing. The old man was the last one to empty his sack. He was obviously reeling and so exhausted and frail after seven days on the road with no food. Handsome punched him viciously.

'Stop it,' Jake called. Handsome ignored him. 'Stop it, you bastard!' Jake sat up and shouted louder. 'He is an old man. He's had enough.'

For a second, Handsome didn't even seem to have heard; but then he turned sharply on his heel and charged towards Jake. Frothing at the mouth, his face contorted with rage and, without stopping to draw breath, he transferred his anger from the old man to Jake and kicked him hard in the ribs. Silke woke up and started screaming. Anna began shouting abuse and curses at Handsome. Jake could see her trying to free herself from her ties to help him.

'No, Anna, don't!' He curled into a ball to try and protect his head from the blows. He knew the less they did, the better it would be. Handsome reached down and pulled Jake up by his hair. Jake's hands were tied to Lucas and Lucas was dragged with him as Handsome held him by the throat and squeezed tightly.

Sudden shrill whistles resounded around the camp and Jake felt the floor reappear beneath his feet as Handsome dropped him. There were intruders.

38

A unit of twelve heavily-armed military men wearing the Burmese army insignia, SPDC, on their arms came into the camp.

Their leader had an air of authority in the way he strode into the camp. He was big, broad shouldered and upright. He was a smart man who took care with his appearance. He had a handsome face and a thin moustache that traced the outline of his mouth. He kept his army cap on his head throughout. He seemed to want to hide his face. On the occasions he looked in the direction of the five, he quickly looked away. He smoothed his moustache with his forefinger: a nervous habit that also served his vanity. Behind him his men stood with their guns at the ready. Saw's men hovered menacingly.

'Tell your men to back off, Saw,' the commander said as he signalled his men to wait where they were as he walked forward. 'I want to talk man to man, in private. There are things a leader should not share with his men.'

Saw cautiously waved his men back. They reluctantly retreated. Saw looked at the commander as he talked and smoothed his moustache.

'Everything has changed now,' the commander said as he looked Saw square in the eyes. If he was afraid, he didn't show it. 'You killed some important men in the mountains. Kasem and his son had many friends in the government. You forget the army runs on drug profits. I have to watch my back. I have a good thing going. I don't want to lose it. The idea was to expand it, not lose it all.' Jake could see that Saw was nervous. He listened, visibly uncomfortable, whilst the other man talked.

'We go back a long way, Saw. I have known you for many years. I knew you when you were running this refinery.'

'I passed a lot of business your way.'

'Yes. We have been useful to one another over the years, but now . . .' He stroked his moustache and looked up at Saw from beneath his cap. 'You are forgetting what is important. Business is what matters, Saw, not personal vendettas. You have become a liability. You had better hope a new deal comes swiftly.' His eyes flicked towards Jake and the others.

'It will come,' Saw barked, his hackles up.

'If it doesn't,' the commander stood and indicated to his men they would be leaving and then he leant over and whispered, 'I will have to kill you and the hostages. The Burmese junta doesn't want the world knowing the truth. They will blame the death of the hostages on the Karen and the world will hate them and the Karen will have no place to hide any more. They will be wiped out . . . but so, my friend, will you.'

39

'Sawat di kha.'

Mary was a pretty-faced woman, a Big Mama type, who looked like she could have come straight off the set of *South Pacific*. She kept one eye on Mann as she delivered the traditional Thai greeting and pressed her palms together as if in prayer and bowed. 'This my place.' She opened her large arms. 'Next door restaurant . . .' She waved her hand at a place behind him. '. . . and here internet.' She pointed to the far end of the reception area. 'If you want you can hire bike from me. You want, you ask, okay?'

There was something likeable about Mary; she was the 'cut-throat with a kind heart' type.

'My three daughters help.' She fixed a look on Mann that he had seen many times before. It said, I have unattractive daughters that I can't get rid of, I am selling them cheap – interested?

'Three? How lovely,' he replied politely.

'One is marry. Two no.'

161

As they were talking a young, over-fed, over-preened woman with a pretty face approached the desk. Mann knew it was one of Mary's daughters, summoned by a discreet whisper through a gap in the door behind the reception desk.

'My daughter, Cantana.' The young woman bowed and giggled. 'She take you to your room.'

Mary had one face for Mann, and the opposite for her daughter, who received nothing but scowls. 'Best room in hotel – bathroom, shower, very nice, you see.'

'How many rooms have you got here?'

'Have ten rooms.'

'Are they all full?'

She shook her head and her neck fat quivered. 'These are very hard times. Just have three rooms with guests.'

'Most of your guests are volunteers?'

She nodded, looking a little worried about Mann's line of questioning. Mann had read the local police report. After they were kidnapped from the refugee camp the five's belongings had been removed from Mary's. It appeared that they either came with very little cash or that someone had removed it after they disappeared. But then, it could have gone into any one of a number of pockets along the way, Mary's apron pocket was only one possibility.

Cantana beckoned for Mann to follow. She spoke no English but she smiled a lot. He followed her through to the backyard and up a flight of stairs that led to a row of rooms on the left. Mann's was the first door – the number six hung by one screw from the battered-looking door. They stood on the peeling

162

linoleum just inside the room and Cantana started sweeping her arms around in a 'how about this then?' gesture. Mann looked around the room. It certainly was a shit hole to be wondered at, thought Mann, but he smiled dutifully, feigning delight as Cantana stepped backwards, bowing, hands clasped, and backed out of the room. She was still smiling at him through the diminishing gap in the door as he finally managed to close it on her.

He put his bag on the bed. It was hard to believe that this was the best hotel in Mae Sot. The room appeared to be directly over the restaurant, flooded by the smell of food being cooked from underneath. Any stray light found its way in through massive gaps where the curtains didn't fit. The room was partitioned from the next one by a blocked-out window, covered in cardboard. It blocked out the sight but not the sound of next door's love-making session. He switched on the ceiling fan and pulled back the cover of the bed to have a look at the state of the sheets. It looked like a couple of sumos had been wrestling in the bed. He took out the trusty *kikoy* that he always carried; along with Delilah, it was the most useful thing he owned. Ever since his surfing days, he had travelled everywhere with it. It served as a towel, clothing, windbreak, sun shield, and now a sheet. He was tempted to look under his bed but decided it was probably best not to know what lurked there. Plenty of lizards on the walls – that was a good sign as any bugs might be eaten before they could start eating him. A big gap under the door, the perfect size for a snake to come in looking for somewhere cool to lie – not so good. Just as he finished stuffing a rolled towel into the gap, his phone went.

'Shrimp? How's it going?'

'It's an awesome place. It must have been paradise before the tsunami. Lots of the small businesses have lost everything though. The government hung on to the aid money. They sold off the villagers' land around the coast and didn't let them return. Now the place has more high-rises going up than homes. It's the same old story – the little people suffer, the big people cash in.'

'Who's there with you?'

'There are five of us here. The others have been here for ten weeks. They were glad to see me, new blood.'

'Who are the others?'

'A bunch of middle-agers "living the dream" – which has turned into a bit of a nightmare. They came over to build this school but now we have all this trouble and unrest. The project manager pulled out, which is why I got the job. They say we'll all be pulled out if things don't resolve themselves in a week. Basically, I am organising morale-boosting projects rather than building ones. I have left that to the Thai workmen and am taking the volunteers off for a picnic tomorrow, and tonight I have got a quiz night organised. My two categories are fashion through the ages and the history of guns.'

'What's their take on NAP?'

'They're a bit reluctant to badmouth it, they paid a lot of money to come here, but they obviously feel it's all a bit of a con. This school is no way looking like it will be finished and it seems to be the same all over.'

'Yeah, well, I don't know where the money's gone, then,' said Mann. 'We know that millions were raised to help after the tsunami. Magda told me she was involved with the fundraising. It was going to rebuild small hotels, shops, beach bars. What's happened to it? Find out exactly what NAP has been doing out there for me – and try not to have too much fun.'

'Okay, boss, will do. How's it going with you?'

Mann looked around the room.

'I'm in Camp Cockroach. It's forty degrees and I don't have aircon. And the couple next door are on a shagging marathon. Apart from that, great . . . I'm off to the refugee camp tomorrow but so far I have a list of possible but no clear suspects . . . Oh and, Shrimp?'

'Yes, boss?'

'I am hiding two million US dollars here.' Mann looked across at his bag. He'd been carrying it around since Hong Kong. He was keen to find a safe place for it now. 'I will text you the details when I know where. If something happens to me and there's any chance of still getting the kids out, I am relying on you to come and do it.'

'No problemo, boss.'

Mann went to liven himself up with a shower. He wanted to chat to the other inmates along the landing but, as the session next door was still in full swing, he decided now was not a good time. Instead, he headed down and stopped at the front desk on his way out. Mary disappeared suddenly when she saw him coming but soon reappeared, dragging a sullen-faced girl with

165

the traditional crusty yellow sunblock that the local girls liked to smear on their cheeks. It was regarded as a beauty enhancer but as far as Mann could tell it either hid or caused bad skin, because hers looked like the lunar landscape under the yellow crust.

'Mr Mann – this is my number two daughter, Nissa.'

This girl was obviously the brains of the outfit. Her English was good but her face would have soured milk. She stood blinking at him for a few minutes until her mother nudged her in the ribs, then she smiled reluctantly. Mann could see why she didn't do it willingly; she had the worst teeth he had seen in a long time.

'Pleased to meet you.' Mann smiled and winked. She panicked and remembered that she'd dropped something on the floor behind the counter. She didn't come back up. Mary flapped her arms and, to judge from her jerky body movements, gave her daughter a few sharp kicks beneath the desk. Mann left: the girl had suffered enough.

He walked out of the front of the guesthouse and crossed over to find some shade and to get a look at Mae Sot. Gee was right, the place had every creed and colour. As he walked down the busy roads, stepping on and off the pavement as it crumbled beneath his feet, a tall black African walked by, his wife in full burka walking behind him. Mann watched him as he shook hands with a man wearing a fez. Sikhs rode by on bicycles with turbans on their heads and Hindus in white robes sat with Burmese, Thai, and Indian men drinking coffee in cafés. Chinese men shared shisha pipes with Africans. The odd pale-faced westerner darted past.

Mann came off the main street and headed towards a covered market area. He was swallowed up by the stalls that touched one another overhead, and a dark wet world of life and death blinked up at him from below as he passed stalls groaning with the weight of butchered pigs, piled high and buzzing with flies. Pink-eyed white rabbits in cages on the floor stared up at him. A crusty-faced woman thrust a live disembowelled frog into his face. It was then that he saw Louis rushing through the market. He wasn't stopping to buy. Mann slipped in unnoticed behind him. He had tailed him to the end of the first set of stalls, across a small road, and back into darkness when Gee stepped into his path. His face was grave.

'You are lost, my friend. You do not want to go that way.'

40

Shrimp left the middle-agers to sleep whilst he went in search of a bar and some locals to talk to and find out the truth behind the tsunami rebuild. He came out of his hotel and walked away from the beach towards the town and the sprawling market that sprang up every evening. It was filled with noisy bars and garishly-lit avenues of stalls selling fake bags, sunglasses and Calvin Kleins.

Shrimp was about to sit with some lobster-faced Aussies who were wearing vests and talking about boxing with the Thai barman – all friendly enough but not exactly enticing. Then he heard the familiar strains of Madonna and 'Like a Virgin'. Out of the corner of his eye he spied a mirror-ball. Three girls in sequin hotpants and glittering heels beckoned him over. He gave the Aussies a wide berth and linked arm in arm with two of the girls as they escorted him to the bar. It was a small semi-circular space done out in a glitzy seventies style with an impressive collection of mirrorballs and Kylie memorabilia. Lava lamps decorated the bar. Shrimp felt at home.

'What can I get you, good-lookin'?' the tallest of the

three girls asked in a clear voice as she moved behind the bar to serve him. She had long thick hair, heavy makeup, but good bone structure, thought Shrimp – and great legs.

'Do you have Diet Coke?'

'Sorry, hon, we only have regular. We have a great champagne cocktail, half price and, as it's happy hour, you get two for one: one for you and one for me.' She smiled cheekily.

'Okay.'

'Fab.' She gave a giggle before turning on her heel and bending over into the fridge at the end of the bar. She pulled out the bottle of fizz and popped it amidst giggles and mock shrieks from the other girls. Shrimp had seen her give it a little shake before she popped it. He didn't blame her, from the sound of the girls, a lot was expected of a cheap bottle of fizz. She popped the cork and a plume of fizz obliged, much to the delight of the girls. She poured him out a flute and one for herself.

'Salut, baby!' she said.

'Cheers.'

'What's your name, hon?' she asked as she wet her lips with the fizz.

'Li,' Shrimp answered. 'Yours?'

'Mine's Summer. Over there are June and July.' She motioned to the shrieking girls.

'Nice place you have, Summer.'

'Thank you, hon, but I used to have a real smart place before the tsunami.' Summer retouched her makeup, snapped the compact shut and threw it back in her handbag. 'I lost everything in that wave.'

'Didn't you get help from any charities? Didn't the government help you rebuild?'

'Sure, they made promises but the money didn't come. I made a big mistake and made a private deal with an investor. They promised me money to rebuild it. They made me sign it away – the bar, everything. I had something special then. Now I just have this . . .' Summer rolled her eyes around the makeshift bar that she assembled every evening and took down at dawn.

'Who made you?'

'The people who run this Thai boxing place. Built a brand new stadium at the end of the beach.'

'Where did they get the money to build that?'

'Those Thai boxers have friends in very high places. They muscled in on lots of the small folk. They got the backing of the police, the local government. They took it from me.'

'How did they manage to do that?'

'After the tsunami the government just hung on to the money. It wasn't just people here in the town who lost out. The fishermen all along the coast? They all lost their homes and the government wouldn't let them come back. They sold off their land to big developers.' Summer shook her head sadly. 'I put my heart and soul into making that bar work. Ah well . . . that's the way it goes. They did it to a lot of people along this beach.'

'Have you got the forms that you signed – can I take a look?'

Summer rolled her eyes and shook her head.

'So dumb – they took it all off me. I never had anything to show in the end. It's the same with many of us here in the market. We had nice places by the beach but after the tsunami it's all gone. So, tell me, honey, what's all this to you? Smart dresser like you? You just on vacation here or what? Why do you care about us?'

'I am looking into some charities. You say those Thai boxing people have done the same to others?'

'Yeah. It wasn't easy after the tsunami. We should have waited. It's just the government money didn't come quick enough and we trusted them. People are really scared of them now.'

'Who else got cheated? Can you take me to them?'

'Sure.'

They left the bar and walked through the bars and the stalls until they came to a stall on the edge of the lit area. They found a couple with a sleeping baby lying on a piece of cardboard. Their stall was a small one, the usual tat mainly: necklaces, shell ornaments but also some beautifully carved wooden figures. The man was sat on a stool carving one, and the woman was making a silver wire necklace.

They looked up and smiled but looked concerned at the sight of Summer with Shrimp. The man stood to greet them. Summer spoke to him in Thai. Then she turned to Shrimp.

'This is Yada and his wife. They had a business on the beach before the tsunami.'

Yada nodded furiously. 'It was a good business, sir. We had a shop, it was my grandfather's shop. In our family many years. My father too, he was a furniture maker. Very beautiful.' He pulled out a catalogue with glossy photos of ornately carved pieces of teak furniture. 'Can make all these things.'

'What happened?' Shrimp took the folder and politely turned the laminated pages.

'We were waiting for the money from the government and two people from NAP came and they said we could get money quicker if we let them help. I trusted them. They said that lots of people from the Netherlands collected money to help.' Yada looked across at his wife. She looked as if she had lost her faith not just in the world but in her husband. Her silence spoke volumes. 'I know I should not have. I thought I would get more money. I listened to them . . . I lost everything. They make me fill in forms. The money comes through and they show me a piece of paper that say I no longer own my shop.'

'Did they bring a lawyer with them?'

'Oh yes, sugar.' Summer answered while trying on a brass bangle. 'They have a whole team.'

'Yes, yes.' Yada nodded in agreement and looked back at his wife, whose demeanour remained hostile. 'There was nothing I could do. The lawyer came, two policemen.'

'Local police?'

'Yes. We see them every day, walking up and down the beach. They must have been paid big.'

Summer and Shrimp left Yada and his wife and they headed back to Summer's bar. They had another cocktail. By that time two British lads had wandered in and were being fussed over. Summer sat at the bar, next to Shrimp. He suddenly realised he was starving.

'Do you know of somewhere good to eat here, Summer? You hungry?'

'Sure.' Summer smiled sweetly and it was as she reached over to get her handbag from behind the bar that Shrimp saw her Adam's apple. He looked from Summer to the other girls with their arms around the lads. Yep, they were all tall girls, deep voices, big hands.

Shrimp had heard about it, he'd seen a drag act in Hong Kong but he'd never talked to a ladyboy before.

'What? Something the matter, honey?' Summer got off her stool; Shrimp was staring at her.

'Are you a man, Summer?'

She giggled nervously. 'Not a man, sugar. Didn't you know there are three sexes in Thailand – man, woman and ladyboy? I had the operation, see?' She patted her flat crotch. Shrimp looked horrified. 'Don't worry. Even have the vagina, clit, everything – so clever, these doctors. Feel everything, if you know what I mean? Real tight fit, sugar.'

'Okay, I have to go now.' Shrimp got quickly down from his stool.

'Look!' She wiggled her shorts down around her narrow hips and pulled down the front of her panties. There was a triangle of pubic hair but no appendage. 'Let me show you the man in the boat.'

'Not right now, thank you – have to run, just remembered something.'

Shrimp skipped past the girls, June and July, who were waiting to hug him on the way out. He was in such a hurry he didn't see the two men who were armed with baseball bats.

41

The men skulked around like beaten dogs as Saw continued to sit by the fire and drink alone after the Burmese commander had left. Jake wondered who would dare approach him first. Toad moped around the edge of the fire. Handsome came nowhere near. He was busy; he had resumed pestering the female porters. But Weasel was most in need of reassurance from his leader and he was too stupid to know better. Jake watched him approach Saw. As soon as he was within range, Saw lashed out at him. He stood and caught Weasel by the throat and, although he was shorter than Weasel, he was at least a third heavier and broader and he picked Weasel up by the throat and threw him across the fire. Handsome stopped to watch as Weasel rolled away from the hot embers and lay panting, a wheezing noise coming from his chest, a look of consternation on his face as he waited to see what more would come his way. Saw bounded across to him and, for a moment, Jake thought he was going to finish Weasel; and he could see that Weasel thought it too and suddenly looked as if he might fight back.

His body stiffened and he raised himself on his elbows, but his instincts told him it would be the last strike he ever made. Handsome started laughing. He drank from his rum bottle and he laughed at Weasel, smouldering, covered in ash. Handsome knew he was the only one who could come close to stepping into Saw's shoes. He was like Saw in so many ways: clever, ruthless and evil. But Saw was still the dominant male in the pack. Handsome would have to wait a bit longer before he could oust Saw.

Saw stood for a few minutes, swaying on unstable feet but his eyes held a look of triumph as he grinned at Weasel and then at Handsome. He lifted his rum bottle towards him as a salute and Handsome returned it. They howled to the rafters and bats flew. Saw's eyes filled with menace. He strode over towards the porters and picked up the youngest of the female porters by the arm and he tore open her top and exposed her small breasts. She clutched desperately at her clothes and tried to cover herself. Scrabbling across the ground the other women screamed and moved as far away as they could. Saw's men gathered around. Here was what they had been waiting for – a return of the master they knew. As the young woman tried to get away from Saw he pulled her skirt off and pushed her to the ground. She crawled on all fours as he tore off her underwear. Saw's men gathered round, chanting and jeering at the waiting porters. Their faces were lit with madness and lechery. Jake and Thomas moved closer to the girls and tried to hide them from the men's view. The young porter crawled naked around the platform, like a spider with half its legs pulled off. She couldn't escape. She couldn't get past Saw's men. Saw began throwing objects at her to make her move as she crawled around the platform, pleading for her life. An old pot broke as it bounced from her back onto the floor. She collapsed momentarily with the impact of it and lay for a few seconds, bleeding. In that instant Saw seemed to lose interest in her. He stopped, his chest rising and falling, the veins standing out on his neck muscles, the sweat gleaming on his body – and he looked across at Anna.

42

Alfie ducked into the doorway of the Prostitute Information Centre. He looked inside; Magda was showing a group of tourists around. She was doing the usual: 'Here is the bed . . . here is where we wash the penis . . .'

Magda waved at him, obviously confused as to why Alfie was hiding in her doorway. She went to call to him, but he tucked himself further in the doorway and shook his head and made a face as if to say 'not now'. Magda shrugged and went on with her tour, then she realised what Alfie was doing there – it must have to do with Katrien walking past minutes earlier. Magda had heard her heels all the way down the street. Her nose in the air. Her vampire makeup. She had been all smiles when Magda first met her; now she pretended she didn't even know who Magda was.

Alfie stayed there a few more minutes before he ducked to the other side of the street and moved close to the walls of the Auld Church. Belle, the brass statue memorial to prostitutes everywhere, still had a bike chained to her. Alfie knew that would be what Magda wanted to tell him – she wanted to tell him to get the bike removed. She was a stickler for the rules and she felt she owed it to the prostitutes to make sure they weren't forgotten. Alfie would do something about it later but, for now, he had to keep after Katrien who was walking past Casa Roso. Just when Alfie thought she would turn into one of the side roads, he saw her turn instead into the entrance to the Erotic Museum. He walked across the canal bridge and watched from a doorway as she walked straight in to the ground-floor shop and then disappeared right. Alfie waited a minute then followed her. He peered in. The shop looked empty. There was no one along its two congested aisles crammed with chocolate willies and flavoured condoms. The attendant wasn't there. Nothing unusual in that, thought Alfie. He knew the woman who ran it. She was on her own most days and had probably been caught short and was out the back. He passed the mannequin on a bike hovering over a penis-shaped saddle and modelling tacky red fishnets and suspenders and came level with the stairs up to the museum itself.

He heard the sound of voices as he stepped over the rope that acted as the gate to the museum. He crept silently up. The stairs swung sharply back on themselves in the typically Dutch tall, thin canal-house style. On the walls were beautiful drawings done by John Lennon – intimate portraits of Yoko.

Alfie heard a man and a woman, arguing. He recognised Katrien's voice, but not what she was saying; she was speaking in another language, but he could hear by the tone that it wasn't friendly.

Alfie stood on one of the ancient worn floorboards and it creaked. The voices abruptly stopped. Alfie turned and ran, straight into two English lads who were about to climb the stairs to the museum. He deftly stepped aside and the lads walked on up, straight into the wrath of Katrien and her friend. Alfie heard the shouting. Alfie'd been lucky. He crossed over the bridge nearby and went inside the Banana Bar opposite and watched through the window. The bar was one of the few left in Amsterdam that the Eastern Bloc mafia hadn't been able to muscle in and take over. They did a great line in intimidation. They were responsible for the imminent demise of De Wallen with all their brutality in humanity and pimping. He ordered a coffee and sat watching. First to emerge, looking flustered, it amused Alfie to see, was Katrien. Then came her companion. Alfie didn't recognise him. He was a short, dark-skinned man, well dressed, Asian. Alfie slipped out of the Banana Bar and followed her friend. He was crossing over the bridge to Alfie's side of the canal and then headed down towards Central Station. Alfie followed.

Katrien walked quickly away in the direction of the New Church and the Jordaan. She looked behind her and caught a glimpse of Alfie's blond curls, his leather jacket. Now she knew who was behind the hidden camera. She headed home to pack. She was going to have to leave sooner than she planned.

43

Alfie followed the man to a bar just near Central Station and sat drinking a beer as he watched him having what looked like a business meeting with a local. Alfie made sure he got close enough to take some good photos with his phone and then he sent the photos to the station to be put through the computer files. Alfie left them to it. They looked like they weren't moving and Alfie wanted to get the most out of the day. He had things to do. Firstly, he wanted to head back and check on Magda. He was nervous since the burglary. It had been a personal attack on Magda.

He had got as far as Belle when he saw the two men – smart, expensive coats, business suits. He stared hard. They had separated slightly. They were coming at him from both sides. They glanced around but always their eyes came back to stare at Alfie and they were headed straight for him. They looked familiar. Alfie kept walking forward, his mind whirring, matching faces in his memory. His mind spun him back to the night that Mann had arrived, when he was throwing a joint over the balcony. He looked down to see two men, one helping the other up from the ground. These were the same men. The men who had followed Magda and who very probably were responsible for breaking into the flat.

Alfie kept walking and his eyes instinctively flicked over to Magda's window to make sure she was safe. He could see her talking to customers in the PIC. She looked up at that second and saw by Alfie's expression that something was very wrong. Her eyes went to the two men approaching him; they had passed her now and she was staring at their backs. They were reaching inside their coats and Magda watched Alfie's expression and she saw the flash of a knife. She saw Alfie stop dead and go to turn and run and she saw the blade in the air as the man's arm drew back and lunged forward at Alfie.

In that instant Magda did what all the window prostitutes would have done in De Wallen. The one thing that would get everyone running onto the streets and to her aid. Magda pressed the panic button.

44

Late in the afternoon, Mann walked into King's bar. The place was empty except for the barman – a happy chap named Eric – an Indian with a predisposition for Americans and classic rock. The smell of garlic and ginger being fried wafted in from the kitchen at the back and there was a good degree of chilli in the air that burnt the eyes. Mann ordered a large vodka and a bottle of mineral water. He didn't trust the ice. Eric was all smiles. He looked like he loved his work. He marched up and down behind the bar and tinkered away as he hummed along to Bruce Springsteen singing about being born in the USA.

'Something to eat, sir?'

He handed Mann a well-thumbed menu – it looked like it doubled as a plate when necessary. There was a massive selection of faded photos of curries of the same colour and looked like washed-out cowpats.

Whilst Mann took his time considering which photo did it for him, the place filled with a bunch of freshly showered volunteer workers all chatting about their day: how much salted fish had arrived, how many more stacks of muslin were needed. Cutting his way through them, a lone tourist came shuffling in, a young lad with a backpack so big it got momentarily wedged in the door frame. Mann watched him sidle up to the bar. Eric homed in on him and negotiations began. It seemed the lad was looking for something that Eric just happened to have.

'No problem, my friend.' Eric was trying to look nonchalant whilst keeping his voice low. 'This I can do for you . . . for a very small fee. I can arrange for it to happen tonight. No need to wait. I make a phone call to my friend and he will take you to get your visa renewed tonight, no problem.'

The backpacker thanked Eric. Eric was on a roll. He could do this for the lad and that for him. But the backpacker wasn't able to hear so well over Bryan Adams and Eric had to shout louder than he really wanted to. He started to look like he was trying to hurry the deal along. 'Listen, let me tell you, visa renewal very dangerous at the moment. Cost normally five, six thousand baht. But, for you . . . I make deal, get it cheap – three thousand, my friend, very good deal.'

'Okay – I'll have that one.' Mann beckoned Eric over and pointed to a green pile on the middle page whilst he asked, 'Is Riley around?' He looked up from the menu.

Eric paused, rolled his eyes skyward, and smiled. 'Mr Riley? He will be here any minute now.'

Mann picked up his drink and went to sit at a table. When the curry arrived ten minutes later, it was surprisingly good. He was halfway through it, watching Eric still working his magic on the young backpacker, when a group of what Mann thought must be medics came in; they were still discussing the day's casualties as they made their way through the door. There were three of them: one woman and two men. The two men were olive skinned, dark haired, possibly European or South American, thought Mann. The woman was Caucasian, in her late thirties, Mann guessed. She was the one doing most of the talking. She had long blonde hair that she had tied in a thick rope plait and kept back from her face with a small, red-spotted kerchief, like the kind old bikers wore. She was the most animated of the bunch; her hands skipped in the air as she talked. The men listened and nodded but Mann could see they were on a mission to get to the bar and to switch off for the day.

Eric leaned across to her and nodded Mann's way. As the two men picked up their drinks and decided where to sit, she left them and approached Mann's table.

'You asked for Riley?'

'I did and, to be honest, you're better looking than I thought you'd be.'

She smiled. 'I'm Sue. I work with Riley.'

She reached across and shook Mann's hand. Her hands were long and thin – piano-playing hands, strong with long fingers. He looked into her eyes as they said hello. She must have been a beautiful child, thought Mann, with big blue eyes and blonde curls. Now she had grown into a very attractive woman with laughter lines and eyes that sparkled with confidence and something devilish. She sat down opposite.

Eric appeared beside them. 'This lady will help you

find Mr Riley,' he said, grinning, his head bobbing like a Bollywood dancer, obviously pleased with himself.

'Thank you, Eric, good job.' Mann kept a smile on his face as he waited for him to leave before he turned back to Sue.

She sat back in her chair and her eyes sparkled with intrigue as she eyed Mann.

'Let me guess. You are an arms dealer who needs to find a guide through to Burma and the supply chain?' She waited for a reaction and got nothing from Mann but a smile. 'No? Okay then . . .' She scrutinised Mann for a few seconds more. 'You sure as hell aren't a missionary – too sane looking. You don't smell like a medic and, although you have a few scars, you're too well dressed to be a mercenary. That leaves us with a misfit and we have plenty of them here. By the look of you, I'd say you are part Chinese. The main business with the Chinese in these parts is drugs. Most of them own the methamphetamine and the opium businesses around here. Okay then . . . I guess you're having trouble getting to your refineries and you need to find a new way in and out?'

Her eyes hardened. Mann sat back in his chair, took a drink and smiled at her. Bon Jovi began singing about living on a prayer.

'Good . . . very good.' Mann smiled. 'But it's not right.'

Mann jerked his head in the direction of the back-packer who was unloading his heavy pack. 'What is the lad buying, a visa?'

'He is probably *extending* his visa. The kids come

here all the time to do it. Anyone here for more than six weeks needs to get out and get stamped back in. Burma is the easiest way.'

'Everyone has to learn some time,' Mann replied taking a drink.

'What do you mean?'

'He's making some deal with Eric that involves him leaving his pack here and going outside to meet Eric's cousin. I'm guessing *he'll* take this lad's money then set him up with his cousin who will slit his throat.'

'No one goes near the Burmese border or Friendship Bridge, as it's laughingly called, at night, especially with all the tension here at the moment.'

'Then I think this lad is about to buy a death trip. Travelling is all about learning but there's learning and there's getting your throat cut.'

Eric caught Mann and Sue looking at him and he grinned haplessly. He looked very much as if he'd been caught out.

'But not safe now.' He leaned over and spoke in a stage whisper to the young backpacker and began furiously backpedalling: 'Stay next door. Cheap room there. In the morning take this road straight to bridge and you will find it no problem.' He held his hands up, palms to the ceiling, and wagged his head in Mann's direction.

'What do I owe you?' The youth looked perplexed.

'For you, my friend, no charge.' He set a beer down on the bar for the lad. 'Nobody gets cheated in King's bar, my friend.' Eric smiled and jiggled his head at Mann.

Mann nodded his approval and returned the back-packer's bemused smile with a wink.

Then Mann leaned forward across the table, rested his elbows and stared into Sue's face. She stared back, unflinching.

'Guessed it yet?'

'The foreign kids . . . that's what you're here about, isn't it?'

'Right third time.'

'What are you – a policeman?' Sue asked incredulously. 'Don't think I have ever seen one in these parts. Not a foreign one.'

'I am helping the Dutch parents of the five missing volunteers, but I need help. You obviously care about these kids.' Mann nodded in the direction of the back-packer sipping his beer and looking happy. Eric appeared with a curry for Sue.

'Have you eaten?' Sue asked.

'Yes, thank you, I think I had what you're having.'

She laughed. 'There is only one meal. It's curry and rice or curry and noodles.' She had a strange hint of South African in her voice, a soft roundness that gave it a melodic lilt. She held his gaze. She pushed the wispy curls at the side of her face back. Her cheeks were flushed from the warmth of the bar, her eyes were shining.

'So, an international detective, how exciting.' She smiled mischievously. 'Like James Bond.'

'Exactly.' Mann winked.

She gave a small, throaty giggle. 'Show me your gadgets then.'

Mann reached into his pocket and produced a small red-enamelled pocket knife.

'A Swiss army knife,' said Sue. 'Very impressive!'

'*And* it's the one with the hoofpick.' He grinned.

'They must have a lot of horses in Switzerland.'

'I've gone there many times looking for a horse,' said Mann. 'When I eventually found one, it was just my luck – someone had just done their hooves.'

Sue gave a deep laugh, slightly late, as if she'd got the punchline.

'What about you?' Mann asked. 'Do I detect a hint of Afrikaans?'

'You do. I spent my first ten years in Cape Town. My parents were South African but we moved around a lot after that.'

'How long have you been here?'

'Over five years now. My main job is as a medic working in the hospital here. I work alongside the foreign medics who come and help. Like the two South Americans that I came in with. I am also a backpack medic.'

'I met one of those – a guy called Louis?'

'Louis's a good friend. We go out into the hills, usually about eight of us. We take medical supplies to the remote villagers. We help wherever we can. Most of the injuries they suffer are from landmines, it's the most heavily mined area in the world, after Cambodia. If the malaria doesn't kill them, then landmines do. Our main job is to train them to treat their own. We have such a battle stopping them putting cow shit on open wounds or ripping out the placenta so they can take it to the woods to bury before it brings evil spirits to the house.'

'Animists?'

'You've done your homework. They will always cling to their ancient beliefs, which is fine, except when it's killing them, and the Burmese don't need any help doing that. Whenever another village is attacked across in Burma some of the villagers escape and the lucky ones find themselves here.'

'How often does that happen?'

'Weekly usually. It's daily persecution at the moment.'

'I've heard about the Shwit.'

'Yes, they are merciless. It's a grinding away of hope, a slow genocide. They just carry on doing what the Burmese junta do best. The ones who are determined to stay in their own land are the bravest but they're slowly being wiped out. We do what we can. The backpack medic team are vital to the villagers.'

'That must be dangerous, crossing into Burma? What about the Burmese military?'

'The KNLA help us.'

'Which ones?' asked Mann. 'I heard that some of the Karen are divided by religion. Buddhist against Christian, even within the army itself. Religion and killing, the two go together.'

'Yes, exactly, we see it all the time . . . even the crucifix kills. No one knows what goes on here. Even the journalists who care, who live here, who write about it, can't make sense of it and cannot offer a clear solution to the world. Have you been out to the Mae Klaw refugee camp yet?'

'I intend to go tomorrow. I want to meet with Riley.'

'Ah, Riley . . .' She gave her rasping giggle again. 'I know him very well. Come with me, I'll pick you up. I work there once a week. I hold a clinic for the new mothers. Then you'll see what the attack left behind. Of course, you won't see the men's decapitated heads and you won't see the raped and murdered women, the butchered children; they are buried already. Let's hope we will get in and get out safely. It's guarded by the same guards who took the blood money six weeks ago.'

The door opened again and a new group of volunteers breezed in, dressed in baggy shirts and original seventies high-waisted jeans. Sue looked at them, smiled and waved as she said under her breath:

'Here they come – the saviours of the human race. Their mission is to go anywhere in the world, to solve a given problem and to get out feeling much better about themselves. They don't really care about the culture of the place, the cause, or the people.' The group were talking noisily, oblivious to the rest of the people in the bar. 'The NGOs play games with the refugees like they were children. They have the money allocated but they give it with so many conditions – they have to fulfil this and that criteria. The main one is that they can't use it to fund the war. But it's impossible when their brothers, fathers, husbands and even mothers are in the fight and the only thing they have in life is to struggle. Of course they are going to – fighting is the only job most of them have. Do the NGOs seriously think they are not going to take every last penny to continue the fight? The NGOs just play God – it's part of the thrill for them.'

Mann studied her curiously.

'But weren't you all NGOs in the beginning?'

She smiled. 'Yes, of course. We are a necessary evil.' She grinned. 'But some of us care more than that. For me, this is an obsession, it's my reason for living. I found such kindness here – I'd never seen that before. I would die for these people. They have endured hell and worse.'

'You support the KNLA?'

'Of course.'

'You know that the world is blaming the KNLA for the kidnap of the five?'

She stared at him, amazed.

'How can that possibly be?'

'The Thai government has issued a statement supporting the Burmese junta's accusations that a group of renegade KNLA is responsible.'

'Why would the Karen want to risk losing the only help they get – the NGOs?'

'They are saying that it is a way of drawing attention to the conflict and getting funding. They are claiming that ransom demands have been made by a group claiming to be supported by the KNLA.'

She shook her head, despondent. 'Sometimes I think everyone is against us and what we are trying to do here.'

'A commander called Alak was mentioned. You know him?' Sue nodded. 'Could he have gone bad?'

'Maybe.' She looked pensive. 'In a world like this one, everyone has a price.'

45

The young porter girl was frantically trying to find her clothes and cover herself. Her back was bleeding, her body shaking so violently that her hands could not tie her sarong. Saw's men were banging their fists on the platform and shouting for Saw to rape the woman. Saw pulled Anna up by her arm. There was no stopping him now. He had reached the point of no return. He was like a wounded animal and wanted to hurt others.

'NO!' Jake kicked out at Saw as he dragged Anna up to her feet. 'Let her GO!'

Jake's voice came out so deep that it sounded strange to his own ears and Saw turned to look at him, almost as if he had never seen him before. Then he turned back to Anna. Anna looked him in the eye and spat. Saw closed his eyes and, when he reopened them, Jake thought that he would kill her – but instead he smiled and savoured her phlegm as if it were a flurry of snow on his face on a hot summer's day. Laughing, he pushed her to the floor and walked back across to the young porter who was sobbing as she saw him coming. She had nowhere left to run. Saw held her down and ripped her sarong away. He held her face to the ground as he pressed his weight on her and raped her. The girl's screams turned to deep guttural sobs as she endured the agony of her first sexual encounter and her last. After Saw was finished she lay where she was, her body shaking from the attack, her face still squashed into the ground, her legs open. Blood seeped into the floor beneath her narrow hips. He looked at his men and nodded towards the other female porters and the fight for them began.

But Saw's disappointment and his anger were unappeased. The porter girl had been just an appetiser for him and now his eyes and his thoughts turned back to Anna and Silke. Saw looked over and Jake could see his eyes searching and finding what he wanted as he pushed his way through his men. He strode over to the five and stood panting, his eyes rabid, his body sweating. He looked first at Anna, grinned and then he reached down and cut Silke's bonds and dragged her out from where she hid behind Thomas. He pulled her, screaming, across to where the men were fighting over the porters as if they were scraps of meat. He threw her down with the other women. The men ceased their squabbling for a few seconds as they twisted their heads this way and that and watched who would claim Silke – the best prize. Handsome stepped forward and the rest of the men stepped back. Handsome ran his hand over Silke's blonde hair and then he twisted his fingers in it and dragged her to her feet. Saw moved to stand beside him. His eyes were alight with madness. Handsome waited for Saw's decision. Would he be allowed to claim the prize? Would he be shown the favour he craved?

Saw laughed. A grin spread across Handsome's face, but not for long.

'Tie her up,' Saw ordered and Silke was dragged away to the far end of the platform where she was stripped and tied to one of the roof struts. She stood naked, her head bowed, shaking with the fear as she pleaded for her life. Across from her, Thomas screamed and frantically tried to untie his bonds but his wrists and ankles were bleeding and all he could do was sink to his knees and scream at the men to stop. All he could do was cry for his sister. He could not help her, none of them could. Silke looked over to him.

'Be brave, Thomas,' she mouthed. 'I love you, little brother.'

46

By the time Shrimp came back the next afternoon, there was nothing left of Summer's bar: bottles, mirrorballs and plastic palms lay broken in piles on the pavement. Summer was sweeping up the worst of the mess.

'Summer?' Shrimp stood at the entrance.

'Yes, honey?' Summer stopped and looked up.

'What happened?'

'Two men from the Thai boxing stadium showed up after you left. Big ugly types, one was the main fighter down there, the other is his coach. They trashed my bar and said I shouldn't be mixing with trouble makers.'

'I'm so sorry, Summer.'

Summer shrugged and smiled kindly at him as she resumed her sweeping.

'You didn't do it, honey. It was those two animals.'

'Yes, but I should have known they'd be watching. Did they hurt you?'

'Just a little.' She turned her face to one side and Shrimp could see that, underneath all the makeup, her face was swollen. 'It's the end for me now, honey.' She stopped and looked around at the remnants of her bar and then she looked at the pile of debris. 'I have no money and no way of doing it all over again. Those thugs have finished me this time. They won, I lost.'

'You haven't lost yet, Summer. Get around all those who have been cheated out of their livelihood. One of them must have some record of it all. I need to know who is behind this and who was responsible for swindling you and the others out of your businesses. It isn't right. When people give to charities they expect it to go to the people who need it, not to local bullies and corrupt police.'

Shrimp was mad angry when he left Summer and headed down towards Patong Beach. People all over the world had given money towards the tsunami relief – the last thing they wanted was for it to end up destroying lives rather than rebuilding them. The beach was straight ahead, at the end of the road. For a few seconds Shrimp's anger vanished as he spied the rectangle of heaven: white sand, blue sky and turquoise sea, sandwiched between the buildings. He pushed his sporty Ray Bans up on top of his head where they rested on the stiff peaks of hair gel. The beach was just beginning to empty a little. The sun loungers were being dusted off and moved back into orderly rows.

He was about to cross Thaweewong Road, the main road that ran alongside Patong Beach, when he was almost trampled by the entourage of promoters and trainers who were handing out leaflets advertising an upcoming Thai boxing bout. On the top of the brightly decorated van that was accompanying them down the road was a tough-looking boxer sparring with an imaginary opponent, 'El Supremo' written on his bright blue shiny shirt. A man whose T-shirt proclaimed him to be the coach and who was holding a loudhailer was announcing, in his none too perfect English, 'Thursday, six o'clock, ten thousand dollars to win. Anyone win. Come, be lucky . . .'

Shrimp stared hard at them. From Summer's description of them, these looked to be the men who had beaten her up and trashed the bar. Shrimp followed the van for a bit as it carried on towards a brand new Thai boxing stadium that he could see at the end of the beach. Once he was certain it was the right people, he turned right and walked along past a salsa bar where a few lads were enjoying a hair of the dog, and past the police immigration department. It seemed to have been made of sterner stuff than anything else along the beach, and had needed very little repair after the tsunami. He came to Patong Beach Road and followed it up and off to the left where it branched out. He'd already passed two Indian tailors, who seemed to be able to survive any world disaster. Shrimp had already spent all his money with them, buying a bespoke suit in three different styles. The only bar on the lane that he could see had an open front and heavy wooden stools. An old wooden carved Cherokee Indian stood outside.

A young Thai waitress in a very short version of the traditional leather-beaded dress, a string of white shells around her neck, stepped out and greeted him with an open arm and a bow. He looked at the name above the door. Wampums.

'Sawat di kha.' She bowed. 'Please come inside, sir.'

Shrimp looked at his guide book. 'I was looking for a bar named Summer's. It was supposed to be up here.'

The girl looked like she either hadn't heard or hadn't understood – he didn't know which.

'Summer's,' Shrimp repeated, taking a step closer inside the entrance to the bar.

'Sorry, not here now.'

'But this *used* to be Summer's bar before the tsunami?'

The girl looked nervous and gave another plastic laugh, but she didn't answer.

'That's okay. I'll come in anyway,' said Shrimp.

The waitress stood back to allow him to enter, bowing as he passed. Ahead was a carved bar with totem poles as struts. The barman was a young Thai. He was in the process of trying to grow a moustache but it just wasn't happening. He had an explosion of acne over his forehead that had formed into crop circles.

Shrimp sat at the wooden bar and read the barman's name badge.

'Hi . . . Lamon. How ya doin'?' Lamon didn't answer. 'Diet Coke please.'

Whilst the barman fixed Shrimp's drink, Shrimp picked up a pen from the other side of the bar and wrote 'SUMMERS?' in large letters on a barmat. Lamon walked over, Coke in hand, and went to put the glass down on the mat. Then he read what Shrimp had written. Lamon scrutinised the mat and quickly pushed it back across the bar towards Shrimp. 'This bar is Wampums.'

'This . . .' Shrimp tapped his finger on the bar. 'This used to be Summer's bar?'

The barman shrugged. Shrimp was feeling irritated now. 'Seems to be a problem with getting information here,' he said. As he did so, he saw Lamon's eyes focus on something behind Shrimp's shoulder. Shrimp realised he wasn't alone. A voice came from behind.

'What information you need?'

Shrimp turned to see two men stood close behind him. He recognised them from the Thai boxing van. One was the boxer, El Supremo, the other was the man with the loudhailer. El Supremo had obviously taken a few less blows to the head than the other man, but he'd evidently not worn a mouthguard and had had to have most of his teeth replaced with gold ones. Coach clearly hadn't been able to afford it, so he tried not to smile. Shrimp swivelled around to face them.

'I am on holiday here. I was told to look up Summer's bar. I was told it was a great place to hang out, meet nice people – like you guys.' Shrimp smiled his most pleasant grin. It worked on Coach – he smiled back enthusiastically whilst trying to keep his top lip down to hide his lack of teeth. El Supremo didn't look like he knew how to smile. He also looked like he had once failed to notice a particularly nasty right hook coming at him; it had all but collapsed his eye socket and meant that he had to turn his head just slightly to the right to get Shrimp in focus.

'No more questions. You have finished your drink. Time to go.' El Supremo took a step closer towards Shrimp.

Shrimp looked at his half-drunk Coke and shrugged. He looked over at Lamon who was smudging the glasses with a cloth rather than cleaning them.

'It isn't Diet you know. You've given me regular.'

'Finish?' Coach asked.

'Sure. No lemon, no ice, regular Coke – not much of a first impression. And the girl's outfit? Yuk!' Shrimp hopped off the stool.

He walked back along the beach and into the police station. A couple of roughed-up-looking Thai lads were sitting in the corner, staring at the floor. The officer behind the desk looked up at Shrimp, puzzled.

'I want to report an assault.'

The policeman looked past Shrimp and grinned. Shrimp turned to see two heavily-armed policemen were waiting for him to finish.

47

Magda held Alfie's hand tight as she listened to the sound of his breathing. She leant forward and kissed the back of his hand as she whispered his name. His eyelids twitched. She knew he was struggling to come back to her. A minute later he managed to lift his long blond lashes and smile as he squeezed her hand.

Magda gasped with relief. 'I thought I'd lost you, Alfie.'

'No. I am still here.' He smiled sleepily. 'How long have I been out?'

'Twenty-four hours. You had to have a blood transfusion and an operation. You were in a bad way. You nearly lost a kidney.'

'Only nearly?' he grinned. 'They could have made an effort.' He tried to laugh but grimaced instead as the pain registered.

'It's not funny, Alfie. You were lucky you were wearing your old leather jacket.'

Alfie looked cross. 'Did they wreck it? Fucking bastards. I've had that jacket since I was a boy. It's my lucky jacket. I pulled you when I was wearing it.'

She smiled. 'It saved your life, Alfie. That's what I call really lucky.'

He lifted her hand to kiss it. 'I am sorry to make you worry. I'll be home later today.'

'Alfie, don't be ridiculous. You're going to have to stay in at least a couple of days.'

'Tell them I'll sign myself out. Listen to me, Magda. This takes the whole thing to another level now. Something is happening here, to us, to Jake. I want you to look at what that bitch Katrien is doing.' He stopped talking and looked at her face. 'What is it?'

Magda reached into her bag beside the bed and pulled out a newspaper. 'I got the paper this morning on the way here.' She unfolded it and looked at the front page. 'It's about Schiphol airport and the planned extensions. I was looking at the photo to see if my friend Lena was amongst the protesters yesterday – she usually is – but then I looked at the picture closely and I saw this . . .'

She showed Alfie the photo. In between two protesters with placards he saw someone he recognised, on her way into Departures. It was Katrien.

'Fucking hell! The sneaky little bitch. Right, I am getting up,' he said, sitting up too fast and wincing with the pain in his back and side. He leant back on the pillow and closed his eyes for a few seconds to allow the pain to ease. 'Contact the paper and ask them what time this photo was taken, contact the editor and ask . . . Ouch!' Alfie grimaced as the pain in his side increased.

'It's okay, Alfie. I rang the airport already. The only flight leaving for Asia during the following six hours was going to Kuala Lumpur and I checked on the internet. They are still running flights to Thailand from there. It must be something to do with Jake, Alfie. It has to be.'

48

Katrien stepped out onto the tarmac and smiled to herself; it was good to be home. Now she was back for good. She hadn't expected to have to get out of Amsterdam on such short notice. She had been hoping to tie up a few loose ends – but she'd managed one at least. Now she'd burnt her bridges and she was home for good. They could investigate her all they liked. They'd never find her in the Burmese jungle.

She checked in her bag and pulled out Johnny Mann's card. His mobile number and his satellite phone number were on it. When the time was right, she would make that call.

She looked around for her ride. She had someone special waiting for her. This was the start of her new life. She smiled to herself. She had done a good job of playing the men. She prided herself in being able to juggle them all and come out the winner. But then, after all, men were like dogs, they only ever wanted the same things. If you knew that, you could lead them anywhere. She looked around for her lift and saw him. He was out of uniform. Shame, he never looked so handsome out of it. He was touching his moustache the way he always did when he was nervous.

49

After leaving King's bar, Mann went back to Mary's. The evening seemed to have livened up there. The volunteers that he had seen in King's were now carrying on the party back at base. There seemed to be an open-door policy up and down the corridor and there was a lot of giggling coming from the rooms. Mann wasn't bothered by the noise. It was the quiet he couldn't stand. That's why he never liked going back to his apartment. It was just so empty. He knew that he could have someone in there, a woman to share his bed and make him feel wanted, but Mann didn't intend to fall into that trap; it wasn't fair to anyone. He had seen too many men do it. Just live with anyone rather than be on their own. What was it with men? They couldn't bear to be alone? They left their mother's house and moved straight in with a woman? As much as he loved women, mothering was something he had never needed from them.

He closed his door and walked along the corridor. The first door was open but no one was there. The second was open and a woman stood looking at Mann as he appeared in her doorway. She had on a loose cheesecloth blouse and a sarong wrapped around her hips. She had the look of a middle-aged hippy with money. She had a thinness to her that smacked of years with no appetite left for anything but alcohol and sex.

She stopped mid-swig of a beer and put the bottle down.

'Hello,' she said. 'I saw you talking to one of the medics in King's. I was there with the rest of the NGOs.' Her voice was raspy from too many cigarettes.

Mann leant on the door frame and waved a hello with one hand, brandishing a pack of beer with the other.

'Johnny,' he said. 'Can I come in?' He handed her the beers.

'A stranger bearing gifts – fantastic. Sit down.' She pointed to the bed. 'I'm Hillary.'

'How long have you all been here?'

Mann sat, she stood, Hillary shook her head and screwed up her face. 'About six months. This is our last night. They're flying us out because of the troubles. What about you? Strange time to arrive when everyone else is leaving.'

'Ah, well, never could plan a holiday right.'

'Is that what this is, a holiday? We thought you must be a new medic of some kind.'

'No, just a traveller. So, you've been staying here for six weeks?' Hillary nodded. 'At Mary's?' She smiled and nodded again as she opened a beer. 'So you were here when the five volunteers were kidnapped?' Hillary stopped drinking.

'Oh, so that's it?' She rolled her eyes. 'You're a reporter of some kind?' Mann didn't answer. 'Well, thanks for the beer, but I've already said all I know about it.'

'What if I told you I am here to help find them?'

'Then I'd still say, sorry, no comment. I was interviewed by the police. NAP have been very good to us. I've said all I will.'

'So you don't give a shit, basically?'

The atmosphere in the room was tense.

'Please leave.'

Mann went back into his room. There was certainly no more party going on now, his presence had definitely put a dampener on things. He checked his phone. He had a message from Alfie. He called him back.

'What is it, Alfie? You all right? I can hardly hear you.'

'I am not supposed to use my phone. I am in hospital. I followed Katrien when she met up with the guy she was emailing. I got knifed. I took a photo of him – he's been identified as one of a ring of drug traffickers under surveillance here. It's a Burmese connection. They import massive amounts of heroin and methamphetamine, ice. She's into the big league.'

'Is he the one who knifed you?'

'No. It was the two guys that you met outside Magda's flat that night, the Asians . . .'

'You must be doing something right to piss Katrien off so badly she's called in her friends. What about the two-million ransom money? How did she take that?'

'She was straight on the webcam, wetting her knickers and telling someone how it was all going to work out peachy for them. But she has left Amsterdam in a hurry. She was about to be hauled into an investigation about where the money from NAP has gone. I think things have got a bit sticky for her. She decided to get out while she could. Anyway, she's headed your way, Mann.'

'She must have a plan for getting her hands on the two million.'

'Yes, she's too greedy to fuck it up now.'

50

In the morning Mann sat next to Sue in her old Toyota as they drove along the main road out of Mae Sot, towards the mountains and Mae Klaw. The road began to straighten and level out and they crossed a wide bridge. Mann looked down and saw the people beneath the bridge by the side of the river, flanked either side by thick forest. People were washing themselves and their clothes in the shallow banks of the fast-flowing river, children were playing, and downstream a man was cleaning the wheels of his scooter. Palm-thatched roofs started appearing on the left, rising as if organically from the wide leaves and verdant greenery. From far away it looked like an idyllic jungle village. But Mann had been in refugee camps before – they were only one up from squatter towns like the ones he knew well in the Philippines. Here the houses weren't made from cardboard boxes or flattened Coke tins, they were made from recycled forest material. There was not a corrugated iron sheet in sight, just thousands of tiny bamboo huts on stilts ringed in by a barbed wire fence. It was a pretty place – but was still nothing but an overcrowded prison.

'It's a big camp. How many people live here?' asked Mann. He could see that the huts stretched as far as the horizon and the start of the mountains.

'At the moment there's two thousand but more arrive all the time.'

'Is Riley a medic too?'

'Not officially, but he's sat in on enough operations to make a good go at sewing someone up or delivering a baby if he has to,' said Sue. 'Riley has been here for so long that he has had to learn to do everything. That's the way it is here, people can be what they want to be, you can reinvent yourself, start afresh.' She looked across at Mann and he could see that her eyes were shining, whether with pride or with love, he wasn't sure. 'There is no one else who cares about these people as much as Riley. He lives, eats and breathes the refugee camps and the Karen people; it's all he really cares about. They have even made him an honorary Karen. You'll like Riley. He's a good guy.'

'What's his history?'

'He's lived all over the place before he came here, speaks French, Spanish, as well as Thai and the Burmese dialects. We've known each other for years. We used to be . . .' she flashed Mann a sidelong glance '. . . together. Now, we still share a house but we are not, you know, a couple.'

This information altered Mann's perception of this man he was about to meet. Riley had been on the list given to him by Katrien at NAP. All he'd managed to find out about him was that he was a long-standing charity organiser who had lived in the area for the last fifteen years and who knew everything there was to know about the refugee camps. Mann had seen his name mentioned in several reports about volunteer workers in the field. He was a champion for the needs of the Karen refugees. He seemed to never stop lobbying on their behalf, raising a lot of money for them over the years. In his head, Mann had an image of a worthy, khaki-shorted, comb-over type running around frantically organising, whilst the volunteer kids sniggered behind his back. Would Sue have been involved with a guy like that? Unlikely – though you just never knew with women and father figures.

Sue turned off the road and stopped just in front of the gated entrance to the camp. Its name, Mae Klaw, was spelt out with sticks of bamboo and mounted across the top of the gate, ranch-style. Two Thai policemen were smoking cheroots and watching the comings and goings of the camp with their guns resting in their holsters. They were sitting on sheets of bamboo that had been split and cut into lengths and bound together. Sue waved at them as they turned in.

Just inside the gate was a checkpoint, a small hut and two more policemen. Sue kept the car running whilst they waited for one of the officers to come over. He sauntered over deliberately slowly whilst the other one remained where he was, leaning against the side of the door frame of the hut and scowling.

'Papers?' He leant in the open car window and rested one hand on his holster as he addressed Sue but stared at Mann.

She answered him in Thai and a banter began

between them. Mann could see Sue wasn't fazed by his show of testosterone. She was all smiles, hands skipping in the air as she explained what Mann was doing there. Whatever she said seemed to please the officer who beamed in at Mann, his demeanour transformed from a sullen-faced, trigger-happy thug to that of a starstruck teenager.

Sue turned to Mann, a frozen smile on her face.

'I have just told him that you are a film maker and are looking for locations and extras.'

'Why did you do that?' said Mann, returning the gritted-teeth smile and nodding.

'Because otherwise they would have pretended to cooperate and then shot you or me or maybe both of us. Either way, it's best to lie. This way we're all happy.'

'You're a little too good at the lying bit.' Mann smiled and he leant across to shake the policeman's hand and wave at the other officer, who was watching closely.

'Only when dealing with Asians; it's the loss of face thing. Better to lie than to risk making them look stupid.' Sue drove through the camp gates and they parked up.

'That's what worries me. I *am* Asian.'

'You don't fool me. You're whatever suits you at the time.' She smiled.

One of the policemen who had been sat outside on the bamboo logs approached Mann's side of the car. His face was stony. He was obviously not impressed by Mann's movie-making ambitions.

'Passport.'

Mann gave it to him and watched as his eyes flicked

back and forth from Mann's face to the photo. He called over to the policeman who was still leaning on the door frame of the hut.

'Shit,' muttered Sue. 'Trouble. He wants your details checked. The other policeman thinks you are lying. If he gets on the radio, we are all screwed. They want us out of the car.'

Mann looked over to the gate. There were a lot of people around. A pregnant woman, selling a stack of dried leaves for thatching. Kids marching past for school. They'd never make it out, it was way too congested. They would have to deal with it. All four policemen were now standing by, their hands resting on their holsters. The policeman at the side of the car was more animated this time – he wanted them out of the vehicle now. His face had turned angry. He unclipped his gun.

Before Mann opened the door he slipped the set of twelve three-inch-diameter throwing stars into his left hand.

51

'So, Deming came to visit you, how often?'

Alfie had been home from the hospital a few hours. He had just got off the phone to Ng.

'Once a month,' answered Magda. She was emptying the drier and had her back to him. 'I told you all this before, Alfie. It was never an issue then.'

'It was never an issue before because he was just the man who impregnated you when you were a teenager. Now his son goes missing and we are being threatened. Was he a violent man?'

'Of course he wasn't, Alfie. He was gentle and sweet and very caring.'

'Did you love him?'

'Yes.'

'But he was an old man compared to you. How could you have a proper relationship with an old man?'

'He wasn't an old man, Alfie! For God's sake, it happens every day. Young girl falls for older man – so what?'

Alfie was about to say something but thought better of it. He was pushing Magda. She hated criticism, she hated discussing her feelings. She hated the way her past came back to spit at her sometimes. She had built this big wall around her life. But Alfie had been allowed to scale it. By now he knew every chink in it where daylight got through and he knew where to get a foothold. But he also knew where it was crumbling.

'All right, but we must do what we can now, Magda.'

Magda turned her back to him and he watched her head and shoulders drop as she thought about what he said. He knew she was only going through the motions of sorting towels from the drier.

'You are right.' She turned to face him. 'What do you want me to do?'

'I want you to think back. Go through your things, mementoes, photos. I want to see if there is anything in there that will tell us more about him and his associates. Someone thinks we're hiding something here, Magda. Maybe we are without knowing.'

'Okay. You're right.'

'I'm right?' He leant forward and felt her forehead. 'I'm right? Twice? You sick?' She smiled at him sheepishly.

'You know I love you, Alfie.'

'I know.'

After Alfie had left, Magda sat at the kitchen table and she let her mind drift back. It was something she hated doing, even more so now that she was dying. She had never liked to live in the past. Even thinking about the boys was just too painful. But now, she knew she had to do it and she sat and stared into space and thought about Deming. She thought first of how she had heard of his death. A solicitor had written to inform her. Magda had been breastfeeding Jake in her bed when she opened the letter. She hadn't heard from Deming in two months. She had been beside herself with worry, without even a contact number to reach him. The letter said he'd left instructions in the event of his death and that he had died, simple as that. It wasn't until six months later that she managed to find out the truth about his death – that he had been murdered. She was a mistress, after all. She had no rights.

Then Magda's mind skipped back to the first day she saw him, looking at her through the glass. He had just stared. She hadn't known what to do for a minute. He didn't want to buy her services; he was just staring at her as if he knew her. There was a silence inside the window, its glass was thick. Even dressed only in her bikini she was hot beneath the neon lights. Deming hadn't even looked her up and down as they usually did, imagining her naked. He had just stared at her face. She remembered that she'd smiled at him and his smile began slowly, his eyes still intently studying her face, but then it broadened and she remembered feeling embarrassed, as if they shared something beautiful. And at that moment she knew that he had fallen in love with her and she with him.

Magda got up to unload the dishwasher, which had begun to beep that it had finished its cycle. She was glad of the interruption. She looked out of the window; the sky was blue, and she wondered if the sky was blue over Jake. Deming had loved his sons; he had lavished them with gifts. Deming had given her more than she ever thought she would have – love, a family, a home. He had bought her the flat. He had encouraged her to start up the PIC. She owned the lease to the ground floor of that building. It never made any money – it was a charity – but it would be an asset to sell one day and it was a place where she could store things.

Magda nearly dropped the glass she was holding. She gripped the edge of the sink and screamed with joy. Yes! Her precious boxes of mementoes hadn't been lost in the burglary at all. She had stored them at the PIC.

52

Mann was almost hoping they would put his cover to the test. The passport he gave them was fake. Ting from the Anti-Fraud division had done a great job on it but it didn't list his occupation as 'film producer'. Ting's warped sense of humour had come to the fore and he had put him down as a psychiatrist.

'What's the problem, mate, no signal?'

'Here's Riley,' whispered Sue, sighing with relief.

A tall, strong-looking guy was approaching from within the camp. He walked with a slight swagger. Even though he must have seen a few hard winters, he was still young-looking, with a muscular but agile build. He was wearing army shorts, an ancient Billabong T-shirt and thong sandals, the kind made from recycled rubber tyres. He went straight over to the policemen and offered them cigarettes. They all took one and the one who had started the trouble motioned Mann's way.

'Him?' Riley shook his head as he pointed to Mann. The officers looked to Mann to be backing off. The first policeman, the budding actor, was laughing now, nodding enthusiastically and slapping Riley on the back. Riley walked over. The radio was put back inside the hut.

'All right, mate?'

Riley shook his hand warmly. Mann hadn't expected Riley to be an Australian. He had a Desperate Dan look about him with a stubbly long lower jaw like that of a hungry bear. He had short, bristling hair that was silvered at the temples and his green eyes had deep laughter lines around them.

He wiped his forehead with his sleeve; his tension was showing, but he kept a smile on his face. 'Let's get out of here.'

Sue reached into the back seat and pulled out her bag.

'I'm off to the clinic.' She gave Mann a smile and waved goodbye to Riley. 'See you boys later.' She walked away from the entrance, up to the right, and further into the camp.

Riley called after her. 'Sue, any trouble, send word and I'll come straightaway, okay?'

'Don't worry. I'll catch up with you as soon as I'm done.'

'Let's go, mate.' Riley turned away and led Mann into the main part of the camp. Once out of earshot of the policemen he muttered: 'They are making a big display about security. Bunch of corrupt wankers. They would let anyone in if you paid them enough, they already did. We can talk and walk; I want you to meet someone.'

'The overcrowding always this bad?' asked Mann,

looking around as they walked. It was as hectic as a small city and the place had a chaotic air, as if of implosion.

'It varies. They have to make the most of the daylight hours. With no plumbing and no electricity, things shut down here early every evening.' Riley stopped to speak to a youth as they walked on down the road. He was obviously getting a mild ticking-off of some kind, but it ended with smiles and handshakes. Riley turned back to Mann. 'There's a whole generation of teenagers who only know refugee life. They turn to what bored teenagers all over the world turn to – dope, drink and fighting over girls.'

'How do they live?'

'They get a government allowance of two kilos of rice per person a month. The rest they barter and hustle for.'

'And work? What do they do all day?'

'They are not allowed to work. Sometimes they sneak out to find work as labourers but the most they can hope to get is a hundred baht a day – it wouldn't even buy a beer back home. Most don't risk even looking for work because the penalties are too harsh. Did you see the road blocks on the way up here?'

'There are a lot of them. The area seems to be well policed.'

A small child ran past their feet chasing a plastic ball.

'Well policed in one way, but not in another. If you get caught by those guys they want a big payoff. Corruption is always a major factor out here. It takes a small fortune to bribe their way out of here. Otherwise they risk being marched back to the border and handed back to the Burmese – and believe me, there's not going to be a good ending to that story.'

Mann kicked the ball back to the child who laughed and ran alongside them, dribbling the ball as he went.

'How are they supposed to become less of a burden if they're not allowed to work?'

Riley groaned with exasperation. 'Exactly. Whilst we thank God for the Thai government's generosity, it's no life for these people. Many of them were born here. They live like rats in a barrel. They're only allowed a four-metre square of dirt to build on. It's not a lot for eight of you and more arrive every day.'

Mann's young footballer had attracted two more lads keen to show off their footballing prowess. One of them kicked the ball high. Mann headed it back.

'There is no hope for these people except to give what little they have to the KNLA and hope that they will achieve something with it.'

'That's some hope, Riley, isn't it? They don't have the money or the resources to win. It might be the longest running civil war in history but it's one that they are unlikely to win. And now the world will be against them. Did you get to know the five volunteers?'

'Yes. They were a good bunch of kids – willing, eager. Nothing was too much trouble for them. I liked these kids – the best we've had, shame it had to be them. Sometimes we get real whingers – some people I would have paid good money to have kidnapped – but they were young and enthusiastic . . . a breath of fresh air.'

'You were responsible for what they did on a day-to-day basis here?'

'Yes, to a degree. They were sent out by a company called NAP – a load of wankers, cutting corners, charging their volunteers a fortune and then ripping them off. They send them out here and the support stops and we're supposed to take over for free.'

'You don't get paid for that?'

'Okay, yeah, I get paid . . . but not much compared to what they're making and they're supposed to be a charity. Fuckers!' He stopped and faced Mann. 'My biggest regret is that I wasn't here when the camp was attacked. I get bouts of malaria and I was in the middle of one when it happened. But they shouldn't have been here either. Normally the volunteers arrive here by nine and leave by mid-afternoon. Nobody but the refugees are allowed to live here at camp. All the NGOs disappear by sundown – they usually have their own transport.'

'A guy called Louis looked after them in Chiang Mai. Do you know him?'

'Not well,' Riley replied and he gave him a sidelong glance. Mann knew he was lying but he didn't know why. 'What about your background? Do you have special training in this sort of thing or are you personally involved?'

'I am officially on vacation. I was asked to help by a friend who knows one of the girls' mothers.' Mann had decided that the less people who knew the truth, the better.

Riley looked out towards the mountains. The cloud

223

was lifting; soon they would feel the blistering heat. 'Christ, I hope they're okay. I don't suppose anything in their life has ever prepared them for *this*.'

Mann could see by Riley's face that guilt was eating him up. Mann could imagine Riley would have put up a good fight. They would have got more than they bargained for if they had chosen a different day to attack, but then, maybe that's precisely why they chose that day.

'But the reality is I couldn't have stopped it happening.' Riley picked up a stone that was nudging his toe. 'I am just glad that they are all together. Let's hope they will support one another and come through it.'

He glanced to the far horizon; the hills were beautiful, almost sheer as they rose majestically above the plains. Mann was staring towards Burma too, the mountainous Shan homeland where the Karen state begged to be allowed to exist. Mann wondered where in those dense woodlands his brother was and whether he was still alive.

53

'She is gone now, Thomas. They can't hurt her any more.'

The grey mists of morning gave a ghostly quality to the still air around the twisted bodies of the murdered women, now unearthly and ugly forms.

Thomas lay curled on his side, still watching his sister even though she had died in the hours before dawn. He could not take his eyes from her body, tied to the roof strut, now stiffening with rigor mortis. Silke's head was slumped forward and her blonde hair hung over her face. Thomas was glad he did not have to see her face.

At the far end of the platform the old porter said nothing as he crouched and stared at the carnage; his daughter was one of the dead before him. From outside came the sound of drunken snoring.

Jake reached over and laid his hand on Thomas's back.

'Thomas?' Jake did not know what he was going to say to Thomas, but he only knew he had to reach him. 'Thomas . . .'

But he stopped as he saw a shadowy figure appear at the edge of the platform. Even in the dim light Jake knew it was Saw. He had come to know the way he stood, the way he walked. He had come to know *him*. Saw scanned the platform, taking in the details anew as if he too had thought it had only been a dream and his eyes were only now gradually unveiling it as more than a nightmare. For a minute he reeled as he stepped up onto the platform and then he focused on Jake and walked slowly towards him. He squatted beside him. His body stank of sweat and his breath was foul with rum.

'You see . . .' Saw flicked his head in the direction of the bodies that lay behind him. 'All this, your fault, boy.'

Jake stared back at him but said nothing, his heart hammering in his chest.

'What do you want?' Anna said, her voice quiet, soft, devastated.

Saw twisted his neck to look at her with contempt.

'From you? I will have what I want soon enough. From the boy . . .' He turned back to Jake. 'I will have my life back or you will die like her.'

He pointed to Silke whose body was already crawling with flies.

54

Magda unlocked the front door of the PIC and locked it behind her. She pulled down the blind and went through to the back. There was a kitchen area and a small office with shelves where she kept the accounts and receipt books. Above those shelves there was a large cupboard that Magda had completely forgotten about. It was full of old records, press cuttings about the PIC, paperwork leading to the erection of the statue of Belle. Anything that needed to be stored long term was kept in this cupboard. Magda dragged a stool over and stood on it to reach down three shoe boxes that she hadn't seen for fifteen years.

She sat on the floor and opened the boxes one at a time. One held mainly baby mementoes of the boys – a lock of Daniel's hair, a photo of her carrying Jake when he was first born. She couldn't remember who had taken the photo. It wasn't Deming. He had been on the other side of the world when she had given birth. The next box was older. There were photos of her as a baby and as a child, growing up. Magda didn't like to think of those days. She looked at one of the photos – she was standing with her new bike, the bike her father had given her for promising not to tell what he'd been doing to her. Magda closed that box and pushed it away. She neither had the time nor the desire to go down that particular memory lane.

The third box contained things from her time with Deming. There were photos of them together. Magda smiled as she looked at them. He had been a handsome man. And yes, she had to concede, she did look so young, but Deming didn't look too old. She put the photos to one side to show Alfie later. Then she picked out some newspaper clippings, neatly folded and now pressed flat over the years. Magda did not even recognise some of the things in the box. They must have been Deming's and she had just kept everything of his. She stared at one of the clippings. It was a picture of Deming standing next to an Asian man. On the back was scribbled a date and a name that Magda didn't recognise. At first she also didn't recognise where they were standing, and then it hit her. They were outside the NAP offices.

55

All around Mae Klaw, rebuilding was going on. It was full of the sound of construction and men calling instructions to one another: at least a hundred houses were being rebuilt. The air still held the smell of burnt homes and ruined lives and the men worked without laughter or joy to try and regain some normality for themselves and their families in their fragile existence.

Mann and Riley turned onto a side road on the right and stopped outside a hut on the edge of the decimated area.

Riley lowered his voice.

'Okay, this is it. This is the person I wanted you to meet. We will have to be brief and be discreet – there are always people willing to sell information for a decent meal.'

They took off their shoes and climbed the ladder into the hut, bending their heads as they entered into a dark inner room. There was no light except that which filtered through the split bamboo walls and from the entrance. In the corner Mann could make out a young woman sitting next to an infant sleeping on a mat on the floor. As they entered, the woman stood slowly and gracefully, and greeted them in the traditional Thai manner.

'This is Run Run,' said Riley. 'She wants to help us.'

The baby did not stir as she stood. Run Run was beautiful: big eyes set in a small triangular face. She was light skinned with dark hair swept into a side parting, across her forehead, and then tied back with a series of bright scarves. She wore a simple dark red top and a homespun sarong was tied around her waist. She was a petite member of the Long-Neck Karen tribe, one of the most beautiful of the hill tribes. The women traditionally wore coils of brass around their necks, adding more coils to them each year as they grew up. It was believed to stretch the neck but actually crushed the vertebrae and collarbones, instead of achieving the desired aim of making the neck look longer. This tribeswoman had chosen not to wear the brass coils but that hadn't stopped her neck from looking swan-like. She stood with her narrow shoulders square and held back. Her every action, her every movement was calculated, and yet somehow fluid.

Mann looked first at her and then at the sleeping baby. Run Run read his thoughts.

'Do not worry, the infant is not mine. His mother died in childbirth; now all the women take it in turns to care for him. I understand the risks and I am willing to take them.'

Mann gave a small nod and a smile of thanks. Here in the gloom, Run Run seemed to Mann to strike a tragically defiant figure, fragile looking and yet strong, like a reed that bends and is flattened by the storm only to rise again with the sunshine.

'Your English is very good.' Mann smiled at her.

'Thank you,' she answered and bowed again. 'I was a teacher in the Shan State before the Burmese came.'

'Have you been in the camp long?'

'Five years.'

'Can you tell me what happened the day the camp was attacked?'

She gestured for them to sit. Mann looked at the baby, swaddled in muslin; it had begun to stir a little. Run Run patted its back as they talked.

'We had no warning. They came in at sunset, in army trucks.' Her eyes drifted towards the hut's entrance as she spoke, as if she feared for her life all over again. 'They were wild looking – bare at the chest, painted. They were mad like animals. Everywhere there were fires starting. People were begging them to stop. People were running. Behind them came the men like dogs, whooping, barking like howling wolves. People were trying to get out of their houses. I saw Mongkut. He shouted to me to run and hide. I heard them call his name.'

'Mongkut was one of the elders here,' Riley explained. 'He was a great fighter in the KNLA once but was too old to fight any longer.'

'They shouted his name. I heard Mongkut calling them dogs, animals. I picked up the baby and ran. I ran away down the road and I hid beneath the new school.' She stopped for a minute to calm herself. Her sentences had become short and breathless. Her face was flushed as she looked once more towards the door as if at any second her attackers would burst through once again. She took a deep breath and looked up at

Mann. 'I had to bury myself amongst the dirt and pray that the fire did not reach us. It was choking us and the baby was coughing but all around was so much noise that they did not hear us. For an hour I listened to the screams and I heard people dying. When I came out I found Mongkut dead, his head on a pole, his body beneath.'

The hut was silent except for the sound of the baby grizzling. Run Run picked it up and held it over her shoulder as she soothed it.

'Do you have any idea who they were?'

Her eyes flicked towards Riley before she answered. She shook her head.

'I have said to Riley that I am not certain, but they were not Burmese army. They were wild men without uniforms. There are some here who might know them. They spoke the dialect of the Shan people. And someone bribed the guards to leave that evening.'

'Did you see the five volunteers?'

She shook her head. 'No, but when they were shouting for Mongkut I heard them calling to each other to look for the five and to bring them alive.'

'Do you remember what the five were doing when you last saw them that afternoon?'

Run Run looked at Riley. She seemed suddenly flustered or confused, Mann didn't know which.

'They were waiting.'

'Waiting for what?' asked Mann.

Run Run tried to recall. 'I asked Anna, one of the girls, what are you doing still here? She told me they were still waiting for their lift, it was late.'

Mann turned to Riley. 'You said they had their own transport.'

'Not these kids. They got a lift with me. That's what I mean about NAP – they just expected me to do everything for them.'

'But who gave them a lift that day if you were ill?'

'Some other volunteers staying at Mary's offered.'

The baby had started grizzling in earnest and Run Run could not placate him.

'They will kill many more if they are not stopped,' she said. 'I want to help you in the search for the volunteers. But we will need money if we want people to help us. We need supplies.'

'I have money,' answered Mann.

'Bring it later. I will buy what you need with it.' She turned to address Riley. 'Can you get me a pass to leave the camp tonight?'

'Shouldn't be a problem. I will say I need you to help with some translation.'

She stood and picked up the baby. He was no more than three months old. His cry was quivery, his mouth like a young bird's as he turned and searched for food at her breast. She stood, kissed the baby's head and handed him to Riley.

'Please give him to Dao. He wants something I do not have it in me to give him. You will find her across from here. She will feed him. I will see you later.' She said, bowing again, 'Tonight I will take you to meet the last of the great KNLA leaders. His name is Alak.'

56

With a look of disgust, Shrimp walked past the armed men on the door and exited the police station. He headed down the road to the Thai boxing stadium. Posters were pinned all over the entrance and the outside walls.

El Supremo remains unbeaten. Thursday evening free-for-all challenge to win the thousand dollars.

Inside the place all was quiet except for six youngsters and their trainer sparring with one another.

'Hey.' Shrimp nodded in the direction of the trainer. 'Mind if I watch?'

'You are welcome.' The trainer walked towards him. 'My name is Pan.' He reminded Shrimp of the man who had taught him Taekwondo when he was a boy. He had been a dedicated kind man and a wise person. Someone who the children could aspire to be like, certainly not a bully.

'And mine is Li. It's a great place you have here.' Shrimp scanned the large auditorium. It could easily seat three hundred people.

'It's not mine,' Pan smiled. He left the boys sparring. 'I wish it was.'

'Who owns it? El Supremo and the coach?'

'Ha! No . . . They wish they did too. They just run it for the owner. They're from overseas.'

'Can you teach me the basics?'

The boys started laughing.

'Shush . . .' Pan admonished. 'Don't be rude.' He turned back to Shrimp. 'I see by the way that you move that you know martial arts.'

Shrimp nodded. The boys' stares became more respectful.

'I have had some success, yes. But I know nothing about this particular discipline.'

'I will teach you the basics – it will be good for the boys to see how others fight. Thai boxing is all about hands, knees, elbows, kicks and punches. Here.' He called two of the boys forward. 'Show Mr Li how it works.'

The young boys began sparring. There came a voice from behind Shrimp.

'We'll show Mr Li how it works.'

El Supremo, Coach and the two policemen Shrimp had just seen at the station had entered the boxing stadium and were now closing the doors behind them.

Pan stepped closer to Shrimp and bowed respectfully to the men at the door. 'He is having instruction, that's all. There is no need to threaten him.'

'Get the children out. Lessons are over for today. This man is causing civil unrest here. Thailand is full of political activists causing trouble – he is just one more.'

'I am sorry, my friend, you are on your own,' Pan

whispered under his breath as he bowed again and backed away. 'I cannot help you now.'

Shrimp looked at the policemen. They looked like they were dying for an excuse to try out their guns. Pan started to back away. 'I suggest you allow yourself to take the beating and try and survive it. You fight back . . . they will kill you.'

57

'Alak is the number one suspect at the moment,' Mann mused as he and Riley left Run Run's hut. 'Can we trust him? Can we trust Run Run?'

They crossed the lane with the grizzling baby to interrupt Dao from her weaving. Her own baby was sleeping soundly in a basket beside her. Dao took the infant from Riley and lifted her top to allow him to suckle as she carried on weaving one handed. Riley led Mann onwards through the camp. Mann said, 'If it goes wrong tonight this could turn out to be a very short trip for me.'

'You can trust Run Run. I can't vouch for Alak. I have never met him. But he's a hero round here. Normally he spends his time carrying out raids behind the Burmese border but Run Run says he is willing to meet with us in the mountains to the north and see what can be done. He is taking a big risk – if he's caught he will be handed straight over to the Burmese junta to be executed. Run Run says he wants to help you to find the volunteers.'

'Run Run knows him personally?'

'I think she knows him *very* personally. I think they were childhood sweethearts, they grew up together. There was talk of them marrying but her mother put a stop to that – he's a Buddhist and she's a Christian. But Alak will die fighting, that is a certainty, and Run Run will probably live out her life here in the camp; that too is a sad fact.'

'How did she end up in here?'

'She was on the run for most of her life because of her mother. Run Run was brought up fighting the Burmese. Her mother is a famous fighter. Her name's Mo. She once commanded a platoon of fighting women who were feared all over Burma. They took out many armed Burmese units. Sometimes through direct combat, other times they were used as decoys. Either way, she was feared and revered. She was a force to be reckoned with. She and her children were on the run from the Burmese for many years but, to keep them safe, Mo went into hiding and has remained there. She can have nothing to do with her children if they're to have a hope of staying alive. They would be prime targets for assassination by the Burmese. Run Run settled here and looks after abandoned kids, women without families, those who are disabled, rape victims, victims of sex trafficking . . . she is a great woman. Never says much, just gets on with it. She's a tough cookie. She maintains strong links with the KNLA.'

'Is that why she isn't married, Riley – because of Alak?'

'Partly, and maybe because when she was a teenager the Burmese sacked the village she was staying in, and they took her and six others as porters and comfort women. They were imprisoned in the camp for six months, made to carry forty-kilo loads all day and service the men at night. Most of them died. But Run Run managed to escape.'

'How?'

'One night she persuaded one of the guards to take her to an area at the edge of the camp. Whilst he was raping her she smashed his skull with a rock. They didn't discover she was missing for twelve hours. By that time she had been found by the KNLA. The man who rescued her was Mongkut. He was a ferocious fighter. He was a good man. He didn't deserve to die.'

'Are we sure he was targeted?'

'Yes.' Riley stopped in his tracks and looked hard at Mann. 'As were the five volunteers. Someone chose them for a reason, Mann.'

58

Mann wiped the sweat from his brow. They had been waiting for nearly an hour. Mann was out of sight in the back of Riley's battered old Suzuki jeep, opposite the camp entrance watching the four policemen sitting on the logs, eating their dinner.

Riley switched the headlights off and they sat and waited. It could be a while; time arrangements were never an exact thing in refugee camps. Night descended so fast that only the mosquitoes saw it coming – they were out in force tonight. Mann could hear them as they did the rounds of the car, searching for warm blood. Mann was lucky – for some reason they never bit him. Riley was not so fortunate; he slapped his neck and squashed a fat one as it sat feasting. Then they saw Run Run. Riley switched the lights back on. She appeared at the camp entrance.

'If she has any trouble getting out I will go over and try and help but I don't want to unless I have to – sometimes it just makes it worse to interfere, especially when they've been drinking. They can turn nasty.'

Mann watched Run Run negotiating her way past

the policemen. It was a curious thing to watch. They wanted to make sure she wasn't carrying anything, they wanted to frisk her. The inspection would not be hurried; they had all night and nothing to do but talk about women and get drunk. Run Run knew the best strategy to survive. She used it now, laughing and flirting coyly with the eager-faced guards. As she walked away Mann watched them grin gormlessly at her disappearing back as their eyes slipped down to watch the merest suggestion of a wiggle. Her body might be still playing the game but she had stopped smiling the instant she turned her back on them – job done. She was one of those women whose beauty was just a tool for her. It had not brought her happiness. She made her way across the road to Riley's jeep. She walked, purposefully but unhurriedly, to the car.

Riley turned the engine on and gave the police a friendly wave, muttering 'wankers' under his breath. Mann kept out of sight. Run Run got into the front passenger seat.

'Wait a few minutes. The women will help us,' said Run Run. 'We cannot be seen to go into the hills. They will make a diversion.' On cue there was a rush of action and screaming and a plume of smoke began rising from the far end of the camp. The four policemen ran off in the direction of the new building. 'Now we must turn around,' she said. Riley did as he was told, spinning the car quietly round and heading away from the camp and further north into the hills. As they set off Mann saw Run Run reach inside her shawl and take out a small wrapped cloth bundle she had been hiding.

Either side of the unlit road was thick darkness. They drove for an hour and a half before turning onto one of the tracks that cut a narrow road up into the hills. Their headlights flashed vivid green over fleshy leaves and myriad small eyes peered back at them from the canopy of trees. Mann was starting to wonder how much more the old jeep was going to be able to take – this was definitely all-terrain country and the road was losing its battle to cut a clean path through the hillside. But as they climbed the trees got sparser and stars appeared overhead. Run Run tapped Riley's shoulder. In the distance, between the black under-growth on the far side of the slope, a torch was flashing. Riley dimmed the headlights to signal he had seen and they wound their way carefully off road and down to the edge of a wooded area.

A face lit by torchlight appeared at the driver's window. The man was minus one eye – a scar sliced his face diagonally in half, so that one side no longer fitted the other. Another face peered in at the passenger side, an M36 rifle raised and pointed casually at Mann as it nestled in the crook of an arm that narrowed to a callused stump. The man wore a short-sleeved army shirt and on it was the badge of the KNLA: a white star on a blue background, topped by a red rising sun.

The man pointed his rifle butt towards a clearing further down and across the hillside. Riley inched the jeep slowly forward, over and down the edge of a cleared forest, where once a thriving village had stood but now nothing but the skeleton of a community remained.

In front of the jeep, more men started to appear. Some were dressed in combat trousers and shirts, others wore dark T-shirts and cut-offs. They were all heavily armed.

Mann could see that these were hard, battle-torn men. Most were young, their sinewy forms moving slowly around the edge of the scene. Their faces were lit by the green cheroots they smoked, their eyes alert with tired wariness. These were men who were born to run and knew nothing but army life; they never got a day off and they never got a homecoming. They were men who looked as if they had lost their souls along the way and now had no idea what a life without struggle was like. They lived in an unreal world where the only hope was in believing that hope was enough. They took it in turns to stare suspiciously into the car. They eventually waved the car on. The jeep was being steered towards the left, down a sharp incline and then onto a level area. Once there, one of the fighters held up his hand for them to stop and get out of the car.

Mann and Riley were frisked. They missed Delilah, tucked into Mann's boot. Escorted by the soldiers, they were led single file into the jungle. The layers of vegetation crackled beneath their feet as they wove their way between the trees. With only torchlight to guide them and the canopy of trees above them, not even the stars were visible. Mann had never been in a forest so dense or a situation so strange. He was a city boy, used to the low life and the high rise, or being on a beach with a surfboard in his hand, but he had never been so lost in a jungle before. They moved through the forest, away from the old village and deep into the safety of the woods until they could hear the low hum of men talking, the crackling of a fire and the smell of food being cooked. There were maybe thirty soldiers in all, sitting around in small groups. The air was filled with the smell of sweat and guns, the damp smell of steaming rice, and the tangy smoke of cooked chilli and fish paste wafted over to them in waves.

From the darkness a figure in combats emerged and strode towards them. He was a powerful-looking man, wild and handsome in a Che Guevara way, with haunted, hollow cheeks sunken into a broad face. His dark bushy eyebrows came low over deep set eyes. He had unkempt hair and he wore a red bandanna around his head. He walked up and shook Riley's hand.

'I have heard many good things about you,' he said as he took Riley's hand and shook it warmly.

'Same here, Captain Alak.'

Then the man turned towards Mann and Mann felt his sharp scrutiny. Mann eyeballed him back. What Mann saw was a man who was in his prime but who was never destined to get old. Alak was relying on every tissue in his body to keep him alive in the moment. But, to judge by his expression when he had glanced at Run Run, it was every tissue that made up his muscle and bone – but none that lay in his heart. He was a man who could be allowed only to dream of the future. Deep in Alak's dark eyes, Mann saw the demon of doubt.

Then, just at the moment when the situation began to look awkward, Alak gave a smile and he reached out to shake Mann's hand.

'It is good to meet you, Johnny Mann.'

'And you, Alak.'

They followed Alak to a cleared area where logs were laid out for them to sit on. Above his head Mann could see a few stars squeezing through the black jungle canopy. As he sat down Mann eased Delilah out of his boot and slipped her into the palm of his hand, pushing her hilt up under his shirt sleeve. He felt the coldness of her steel against his arm. It was reassuring to him to feel her there. He had the feeling he would need her before long.

59

'I'm all right, Summer, really,' said Shrimp. Summer couldn't stop crying. 'It looks worse than it is.'

She howled louder. She had come to find Shrimp in his digs. He was lying on his bed, the window open, the smell of the sea filling the room. 'Shhh, Summer, please, you're not helping.'

'I am sorry, hon. Truly sorry. Here . . .' Summer opened her bag and took out a bundle of papers. 'It's what you wanted. Some of the people made copies of the legal stuff.'

Shrimp sat bolt upright and took the papers from her. She began overzealously plumping his pillows. He flicked through the documents quickly.

'Perfect,' he said. 'I will come and talk to you later and tell you what I need you to do.' Summer started crying again. 'But only if you promise to stop crying.'

Shrimp spent the next five hours laid out reading the papers from Summer. They all added up to the same thing – the people had been deceived into signing away their homes or businesses. It wasn't just a local fraud going on. Lots of the buyers for these businesses or strips of coastland were from overseas. Even if they had not wittingly thrown a farmer off his land, in the end, they had built a hotel on what used to be his home. Someone in the middle had brokered these deals. Shrimp was positive he could find enough evidence to take their cases to an international court. He was also positive that the charities commission would want to know that one of their Dutch charities had been the middleman on some of these deals.

Later that day he managed to rouse himself from his bed. Very slowly and gingerly, he walked down Patong Beach and along to the boxing stadium.

The children looked up as Shrimp entered. One of his shoulders hung lower than the other where it had been dislocated. His battered face was unrecognisable. Only his hair gave him away – gelled into a peak at the front.

Pan came towards him.

'You are a brave man. I am happy to see you alive.'

'Yesss.' Shrimp could not speak properly, his lips were so swollen. He walked slowly forward. There was no part of him that hadn't been bruised by the beating.

'What do you want here?'

'To learn how to Thai box.'

'Still?'

Shrimp nodded.

60

Mann looked at Run Run. Her eyes were locked on Alak's, shining in the firelight. One of Alak's men brought over some glasses and a bottle. Naked to the chest, the skin on his back was cut and there was a folded area where he had lost muscle and flesh from a massive injury. Alak poured them each a shot of rum.

'To the fight!' The mood was sombre.

'To the fallen.' Alak's eyes burned as he looked in turn at each member of the group gathered there. Around him his men stopped to join in the salute.

'Yes, to Mongkut and the others.' Riley raised his glass high. They drank. Mann studied Alak in the dim light. This was a man who never relaxed. His back was strong, but his shoulders were over-muscled from carrying heavy packs as well as tension all his life. He was a man who never slept, who never let his guard down, he didn't dare.

Alak brandished the rum, waiting to refill Mann's glass. Mann drank it down and held out his glass.

'Mongkut died the right way. Born a Karen, die a Karen,' said Alak. The tension showed in his jaw when he talked. 'It is the job of every Karen to play his part, to do what he can to fight for our right to exist, to regain our homeland and to live in peace.

'We live by the four principles spelt out in 1950 when the Karen National Union was founded. They are . . .' He counted each one off on his fingers. 'Number one – no surrender. Two – the recognition of the Karen State. Three – the Karen shall retain their arms. And four – they shall decide their own destiny. Nothing changes those principles.'

Alak leaned forward to refill Mann's glass and stopped mid-pour as he looked into Mann's eyes.

'You are a long way from Hong Kong, Detective Inspector Johnny Mann.' From the corner of his eye Mann could see Alak's men watching.

It didn't surprise Mann that Alak had done his homework. It would represent a big risk meeting a stranger. But Mann had done his homework too. Alak was the man Mann had been hoping to meet. He was the captain whose name was being bandied about as the abductor, the organiser of the attack.

'I owe someone a favour. That's as personal as it gets – I am here to find the missing volunteers. That is my only reason.'

'You are not here to take up arms with us?' Alak laughed and sat upright. He spoke clearly, as if making sure his men could hear. 'To fight by our side? If you are not with us, then why should we help you?'

'You have no choice. They say that you are the rebels who attacked the camp. They say you are taking payoffs from the drug barons.'

There was a loud intake of breath all around and Riley choked on his rum.

In the instant Alak reached for his knife, Mann already had Delilah flipped out. Like a chameleon's tongue catching a fly, she winged silently through the air, her cord still attached to the hilt. She knocked Alak's knife clean out of his hands, nicking his forefinger, before safely flying back to Mann's hand.

As Alak's men rushed forward, he held up his hand for calm. He looked down at his finger and laughed as he sucked to stop it bleeding. He nodded his head, as if pleased with the outcome. Then he turned to his men, speaking in Shan, and one by one they broke into laughter. He turned back to Mann.

'Pity.' He grinned. 'We could do with a man like you.'

Mann bowed his head in thanks.

'But I don't think you believe I took the five volunteers, otherwise you would not have come here tonight. But I do believe you need my help to find them. Run Run, what do you know about the attack?'

Run Run reached beside her and lifted the package she had brought. By the light of the lamp, she unwrapped the cloth bundle and spread out the items one by one on the jungle floor. First, a red bandanna. 'I took this from around Mongkut's head.' It still held the shape of his skull; it was stiff with blood. Next, she placed a knife and a small square of cloth, ragged at the edges, with writing on it. 'This note and this knife were embedded in his eye.'

Alak reached over and picked up the note. As he

read it, his eyes locked onto Run Run's. He seemed transfixed by the words he had read.

'This is a personal challenge to me.'

'You know the man who wrote it?' asked Mann.

'Yes. I know him very well. His name is Saw Wah Say.'

'What does the note say?'

'It says . . . the day of reckoning has come.'

61

Mary watched Mann go with a curious look on her face. He wasn't sure whether she was worried about the bicycle or about him – both probably. It was late – too late for a tourist to be riding around Mae Sot. But Mann had an appointment to keep and it had to be done under cover of night. Someone wanted to join their party and they wouldn't take no for an answer.

Mann cycled past the roaming bands of wild dogs skulking furtively on the roads. By day they pretended friendly indifference to the wandering goats that grazed at the roadside, but by night they salivated at the sight of the young kids inside their bamboo pens. At night they killed each other and anything else that got in their way for the right to feed and fornicate.

Mann picked up a stick from the side of the road, that would at least serve to give him time to escape if a pack attacked. On either side of the road the restaurants and bars, workshops and shanty houses, were beginning to disappear and the blackness appeared in their place. It was a straight road to Burma. Trucks were moving along in a constant stream. The nighttime had begun in Mae Sot. The night market would spring phoenix-like from the ashes of the day market and Mae Sot would sell its wares: diamonds, rubies, gold and sex.

Mann stayed out of the way of the traffic. He had no lights on his bike, which was just as well as he didn't want to draw attention to himself. As he neared the start of the bridge that spanned the river he saw the place was heaving with activity. Small fires lit it up as hundreds of people stood along the river. A busy market already existed along the banks of the Moei. But now in the night it had taken on the look of a thriving night bazaar. The river was low. By the light of the moon Mann could see the shadowy figures of people floating across on tyres to sell their cigarettes and opium. Roadside kitchens served steaming food whilst men stood around haggling.

Mann didn't need to get too close. He was waiting for someone but he knew that person would have no trouble finding him. Ten minutes passed as he watched the constant traffic along the water's edge as boats pulled up to offload their wares. Then he became aware that he was being observed. He turned to see Gee slouching covertly near the bridge and dragging heavily on his cigarette. His red baseball cap was still firmly pulled down on his head, his gold chain gleaming in the dark.

'Hello, my friend.' Gee walked over to him. 'Thank you for coming. I am sorry to bring you to the bridge but I am waiting for my cargo.'

They walked to the water's edge where they looked down. Beneath the bridge, a boat was unloading boxes.

'And I know that you are making plans. Follow me please. We will talk in private.'

Mann ducked as they entered the covered market. Within was an Aladdin's cave of treasures. A tall black African with yellow eyes looked up and watched Mann pass, his rubies and sapphires laid out on a velvet mat in front of him. The potential buyer, a wizened man, was huddled over examining them with an eyeglass. Mann could hear the sound of stifled screams, the laugh of excited cruelty, and from the corner of his eye as Gee marched him through, he saw sex slaves being herded into another part of the market, ready for the auction.

Mann followed Gee as he weaved through the stalls. They exited at the side and stopped at one of the doors in an alleyway of lock-ups. Each one had a notice of which merchant it belonged to and a number. Gee's lock-up had something extra – a Buddha looked out at Mann from a small altar next to the entrance, where there had once been a window. Incense burned in a brass holder and a plastic elephant joined Buddha next to some nuts. A rat skittered away with one in its mouth as they neared.

Gee unlocked a hefty padlock. 'Did you make your arrangements to find the five young people?' he asked.

'I leave at dawn tomorrow,' Mann nodded. 'Did you get your business done?'

Gee flicked on a light. One bulb hung down from the centre of the space, which was mainly empty apart from a few boxes in the corner. There was a stack of teak chairs and a trestle table. It had one window, which overlooked the alleyway that ran alongside the market.

'This place should be full. But business is bad. This market is normally a hundred times busier than tonight. Everyone is suffering whilst these troubles continue. But that is not what I wanted to see you about. My village has many troubles. Soldiers have come and they have killed many and destroyed the rice. So many problems there.' He sighed. 'It's worse than I thought. They have been attacked and most of their elephants killed. I must take what I can to help them.' He stopped and looked at Mann. 'I am asking if I can come with you part of the way. You will be stopping by my village because it is a central place and all people pass by. I need your protection. I will make a donation to help your cause. I will not be a burden to you. I will provide porters from my village. They will be waiting at the other side and I will organise a boat. I will give directions tomorrow when we meet.'

'You can come, Gee, but any trouble and we leave you. We can't carry anyone.'

'Ah ha . . . I understand exactly. I will be no trouble to you, I promise.' Gee finished securing the lock-up as Mann waited outside. There was no sign of the rat. The Buddha's fat little face smiled serenely out behind a plume of incense. Above the Buddha's head was an inscription.

'What does the writing on the altar say?' Mann asked.

'It says – let me think – in English, "What is in your head, thoughts, good or bad, that is what you will become."'

They walked around the outside of the market and down to the river. A boat pulled alongside and Gee nodded discreetly to its captain. 'I will meet you outside Mary's,' he said to Mann. 'Now I must make my arrangements first. I must get to the night market and buy what I need. You may go now, my friend. I see my cargo is being unloaded. Better you do not stay.'

He was eager to get rid of him. Mann could see the boxes on the boat. Whatever it was Gee imported, it came in wooden crates with the stamp of the Burmese army on the top.

62

Mann was showering when his phone rang. It was Riley.

'Alak will send some of his men to help us. They will meet us at a village a half a day's walk from the Burmese banks.'

'What do you mean, *us*?'

'Sue and I will be coming along. People know me, they trust me. We don't know what state the kids will be in if we find them. We may need Sue to help with any medical emergencies. She can handle it better than we can and she knows that part of the jungle very well. And I have found us a guide – an expert tracker. We will be picking you up first thing tomorrow, five a.m. We'll wait for you on the road around the corner from the hostel.'

'There is another person coming. His name is Gee.'

'Gee? From Chiang Mai?'

'You know him?'

'Everyone knows Gee. He does nothing unless there is a profit in it. Why is he coming?'

'He needs to get back to his village. He wants

protection and he can offer us money, porters and a boat. I figured it wouldn't hurt.'

'Okay. So long as he understands that once we start we are committed. What goes on is dealt with on the spot. He needs to understand that.'

'He will.'

Mann hung up and called Ng. Hong Kong was one hour ahead of Thai time.

'We start the search tomorrow, Ng.'

'Do you know where to go?'

'I know where to start. That's as good as it gets. The only help I can expect here is at ground level. I get more questions here than I get answers, and dealing with the politics is an added problem. What's the latest?'

'It's not so good. It seems that the Thai government are headed for a military coup and they are making deals with the Burmese. They are handing over responsibility to Burma to find the kids. They say the Burmese will be intensifying their efforts to track down the KNLA rebels who have abducted them. Will you be able to keep in touch?'

'I am taking my satellite phone but the battery doesn't last forever. Don't suppose there are many places to charge it in the jungle . . . Whatever happens, Ng, I'm out there till this ends. I suspect, one way or another, it will be over fast. Oh, and Ng, did you get anywhere with that other matter?'

'I have started. Deming had stakes in several companies that no longer exist today or have changed names. It will take time.'

'Thanks, Ng.' There was a knock at the door. 'Got to go . . .'

'Good luck, Genghis.'

Hillary stood at the door in a cotton sarong, very loosely tied. She had a bottle of vodka in her hand.

'Can I help?' asked Mann.

'I think I might have appeared rude earlier on.' Hillary looked very awake for someone about to go to bed.

'Don't worry about it. I don't take offence easily.' Hillary giggled as her sarong slipped down and she clutched at it half heartedly.

'It's just that NAP have been really supportive. They paid for us to finish our projects here and everyone is really shocked about what happened.'

'Just tell me one thing, Hillary: did you give the five volunteers a ride into Mae Klaw that day?'

'Yes. Riley was ill.'

'But you didn't bring them back later on?'

'No, that's the thing. We were sent home early that day. We were doing the run of all the camps in the area. We were on our way back to pick them up when we got a call to say we didn't need to.'

'From whom?'

Hillary looked around a little nervously. 'Look, can I come in? I feel a bit *exposed* out here. We need to talk in private.'

Mann got up and checked the corridor before closing the door behind her. The young backpacker who had narrowly missed a death trip in King's bar was grinning at him from down the corridor.

63

Mann waited until Hillary had disappeared back into her own room before he began making his preparations to leave. He stripped to his waist and strapped his shuriken belt around his chest and another to his arm, which held his throwing spikes. The weapon holders were like a second skin to him. The largest one he owned was the Death Star, a four-pointed throwing star measuring six inches in diameter. It was custom made from steel. Each of its four blades was razor sharp and reinforced with steel rivets to give precision, balance and performance. It was not just a beautiful thing to hold but also capable of decapitating a man in one shot. He slipped it neatly into a leather pouch nestled beneath his ribs.

He picked up his bag and crept out of the door and went down the stairs. The air had the heavy weight of pre-dawn to it and there was the smell of a new day coming. The darkness was permeated only by the sound of the kitchen staff chatting as they prepared the food for the day. Mann dropped his key behind the empty reception desk, and walked silently across the stone tiles, past the caretaker asleep on a bench by the door, and out the front entrance. As he stepped out onto the pavement, a lorry rattled past on its way back from Friendship Bridge. Frightened eyes stared out at him from the back. A dog crossed the road, its sand-coloured eyes gleaming in the headlights as it stopped and turned to glare at the lorry with contempt, before sauntering to the side.

Gee was waiting for him across the road. Beside him were two large canvas bags. He was talking to someone; Mann couldn't make out whether it was a man or a woman. As soon as Gee caught sight of him, the other person scurried off and he came across the road to Mann, lumbering under the weight of the bags.

'What's in there?'

'My contribution.'

'Couldn't you have given something lighter?' Mann took one from him. 'This weighs more than you.'

'Believe me, my friend, I have brought along the perfect present,' he said, struggling with his remaining bag as they walked down the road together. 'All night I have listened to the stories of a group of men who are devils, and the worst kind of Shwit – they slice through the necks of men, women and children, just to hear the sound it makes. These men are not human. They are wild animals. Now, where is our lift?'

'Over there.'

Mann gestured with his head. They had just turned a corner in the road; ahead, a VW van winked its head-lights at them. Riley was in the driver's seat. Mann and Gee walked over, slid back the side door, and heaved their bags up onto the van floor. Run Run and Sue were sitting in the back with Louis.

'Ah – the expert guide.' Mann nodded at Louis.

'I got an offer I couldn't refuse. Anyway, I thought you might need me.'

'Whatever your reasons, it's good to have you on board. Everyone here know Gee?'

There were mutters in the affirmative as Gee got into the back. Mann sat in the front beside Riley. As they drove away from the hostel, Mann turned around to look at Run Run. Her hair swept across her face and knotted at the nape of her neck. She was dressed in trousers and a dark T-shirt, with a simple scarf knotted around her head. From a distance she could have passed for a pubescent boy, but up close her beautiful face with its delicate features gave her away. He knew that she was putting her place in the camp at jeopardy; if caught, she risked being kicked out of the camp and being deported back to Burma. Mann turned back to Riley.

'How's it going to work for Run Run? Were you able to sign her out?'

He shook his head. 'Too risky, mate. Too many people would start asking questions. They would want to know why all three of us were going away for a few days. And, who knows, it could be longer. We discussed it but we decided we couldn't afford to jeopardise the mission. Run Run was the one who had the final say. She knows the risks.'

But, as Mann looked at her in the gloom and the silence, he could see that her eyes were bright and shining, alight with life. She was out of the camp and she was doing what every Karen should do – fighting for the cause.

'Thank you.' He smiled at her. 'Thank you for helping us.' She did not answer him, but Mann saw a flicker of a smile cross her face as she bowed her head and acknowledged his words.

'What's Gee along for?' Louis asked.

'Gee is tagging along till we get to his village,' answered Mann. 'He is going to provide us with porters from his village and organise supplies for us along the way. He is making a substantial contribution.' Everyone's eyes went down to the canvas bags by Gee's feet.

'There's no money to be made out of this, Gee,' Louis said. 'Are you sure you want to come?'

Gee spoke up. 'I am coming along to get safe passage to my village. They need me. Anyway, no money to be made, but money will be lost if you do not find these five young people. The world will start with its sanctions and we will have a hard job shifting goods.'

'Huh! I can smell bullshit a mile off, Gee,' said Louis. 'All you'd do then is make even more money on the black market. What's your *real* reason for coming on this mission?'

The van fell silent. Run Run curled her legs beneath her and rested her head against the window. In the darkness Gee hid his face beneath his cap.

Mann watched his profile as he eventually spoke.

'It is time for me. Now, I feel in my heart, I owe my village. I owe my people. I am old now. It is time

I paid back. It is time I thought about my death and made payments for my afterlife.'

'Huh,' Louis scoffed. 'That bit sounds right. So, ultimately the goal is selfish – you've become scared of dying and you're trying to secure yourself a comfy ride into the next life?'

'Yes. Yes. I admit it.' He lifted his head and glared at Louis. 'But also I feel it is time for me to go home.' He spoke softly and with conviction. 'And I want to go home to a country where I am allowed to live in peace. Politics is our only way for that. We must make the world care about us. We will not do that by killing the people who come to help us. Even if it only *appears* to be our fault, it will be enough to damage. I am sick of having no home.'

'What's the news from your village? Have they seen the five?' asked Riley.

Gee nodded his head, solemnly. 'I have been told that five weeks ago, a band of wild-looking Shwit came through the village. They shot elephants, destroyed crops. They took some of the women for porters. They killed a hundred people in the village – many women and children. The way they describe these Shwit, they are animals – wild dogs, savages. There were twenty of them. They had the five young foreigners with them.' There was silence in the van as Gee continued, his head bowed; he looked suddenly much older than his sixty years.

'I grew up with fear in a farming village, growing rice in the paddy fields. Each year, before the harvest could be picked, the Burmese army came. They came

264

for porters, for food. They promised payment that never came. One year they took my father and when he became sick they left him to die, without water or food. *Thay-ne*, they call the porters – it means ghosts; they become the walking dead. Their bodies litter our forests, still carrying the sacks that killed them, they melt into one. I was taken as a boy to fight in the Shan State Army, as it was then, under the Opium King. We learnt how to fight. I grew up to believe that we had a chance. We had the arms then, we had the backing of the Opium King. We had the money to buy weapons, but when the King deserted us and we lost our last battle at Shooting Dog Hill, we no longer had a homeland to defend so I left the army and travelled through Thailand and into Europe. After some years I became the businessman you see today. But I know these men – the Shwit. I have seen what they do to the villagers. They rape and torture for nothing – and why? The villagers have nothing to give them. They are devils who eat the flesh of others.'

Mann looked across at Riley and at Sue. Sue blinked back.

'It's a rumour,' Riley said dismissively. 'Some animist tribes do it in Vietnam. But not here. People say it to scare the children. It's "the Bogeyman will get you" stuff. Somehow the rumour has grown in the jungle.'

There was an uncomfortable silence from the back seat. Run Run was asleep or she was resting. Either way she had curled into a ball, unwilling to substantiate or deny the rumour; it was clear she didn't want to participate in the discussion.

'It's no rumour,' Louis said, and Sue muttered her agreement. 'When we are out in the villages we hear a lot about it, firsthand accounts. It has to be believed.'

'Believe it!' Gee lifted his eyes beneath the rim of his cap as he looked at each in turn. 'I, myself, have tasted human flesh.'

All eyes turned towards him in the gloom of the van. Even Riley kept quiet. They all looked at him expectantly. 'Sometimes it is not enough to kill the bad man. They kill your family – you want more. You want to make them suffer like your family did. There are some men, some army captains, who capture enemy and eat them, cut their flesh while they live. One time our captain caught a man – another captain – a Burmese. He was responsible for the death of many villagers. Many of the men in our unit had family who were killed by him. He was a fat man. Our captain tied the man against a tree and he cut off his . . .' Gee leant forward slightly and cupped his chest. '. . . Here. He cut off this . . . this, breast. He chopped it and mixed it with rice wine, with soy sauce, ginger. He placed it in bowl and gave it to us. We all must eat and share. I did not eat much. I was frightened to get a taste for it. The men were happy to see the Burmese captain suffer. It was good to eat from the man – to watch him in so much fear, so much pain. It was good. You understand?' No one answered.

Strangely, a part of Mann did understand. Not that he ever wanted to eat another human being but did want to enact the most terrible revenge he could for his father's death. He still burned inside with the pain

266

of unrequited revenge. He wanted his day in front of the devil that he had put many faces to. He not only wanted revenge on the person that carried out his father's death, but also on the man who ordered it. That man had condemned Mann to a life of endless searching, a life that would always be freezeframed in that terrible second in which he was made to watch his father's execution. In those final few seconds as he waited for the axe to come down on his father's head, Mann had known that he would never be the same again. Outside he grew strong and fit and he studied weapons and martial arts but inside he remained a broken youth, always searching for resolution, for justice.

Mann looked back at Run Run. She was no longer sleeping – he guessed that she had never been – but was sitting up, her hands clenched in her lap. Mann could see that in the dark her eyes were wet. He knew that Run Run had seen more dreadful things than any man in that car.

64

Thomas stared at the ground. Jake had watched him drag his feet all day. He had said nothing. Jake knew that there was nothing to be said. He cried constantly. They had all watched Silke being raped so many times that she had stopped screaming hours before her long night was over. All night Thomas hadn't taken his eyes from her. Jake knew what it was. He had to suffer with her. He could not let her die alone. Saw's men had been animals. They had painted Thomas with his sister's blood. Now Thomas was no longer part of the living. He was nearer to Silke than he was to them. Jake saw him stumble time and time again and Saw's men came behind him and dragged him to his feet and hit him and punched him but he didn't flinch or make a sound this time. He was walking in a nightmare.

Lucas was slumped over, tied to the donkey, his body rocking and swaying with the movement. He took the water Jake gave him and tried to speak but nothing coherent came out. Anna kept walking. She said nothing. She didn't cry like Thomas but she was in shock, screaming inside, so terrified. Suddenly, now, for the first time, Jake thought Thomas was right. They were all going to die. The old porter had died today. He had been left to decompose. Jake looked over at Saw who turned and grinned, but his eyes were not smiling. His heart beat with pure hate.

65

By the time they reached the river, the darkness was slipping away and the morning mists rose like steam from the surrounding jungle. The muddy river flowed fast ahead. A boat was waiting for them and a young man sat beside it. He was idling away his time fiddling with a radio as he watched them approach with a degree of cautious indifference. He did not move as he watched them park the VW van on the flat approach to the mooring.

'Ah, there is the son of my good friend.' Gee got out of the van and went to talk to him, returning a few minutes later. 'All is good. He will take us across and others are waiting for us on the other side.'

Once the gear was loaded, the young boatman took them out into the deep channel in the middle of the river and then headed towards the far bank, steering the boat upstream. There was an air of trepidation and foreboding as they watched the navy sky above turn pale blue and the moon sink away. Only the noise of their boat disturbed the still air. Deep below them, a giant catfish stalked the muddy riverbed. Shoals of long eels skimmed the surface, their backs a muddy grey, their bellies silver.

No one spoke. On one side of them was Thailand, on the other Burma. If they were caught in this no man's land, neither country would want them and they would disappear without a trace. Mann looked out over the stillness of the water and up to the dense forest that rose steeply ahead of them on the far side of the river. He wondered what it was hiding. There was no turning back now. Whatever fate lay ahead, he shared it now with a brother he had never met. If the monk was right, then his own death would be linked to the five's. The monk's words wouldn't leave him.

They chugged their way upriver for a half an hour, passing only the fishermen on the Burmese banks who were out checking their nets, before coming to a stop at a jetty. Two porters from Gee's village, Dok and Keetau, were waiting for them. Keetau was the elder of the two. He spoke little and smiled even less. He'd obviously had enough of Dok and snarled at him whenever he spoke. Quickly and silently they all unloaded the gear from the boat. Keetau and Dok transformed Gee's heavy canvas bags into backpacks by the use of bamboo straps and carried them high up on their backs.

They left the boatman by the side of the river and Louis led the way up a path through the jungle. The land rose steeply from the river, the hot sand turning to blackened earth beneath their feet as they climbed. The frogs called an alarm up and down the riverbank.

'Keep to the path,' Louis whispered back along the

line. 'Follow in someone else's footprints all the time. This whole area is mined.'

Mann didn't need to be told twice. He stayed close behind Sue's slim frame as she strode ahead of him. No pretty skirts to hold her up today, no tie-dyed blouses. She looked pert in her military-style dark trousers and long-sleeved shirt, her thick blonde plait resting between her shoulder blades. Sue and Louis carried all the medical supplies. The rest of the gear was split between Mann and the others. Sue was carrying the same size pack as Mann on her back, and he knew it was heavy and hard to balance as the weight pulled backwards, but she was as sure-footed and nimble as a mountain goat climbing the steep bank. She was clearly used to it; backpack medics were renowned for their strength and stamina.

Beneath their feet, the dried leaves crackled and the bank climbed sharply up into the jungle. The going rapidly became difficult and Mann had to pull himself up using the branches and vines, careful not to step out of the others' tracks. When the way became impassable, they took it in turns to machete their way through the thick foliage. The sweat poured from them as the heat from their bodies was trapped in the denseness of the lush vegetation. Somewhere above the canopy of the jungle there was a midday sun overhead; but it hardly broke through the tops of the teak trees.

By late afternoon they had reached the beginnings of a village. Directly in front of them was a wooden arch, roughly constructed. On one side there was a carved wooden figure representing a man with a massive erect penis, on the other a carved woman's vagina.

'Animists,' said Riley, by way of explanation. 'Don't ask . . .'

'Don't really think I need to,' smiled Mann.

Hidden amongst the forest, the dwellings came gradually into view – about thirty or more houses built at odd angles to the hillside and to each other. A stream ran down the centre of the village.

A white dog barked at their approach and raced up to Run Run, his tail wagging furiously. She called out a greeting and there came the sound of an excited rush of giggling voices from the forest around. A group of young children of differing heights and ages appeared in their path to greet them. One of them shuffled after the others on her bottom. Her head was misshapen and her legs malformed. The children crowded round Run Run as she scooped up the little shuffling girl and carried her on her hip into the settlement. The others wrapped their arms around Run Run's waist as they pulled her forward and the group followed. As they passed the first dwelling, a stout-looking older woman emerged. She had a rifle in one hand and a bloody bandage in the other. She frowned when she looked at Mann and the others but, when she looked at Run Run, a small smile twitched at the side of her mouth.

'And how is my daughter?' she asked.

'I am good,' Run Run answered. 'Mr Mann, this is my mother, Mo.'

Mo greeted them with a sharp nod before turning briskly back inside the hut. Run Run beckoned Mann to follow her. They left their shoes outside and entered into the inner room where there was a smell of antiseptic and rum. There they found a young girl and a soldier, who was sitting in the corner looking the worse for wear as he leant against the side of the hut. He held one of his arms close to his chest. Mo went over to him and continued her work of stitching up a large gash on his temple.

Mo looked at them. Her eyes were small and hard; her face must have been pretty once, but now it was scarred by years of fighting.

'And this is Phara, who is like a sister to me.'

Phara was a slim, beautiful, fair-skinned girl, who wore the traditional brass rings around her long neck. She beamed at Run Run. She looked as if she would have loved to stop what she was doing to rush over and hug Run Run. Instead she held a cloth up to contain the stream of blood that dribbled from the cut in the soldier's head into his eye as Mo stitched, and smiled a big grin.

'And this little girl . . .' Run Run kissed the head of the little girl, who was still sitting on her hip '. . . is Kanya.'

Mo took a minute to study Mann whilst the soldier repositioned the bloodied cloth over his eyes and Phara held the wound together.

'You are welcome here, Mr Mann. Now, Run Run, make your friends some tea and I will send our brave soldier back to die with his comrades, hey?' Mo's English was even better than her daughter's. 'Send in the medic, I need her.'

She eyed Mann closely. 'And show *him* and the others where they will sleep. I have cleared the hut next to mine – it is dry, at least.' Mo gave Mann a wry smile as she hovered over the soldier. 'Dry is all we can ask for, isn't it, Mr Mann?' She turned back to her patient before Mann could answer, even if he had intended to. Then she called after him: 'Of course, there's plenty of room in *my* hut if you get lonely.'

Her shoulders and chest rose together as she laughed silently and the soldier winced as her hand jerked at the other end of the needle.

'Hold still!' She swabbed viciously at the wound. 'Otherwise I'll call the healer from the village and he'll put some cow shit on it and you'll lose half your pretty face.'

Mann turned to leave. He stopped in the doorway and nodded at Mo.

'I'll bear it in mind, if I have trouble sleeping . . .'

Mo laughed again and looked pleased with herself as she bit off the end of the thread with her teeth.

Mann followed Run Run outside. Sue was already washing her hands and had her medical kit open.

'You've been summoned,' said Mann.

Sue chuckled. 'Delighted to oblige. Mo is one of the people I trained and she's my star pupil. She's the local casualty department in this area and not someone you can ever say no to.'

'That's worrying.' Mann turned to wink at Mo who was watching him through the open door of the house. Her eyes had been glued to his arse as she watched him walk away. 'Great bedside manner,' said Mann. Sue laughed.

'You wait till she's had a few drinks,' she muttered quietly. She picked up her kit and went inside.

The rest of the villagers came out to look at the newcomers. They were nearly all older women, most of them strong looking. They stared at Mann and the others, not with hostility, but with some suspicion. They looked like they had fought in many battles. Some had lost limbs, others had massive scars.

A few feet away, Louis was stood in the shade chatting to a soldier who was smoking a cheroot while he waited for his companion to finish being seen to. Riley was nearby, kneeling on the floor with some of the village children as he unpacked gifts of paper and crayons for them from his rucksack.

Mann followed Run Run further into the village. They walked fifteen metres to what looked to be the largest of the dwellings. Like most of the houses in the village, it was built on stilts. However, unlike most of the other houses, there were no pigs or goats beneath this one. They climbed the ladder and set their packs down in the hut that was to be their home for the next night at least. Mann looked at Run Run.

'Your mother was a great warrior, Run Run, is that right? It looks like the other women in this village were also fighting women.'

Run Run inclined her head in a small bow of agreement.

'Yes. My mother was and is a fighter, Mr Mann. She is that before all else. She will fight till she dies, like all of us. Her unit retired here. They killed many Burmese army between them.' She started to sort out the contents of her bag. 'It is her life.'

'And what about you, Run Run? What are your hopes and your ambitions for your life?'

She turned towards him and seemed to study him, and he could see she was deciding what his intention was by asking a question that would be considered too personal and therefore rude in her culture.

'The job of every Karen person is to fight for their homeland. That is what I do, in my own way. I will play my part before I die, just like my mother has played hers. She has killed many Burmese and she has helped many villagers.'

'How will she be involved in this mission to find the five?'

'She will pick up arms again if she must. We all understand that it is vital we find the five volunteers, otherwise there will be no more money to feed the refugees, to fight for our homeland.'

Whilst Run Run was speaking, Mo had appeared at the entrance. 'My daughter is correct. We are beggars, living on handouts. We all know that we are approaching a time when the Karen might be forgotten, might be hounded out and murdered so that we will be no more. If the world thinks that we took these five young people, then the world will turn its back on us altogether and we will have no chance. I cannot allow that to happen. We can never give up and we can never surrender. That is what the Englishman said, wasn't it . . . Churchill? He was a good man in history; he supported the Karen people. The five principles must stand and those are the code we live by. Are you a man of principles, Mr Mann?' There was a hint of intrigue in her eyes. 'What is your code?'

'I have strong principles. I try and get justice for people who cannot get it for themselves,' he replied.

She studied him for a minute before she smiled and nodded her head approvingly.

'Good. Then we will be fellow soldiers, you and I. We will fight alongside one another. You will watch my back and I will definitely watch yours.' A grin spread across her face and her silent laugh grew into a coughing fit that rattled her lungs and produced a mouthful of phlegm that she spat over the balcony. Then, without waiting to be asked, she went to Run Run's pack and emptied it out. From inside the bundle, she spread out the contents: a pack of explosives, a belt of grenades, ammunition, detonators, knives and medical supplies. Mo said something to Run Run in Karen. It looked like she was expecting more. Run Run began to argue back, but Mo held up her hand for silence and shrugged, resignedly.

Mo looked at Mann, and smiled.

'Do not worry, Mr Mann. We are a peaceful people. We only defend. We will need these weapons to save the young people's lives.'

The dog was barking. She stopped to call over her shoulder for quiet. The jungle was sending up its alarms through birds and trees. Someone was coming. Mann followed her eyes towards the jungle. The dog had found more intruders. A troop of KNLA soldiers were walking single file out of the jungle. Alak was at the front. Mo turned and glared at Run Run. Mo obviously hadn't been expecting Alak to come in person and neither had Mann. But, from the expression on her face, Run Run obviously had.

66

The darkness descended fast in Mo's village. All around the sounds of women soothing their babies for the night could be heard. Alak's men were washing in the nearby stream. The smell of cooking began to permeate the thick, hot night as blackened cooking pots were stacked over red coals and the evening meal of fish curry and sticky rice was prepared.

Mann stood on the platform of his dwelling to check his satellite phone. He heard a giggle behind him.

'Men and their gadgets. Who are you trying to call?'

He turned and grinned at Sue as she came up the ladder. Her hair was wet from the wash in the stream and hung down her back in flaxen strands.

'Just wanted to make sure it worked.' He grinned sheepishly. 'No, actually, you're right – new toy, dying to use it.'

'Don't suppose it will matter but satellite phones are illegal here. The Burmese junta can't tap them so they ban them. We never carry them just in case we run into the military. Especially if you're a woman; they have a habit of planting stuff on women for the guys down the road at the next road block to find. Gives them the excuse to hold on to the girl and rape her.'

'Don't worry. I will take full responsibility if we get caught with it.' He shut down the phone, put it back in its case and stowed it away in his bag.

'In any case . . .' Sue said, 'there will be no one to call for help. There will be no one to rescue us if we run into trouble. Normally, as backpack medics, we spend weeks on the road with just the bush telegraph.'

'I'm beginning to think I should have made a will.'

Sue laughed. 'I'm counting on you to keep us all alive.' She stood in front of him and looked up into his face and gave a sweet smile. She had the fresh scent of jasmine soap on her, along with the bloom of fresh sweat. He had a sudden urge to reach out and pull her close.

'I would like to get to know you, Johnny Mann,' she said, as if she had read his mind. Then again, maybe the look in his eyes wasn't too hard to read. She took a step closer towards him.

'Sounds good to me.' He put his hands on her waist and pulled her in towards him. She pressed her hips against him and gave a playful grind. Just then Riley appeared. Sue quickly pulled away.

'Did you manage to get your hair washed, Sue?' Riley said, looking from one to the other.

'Yes, thanks.' Sue had looked momentarily embarrassed but she recovered quickly. 'What about you, Riley, did you talk to Mo about setting up a school here?' Mann had the sense he was watching two people who had known each other intimately for many years.

He shook his head. 'I will try again later. She's not in the mood for learning at the moment. She's busy with Gee.'

'What about using Alak's radio?'

'I'll do that later, too. He hasn't set it up yet.'

'Here, use my new toy.' Mann pulled his sat phone back out from the bag and handed it to Riley.

'Ah, been dying to get my hands on one of these. I bet this was expensive, wasn't it, mate?'

'I live in Hong Kong, remember? Go ahead, be my guest. Just don't chat for long.'

'I will then. Thanks, mate, I'll grab it later.'

Gee appeared at the top of the ladder looking smug. He was still wearing his red baseball cap. He hardly seemed to sweat, he was so used to the climate. He spotted Sue's mosquito repellent that she'd left out beside her bag and began slapping it on his arms and face.

From down below, Mo bellowed: 'Come and eat. Come to my table.' She looks in a good mood, thought Mann, looking down at her over the edge of the balcony.

'Happy lady.' Gee grinned up at Mann from under his cap. 'She likes my contribution.'

Gee's bony shoulders shook as he chuckled.

Mann watched from the balcony as Mo wandered back in the direction of her house and began inspecting the contents of the canvas bag lying outside it. She had a Kalashnikov AK-74 in one hand and a grenade launcher in the other. Sue took the mosquito repellent off Gee and replaced it in her pack.

'Okay, let's not keep her waiting,' she said, adding

under her breath, 'She's not the kind of woman I'd ever want to piss off, frankly. And now she's trigger-happy – great.'

They walked across to find Run Run helping with the food preparation, still carrying Kanya on her hip. Alak was sitting nearby, talking with some of his men, though Mann noticed he still kept a close eye on Run Run. It could easily have been the usual village domestic scene, thought Mann – the husband watching the wife as she made dinner, a child on her hip, another running around at her feet. Childhood sweethearts they may have been, but it didn't look like the love had gone away. Whatever bond they once had was still there. Mann watched Sue walk on ahead. He wasn't the only one watching. Alak's soldiers paid her more than a little attention. Mann had a feeling she encouraged it and he smiled to himself. That didn't bother him. Mann's thoughts were interrupted by one of Alak's men who finished watching Sue walk by and then grabbed Phara and pulled her onto his lap. She struggled to release herself.

Mo looked up from her canvas bag. Alak ordered his man to release Phara. Either the man didn't hear, or he didn't want to hear. Riley marched over and pulled Phara from his lap. He picked the soldier up by his shirt.

'Step out of line again, and I'll deal with you personally.'

The soldier looked at Alak. Alak glared back at him. The soldier backed down with a dismissive shrug of indifference.

Mo's eyes lingered coldly on the soldier and then on

Alak. She gave a flick of her head and went back to examining her new toys.

Alak and his second-in-command, Captain Rangsan, got up, leaving the rest of the men eating their dinner, and came to join Mann and the others as they gathered in front of Mo's hut. Mo held up one of the rifles to her face, closed her eyes, and breathed in its smell as if it were a newborn baby.

'Ah . . .' She waved it in the air triumphantly. 'It's been many years since I held a new rifle, many years. All thanks to my new friend here.' She reached out and pulled Gee close to her, squashing him to her large breasts. 'I think I have a new lover.' She kissed him hard on the cheek, squashing his face in her hand. Gee looked terrified.

Riley didn't look happy.

'Didn't know we were gun runners now.' He stood with his arms folded across his chest. 'I thought we were on a rescue mission, not a military one.'

'The two will be hard to separate in the end, Riley,' Mann answered. 'We can't afford to meet up with these men unarmed. We will need all the help we can get to rescue these kids. These guns were not bought with NGO money – they were a private donation, hey, Gee?'

Gee gave one quick sharp nod of affirmation. He was still restrained by Mo's vicelike grip and was frightened to make a move in case she crushed him further.

'Food!' Mo was hungry. She picked up a bottle of rum in one hand whilst still maintaining her grip on Gee with the other. She signalled the way and propelled Gee forward to the other end of the compound.

Alak and Ransang followed them. 'I will show you my new building,' she announced.

'You've been building since we were last here?' Riley asked. He stopped in his tracks as they came to a newly cleared area in the forest and they saw an open-sided building with a raised floor, furnished with benches and tables. 'What's this, Mo?' He looked amazed.

'You don't know what this is?' Mo looked slightly put out. 'This is the school you keep telling me to build.'

Riley nodded approvingly, a wide grin splitting his face. The group moved to sit at some of the long rows of desks.

'So, we are the first to sit in this school,' beamed Mo. 'Let us hope it will not be burnt to the ground next week, huh? My heart tells me that my village will soon be moving on. We are running out of places to hide in this world. We are running out of friends.'

Mo poured herself a glass and then put the rum bottle in the middle of the table. Louis came to join them. Mann had seen him talking to the villagers earlier. He was preparing for his job of guiding them and tracking the five. It was a big responsibility. Louis acknowledged everyone with a grunt, but didn't speak. Lamps were dotted and incense sticks lit to keep away the mosquitoes. Lizards ran across the tables and up the beams of the open-sided school.

Phara brought over bowls of rice and sweet hot curry for them. Mo finished her rum, poured herself another, and then handed the bottle around. Mann didn't have to know Mo well to read her expressions. She was in an aggressive mood that had been exacerbated by Alak's appearance, and the drink was bringing it to the fore. She drank plenty during the meal. Once they finished eating, Phara cleared the table and Alak spread a well-worn map in front of them. Run Run placed a candle in its centre.

Alak said, 'Since we left you, we have been talking with the hill people.'

'Do they think the five are still in the area?' Mann asked.

Alak nodded. 'They have been seen here.' He used a stick to reach over the map to point. 'I have sent six trackers out looking for them. Three have returned and say that the kidnappers have journeyed as far as the Laos border, up to the opium hills of the Golden Triangle. But now they keep moving, only staying one night or two in each place, and they force the villagers to help them carry their loads. That's how we will find them.' He traced the line of dots already drawn onto the map. 'The villagers will tell me. They have taken porters and demanded food and somewhere to sleep here on their way north, but not straight north – they take a twisting path. They are not trying to escape, they are waiting for something . . . someone.' Alak pointed out the kidnappers' course with the tip of his stick as it zigzagged across the hills. 'They move every day, but they go nowhere. The mountains of the Golden Triangle will hide them.'

'What about the hill tribes?'

'These are people high up in the hills, opium growers. They will say very little as the food in their children's mouths depends on silence. The people will be too afraid to stop them. You cannot stop the Shwit. They will keep going and not care whether people like it or not. They will push the five until they get what they want.'

Mo wiped her mouth with the back of her hand. Her lips looked burned from the strong dark liquor. In the firelight her eyes were hard and her face jowly. She had been drinking for hours and now her drunkenness slurred her words and she growled rather than spoke. Her demeanour turned cold as her shoulders slumped and she stared at the map.

'Pah! We have killed plenty of Shwit in our time.'

'It's not *just* the Shwit.' Alak looked across at Run Run. 'They are led by an old enemy – Saw Wah Say is their leader. He left a message for me when he killed Mongkut. He is challenging me.'

Mo's expression changed. Her eyes narrowed with hate as she glared at Alak.

'See!' Mo stood, swaying, and banged her glass down onto the table. 'All the bad things come back to you in time.' She spat her words at Alak who did not move. 'Mongkut died because of *you* . . .' She slumped back down onto the bench, her fire disappearing as quickly as it had flared. 'He was a brave man, a good man; he was my friend. I knew him all my life. I fought with him in many battles. You killed my only son and you killed Mongkut.' Her voice trailed and her eyes filled with tears. She poured herself another drink, and then turned, her eyes flashing with hate in the darkness. 'You have caused so much suffering in your worthless life.' Mo glared at him. Her fire had returned. She was suddenly upright, poised and spoiling for a drunken fight.

There was an intake of breath from Run Run as

Alak's shoulders stiffened and he glared at Mo. For a few seconds he seemed ready to leap across the table at her throat; but instead he remained in his seat, fuming but controlled.

'When Saw and I were taken away to fight for Khun Sa we committed terrible crimes. We were wild and lawless. But I have paid for my crimes, Mo. I cannot pay for them for the rest of my life. I am a Buddhist. I have made amends.'

'Hah!' Mo laughed sarcastically as she turned and spat into the darkness. '*Your* God? *Your* God divided the Karen people. *Your* God works for the Burmese junta and kills his own people.' She rocked forward and waited, daring Alak to retaliate. Mann waited too, watching Alak, who gave him a resigned smile and shook his head slowly. Then he reached for the bottle and poured himself and Mo a drink. He gave a small sigh before he raised his glass to Mo.

'To the fight. To the four principles and to the gods – we beg their forgiveness. And to Mongkut – he was a brave man and a good friend to all of us.'

'Pah!' Mo did not raise her glass. Instead she wiped her mouth as if there were a bad taste in it, before sitting back down and reaching over and snatching up the bottle once more.

Mann kept his eyes on Run Run. She remained silent but her eyes, her shoulders, her soul seemed filled with a sad hopelessness as she watched Mo and Alak, still fighting after all the years. Alak sat back against the bench and he took a few deep breaths. He was a man well versed in the art of warfare but he would back down from Mo.

Not only because he had too much respect for her, but also because he returned Run Run's love and her eyes were begging him not to retaliate. But whatever it was that Alak had done to offend Mo, it wasn't something she was ever going to forget, Mann thought. The evening seemed in danger of degenerating into a slanging match and Riley got up and excused himself. Mo sat muttering under her breath as she watched him go.

In the rest of the village, a quiet was descending. People began to excuse themselves and drift away to find a few hours' sleep before dawn. Only the dog still continued its wakeful patrol, and now he began to growl at the undergrowth. As they all paused to see what the concern was, Mann could make out Riley talking on the phone to someone. Mo picked up a stone and threw it at the dog to shut it up.

'We must rest now. We set off at dawn,' said Alak. 'Two groups, to cover more ground. My men will travel in one and we will travel in the other. Mo will remain here. We need someone to coordinate and Mo has the radio.'

Riley rejoined them. From the corner of his eye, Mann could see the shape of someone moving through the undergrowth. He looked around at the others. Only Louis seemed to be looking in the same direction as him but he looked away. Mann looked again and he knew he was right – two eyes were staring back at him from the blackness.

67

The day was just beginning to surrender its nighttime moisture to the air. It was already warm. There was a pre-dawn stillness, broken only by the coughing coming from Mo's hut as she stirred from her bed to spit her phlegm off the side of her platform.

'Are we set?' Sue was looking at Mann as she stood beside him on the platform while he drank the last of his coffee. She followed his eyes out to the jungle. Mann was still looking for any trace of what it was he'd seen the night before. 'What is it? Didn't you get any sleep?'

'I slept okay . . . you?' Mann turned to see that Sue had got herself kitted out in her jungle outfit once more for the day's journey.

'You must be kidding, it's an oven in there.' She looked back towards the entrance to the inner room of the dwelling. 'You feel like your skin is crawling. But at least everyone goes to bed early.'

'Yes, no chance of catching a late movie here.' Mann was still distracted by the forest, still hoping to catch another glimpse of whatever it was he had seen.

'What is it?' she asked again.

He turned and smiled at her. 'Just thinking, that's all.'

'About?'

'Last night mainly. What is it with Mo and Alak about him having killed her son?' He looked down from the platform. He could Run Run playing with the children; Alak was talking to Captain Rangsan in the clearing.

Sue lowered her voice. 'I'll tell you later.'

Beneath the ladder, the rest of the parties were beginning to congregate. Gee was sat on a log smoking in his self-contained manner – same red T-shirt, same red cap on his head. He looked to be in a contemplative mood. Nearby, Dok and Keetau were packing the provisions into their bundles and tying them onto bamboo straps. Mo had kitted them out with enough food to last the next five days of their journey. By then they should be at Gee's village and able to get more supplies. Mann threw the rest of his coffee into the undergrowth. 'Okay, I'm ready.' He made a last check of his bag and followed Sue down the ladder.

'Alak and I are discussing tactics.' Louis looked up as they approached. They were hovering over a map drawn in the earth. 'Alak has more news this morning,' he added.

'Yes. My scouts came here before dawn. Saw and the volunteers are no longer in the Golden Triangle. They have returned to this area. They are somewhere in these forests.'

'That's good,' said Sue. 'Isn't it?'

Alak looked pensive. 'Perhaps. But we do not know why.'

Louis pointed his stick in the dirt and etched a map. 'Alak's men will sweep around to the west; we'll go east and meet in five days at Gee's village. We will keep in touch by radio.'

'Where's our first destination?' asked Mann.

Alak answered. 'The old refinery, two days' walk from here. I think Saw will have gone there.' Alak had a final word with Captain Rangsan before he and the men picked up their equipment, strapped on their new weapons, and disappeared stealthily through the village and out into the jungle. The others stood in silence and watched them go. The silence was broken by Mo's booming voice, berating Run Run about something. Run Run walked quickly towards them, her head bowed and her face set in stone. She had obviously heard enough from her mother.

'You do that and you are no daughter of mine.' Mo scrambled after her, hurrying to keep up with her. Run Run wheeled back around to face her.

'I will not live my life like you, Mother! I want to be happy. I want to feel love. I would rather die than live a life without love . . . I am a *thay-ne* to you – a walking dead. I mean nothing to you.'

Mo had stopped dead in her tracks, shocked. She watched Run Run pick up her pack and throw it over her shoulders, stopping only to hug Phara and Kanya before starting out towards the jungle. She didn't look back at her mother. For a few seconds Mo stood where she was, bewilderment and hurt on her face, then she swung around and scowled at Alak.

'Pah . . .' Mo looked at him and spat. 'Don't fuck up.'

Just as they started after Run Run, the dog began barking furiously, just out of sight on the edge of the camp. Everyone turned to look and to watch Mo's reaction. She knew its barks as if they were a language. She started slowly towards the direction of the dog. This bark was of alarm, not an intruder, but something was frightening the dog.

Alak removed his gun from its holster. Mann moved Delilah from his boot to his hand and Alak, Louis and Mann walked towards the spot where the dog was still barking. They fanned out as they came near, approaching from three directions. Louis was the first of them to spot the soldier's body.

68

He was slumped over at the base of a tree. His head was bent back where he had fallen awkwardly. His eyes stared vacantly upwards. His mouth hung open, forming a cave for the flies to explore. His trousers lay around his ankles. It was the soldier who had pulled Phara onto his lap.

Louis knelt down to look him over. Mann bent down beside him.

'Fucking religious crap.' Louis snatched something from round the soldier's neck and threw it into the bushes.

'What was that?' asked Mann.

'Animist charms,' said Louis. 'Spirit appeasers. Fucking voodoo beads.'

He looked up at Mo, who had followed them with Phara. 'How did he die?' asked Riley.

Louis and Mann searched his body. They found one wound on the soldier's chest. 'This is what killed him,' Mann said as he examined the wound closely. 'It's a clean deep cut, made by a fine stiletto-type blade, about an inch wide. There's bruising either side of it, the knife had a hilt of some kind.'

'Straight into the heart,' said Louis. 'Why wasn't he missed this morning?' Louis turned to ask Alak.

'I sent him to look for the scouts last night. He doesn't see many women. I didn't want him causing a problem here in Mo's camp. The scouts arrived without him; I knew he must have hit trouble. I did not expect it to be so close.'

'It looks like he came out here when he was caught short,' said Riley.

'Not exactly,' answered Mann, looking at the dried semen on the soldier's leg.

'What shall we do?' asked Sue, her voice sounding panicky.

'We have no time to find out who killed him or why,' said Mann. 'We'll have to leave his body here for Mo to deal with. We have no choice. We are together now for good or bad. If one of us is a murderer we will find out soon enough.'

'Yes,' Alak agreed, picking up his gun and slinging it over his shoulder, ready to leave. 'We must hurry now.'

They carried the soldier's body to the medical hut and now, with the sun already high in the sky, they had to hurry to make up for lost time. They picked up their packs and followed Alak as he turned and led them out of the village. Mann looked back to see Mo cutting an anxious, lonely but stoic figure at the village entrance as she watched them go.

After they left, Mo went to tend to the soldier's body. It must be given the proper rights to appease the spirits. His death, which had taken place in such a violent manner, would bring a curse on the village and his spirit would haunt them all. Phara helped her and together they removed his clothes and prepared his body. They washed him and removed his intestines, then anointed his body with palm oil before wrapping it in strips of white fabric.

'A blood sacrifice must be made.'

Mo picked up her knife and went to the pig pen below her house. There she grabbed one of the small pigs and thrust the knife into its heart.

'Tonight we will eat the pig and appease his spirit. We will give it passage to heaven.'

The soldier's body was carried to a funeral pyre, high up on a sacred mound a half a mile away. Ten of Mo's women accompanied her whilst the rest stayed in the village.

The brightness of the soldier's body as it burned lit the evening sky. It was the inadvertent signal that the Burmese army captain, Boon Nam, needed. Mo had taken her best fighters to carry the soldier on his long journey up to the sky. She had left behind Phara to cook the pig in preparation for the evening and to look after the camp. The camp was unprotected.

From their positions on the ground Kanya and the dog were the first to feel the earth beneath them tremble at the approach of many feet. The dog listened; it twisted its head and gave a series of small alarmed barks and then it looked at Kanya. Both of them looked towards the sky. Birds were rising, monkeys were squawking. The dog's hackles went up. One by one, the other children stopped playing and came to stand with

Kanya and the dog. An old woman stood in her doorway and called to them.

'What is it? Is it Mo returning already?'

Phara stopped turning the pig on its spit. Her eyes went first to one side of the camp and then the other. The jungle was moving all around them. Then she saw the flash of a gun, she heard the crack of twigs breaking beneath army boots, and she shouted to the children, 'Run, run, run!'

They scampered into the jungle; most were hacked to pieces as they ran into the waiting soldiers. The old woman was killed where she stood. Phara was pinned to the ground by Boon Nam's men and gang-raped whilst her face was forced towards the fire to watch not the pig on the spit, but Kanya, suspended upside down and roasted alive.

69

Mann and the others headed west and followed a small tributary of the river. The night came thick and fast and Alak called a halt to the march when they could no longer see well enough to walk. They cleared an area of the bank twenty feet from the fast-flowing river and made a makeshift camp. The place was cleared of snakes and insects, hammocks were slung between trees and a fire was lit. Run Run and Gee took out the pots from the porters' packs and began preparing the meal of rice and a thick vegetable sauce. The mood was pensive. They had spent much of the morning discussing the soldier's death and come to no conclusion. They were all together now for good or bad, till the end.

An hour later, Mann found himself with Sue in the river. Her clothes were already hanging from a branch. As he approached, she waded deeper into the water.

'So, tell me the story,' Mann said. 'What was that all about with Mo and Alak?'

Sue kept her shoulders submerged beneath the skin of the water as she answered him.

'Run Run, Alak and Saw Wah Say were all friends as children. Like Alak said, he and Saw were taken away to fight as youngsters and then to help run the refinery. It seems that Saw was in love with Run Run and so was Alak. Alak is a Buddhist and Mo wouldn't allow the marriage. Saw was a Christian and she said yes, but Run Run didn't want it. The two men lived side by side like brothers both after the same girl.

'From what I heard, in their years at the refinery, they committed many terrible crimes between them – raping, killing, high on drugs – it was a mad time. After the refinery changed hands and they were kicked out, they returned briefly to the village. As Alak said, there was nothing to return to for Saw; his family were all either dead or gone. He stayed with Alak but that brought everything to a head, and he tried to rape Run Run. Alak nearly killed him but, in the process, Run Run's brother tried to help. He got in the way and he was killed. We don't know how. No one knows exactly what happened that day, only the three of them. Since then, Saw has been on the run, getting wilder, apparently. Mo will always hate Alak. All I know is that Alak and Run Run can never be together – it is forbidden. But it doesn't mean they don't love each other.'

As Sue was talking, Mann was staring at her. She looked beautiful, like King Arthur's 'Lady of the Lake', the moonlight tracing the curve of her breasts and silhouetting her bare shoulders. Her hair, loose now, pooled on top of the water, gold turned to liquid platinum in the moonlight. Mann was almost lost for words.

'Talking of love . . .' said Mann. 'You've known Riley for a long time, haven't you?'

She smiled. 'We are good friends, Johnny. We have been through a lot together. I love him like a brother now.'

'Does he know that?'

'Yes, he does. We split up ages ago; we only live together out of convenience.' Mann took a step closer towards her and she rose a little out of the water. He cupped some water in his hands and poured it over her shoulders. The water dripped from the tips of her erect nipples; her breasts had goosebumps. There was a rustle of noise behind them.

'Dinner is ready.' Riley appeared on the riverbank behind them. Sue dived back under the water.

'Thanks, Riley, coming.'

'Okay, look away, boys, I'm coming out . . .' She waded out of the water, naked.

Mann had no intention of looking away. Riley scrabbled to find her clothes but Sue was in no hurry to cover up. Riley looked as if he was seething, and he wasn't going anywhere.

'Did you need to borrow the phone again?' Mann asked him. 'Go ahead, it's in my bag.'

Riley hesitated. 'No, you're all right, mate. Not tonight. Thanks for lending to me last night, hope you didn't mind. It all got a bit lively at the table.'

'I don't mind. As long as we keep it to emergencies. The battery on those things isn't massive and there's nowhere to recharge it out here.'

'Oh yeah.' Riley paused. 'I needed to speak to a new

guy in charge at the camp . . . I just have to keep an eye on stuff, that's all . . .'

'Just wanted to make sure there haven't been any more incidents.'

'Face it, Riley. You're just a control freak, aren't you?' Sue smiled at him affectionately and gave his arm a squeeze as she finished dressing. She picked up her bag and started walking back up to the camp. 'The camp will be fine, Riley. They won't attack it twice in such a short space of time.'

He shook his head and shrugged as he smiled after Sue. 'Yeah, you're right – as always. But you know me – I just have to make sure.'

'You coming?' Sue asked them both. Mann shook his head; he didn't intend to be hurried. He walked out of the water and started drying himself.

'Five minutes,' answered Riley. 'I just want to have a word with Johnny.'

Mann started getting dressed. Riley waited until Sue was out of earshot before he spoke.

'Look, mate, this isn't some fucking camping trip for singles dating. We are here to do a job. I know Sue. She can get hurt easily. She looks tough but inside she is very fragile.'

Mann held up his hand.

'Let me stop you there, Riley.' Mann's temper was like a lit candle inside him, always burning, never going out; and occasionally someone came along to breathe gasoline on it. 'Don't ever fucking tell me what I can and can't do. I will do my job and anyone else's who doesn't make the grade and don't think for one second that I will take my eye off you, Riley. You lied to me when I asked you about Louis in the camp. You said you didn't know him very well – that's bollocks. You lied to me about the kids having their own transport. The soldier who you had words with yesterday was murdered just feet from where you were on the radio last night. To my mind, you have to be the number one suspect here.'

'It's not how it looks. I didn't want to get Louis or myself into shit for maybe bypassing a few rules when it came to qualifications. Louis isn't the normal type but I wanted to give him the work. And don't talk to me about that soldier's death. You carry a knife just like the one used to kill him.'

'Yeah, but you know who the killer in stories never is, Sherlock? It is never the fucking detective who comes halfway around the world to help. Who it turns out to be is a local with a motive. And maybe that's you, Riley. As far as I can see, you're a liar. You lied to me once and you will do it again. Now, until I make sense of what's going on, I won't believe a word you say. We have five missing kids and as many loose ends as a bowl of spaghetti right now. I still don't know where you fit in to all of this, or why you wanted to come on this mission, but, believe me, I will. By the end of this "camping trip", as you call it, we will all know each other much better. And, Sue and I? That's none of your fucking business.'

Mann finished dressing and picked up his bag before heading back up towards the camp. Riley was left at the water's edge. He stood there for a moment, then ran to catch up with Mann.

'Sorry, mate.' He held out his hand for Mann to shake. Mann did not take it and he retracted it after an awkward few seconds. 'Believe me when I say I had nothing to do with the soldier's death. I haven't got a fucking clue who killed him or why. But you're right. Sue and I have been over a long time. I just feel protective towards her, that's all. But, of course, she can more than handle herself and it's no bloody business of mine.'

'Let's just get on with the job, Riley. Even if you did come on this mission just to stop me making advances to your ex-girlfriend. A handshake won't get you off my list of suspects.'

'Don't be bloody ridiculous,' Riley scoffed. 'I came because I thought you might need me. Whatever else you think of me, you have to realise that this is *my* world. I don't want it shat on. Where do I go if all this disappears? If we don't find those kids alive then nothing will be the same here and *here* is all I care about. I will do everything I can to preserve it.'

He was right, admitted Mann. Thailand attracted people like Riley. They might be escaping from the past but they cared passionately about hanging on to their present.

As they rejoined the others, Alak was busy talking on the radio. Sue was waiting for them and scanned their faces anxiously. Mann gave her a smile and shook his head, as if to say there was nothing to worry about. She looked relieved. Riley was about to say something when Sue put her hand up for silence.

'Wait . . .' She was listening to Alak's conversation.

'Something's wrong. Alak's on the radio to Mo. I heard him ask her about details of an attack.'

Run Run was waiting at Alak's side to speak to her mother. She bowed her head and her shoulders shook with sorrow as she listened to her mother's account of the attack, then she handed the receiver back to Alak. He wound up the conversation, stooped briefly to comfort Run Run, and then came over to update the others.

'There has been an attack on Mo's village.' His face was dark with anger. 'Boon Nam has killed many women and children.'

'Mo?' asked Riley. 'Is she all right?'

'He could not have known who she was. If he had known she was the infamous fighter, responsible for wiping out many Burmese army regiments, he would have made sure he killed her. As it was, he sought to punish her for allowing foreigners to stay in her village.'

'How many dead?' Riley asked.

'Thirty. The school burnt. The houses destroyed.'

'Bastards,' said Riley bitterly.

'That means they are on to us,' said Mann. 'They know we are here and why.'

Alak nodded. 'It means that the Burmese junta knows about the kidnapping and is helping Saw. We are going to be attacked from all fronts – anyone who knows or helps us will be slaughtered.'

70

The next morning the atmosphere in the camp was subdued. No one had really slept except Gee, who seemed to thrive on the basics and didn't feel the stress levels. After washing and cooking up some coffee, they headed off just as the dawn was filtering through the tops of the trees. All around, the earth was coming alive with the sounds of calling birds. They struck away from the river in order to stay hidden and crossed over what appeared to be a well-used path. Louis stopped to check for signs that others had been that way.

'Who makes these tracks, Louis?' Mann caught up with him as he was examining some donkey droppings.

'Drug runners mainly.'

'I thought the Thai government had stamped that out?'

'They don't move the drugs by road any more. The only way to move the stuff is by mule.' Louis stood. 'You're never going to stop it. Just because the Opium King surrendered, it didn't mean anything had to stop. He left a fully-functioning supply chain from grower to smuggler. It was never going to stop just like that.

Others slotted straight into a very well-oiled business whilst he made a deal to live the rest of his life under luxury house arrest in Rangoon. The Burmese government are expanding their opium production daily. They have moved their refineries away from the Thai border, that's all.'

'Have you ever been to this old refinery that we're headed to?'

'Yes, I've stopped there sometimes with the backpack medic team. It's an eerie place. Things were just left abandoned. It feels like a place full of ghosts. Doesn't it, Alak?' Louis called softly across to the captain as he passed them, ever watchful, his eyes alert for any signs of trouble. Mann thought again how haunted Alak looked. He had the demeanour of a man who had never known a day without struggle. They caught him up and walked alongside him.

'Why do you think he will go there, Alak?' asked Mann.

'I know him well. I feel his fear. He is scared now. He has had the five for two weeks. Whatever he hoped to achieve, it has not happened.'

71

Alak was getting more edgy as the day wore on. The oppressive stillness of the forest seemed to suck out all the energy and oxygen from anything that tried to move through it, as if they were not welcome there. Alak had halted them many times in the last hour. It was as if he sensed something in the air. As they neared the first set of three peaks, he disappeared. He returned ten minutes later.

'There is a scouting party, out looking for us. It must be part of Boon Nam's unit. We must kill them.' Alak looked at them all. 'Come with me.' He nodded at Mann and Louis. 'No guns. We must have complete silence, understand?'

Mann and Louis both nodded. Mann undid his shirt and added more throwing stars to the pouch he wore looped around one shoulder and across his chest. He held Delilah in his boot. He strapped his six throwing spears – especially weighted, feather-tipped, six-inch deadly spikes – to his arm, and he carried his most lethal star, capable of decapitating a man, the Death Star, nestled in a pouch on his belt.

'How many of them are there?' asked Louis, as he added a hatchet to his already well-equipped knife belt.

'I have seen ten. We will need to strike fast and strong with everything we have, before they have a chance to fire their weapons. Ready?' Mann and Louis nodded again. Alak turned to the others. 'Stay here and stay quiet. If we are unsuccessful and they run this way, use these.' He handed Riley and Gee two handguns. 'Only use them if you have no choice because the noise will bring Boon Nam straight here.'

The three men stayed together as they reached the start of a ridgeway of trees and the first of the mountain peaks. They lay down in the stubbly grass at the edge of the forest and watched the line of soldiers walk stealthily across the clearing on the side of the second rise. They crawled forward on their bellies until they were crouched just in front of the approaching soldiers. Their weapons at the ready, they waited. The soldiers were still twenty feet away, moving warily across the open side of the ridge. Just as Mann undid his shuriken pouch and slipped the throwing stars into his hand, there was one single clap of gunfire that echoed around the hills and sent a flurry of alarm across the canopy of the forest. It had come from the direction of the camp. Had they missed another scouting party? They looked at one another for the answer. The only thing they knew for sure was that the others were under attack.

Up ahead, the soldiers turned at the noise and broke into a jog as they dropped down into the valley and headed towards the sound. Mann reached for his first set of shuriken. He knelt up in the grass and fired off all five at once. They sang in the air as they found their targets and sliced into muscle and bone. Three of the men dropped to their knees. Before they had time to reach for their weapons, Mann had fired off his second set of shuriken and three more fell. Louis and Alak were on their feet charging forward, knives in hand. Alak plunged his knife into one man's chest and he fell to the floor. Louis slit another's throat. Only two of the men were still standing when Mann reached for his throwing spikes and he threw with such force they struck the first man dead. The second man was struck with a shuriken in his neck and another in his chest. Alak plunged his knife into the last man's heart as he lay there twitching then they turned together and ran back towards the forest.

Riley stood, and pointed his gun at the young soldier flying through the forest towards them. He didn't seem to see them. He had lost his senses. He just wanted to escape from the army. He wasn't looking for them.

'Stop,' Riley shouted to him in Burmese. 'Or I will shoot.'

It was too late as Gee fired his gun into the trees but missed the soldier. The young man, beautiful in his youth, came to a standstill before them and stood there panting, his eyes panic stricken as he stared at Riley. He looked desperate to find a way out but he was frozen with fear.

Silently Run Run stepped up on a rock behind him, yanked his head back and slit his throat. His arms flailed wildly but his eyes locked onto Riley's in panic before they rolled back in his head and blood spurted from his gaping throat.

'What happened?' asked Alak as the three men came running back through the forest. Run Run was standing silent with a knife in her hand. Her face was splattered with blood. She bent and wiped the blade in the grass. Gee stood, his hand shaking, still holding the gun. Riley answered.

'The young soldier came from nowhere. Gee shot at him and missed. Run Run killed him.' Riley shuddered.

'It was my fault.' Gee stood, his head bowed beneath the red cap. 'I had the gun ready. I saw a person coming, I panicked, I shot at him. I missed. I am sorry. I was scared.'

Alak looked down at the dead soldier and then at Run Run.

'Was this the only one?'

'Yes,' Run Run replied.

'Okay, it is done. We need to move from this place quickly; Boon Nam is coming.'

72

By dusk the next day, Mann and the others came across the track that led to the old refinery. Louis looked anxious. Mann could see why. It was obvious that many people had been there recently. The grass was squashed; there were fresh mule droppings, covered in flies.

'Keep to the track,' Alak whispered along the line. They followed the lane until they stood above the plant, looking down on the abandoned refinery. The manmade lake below still contained water, though there were holes in the palm-thatched roofs, rust on the corrugated iron. Outside were piles of obsolete equipment and, more significantly, there were glass bottles glinting in the last rays of the sun, signs of recent habitation and a night of heavy drinking.

Mann felt his heart begin to race, a knot in his stomach, his hands sweating. He knew that something lay waiting to be found in those dilapidated buildings. He needed to keep himself calm and his pulse low. He needed to be ready.

He stooped to pick up a cheroot butt from the side of the lane. 'It looks a few days old . . .' Mann said to

Louis and then paused to listen to a horribly familiar sound. 'Something's very wrong here.'

It was a sound that Mann had heard many times before, but he wished he hadn't. It was the droning of thousands of flies.

73

'I am coming this time,' said Riley as he joined Mann and Alak as they made their way cautiously towards the large buildings in the centre. The others stayed to keep watch. They walked in a line until they came level with one of the barns. They followed Alak in silence as Mann kept his shuriken at the ready. As they passed the first of the smaller, open-sided barns Mann stopped to examine a pile of old sacks, their stamps still visible: they were branded with their supplier's brand. As he picked it up, a large spider ran from beneath the hessian folds. He shook the sack and another dropped out, plopped onto the floor, and disappeared back into the bottom of the pile. He spread the sack out so that he could read it. It was Chinese script. He tore off a small tag with the logo on it and put it into his pocket. All around him were the remnants of heroin processing: containers that had once housed the sugar, the chemicals, and the vats for distilling. All around, the earth was churned with fresh footprints and a fire had been burning there very recently.

Despite himself, Mann felt his pulse quicken as they

drew up to the entrance to the longest of the barns. Around them empty bottles of rum lay smashed and crawling with sugar-hungry insects. A cobra danced at them as they approached. The droning of flies was deafening.

'Shit. Jesus Christ!' Riley instantly recoiled as they rounded the corner of the building. A cloud of flies lifted, turned in the air and resettled onto another body.

'There has been a night of madness here,' said Alak quietly.

Flies swarmed over smears of blood and scraps of bloodied rags: women's clothing lay in shreds across the floor. Three bodies lay on the wooden platform and a fourth was slumped over, tied to a roof strut on a raised platform. Its head was slumped forward. It appeared to be moving with flies and feasting insects and its legs were being gnawed at by a wild she-dog and her puppies.

As they mounted the platform and approached the body, the canopy of black flies parted and revealed strands of golden hair.

'Jesus, look, Mann – she has blonde hair . . .' Riley's voice rose.

Alak held up his hand for calm. Mann looked back from the doorway to where Sue and the others were stood. He held up his hand to tell them to stay where they were. Louis nodded back; his face grave. They didn't need to witness it to know that there was something dreadful.

Mann, Alak and Riley walked cautiously towards the

body and stepped up onto the platform. Riley couldn't take his eyes from the body.

'Christ, it's one of the girls. It's Silke.'

The dog stopped to growl at the newcomers. Mann picked up a stone and threw it, it hit her on the rump. She yelped and ran off down the side of the platform, her puppies scampering behind.

'Some people were lying here. You can see their outline.' Alak pointed to the barren floor where the dust was missing. He knelt down and picked up the strands of rope that lay around. 'They were tied together.'

'Why the fuck has he started killing the hostages and why here?' Riley couldn't take his eyes from Silke.

'They did this three days ago.'

'Are you sure?'

'Positive,' answered Mann, as he stooped to look at one of the bodies. 'You can tell by the size of the maggots.'

Alak looked around him, as if the answer to this madness were in the roof, or in the still putrid air, as if it lay in the atmosphere.

'He came here because he is frightened and he sought sanctuary. He came because he had no choice.' He looked across at Silke. 'He left her here for us to find. If we are to save the others, we must hurry. Whatever he wants he has forsaken. Now he wants to make the world pay. Let's go.'

'We can't leave her,' said Riley, visibly distressed.

'We have no choice. If he passes this way again, he won't know we have been here. He will think we are far away and headed in the wrong direction. Then we may have a chance to save the others.'

'I agree with Alak, Riley,' said Mann. 'The less help we give him the better. We need to think of the living now,' he finished quietly as he and Alak began to make their way along the edge of the platform.

'I won't leave her here.' Mann turned to see Riley, his knife in his hand. 'I'm going to cut her down.'

'No, Riley.' Mann stopped in his tracks.

'Stop!' Alak turned and shouted to him.

But Riley was already stepping over the piles of bloodied clothes towards Silke, until he froze and turned to Mann and Alak, his eyes wide with terror. He went to speak but whatever he was going to say was drowned by the sound of the explosion beneath his foot.

74

Mann was blown off the platform. Dazed, he struggled to his hands and knees and shook himself conscious. Alak was doing the same. They raced over to Riley. One foot was badly lacerated, the other leg was opened up like the petals of a flower. A piece of Riley's shin bone was sticking out of his groin. There was nothing left of Silke's body except her arms still wrapped around the roof strut.

'Keep to the right-hand side, the place is booby-trapped,' Mann yelled as Sue and Louis came running into the barn. Alak jumped down from the platform and slipped outside to stand guard.

Run Run pulled out the medical supplies from the bag. Riley was fitting from the shock and loss of blood, but still conscious. Louis strapped a tourniquet around Riley's thigh and Sue tore open the medical pack and pulled out a pack of blood-clotting bandages.

'You hang in there, Riley, you're going to be okay.' Mann kept talking as he worked fast with Sue and Louis to apply pressure to the massive wounds.

'Bring me more bandages from the porters' packs,' Sue

shouted. 'Hold this . . .' Sue gave Mann a pack of wadding. 'Open it, but don't touch it till I say. For Christ sake, Riley, it had to be you.' She paused for a moment, pushing the hair from her face with the heel of her hand. It left a smear of blood across her forehead. 'Riley's not used to looking out for landmines – he's not used to it the way we are.' She looked at Mann, her eyes full of worry.

Louis gave Riley a morphine injection and an antibiotic jab and inserted a saline drip into his arm. Run Run helped Louis clean and close the lacerations of Riley's foot. The floor was saturated in fresh blood and bone fragments.

Louis nodded towards the open medical bag. 'In there,' said Louis. 'You'll find an oxygen converter; it's in a blue bag. Get it out for me.'

Mann wiped his hands on his trousers; they were wet with Riley's blood. He leant across to the medical bag and pulled out the shoulder strap of a blue pack. 'That's it. Now get this stretch bandage around his foot for me whilst I set this up.'

Riley went still as the morphine kicked in. They got him onto a stretcher and carried him outside.

'If I take that out, he's going to die,' Sue said, looking at the piece of shin bone jutting from his groin. 'It's right next to an artery.' She shouted over her shoulder: 'Alak! Radio Mo and tell her to get a stretcher team here immediately.'

Alak was already talking to Mo on the radio. He shouted back: 'There is no team near. We will have to take him ourselves.'

Sue didn't respond. She looked at Louis and Mann.

318

Mann knew what they were all thinking – they would now lose half their team. Louis put it into words.

'It will take four of us to get him down alive. The two porters will have to carry him and Sue and I will have to look after him. We have no choice – otherwise he will die.' Louis started assembling the stretcher. 'That means you have no guide, Mann. I am sorry. You'll have to find another tracker.'

'Somehow I don't think we will need one.' Mann looked at the sky. The explosion had sent a vast cloud of dust and debris upwards. 'I think they will come to us.'

Alak was already preparing to leave. Run Run came over, knelt beside Riley and kissed his forehead. For a second his eyes stopped rolling and focused on her.

'Sorry,' he snorted through the agony. They watched as he was lifted gently by Dok and Keetau. Gee was talking to them, giving them instructions. With anxious voices they answered him, and nodded their understanding. Gee knelt and murmured some encouraging words to Riley. Riley didn't answer but he nodded.

Sue stared, panic-stricken, at Mann then at Riley.

'You need me here,' she said. 'I am staying. Louis will manage to get Riley down.'

Louis looked shocked. He lowered his voice, speaking in an urgent whisper that could be heard only by Sue and Mann.

'There's a good chance he will die anyway, even with us both helping. He will definitely die with just me looking after him. What if something happens to me? It will take three days to reach the river. If you don't come, his chances are next to nil.'

Sue turned to Mann, her eyes full of anguish.

'Louis is right, Sue.' Mann smiled at her. 'You have to go.'

'Yes, of course.' She looked resigned. 'Take care of yourself,' she said to Mann, sadly. 'I want to see you back at King's, you understand? We have unfinished business.' She smiled bravely.

Dok and Keetau were already negotiating the stretcher over the uneven ground as they headed back down into the forest. Sue followed. Mann watched them until they were out of sight.

Gee and Alak were already repacking the bags. Run Run was looking at Mann. He smiled back reassuringly.

'Riley's a tough guy.' He felt in his pocket for the piece of hessian sacking he had picked up with the company label printed onto it. In the explosion, he had temporarily forgotten about it. Its faded lettering was once brightly embossed – the head of the orchid imprinted on top of elaborate Chinese script, signifying the union of China and Thailand. He would ring Ng as soon as they stopped and get him to investigate it. Just as he was studying it, a light flashed and he looked towards the distant mountain. Alak saw it too.

75

From less than a mile away, on the side of a hill, Saw heard the explosion and he watched the cloud of dust rise. His knife flashed in the sun. He smiled to himself. Alak must be getting careless, he thought, to have fallen for the old tricks that they both knew so well.

Toad came alongside him and stood with him to watch the plume of grey smoke rise.

'Alak is soft now,' said Toad, laughing.

'Yes,' replied Saw. 'When the time comes he will be easy to kill.'

'When is that time? When will this journey be at end?'

'Soon. Tonight we camp near the border. We wait for someone.'

The stumps of felled teak trees lay all around them, like a tree graveyard. On the side of the far hill, a light blinked as a farmer cooked his dinner. Jake looked up at the stars and wondered which one was Daniel. He looked away quickly and swallowed, his dry throat cracking. He looked at the sky again and didn't fight the tears this time. He wondered if Magda looked for him amongst the stars. Did she think he was dead like Daniel? Had everyone given up on them? Was there anyone out there in that world that he was staring at, in the massive universe, was there anyone out there who knew they were sat on a hill, between the huge stumps of fallen trees, waiting, waiting for someone to come?

Saw looked at Jake and the others and then back at his men. He watched his men skulking nervously. He knew there were plots against him. They thought he had led them badly. There would come a time when Kanda would challenge him. Saw shook his head and kicked out at a scorpion that had come to investigate his rum. The men needed him to have answers now and he had none. They had run out of places to go. Boon Nam was coming for them. The forest rang with whispers. Saw felt alone. But . . . he lifted his nose to the air, smelling the wind . . . the smell of woman was in the air – a woman with a fire in her heart like his own. She would come and counsel him, in all her wisdom. She had been at the heart of this; without her none of this would have happened. She was as clever as she was beautiful. Saw stood as the whistles ran out around the forest. And then he saw her striding towards him.

'Saw, my darling . . . it could have been over by now, but it wasn't your fault . . . politics got in our way. I am here now.'

'What is to be done now?' asked Saw.

'Now people are scared. Things have become more complicated. But you mustn't worry. We will still make you the new Opium King . . . we will get there, just believe in me. There is a new deal on the table.'

'Will you get me back what was promised?'

'That and more,' she answered.

'But Alak is here. He is tracking me.'

'I know. He is with Johnny Mann. But you mustn't let your hatred cloud your judgement. Don't let old grudges get in the way now, Saw. You will have your revenge when you are richer than all of them.'

Saw howled to the starry sky; her words made him happy again.

'We will have it all, but only if you keep your head now and do as you're told.' She rose and stood close to him and touched her palm to his naked chest and held it there as she smiled up at him from seductive eyes. His heartbeat quickened beneath her hand. He went to hold her but she pulled away playfully. 'Now, my beautiful Saw.' She stood a few feet away from him and began unbuttoning her trousers. She wriggled her trousers down to her ankles, she pulled down her panties. 'Take them to Mae Sot, hide them in the market under the bridge until I come.' She turned and bent over. 'Now come and fuck your bitch.'

76

Alak picked up his pack. 'We will head towards Gee's village just as we planned. As soon we stop again, I will radio Captain Rangsan. We need to meet up with my men quickly. We are too vulnerable now.'

'Yes, yes,' Gee agreed, nodding enthusiastically. 'Just as we planned. My village isn't far now.'

Run Run brought a bucket of water up from the lake for Mann to wash his hands, which were still covered with Riley's blood. Mann splashed his face and emptied the bucket of water over his arms and legs.

'Come,' said Alak, 'we have seen enough here. There is nothing left for us now. We must move as fast and as carefully as we can.'

Mann was ready. They were no longer the ones doing the hunting. They had become the prey. He looked back at the building. The wild she-dog was waiting by the barn entrance, her shoulders hunched, her body poised to scuttle back into the barn.

They headed deep into the forest and upwards into the mountains and made good ground before nightfall.

They took paths where they did as little as they could to disturb the undergrowth and leave a trail.

At dusk Alak signalled for them to stop.

Mann took out his own hammock and found a suitable place to hang it. It was not a night to light a fire. The evening air was full of trepidation as each of them busied themselves in their own way. Gee had put his hammock up and was now settled down for a smoke, cupping the cheroot to hide the glow. He rocked gently and stared at the stars, just visible in patches between the tops of the teak trees.

'The next stop will be at your village, Gee,' said Mann.

'Yes.' Gee crushed the burning cheroot tip with his fingers and threw the stub out into the darkness. 'It will take one more day – that is, if we make it.' Gee swung down from his hammock. 'Coming to the river, my friend? We will need to use tablets for the water; we cannot light a fire to boil it.'

They walked down in the direction of the small tributary of the river they had been following all day. 'We will take it in turns to wash. I know how you must be waiting for it – I smell death on you. Come, I will keep first watch while you bathe.'

Mann picked up his pack. He would need fresh clothes. He had smelt Riley's blood on his body, in his nose, in his hair all day. He emptied his pockets, laying the contents on the bank, and stripped naked. He felt the huge relief of clean water pass over his body. He waded further into the water. Now he submerged his head and allowed the cool water to fill his ears. When he lifted his head from the water, Gee was standing close to him.

'I thought you had drowned, my friend,' he said.

'I'm not that easy to kill.' Mann smiled.

'Not like our poor friend today, Riley,' said Gee as he moved back to his seat on a rock on the bank.

'Riley'll make it, he's a tough guy.' Gee nodded. 'How well do you know Riley?' asked Mann.

'I have relatives in the refugee camp. Everyone knows him. He has been in Mae Sot many years. He is a good man.'

'What do you think we will find in your village?'

'I fear that we will find much that is bad. Dok and Keetau said that I must prepare myself – I will be very sad to see how many people lost their lives. So many elephants dead and now the main route to the village is mined to stop the KNLA coming and helping. But I will be glad to begin my new life. My humanitarian life.'

Mann resisted the urge to smile. The thought of Gee becoming a charity worker didn't really sit.

'But two days is a long time and many things can happen. I came with you thinking that we would be of mutual help to each other along the way. Now I find I have a good chance of getting killed before I get anywhere near my home, and I can't see how that will benefit my village. My ex-wives will divide up my money and my village will name a seat after me, like you do in the UK, and that will be it.' He sighed and shrugged. 'But we cannot expect to live forever on this earth . . . and, anyway, who would want to?'

On their way back to the camp, Mann stopped to look for a signal from his satellite phone while Gee went on ahead. Mann looked up at the starry sky – so many stars. Somewhere up there, the satellites were waiting, listening for his call. He watched a symbol that meant he had a signal flash up on his phone. He looked at the battery icon on the screen. It was low; he had just two bars of life left. Someone, not just Riley, had been using the phone. The battery was precious and it would have to last him. It would be days before he could get near a recharging point.

'How's it going, Genghis?'

Just hearing Ng's voice was a tonic. Mann could picture the scene in Headquarters. It seemed a very long way away at that moment – a different world, aircon, fresh coffee, and the smell of Pam's perfume, the rookie detective, and the feel of a cool crisp shirt on his back. A world away from the heat and sweat he was in now.

'Could be better. We walked into a trap today.'

'Anyone killed?'

'No, but someone had to be stretchered out. We have lost two medics and two porters. That means we are down to four. One of the kids, Silke, is dead.' Mann heard the sharp intake of breath from Ng. 'Things are going bad here. Saw knows where we are and the Burmese army are after us.'

'Alfie told me Katrien is in your neck of the woods.'

'Yes. It seems so. I don't know what she's up to. She can't get the ransom unless she makes contact. Unless she has an insider here in the camp.'

There was a pause.

'What are you going to do?' asked Ng.

'Carry on. We don't have any choice. We are in here till the end.'

'Is there anything I can do?' Ng asked helplessly.

'There is something – I want you to look up a company name for me.' Mann pulled the piece of sacking out of his pocket. 'It's an old company named the Golden Orchid. I am looking at it now. It has Chinese script in the background and the outline of an orchid blossom over the top. It was shipping out heroin from here.'

'No problem.'

'What about Shrimp?'

'He said someone's been using strong-arm tactics down in Patong Beach. People have been forced to sign over their businesses.'

'Tell him to be careful. I don't want him getting killed.'

When Mann returned to the camp, Alak was setting up his radio and trying to get a signal. It was a long process in the cover of the trees. He had had to move, up towards higher ground, and it was already very dark. After a while, Mann could hear him talking to Captain Rangsan.

Run Run had prepared their evening meal. She stood and handed Mann a bowl. He thanked her. She hesitated as she passed it to him.

'You are a good person, Johnny Mann. I see hurt in your eyes but I feel hope in my heart.' She smiled.

Mann was touched. 'Some day, I hope you and Alak find happiness.'

She smiled and shook her head sadly. 'There is no happiness in this life for us.' She turned away.

Alak was in a dark mood when he returned. He packed the radio away and sat down on the trunk of a fallen tree, saying nothing. Run Run busied herself around the camp, but her eyes flicked constantly back to Alak. After he had finished eating, Mann went to sit next to him.

Alak looked up at him as he approached and shook his head sadly as he sighed, 'I should not have gone there.' Frustration and anger flashed across his face. 'The risks were too great. Now there are only four of us and he knows where we are. Instead of tracking him, we have become the hunted . . . We must rejoin my men. I have talked to Captain Rangsan. We liaise tomorrow outside Gee's village. Saw is here – he is all around, watching. We are the only real enemy he has. There is no one else to stop him but us. He will kill us because he can, and Boon Nam will help.'

'Then all we can do is think faster, walk quicker, hide better,' said Mann. 'All we can do is what we set out to do, Alak. We are their only hope but I think we are still a good one.'

Alak nodded, his resolve returning. Mann took the piece of cloth with the golden orchid logo out of his pocket.

'What do you know about this company?' He passed it to him. Alak took it from him and looked at it with an air of reverence as he turned it in his hands and stared at it for a few minutes.

'I first saw it many years ago. The Chinese master

of the refinery talked about the significance of the orchid, the golden triangle, that symbolised the wealth of his company back home.'

'What do you remember about that time?'

'Khun Sa, Lord of the Golden Triangle, took us all as young boys to train as soldiers to fight the Burmese army and regain our homeland . . . Many people believed Khun Sa when he said that the opium was the only way to fund our freedom. But it turned out that the opium was more important to him than the war. He chose some of us to help him run it. Saw and I helped to run the old refinery. We did many things then that I regret. We smoked the opium and we lived our lives in the shadow of it.' Alak looked over at Run Run. She looked back, not accusing, not judging. 'The refinery changed hands several times. At one time we thought we would own it, Saw and I, we were promised a share. We had a lot of dreams then, but they all came to nothing and Saw and I returned to our villages. His village had been destroyed by the Burmese army, his family gone.' Alak looked at Run Run. She held his gaze for a few seconds. Alak looked away and she stared down at her lap. 'Things happened there that I will not speak about. But from that day on Saw and I became enemies. He deserted from the army and I did not know what happened to him. I joined the new KNLA and went back to fighting. I had heard that he made his money from looting and raiding the small drug operations around northern Thailand and Burma, and that he belonged to no cause but his own. He has joined the Shwit.'

'Did the boss of the refinery speak of his home much? Did you know exactly where he came from in China?'

'He said it was an island where buildings were made of gold and where men could lose their entire fortune on one roll of a dice. Hong Kong, I think.'

Mann frowned. 'That is not Hong Kong. But, I know where that place is. It's a place where triads rule.'

He made another call to Ng.

'Go to Macau.'

77

It was a bright sunny morning when Ng stood outside the seventeenth-century church of St Dominic in central Macau. The former Portuguese colony was a small piece of Europe in the middle of Asia. The sun was shining on the front of the beautiful, canary yellow, wedding cake of a church with its bright green shutters and its neoclassical arches. All around Ng in the busy cobbled square, tourists and locals were going about their business in shops, schools and offices. Half of Macau's income came from tourism, the other half from gambling. Casinos were what Macau was most famous for and casinos brought triads in their droves. And where there were losers, there would be loan sharks.

Ng was waiting for a man that he knew well. His name was Split-lip Lok. He recognised him now as the fat old man walking slowly across the cobbled square towards him. He had once been a notorious triad and had served ten years at her majesty's pleasure in Hong Kong, courtesy of Ng and Mann. He had put on a lot of weight since those days. He walked slowly, his frame crumpling under the weight of years and porous bones.

He had risen in the slums of Macau; it hadn't been easy to survive with a hare lip. He'd done it by being funny and cruel. But the years in prison had been too much for his old bones. He now looked like a puffer fish.

'Walk with me,' Split-lip said when he got within range of Ng. He led the way across the busy square and down the steps of the Café Mozart, past the display of beautifully decorated gateaux.

Split-lip chose a booth at the side, from where he could see the steps to the street. Ng sat opposite him.

'Thank you for agreeing to meet me.'

Split-lip shrugged and signalled to the waitress. 'What else do I have to do? Besides, you are like an old friend.' He chuckled. 'More! You have accompanied me on my life's journey. Sometimes you have even forced me down certain paths.' He chuckled again. 'And where is your young detective – the one who looks like a gweilo?'

'Mann? He is busy.'

Ng sat back as the waitress brought the menu, opened it and placed it in front of him. Split-lip held up his hand to indicate there was no need for a menu for him.

'The usual,' he said. 'Extra cream on the strudel.' He gave Ng a wry smile. 'It is good to maintain one's sense of pleasure.'

'Chocolate gateau and tea,' Ng ordered and gave the menu back to the sullen-faced waitress.

'You are looking well, Split-lip. How are you finding retirement now?'

'I survive. Many people are very kind to me.'

'There would be many of them serving time if you hadn't served it for them. They owe you.'

'Debt is not a thing to quantify when it comes to favours; one simply knows when it is paid off. I belong to a large family.'

'The proper word is triad society.'

'It is illegal to belong to such an organisation.'

'It's all right, Split-lip. I did not come here to trick you. I came for information.'

'I do not know how anything I say could be of interest to you. I know very little these days.'

'I need information on the past.' They paused as the waitress brought their order. Split-lip looked at him curiously. 'You were a share holder in a consortium that went under the name of the Golden Orchid.' Split-lip looked startled for a moment.

'It has been a long time since I heard that name.'

'You remember it?'

'Of course. It was one of my first business ventures, a trading company. We brought goods from Thailand and Burma, we repackaged them and sent them over to sell in Europe. Why do you ask now? This company is long dead.'

Ng sipped his tea and hacked away at his gateau. 'But you didn't just sell toys, necklaces, did you? It was a front for processing heroin. You had a refinery on the Thai border with Burma.'

Split-lip stopped spooning the cream into his mouth and looked at Ng incredulously. 'How do you know that?'

'Because Johnny Mann was at the refinery and he found the evidence.'

'All right.' Split-lip sighed and shook his head. 'Yes . . . it was during the days when Khun Sa leased the refineries to us. I did not know at the time, of course.' He paused. 'I did not know that opium was being refined there. I thought we were importing toys, not heroin.'

'Of course. What happened to the heroin?'

'It went the way of all goods, through Amsterdam and on to Europe, or to America via courier.'

'How many of you were in it? Who were they?'

'There were four of us. We all had different roles in the company. Mine was the accountant.'

Ng chuckled. 'They must have been mad to leave you in charge of the books.'

Split-lip smiled. 'I was not well known to them at the time.'

'And the others?'

'Jobs crossed over but basically someone was in charge of the running of the refinery and the others handled the sales and the Amsterdam distribution.'

Split-lip concentrated on dissecting his strudel into sections. Ng had spread his gateau across his plate and, soon, over the table. Ng called for the waitress to take his plate. He hated seeing the crumbs sat there as a reminder that he shouldn't have eaten it.

'The business collapsed when Khun Sa surrendered. That's when I lost my money.'

'I looked it up – it's still trading.'

Split-lip leaned over his strudel and Ng caught the whiff of cidered apple from his breath. He could see the cream caught in the crevice of his hare lip.

'Let me just put you straight on that. Your records

335

are incorrect. The company might be, but in name only.'

'What happened?'

'We fell out.'

'How?'

'I should never have trusted like I did, but I was young. I lost a lot of money. I grew up after that.'

'What about the others?'

'Some lost more than money: some lost their lives.'

'I want the names of those others in the consortium.'

'They are dead now.'

'No . . . someone is still trading. Names, Split-lip.'

Split-lip picked up his paper napkin and wiped the cream from his mouth. 'You really don't know?'

78

Saw eventually called a stop for the night at a collection of half a dozen dwellings where a rice farmer and his extended family lived. Jake got Lucas down from the mule and washed his face and gave him drink. Anna helped Jake carry him inside and Thomas followed mutely. The four of them sat inside the hut. There was no furniture inside, just bare matting. Toad came in to tie their wrists. They sat in the corner of the hut and watched Saw raging outside as he stormed back and forth past the hut. He looked about to kill the opium farmer and his family. There was no food to be had in the place, just rice and a few prawns the farmer had caught that day. The farmer held up the prawns to Saw, who knocked them out of his hands. His wife offered him opium. Saw took the package, wrapped in banana leaf, and opened it. Inside was a sticky brown square of opium. For a few minutes he studied it, smelt it and then he threw it in her face. Saw was incensed. Jake watched him pace. There was no liquor and there was no food. As much as he beat the woman and her husband, they could not produce the pig that he accused them of hiding.

Handsome began tormenting the woman. The farmer stepped in to defend her and Weasel hit him across the head with a piece of wood. The farmer fell unconscious, blood pouring from his head. The woman cried. Weasel mimicked her and pulled at her sarong until it came off and he wrapped himself in it. He started dancing. He touched his own breasts and teased the men as they reached out to touch him and he danced between them seductively. Saw began laughing. Thomas started crying louder. Anna and Jake tried to comfort him, make him hush, but Thomas wouldn't stop. Weasel looked at them and danced his way into the hut with cheers from the men. He started tormenting Thomas by trying to touch him. Thomas curled into a ball. He tried kicking out at Weasel but Weasel just danced around him. Anna screamed at him and Jake lashed out with his feet but they could do nothing to stop Weasel from dragging Thomas outside by his hair, still sobbing. Anna turned away and sobbed into Jake's chest as outside Thomas was made to crawl around whilst Weasel raped him, to the grunting and howling of the men.

When Weasel finished and momentarily lost his grip, Thomas managed to get away and crawled as fast as he could back towards Jake and Anna.

'Come on, Thomas, quick . . .' Anna held out her bound hands to him.

Jake wriggled forward to try and block Weasel from coming back into the hut, but it wasn't Weasel that entered, it was Saw.

He stamped his foot on Thomas's back and held him

pinned down whilst he leant down and squeezed Thomas's bare rump with his gnarled, brown hands. Thomas's fear shook his whole body as he wriggled on the floor and whimpered and then began squealing in terror as Saw pressed him into the floor and he couldn't breathe. For a moment, Jake thought Saw would rape Thomas too but instead Saw wheeled around to his men and said something, gesturing in Thomas's direction. One by one they started to howl.

'The woman say her pig is gone . . .' Saw turned to Jake. 'Run away to the hills and we cannot eat it. I say, her pig has just returned and here he is . . . !'

He slapped Thomas on the rump. Thomas looked at Jake, horror following confusion. Saw started snorting like a pig and soon all his men joined in.

'I say we will have pig to eat tonight.'

79

Ng and Split-lip moved on from the coffee shop into the casinos. The Golden Beach casino was a giant, luxurious, noisy aircraft hangar. From its central gaming floor it climbed four more balconied floors up to the private rooms at the top, where mass orgies were going on between triads and prostitutes, fuelled with methamphetamine from refineries in the Golden Triangle.

'You always bet on number two?' asked Ng, as they sat down at the Fan Tan table. On the stage behind them, two girls took off their clothes to the strains of Britney Spears. Fan Tan was a simple game traditional in Asia. On the table in front of them was a square, its sides marked one to four. Players placed their bets on any of the four numbers, after which the banker emptied a double handful of small golden beads onto the table and covered them with a metal bowl. Ng slipped a hundred-dollar chip to the croupier to place next to the number four, opposite Split-lip's bet.

'Four is a bad number. Death is something I don't want to take bets on and three always loses,' said

Split-lip. The croupier segregated about half with a smaller cup, then removed the remaining beads with a small bamboo stick, four at a time, until four or fewer were left. The number of beads left was the winner.

'Number three wins.' The croupier smiled at Ng and Split-lip, as if her smile would somehow compensate for the loss of their money.

'I prefer horses,' said Ng. 'At least your money lasts a bit longer before you lose it.'

Split-lip didn't answer. He got off his stool and Ng followed.

'Let's eat,' he said as he led the way up the escalator and into a self-service restaurant on the first floor. It was a semi-circular group of ten concessions each serving Oriental fast food. Ng and Split-lip took their card from the cashier and chose the Japanese hotplate.

'Well?' They sipped miso soup as they waited for the lobster to be cooked in front of them.

Split-lip looked all of his seventy years as he sat and sucked on a toothpick, an old habit of his. He tutted and sighed.

'I was double-crossed; I told you, we all were. Someone sold his share on, gave it away, I don't know . . . but all I know is, I don't see a penny of the money it makes any more. He was the one with the controlling share of the company.'

'Who was that someone?'

'Forgive me if I seem reticent, but some things I fear more than prison.'

'Okay, let me give you a hand. Does the name Deming mean anything to you?'

Split-lip stared coldly back at Ng.

'I was hoping never to hear that name again. He was the greediest of us all.'

80

As they prepared to set off the next morning, Mann knew he was getting ill. He shook and shivered as they walked on through the day in what felt like torturous heat and humidity. Every step became difficult for him as his body temperature soared and his energy level plummeted. He walked as if in a dream, not seeing anything through his fog of delirium. His face was red and blotchy. Gee turned to look at him and said simply:

'You have malaria, my friend.'

That night they stopped to camp early. Mann heard his sat phone ring in his bag.

'Inspector Mann?'

'Yes.'

'It's Katrien. You and you alone must deliver the money and you will get your brother.'

'Where is he? Is he with you now?'

'No. But I know where he is. I will bring him to Mae Sot. Hurry or you will be too late.' She hung up.

Mann looked at his phone. The battery was down to one bar. He called Ng.

'What is it, Genghis, you sound rough?'

'I have malaria. Tell Alfie that Katrien has made contact.'

'What did she say?'

'She says to go back to Mae Sot. She doesn't have Jake yet, but she will get him. We need to try and find him first, but I am not sure how I am going to do that right now. I feel sicker than I've ever done in my life. Listen, Ng, If I don't make it out of here, keep an eye on my mother for me.'

There was silence.

'Yes. I promise.'

'Tell me, Ng, did you find out anything about my father? What did you find out about Deming?'

'Not now, Genghis.'

'Yes, now more than ever.'

Mann's sat phone beeped for the last time and then it went dead.

Mann lay back against a rock and stared up at the sky, watching the stars, and he felt the last ounce of energy drain away.

The next two hours saw him deteriorate. He thrashed so much he could not stay in his hammock. Run Run made him a bed on the ground.

'How is he?' asked Alak. Mann heard their voices as if from some faraway place.

'There is little hope for him.' Gee shook his head. 'It will kill him,' he said, matter of factly.

Mann saw Helen. He saw her smiling at him. Her face freckled, her blonde hair streaked from the sun. She was laughing. They were on a beach somewhere. The sun was hot on his face.

'His fever grows worse. It will kill him.'

'He needs medicine,' answered Run Run, as she lifted Mann's head and rested it on her lap. She dripped water into his mouth.

Helen's arm was around his neck. She was kissing him, her mouth on his.

In the distance they heard gunfire. In the darkness they looked at one another.

'We need to make progress,' said Alak. 'There is no sign of Rangsan and his men. But we are some way off the agreed rendezvous point – we are south of Gee's village.' He took out his radio and tried to find a signal. 'We will make a new rendezvous point with Captain Rangsan. He will find us there.'

'Contact my mother. She has a small amount of quinine,' said Run Run. 'She will bring it.'

Alak shook his head. 'It will take her two days to get here. That will be too late. The next forty-eight hours will see us all dead if we stay here – sitting targets for Saw and Boon Nam.'

Alak picked up the radio and moved to higher ground. As he tried to get a signal, Run Run went back to tending Mann. He was shouting in his delirium.

Helen was suspended by her arms, she was twisting with pain. Mann couldn't make her hear him. He couldn't make the man stop whipping her. Helen was screaming in agony.

'No one is answering and the signal is weak,' Alak said, returning after another attempt to find a signal. 'We need to know what is happening. We must get to Gee's village and find out where Saw is and what he intends. We cannot be here in the break of day. That gunfire was no more than a mile away.'

'We are a few hours' walk from my village now,' said Gee. 'I will go and try and find some help for Mann. I will find out where Saw is.'

Run Run shook her head. Alak knew what she was thinking because he was thinking the same; that Gee might not come back. That they would still not know what was happening and that Mann would die anyway.

'No,' said Alak. 'They know you, Gee. If something is not right they will give you away. I will go.'

'No.' Run Run stood. 'It is better if I go. They will not be suspicious of a woman on her own and you need to keep in contact with Captain Rangsan.'

'What if Saw is there and he sees you?' Fear was in Alak's voice. He was torn.

'He won't see me. I will look and come back, that is all.'

Alak tried to argue back but he knew she was right. Their survival depended on stealth now. Run Run prepared to leave. She bent over Mann. He was quiet now; he was slipping away into a world of darkness and coma. 'Come back to us, Johnny Mann,' she whispered. Mann's eyes flicked open, focused on her, then they rolled away. Run Run stood.

'Head straight for the dip between those hills,' said Gee. 'Then skirt around and come in at the far side of the village. The whole of the approach is mined.'

'Do not worry, Gee. I have lived all my life amongst mines. I will avoid all the paths and stick to the woods.'

Alak embraced Run Run. He whispered in her ear.

'So wise, and so beautiful, *my* Run Run.'

She held him closer and replied: 'I will be, and have always been, *your* Run Run, Alak.' She looked at him in the darkness and reached up to kiss him softly on the mouth before she turned and disappeared into the jungle.

Alak spent the next few hours trying to reach either Captain Rangsan or Mo on the radio whilst Gee took over looking after Mann. After trying for three hours, Alak finally got through to Mo.

'Alak, you must turn back,' she said. 'There are not enough of you now. Too many things are against you – Boon Nam is closing in on you on one side, Saw the other. We will fight together. Turn back, Alak.'

'We cannot move from here. Mann is ill with malaria. Run Run has gone to Gee's village to try and find some help and to scout for us. We are due to liaise with Rangsan very soon. We must carry on.'

'You have sent my daughter to Gee's village?'

'Yes, I have.'

'Then you are a fool. Saw is on his way to attack Gee's village.'

81

Alak loaded up his weapons. He carried his machete on one hip, his gun belt around his chest. Around his head he twisted a scarf that Run Run had given him. He turned to Gee as he left.

'Stay here. I will return by tomorrow, sunset. If I don't, and Mann dies, give his body to the river; you will have done all you can.'

With that, Alak disappeared.

Gee sat next to Mann and looked back and forth from him to the jungle. He looked up at the moon overhead. It was just gone midnight. It would be a long night of waiting. When daybreak came, they would be at their most vulnerable and Gee could not keep Mann still or stop him from shouting. He felt an enormous anxiety. His whole being was telling him he should get out fast. He was stuck in a forest full of murderers with a dying man who was shouting their whereabouts. Because Mann didn't just have a fever – he had malaria – cerebral malaria. And that meant that Mann had been carrying the virus for a while without realising it. Now it was too late and he was likely to die. Gee knew it – he had seen it many times. He knew that Mann's temperature would rise so high that soon he would slip into a coma that he would never come out of. He must leave, he told himself – and yet he could not leave. Gee sighed and fretted, washing Mann's head and talking to him when his eyes opened wide. Gee could see his heart and lungs racing, fighting the fever, fast and stressed. Gee soothed him as he would a baby. Gee had many of those; from his four wives, he had twenty children. Gee wondered sadly whether they would miss him when he was gone. When the Burmese came to cut his throat and Mann's, then what would Gee's life have added up to? Mann convulsed and Gee gave him water and searched in vain through the backpack for any quinine he might have missed. In the haste and confusion at the old refinery, the medics had taken the only medicine they had when they took Riley. Now there was nothing to give Mann. He sweated as Gee held him down.

Mann saw Gee's image swimming in front of his eyes and from a distant planet he heard him speak.

'They say there is nothing to be done – you must sweat it out, dear friend, or you will die.'

Man looked into Helen's face; her eyes stared back at him, through the plastic, lightless. She smiled and beckoned to him.

82

It was the middle of the night when Run Run approached the outskirts of the village slowly and with great caution. As she neared the village she had heard the commotion and she knew exactly what it meant. She heard the crying women and the screaming children and she heard the howling. It was the same sound that she had heard at Mae Klaw – Saw and his men. She crouched low in the undergrowth until the first peek of the sun illuminated her way, then she crept forward just enough to be able to see the track that led to the start of the village. Run Run gasped silently and backed away. Guarding the entrance to the village were frightened villagers, standing beneath poles. On top of the poles were the heads of Captain Rangsan and his men.

She retraced her steps and crept back through the forest, making her way in a wide arc to come around to the rear of the village. There, at the edge of the paddy fields, amongst the dead and dying mown down as they tried to escape, she watched what was happening. The village had been destroyed. Fires were still burning. Slaughtered men, women and children lay where they had been chased down and murdered. The air was filled with the sound of wrenching grief and fear; small children whimpered for their mothers, mothers wept for their dead children.

Run Run moved closer until she could see Saw's men. They looked as if they were preparing to move out. They had rounded up six of the women who were standing huddled together amidst the screams and chaos as their children tried to get near to them. They were killing any child that still clung to its mother. Run Run crouched low, crawled on her belly and moved in again, hiding herself amongst the dead. Now she came to the first of the houses and she could see the young volunteers. She recognised them from Mae Klaw. They were bound, tied at the wrists. She could see the blonde girl, Anna, and she saw Jake. At first she could not see the others. Then she saw another of the boys – Lucas. He was sitting on the mule. He was lashed to its back. His head lolled as the animal pawed the ground with its hoof. She edged closer to look for the other. She hid behind a tree. She held her breath as she saw Saw Wah Say. She recognised him straightaway, even though it had been many years since she had seen him. Not since the day she refused to become his bride and he had tried to rape her. Not since he fought with Alak and her brother died. That day he had run from their village, limping and bleeding from Alak's beating. Now, seeing him again, his body wet and streaked with the blood of others, seeing his once handsome face turned into something so savage and evil that there was nothing left of hope of humanity in him, Run Run wished Alak had killed him on that day. Her mind caught in memories, long buried, Run Run failed to hear the stealthy approach of Handsome creeping up behind her until she felt a rifle butt dig into her back.

'Another whore,' he shouted to the others. 'She was hiding from us.'

Run Run kept her eyes to the floor as he dragged her to join the other women. Saw was standing apart, shouting orders. He did not look at her. He shouted to the women to pick up their packs and start walking. Run Run did as she was told. The huge pack dug into her shoulders. She kept her eyes down and waited with the others. When they were all laden, Handsome came alongside Run Run and tilted her face up to look at his.

'You will be *my* whore.' Handsome had decided the time had come to challenge Saw. He would take a woman and have sons with her. He would leave something on this earth beside his bones.

Run Run stared at him. He stank of rancid sweat and putrid death and his breath was rank on her face. Run Run could not resist the temptation to answer.

'You are no man; you are nothing but a dog.' She looked at his eyes, yellowed and raging, staring straight into them. 'And I would rather die *now* than lie with you.'

For a few seconds Handsome just stared at her, as if she spoke a foreign language. But Weasel had heard Run Run's words. He whooped and howled like a wolf as he pointed his finger at Handsome, who was still smarting from the loss of Silke. He had hoped that she would be given to him. He had thought he had earned her. But Saw did not give her to him, instead he had used her first, let all of them have her and then left her for dead. He had fought by Saw's side for all his adult life – he deserved more than he got from him, he deserved respect. The time was coming to challenge Saw. Handsome knew Saw was starting to make mistakes and maybe fate would smile on Handsome as it sliced a smile into Saw's throat. But, for now, he would not take being laughed at by Weasel.

Handsome's face twisted with rage and he pulled Run Run by the elbow out of the line. She staggered under the heavy weight of the pack as she was pushed forward through the women until she stood before Saw. Still, she did not look at him; she kept her head down. He did not pay her heed; he was watching the path ahead, agitated. It was time to go.

'What is it, Kanda?' he asked.

'She insults me,' replied Handsome.

Saw turned to him and laughed.

For a few seconds Handsome looked flustered, as if he thought he had been wrong to push Saw now and it would be he who would die. The men around them waited to see whether Saw would humiliate Handsome again. But Saw looked at him and grinned.

'Then . . .' Saw wrenched the pack from Run Run's back and threw it down. '. . . Find another whore to carry this. People we have plenty of, food we are short of . . .' Saw turned back to look at her and Run Run kept her head down as she stared along the treacherous path ahead.

'She insults my lieutenant . . . She will clear the mines for us.'

83

Alak flew through the forest, running without stopping until the dawn filtered through the giant leaves and tree tops. He wheeled his machete back and forth and cut through the undergrowth with unrelenting force and speed. He squeezed through gaps, he jumped over fallen trees and he swam rivers. He hardly felt his lungs burning. His legs felt no tiredness. His feet had wings. His heart held a terrible dread.

He followed Run Run's footsteps without realising it as he skirted around the edges of the paddy field at the edge of the village, its waters now turned milky red from the blood of the floating dead. He approached the village from the rear. He saw the young foreigners, just three of them; they blinked back at him from their pale lost faces. The young Chinese watched him; his eyes followed Alak's movements. Alak nodded to him, he nodded back and a smile of relief came across the young man's face.

Alak moved silently up amongst the crying children and behind the female porters until he came behind Toad. Alak took his knife and silently, quicker than a breath, he wiped the blade across Toad's throat, *Shwit*. Toad dropped.

The women turned, startled. One of Saw's men barely had time to raise his eyes before Alak's cudgel came down and shattered his skull. Alak stabbed another between the ribs, twisting the knife deep into his heart as he fell. The women screamed as they tried to get out of the way. Now the rest of Saw's men came rushing at Alak. Every muscle in his body hardened and pumped with adrenalin and blood and survival. All the skills of killing he had learnt in his life worked for him now as his blows came double-handed and he cut through muscle and bone and skull.

Saw turned at the sound of the women's alarm and looked back along his ranks and saw Alak running towards him. Alak looked past him and, as much as Alak's body was a machine, his heart was vulnerable and his eyes did not see the knife in Saw's hand, they looked for Run Run. Saw lunged forward and plunged his knife into Alak's side. Alak saw her, her beautiful face transfixed with terror, standing alone, like a solitary reed on a deserted riverbank, she watched him crumple from the blade that punctured his side and halted him in his tracks. Handsome came from behind and stabbed Alak between his shoulder blades. Alak kept his eyes fixed on Run Run. She stared back in terror, swaying, too fragile to withstand the typhoon coming her way. Saw struck him on the side of the head with a blow that knocked Alak sideways and onto his knees. He shook his head to clear it and stood. He lurched forward as Saw thrust his blade again into his stomach, twisted it and pulled. Alak doubled over in pain and lifted his head and saw Run Run watching her hope, her life and her only love dying before her. They saw only one another as he sank to his knees and Saw turned and followed his gaze to see who Alak was sharing his last vision of the earth with. He saw it was Run Run and with a massive roar, he pulled Alak's head back by his hair and he sawed away at his throat until Alak's head hung down from Saw's hand. Saw looked at Run Run. Her eyes were huge with horror. Saw beckoned her to come to him. She looked at Saw and then she looked down at the path, at something barely hidden in the grass at the side of the road. With his bloody hand he reached for her again and called her to him. Love was in his eyes, love and betrayal and desperation. She held his gaze for a few seconds before she turned and stepped onto the mine.

84

Gee tried the radio; it was dead. He paced about. Sunset was fast approaching. He had waited all day as Alak said he must. He had done all he could now . . . Now he had to think of himself. Mann had been in a coma for hours. There was no more thrashing; he lay silent and his breathing was so shallow that Gee had to watch his chest to see that it moved at all. If he stayed any longer then he would be dead too. Gee gave Mann one last drink. He packed up his bag, looked around the campsite for the last time and left. Mann was alone when the final hour came.

85

'Deming was the most ambitious of us all.' Split-lip picked the flesh out from the lobster claw. 'I knew him from when he was young.'

Ng had already finished his lobster and was eating his rice.

'He was no triad then,' continued Split-lip. 'But he became seduced by it over the years until he was caught like the rest of us – in the grip of greed, power. It's what Hong Kong is all about, after all.'

Ng signalled to the waiter to refresh their teapot.

'It started as a basic trading company; we sent goods over from Hong Kong. We had them manufactured in Burma and Thailand where it was cheaper. Well, the goods became drugs. Then the drug trade was just beginning for us. We were offered a stake by the Opium King. He gave us the rights to process the opium and manufacture heroin. Those were good years for us. We made big money. We expanded and we took over the European routes. The heroin was smuggled to Amsterdam and from there it was distributed throughout Europe.

Deming handled that side of it; he was back and forth to Amsterdam. He was very good at his job – ruthless, even . . .'

86

Sue called to the boatman under the bridge and there was a scramble to get near enough to the boat to pull it in. They needed to get Riley into a car and into hospital as fast as they could. He was very weak but still alive. Riley pulled at Sue's arm; he wanted to speak to her. She leant over to listen. Louis stood near by.

'The meds, Sue. You've forgotten the meds,' said Riley.

Sue shook her head and turned to look at Louis.

'What's he talking about?' asked Louis, as he waited for the boat to stabilise alongside the jetty and for the porters to be able to lift Riley off.

'The meds? He's delirious.'

'Oh shit!' Louis groaned as he caught on to what Riley was saying. 'He means that we forgot to leave any meds behind for Mann and the others.'

Riley looked at Louis. 'Go back out there now. They need you. Sue will get me to the hospital.'

'Okay. I will stop here one night, pick up more supplies and then I'm gone.'

87

Katrien pushed the young man away. She was irritable and he was making it worse. She couldn't get what she wanted from him and she was hot and bothered. Her skin sweated out the coke. Now she only had methamphetamine and heroin instead, and she didn't much care for either. She pushed him away and stood up.

'Go,' she said imperiously, peeling off notes from a wad and throwing them on the bed. He stayed where he was, a little unsure of himself. 'Now!'

He reached for his clothes, picked up the money and left, closing the door behind him. Katrien went into the bathroom to vomit. The heroin always made her puke. She splashed her face with water and watched a cockroach scuttle across the shower tray. She looked at herself in the mirror. Her makeup was streaked down her face. Her eyes were red, her face was sweating. She looked like shit. She went back into the bedroom and checked her phone; she threw it on the bed in disgust.

'What's wrong with this fucking place?' she said out loud. 'No fucking signal. No one is answering their fucking phone.'

Katrien texted another message to Mann on his mobile. Sooner or later, he would pick up the message. He only had to cross the river into Thailand and he would get a signal. Then she would know that he was on his way. She lay back on the bed and watched the ceiling fan whir lazily around. She could feel the heat still in the bed; she could smell the sex she had with the boy. And, as much as it disgusted her, she wanted it again. Her hands moved to touch herself in the heat and sweat; she could not stop her craving for sex. She finished and got up to chop another line of ice. She would save the heroin for later. It calmed her. But right now she needed to wake up. She snorted it and gave a yell of pain as the chemical hit her sensitive nasal passages. Her phone rang. She scrabbled to find it in the sheets.

'Hello, Big Man . . . yes, just leave him to me. I will deal with it. You go back to the hills and wait. When I have the money I will come . . . It won't go wrong . . . Leave him for me. Get out now.'

Katrien hung up. She had another call waiting. She sprang up onto her knees, excited as she answered.

'My love . . . Hello, baby, I thought you were still in the jungle. Are you on the way back? I can't bear it here on my own, hurry . . . I need you.'

88

Mann lay on the ground, on a makeshift bed of soft fern on the forest floor. A monkey looked down inquisitively from the high branches above. The insects walked over him; the mammals came to investigate. He was becoming part of the earth. Leaves fluttered down from the trees above and settled on him.

Mann was dreaming of hot sand beneath his bare feet. He was dreaming of paddling out to sea. Mann felt good; he had a surfboard in his hand. He felt the cool water around his knees as he walked out into the calm turquoise ocean. The sun was warm on his back; he was desperate to dive into the water. It looked like a day in paradise. He couldn't be in a better place . . . But then he realised he wasn't going to be able to surf, there were no waves. Not a wave, it was too flat. Why was it so calm? He didn't know why he would have a surfboard in his hands if he wasn't going to be able to surf. Why were his feet so heavy in the sticky sand? Suddenly nothing felt right. It was taking him forever to get anywhere and now he was not just hot, he was boiling, and the sun was blinding him. Then he looked up at the horizon and saw that it looked strange, it was rising. He watched it growing taller, climbing up out of the sea and then his heart surged and pounded and his breathing become loud and frantic. He tried to cry out, he tried to turn and run, he tried to move, but his feet were held like cement by the sand and he knew there was a tsunami coming and this time it would get him.

Someone touched his arm, as light a touch and as cold as to seem just like a breeze, and a young man appeared behind him, smiling at him and beckoning him to turn away from the approaching wall of water. The youth was dark haired, good looking. He was wearing bright coloured board shorts but they were ripped and slashed, and beneath the torn fabric his legs were cut badly with deep wounds to the bone. A large shard of glass protruded from his chest. The youth followed Mann's gaze to his chest and he smiled at Mann as if to say – don't worry . . . I feel no pain. Mann looked back towards the horizon. Now he could see nothing but the wall of water. No sky was left. Any second it would be upon him, completely crushing him. Already, in its approach, the water had risen to his waist. Mann turned back to the youth and, as he did so, he felt his feet slide out of the sand and move. He looked towards the shore. A monk stood there, completely still, his orange robes turning to dark red as the water rose around his chest. He seemed not to care about the approaching tsunami. He seemed to be waiting for Mann and the boy. He smiled at Mann. It was the same monk he had met that time in the temple at Chiang Mai. The monk was saying something.

'We are what we think. What we think, we become.' The youth was nodding and smiling at Mann, as if agreeing with the monk. Then the youth took the surf-board from Mann's hands and held it flat on the water for Mann to mount. At the same time he glanced over Mann's shoulder and then looked back at him with a reassuring smile. Mann did not dare look behind. He knew that a thirty-metre wall of water was about to take him and swallow him whole. The youth held on to the board and Mann climbed on. Then the wave lifted him high up in the air and he saw the youth far below him, in a tunnel, and he was smiling up at him, his feet anchored in the sand.

89

For a minute Saw seemed dazed by the blast. He lay still on the path. Weasel rushed to his side. Saw pushed him away and got quickly to his feet as he looked around frantically. Run Run was lying beside the path. Her legs were gone, her torso soaked in blood. Saw held her to him and she turned her eyes slowly to him and then to Alak, whose head had come to rest near hers. Saw held her close.

His chest heaved and his shoulders wilted beneath the weight of sorrow.

She looked at Alak and then back to him.

'I never loved you, Saw. Never.'

Her eyes remained open but the light in them disappeared. For a few seconds, Saw held on to her as he knelt in the dirt. His men stood around. They had come because of the blast but they stayed to see something they had never before witnessed. They saw their leader, with his broad muscly back to them, and his arms wrapped around a dead woman; they saw him as a human being, grieving. Alak's head rested near by, his eyes staring accusingly at Saw. Saw laid Run

Run gently back down on the grass beside the path and, shaking, he stood and wiped her blood from his face and turned to Handsome standing near by. Handsome instinctively edged away from him. He had seen many a murderous look before but never had he seen the pain of lost love in Saw's face. But Saw didn't lash out. Instead he stood, head bowed, whilst all around him went quiet except for a crying child and a whimpering dog. When, after several long minutes, he lifted it again, his face was set cold and hard. It showed the ice-burn of hatred branded on his heart. Now he had nothing left to live for except revenge.

90

'I am coming with you, Louis.'

Sue watched Louis preparing for his journey. He was packing medical supplies into his bag.

'No, Sue. It's best I go alone. We've had contact from Mo. Run Run and Alak are dead. It has come down to just Mann and Gee and apparently Mann has malaria very badly. They had nothing to treat it with.'

'Oh no . . .' She held her head in her hands and groaned. 'We took the quinine.' She looked up at Louis. 'Is he dead?' Sue panicked. 'Is he dead, Louis?'

Louis stopped his packing and looked at her.

'We don't know if any of them are still alive.'

Sue stood, a look of defiance and determination on her face.

'I am not asking you, Louis. I am telling you. I am coming.'

'What about Riley?'

'Don't tell him, he isn't my keeper . . . He's out of danger now. He will start getting tetchy soon. I'd rather not be here when that starts. I want to come, Louis.'

'No, Sue. There's nothing you can do now. Your job

was as a medic but we will come up against Saw. And we are going to need some muscle more than anything else right now.'

'Bullshit. I am coming whether you like it or not. If Mann is dying, I need to be there.'

91

When Mann opened his eyes he saw the world in the treetops. He saw the morning light filter and flicker through the tiniest gaps in the leaves. Something moved in the branches high above and he watched it flit from branch to branch. It was a monkey carrying her young on her back and looking down at Mann. Waking to such a morning felt like the best thing ever. Mann lay still. He could not have moved even if he had wanted. His body was all but spent. His head felt like he had been in a boxing match that he had lost, badly. His mouth was parched. The image of Daniel and the monk were still fresh in his mind. He lay there thinking of what it all meant, and before long he had drifted back to sleep. The next time he opened his eyes, the day was well established and there was the sound of something large coming his way through the jungle. Mann lay very still as the noise came straight towards him and he waited, his heart pounding, expecting at best a tiger, at worst Saw. Then he saw Gee. He didn't look at Mann; he went straight for Mann's backpack.

'What's the news from the village?' Mann asked. Gee jumped.

'Ah . . . You are back from the dead? Very good.' He laughed. 'You are strong. Where is your phone?'

'The battery's dead.'

Gee came and knelt beside Mann.

'Tut tut.' Gee shook his head 'We need it now. Things have not gone well, my friend.'

Mann propped himself up onto one elbow and looked about the clearing. 'Where are Run Run and Alak?'

Gee stood and pretended to be busy.

'Where are they, Gee?'

'I am sorry to tell you, but I have terrible news. I went down to my village and found there such awful things. Such terrible things. Both Run Run and Alak, all Alak's men, they are all dead, killed by that man – that half wolf – Saw.'

'Did you see the volunteers? Do you know what happened to them?'

Gee shook his head solemnly.

'They were at the village. They are no longer four, now they are three. One of the boys is dead, another still very sick.' He lifted Mann into the hammock and brushed the debris from his clothes.

'Is the Chinese boy still alive?'

'I asked about him. Yes, he is still alive.' Gee lit a small fire and started boiling up some tea for Mann and himself.

'Drink it.' He held the cup to Mann's mouth. 'It taste very bad but it is very good for your fever.' He grinned at Mann from beneath the red peak of his cap. 'You are very strong. I thought I would be humping your dead carcass back to Mae Sot to sell in the market. Now I will sell you alive – much better.' He laughed.

'Ha . . . is that why you came back?'

Gee looked at him curiously.

'Of course.'

Mann took a few sips of the drink and lay back exhausted.

'Funny, I thought it was because you wanted something I had.'

'No, no, dear friend. We only have us two now. We are the last. It is such terrible times. I hardly know what we should do.' Gee's eyes searched the horizon and he looked as if he expected to be killed at any moment. 'Very bad. Many of the men are killed. The women are taken as porters for the Shwit. Only the children are left and a few old people. The rice is left to ruin and most of the elephants are dead. It is much worse than I ever thought. I left them with gem stones to buy rice and I will go back and help them rebuild the village. But we cannot stay here, it is not safe.'

'We need to get back to Mae Sot.'

Gee looked at Mann as if he were delirious.

'You are too sick. It is a four-day journey to the River Moei and the crossing to Thailand. We must hide further into the hills.'

Mann lay back and closed his eyes. 'We have to go to Mae Sot now, Gee. We have no choice. I have to play the game with Katrien. Whatever it takes, I have to get Jake back.'

At first Gee did not answer, and then he jumped up.

'Then I know what we shall do. I will be back soon.' Before Mann could ask where he was going, Gee had scampered off into the jungle and disappeared from sight. Mann was too tired to try and make sense of it and sank back down to sleep. The monkey watched him as her young clung to her. A few hours later, he awoke to hear Gee calling out of the jungle to him.

'Do not worry, it is just I.' There was a strange snuffling noise accompanying him and the sound of breaking twigs.

'I have brought an old friend with me.' Mann could hear Gee and he could here the sound of something else, something big.

Mann sat up to see Gee riding atop a large flappy-eared, soft-eyed elephant who was looking down at him and nudging him with her trunk. On top of her back was a wooden seat. 'Her name is Brigitte. She is the only surviving elephant after the attack on my village. She was out eating when the attack came. She is very naughty and very greedy, but she is a very lucky elephant. She will carry us to the river. I was trained as a mahout – an elephant handler – when I was young. We will leave now. We are not safe here. They will find us. We need to keep moving.'

Gee helped Mann to stand and he tapped Brigitte's trunk and commanded her to kneel so that Mann could stand on her leg and pull himself up into the basic wooden boxseat, which had a bar across it to stop him falling out. Gee picked up all he wanted from the camp – the cooking pot, the mosquito nets and two hammocks – and then did his best to cover their tracks, before ordering Brigitte to lift her knee again so that he could straddle her neck and guide her.

Mann was jolted back and forth in the wooden box. It was like riding a bucking bronco set at the slow setting. Gee reached back and wedged Mann in with the bags, so that he could sleep. As they made their way through the jungle, Mann looked down on the world and became mesmerised watching the frayed edges of Brigitte's ears, speckled pink on the underside, gently flapping.

Gee looked towards the hills. Tomorrow he would turn towards them; tonight, he needed to stay by the river. He was glad Mann was asleep, so that he would not ask him why they were going the wrong way.

92

Mo was drinking rum, one shot after the other. Sue and Louis sat with her, having arrived a few hours ago. She had gone to Gee's village to recover Run Run's body and had brought it home. Now she sat forlornly snuffling as she wiped her nose with her sleeve and drank her rum. Phara brought her something to eat – she pushed it away. She looked up from her drink, her eyes brimming with angry tears.

'I intend to kill him with my bare hands. If I cannot find Saw, I will at least find that bastard Boon Nam and I will roast his flesh over my fire for what he did here to my family.' She wiped the dribble of snot from her nose. 'Then we will leave this place. We cannot rebuild it now. We have only unhappy spirits here.' She was heavily drunk. She got up and lurched into Louis. She pushed him away as if he had fallen into her. 'Come. Come and see my daughter, Run Run. Tomorrow she goes on her journey to the heavens.'

They walked across the scorched earth, the smell of charcoal still in the air, the melancholy feel of things left ruined and broken.

They came to one of the few houses left untouched by Boon Nam and his men. They took off their shoes and climbed the ladder. There, laid out and wrapped in white cloth, was Run Run's body.

'I will rip his throat out with my bare hands.' She squeezed her fists in the air and her arms shook as her hands knotted around an imaginary throat, and then she started to cry, heaving big drunken sobs, before she wiped her eyes with her T-shirt and looked mournfully across at Sue and Louis.

'I have given you the coordinates of Gee's village and where I think you will find Mann – what is left of him. Now leave me. I need to be with my daughter.'

They left her lying beside her daughter's body, wrapped and embalmed and made ready for the cremation. Beside Run Run's was another body; it was Alak's.

93

'Brigitte must rest now.' Mann heard Gee's voice as if it came from a great distance. 'We will rest a few hours. We will eat something, then we go on.'

Mann was hardly aware of the day. They had been travelling for ten hours. It was too dark to see further and they had no choice but to wait till dawn. Gee helped him down from Brigitte's back. He had already prepared a small fire to boil water and make noodle soup and he now made Mann's hammock ready.

'You will take a little rest and some food now, my friend, then I will leave you just for a few hours whilst I follow the river and see if it is safe and which path we should take in the morning.'

Mann forced himself to eat and then he sank into a deep sleep as he listened to Brigitte's breathing; she sighed as she lay on her side and slept.

Downriver, Sue and Louis were also setting up for the night. They had brought enough provisions to last them four days; after that, they would need to head back.

'How far are we by Mo's coordinates, do you think, Louis?'

'A day and a half, but if we stick to this route we might find him earlier. This is the way we came last time. It is the best route for anyone retracing their steps.'

Sue made a fire whilst Louis set up camp, then picked up her bag. 'I am going to wash,' she announced as she went down to the river. She stood for a few moments looking across to the other side, watching the stars twinkling, the moon gliding on the river. She remembered the last time she had had any time with Mann had been almost at this exact spot. She unbuttoned her shirt and stripped naked and left her clothes on top of her bag as she waded in and washed her body with the cool water.

'Did I come at the right time?'

Sue gasped and ducked down into the water as she turned and saw Louis watching her from the riverbank.

'What do you think you are doing, Louis?'

'What does it look like?' He grinned. 'Don't worry. Just looking. I came down to tell you that dinner is served.'

'Okay, coming. Now . . . if you don't mind . . .' She ducked down under the water until he had left. After drying herself, she returned to the camp. Louis handed her a cup of something as she passed him.

'What's this?' Sue asked. It smelt a lot like rice wine.

'It's medicinal.'

'Really?'

'I was thinking . . . we are out here in the middle of nowhere and this could be our last night. So . . .'

'So nothing, Louis. I have heard all the reasons . . .' She ruffled his hair as she stood and made her way to her hammock. 'The end of the world one never cut it with me. Well, tomorrow is another day. Night, night.'

Sue awoke the next morning as the canopy above their heads came to life. She slipped out of her hammock and re-packed her bag whilst she waited for Louis to get up. She looked across at him, still in his hammock. He seemed to be able to sleep through everything.

'Louis, get up, you lazy bum,' she called. His back was turned to her. Years of being a backpack medic had taught him to be at home in the jungle.

She called again. He didn't answer. She walked to his hammock and bent over him to wake him. Louis's eyes stared lifelessly back at her. Sue looked down at his chest. There was a single wound, an inch across, straight into his heart, with bruising either side, exactly like the dead soldier at Mo's camp.

94

A mile away across two hills, Jake helped Lucas onto the mule. Anna helped to tie him on. Anna had hardly spoken for days. She moved like a zombie. Jake knew that she had given up hope. She lived on the edges of her nerves and every breath she took was pained. She was constantly terrified. Jake knew that, because he felt the same way. Since the fight in the village, Saw was losing control. It was left to Handsome and Weasel to keep the men in check. Every night the men fought and killed each other over the female porters. Now there were only Handsome and Weasel and four of Saw's men left.

'Faster.' Saw came alongside Jake who was leading Lucas. The mule was lame. It had a split in its hoof which every day had got bigger. Now it was so sore that it struggled to keep going over the uneven terrain.

'The animal has a bad leg,' answered Jake. 'It can't go any faster.'

Saw watched it take a few more steps. 'Take the boy off,' he said to Jake. Anna helped lift Lucas from the mule's back. Lucas slipped to the ground. Saw said something to Weasel and he appeared beside them, knife in hand, and slit the animal's throat. Saw turned to Jake.

'Go. We go.' Saw started walking away.

Anna came over to help and between them they got Lucas to his feet. Saw looked back at them and shouted:

'Leave him.'

Jake stood firm. 'No . . . we can manage. I am not leaving him.'

Saw turned and raced back. Lucas dropped to his knees as Saw began punching Jake in the head with several fast, hard blows, until Jake felt his knees go weak and his head begin to spin.

Anna jumped onto Saw's back and bit his shoulder. He gave a growl of pain and threw her with such force that she landed six feet away and lay stunned on the forest floor. Saw stood over Jake panting with rage. It was as if he had finally had enough. His men watched him with nervous curiosity. Handsome walked over to Anna and dragged her to her feet. He threw her over his shoulder and marched off down the track.

'Get up,' Saw shouted at Jake.

Jake rolled onto his knees and vomited. He held on to a tree and pulled himself up and leant against it, trying to breathe.

Saw grabbed hold of his wrists and started dragging him away from Lucas.

'Lucas, Lucas, get up,' Jake shouted at Lucas. But Lucas didn't move. 'No . . . please, please, I beg you, don't leave him,' Jake pleaded.

Saw strode over and kicked Lucas to see if he was still alive. Lucas didn't move.

'Leave him.'

Saw dragged Jake away.

95

Alfie stopped opposite the entrance to a shop stacked with ceremonial dragon heads used for Chinese New Year, massive heads with bulbous fish eyes rimmed with white and orange fur.

He looked again at the details Ng had faxed over to him. The Golden Orchid Company was registered to an address in Chinatown.

Yes, that was the place. He crossed the road. The door clanged with a series of tinny bells as he opened it. The shop was dark and crammed with Chinese wares. They were obviously not expecting customers. A young, slim Chinese woman, who was unloading a box of jewellery as he entered, looked startled.

'Good morning,' Alfie said with a big smile. She didn't answer; instead she rose swiftly and exited twice as swiftly to a room at the back.

Strands of pearls were lying on the counter alongside jade jewellery items and mini Buddhas. Alfie examined the merchandise.

'We are closed.'

Alfie looked up to see a man, similar in ethnicity,

but not the one the Bitch had met. He spoke good Dutch.

'Really?' Alfie looked around.

The man didn't answer. Alfie held a bunch of pearls in his hand and weighed them in the air.

'You have some nice things here. Where do they come from?'

'Hong Kong.'

Alfie looked at the script on the tag attached to the pearls. It wasn't Chinese writing. It was very distinct, ornate, rounded, almost Arabic. The man saw him looking.

'Some of it comes from other countries in Asia. What is your business?'

'Mine? Customs and Excise. I want to know whether you have paid the taxes on these things.' Alfie fished in his jacket and got out his warrant card and flashed it briefly. Brief enough to show it was legitimate but not to show which division.

'We have import papers for it all.'

'I will need to see them.'

'They will take some time to find.'

'I can wait.' Alfie knelt down to look at the front of the box that the girl had been emptying. On it was the crest of the Golden Orchid Company.

'Burma, huh? You still are managing to do business with them despite the troubles?'

The man shrugged.

'The world will always have troubles, my friend. Business must go on.'

Alfie could see that his eyes were black, lightless.

384

He was a man unmoved by human tragedy. He seemed to be weighing Alfie up. Then, clearly irritated, he called for someone from the back room. The slim girl reappeared, looking very nervous. The man spoke sharply to her and she stared at Alfie with a pleading look. The man spoke even more sharply and she turned on her heels and scampered off.

She returned with a few pieces of paper which she gave to the man and which he passed on to Alfie.

'Can I keep these?'

'Why should you need to? They are legitimate import documents. You can see by the stamp.' The man gestured towards the paper. Across the grubby pages was a red stamp and a scribbled signature.

'I want to check it, that's all. I will give you a receipt for them.'

'Take them if you want but there is a lot of work for you here. Surely there is something I can give you to ease your work. I can make a donation to your police fund maybe?'

The man's eyes stayed focused on Alfie as Alfie stared back for a few seconds and then grinned.

'Like I said, I will take these.'

Alfie stepped out of the shop. Folding the papers in his hand, he slipped them into the inside of his jacket and walked back towards the station. He wanted to fax them straight over to Ng.

96

Shrimp stood at the entrance to the boxing ring. An orchestra of five were playing traditional Thai music in the corner. There was a good crowd, maybe around one hundred and fifty, mainly locals – tourists were thin on the ground. A queue of hopefuls was already limbering up at the side of the ring.

Shrimp found himself an empty seat.

The live orchestra banged cymbals and jangled off-key percussions. After an hour Shrimp was no longer sat on his own, he was squashed beside a family who had brought their supper with them. They seemed keen to adopt him and share their dinner with him. There was a change of tempo in the music; something was about to happen. Then Shrimp saw El Supremo, ready for fighting. There was a big roll of the drums and clashing of cymbals as he stepped up into the ring, Coach at his side. Following them into the ring were two squaws, with thonged sandals criss-crossed up their legs and wearing very short, beaded leather dresses. One of them was carrying an open case full of money which she displayed to the crowd as she walked around the sides of the ring. There were gasps of excitement as the crowd surged forward to get a look at the prize money, more than five years' wages for most. Then the list of contenders was read out. A few hopefuls came out and one by one they tried their luck against El Supremo. He annihilated each one in turn. The crowd were becoming glum and disappointed by the time Coach got into the ring and held up his hands for calm.

'El Supremo is undefeated,' he shouted. 'Anyone else want a go?'

There were murmurings but lots of head shakings until Summer stepped into the ring.

'I have someone to fight.'

There was a chorus of catcalls. The orchestra went mad with the cymbals.

'Who?'

Coach eyed Summer's girls, who were standing behind her.

'Me,' Shrimp called out as he shuffled to the end of the row, amidst much support from his newfound family members. El Supremo watched him approach and began to laugh. Shrimp reached the side of the ring and slipped out of his trousers to reveal pink boxing shorts. The crowd went wild. El Supremo threw his arms up and refused to fight Shrimp, who had come without a teacher to observe the proper ceremony.

'I'm here, honey.' Summer stepped up and into the ring in pink glitter shorts and a sequined boobtube. She held the headband, a pink scarf with VOGUE written on the front, in both hands and bowed.

Shrimp returned her bow. 'Thank you, teacher,' he said and there was a roar of approval from the crowds.

'Do you know what I do in this bit?' whispered Shrimp. The music struck up a cheery off-beat jangle.

'You bow to me. Go to each corner, bow, pay your respects. Then go in the centre of the ring, kneel towards your home, Hong Kong, whichever way that is, and look like you're praying. Get up, strike a pose, baby, and then bow three times. Then that's it. Lots of luck, honey.' She leant over, kissed his cheek.

El Supremo was seething. He performed his pre-fight ceremony with ill-grace and when he came to Summer's corner he stamped his foot aggressively. The crowd roared and booed.

'What is it?' asked Shrimp. Summer looked upset but kept smiling for his sake.

'Don't you worry, honey. Here's your gloves.' Shrimp held out one arm at a time for her to put them on.

'Summer?' Shrimp could see the look on her face.

'Stamping means this is not ordinary fight.'

'How?'

'It ain't nice, sugar. He intends to kill you.'

Shrimp heard music, Elvis Presley was singing about returning to sender. 'Wait . . . that's my phone. Check it for me, Summer.'

Summer pulled the phone from Shrimp's trousers at the side of the ring.

'It's a message, honey. From a man named Ng. You want me read it?'

'Yes.'

'It says: "Mann in trouble. Go to Mae Sot."'

Summer put the phone away and tightened up the laces on Shrimp's boxing gloves.

'You all right, honey?'

Shrimp nodded. 'Let's get this over with, Summer.'

'Such a brave boy . . .' Summer kissed his cheek. 'Now just remember, sugar, he may look mean and big, and he's definitely ugly, but you got me and the girls on your side. Just do your best.' Summer's girls were practising their cheerleading routine. Only July really nailed it – June had no coordination at all.

'They're calling you over.' Summer finished with the gloves.

El Supremo made the first strike. He caught Shrimp off-guard with a turn and a flip foot in Shrimp's stomach. As Shrimp doubled up, El Supremo brought his left-hook up under Shrimp's chin. Shrimp hadn't reckoned on it being so tough. As El Supremo launched another series of hooks and upper cuts, Shrimp blocked them with his foot and a screech of delight went up from Summer and her girls. For a second, Shrimp lost concentration and, when he attempted to block an elbow next time, El Supremo caught his foot in mid-air and twisted it. Shrimp felt the pain as El Supremo leapt in the air and brought his elbow in like a spur into the side of Shrimp's thigh. Shrimp spun out of El Supremo's reach to give him time to recover.

It was then that Shrimp began to think that he may have been a little hasty in thinking that he could learn enough, quickly enough to give it a go. El Supremo came forward and Shrimp tried to distract him with a fluttering of arm movements. El Supremo mocked him and goaded Shrimp to punch him. Geed on by Summer, Shrimp jabbed El Supremo in what he thought was a good attempt, but El Supremo ducked and brought an elbow up into Shrimp's throat. Shrimp staggered back and began jogging around the ring, skipping sideways to give him time to recover. The crowd didn't like it but, without being able to throw a good punch, Shrimp was doomed. It had just dawned on Shrimp that he was actually going to be beaten to a pulp if he didn't think of tactics soon. If he couldn't use his gloves, he had to try the knee and, after making a few preliminary small kicks to the side of El Supremo's shins, he leapt forward and brought his knee up into El Supremo's jaw. Summer and the girls shrieked and started pom-pomming with their pink balls. But now El Supremo was hurt as well as irritated and he didn't wait – he held on to Shrimp's head and locked it down as he began an assault with his knee into Shrimp's chest. But Shrimp was used to that. He had hardened his body, his abdominal muscles were like iron, he used the few seconds it gave him to plan his final assault. He could hear El Supremo breathing hard. Shrimp was tiring him out by making him chase him – now Shrimp had to do what El Supremo least expected. He expected Shrimp to use his feet. Shrimp knew there was one place he could cause enough damage to have a chance – El Supremo's left eye, his blind spot. As Shrimp covered his face with his gloves and bent double to guard against the knees pummelling his body, he prepped his feet, made them solid, evenly weighted, and then he bent his knees and jumped as high as he could, knocking El Supremo back a few inches. Shrimp twisted his body in the air. Putting all his strength and force into the power in his arm and glove, he threw a punch into the left side of El Supremo's head. El Supremo's legs began to wobble, his arms went down to his sides; he fell to his knees and then flat on his face.

A massive roar went up and Summer and the girls invaded the ring. A squaw handed him the case of money and Summer lifted his arm high in the air and paraded him around the ring. The girls came in for a group hug.

'We gonna buy you a drink, sugar.'

Shrimp raised up his hands to speak. The crowd fell silent.

'All of you who were cheated into giving up your businesses, cheated by these men . . .' He pointed to El Supremo and Coach '. . . and their masters, the corrupt politicians, the greedy police, the people who cashed in and sold your businesses and your homes from under your feet, they will pay. I want you to know that I have informed the international charities commission and have begun law suits on your behalf. When the world knows what these men and women did they will have nowhere to hide. Their time will be up and the money that should have been yours will be returned. The overseas companies involved, like NAP, will be forced to make amends for what they did. We will get your businesses and your homes back. These men are on the way out.'

There was a big roar from the crowd. Shrimp turned to Summer.

'I have to go, but . . . *I'll be back*,' he said in his best Arnie accent. He handed the case of money to Summer. 'Buy yourself a new bar and save me a stool.'

97

Sue felt the eerie stillness of the forest and eyes watching her as she pushed Louis's body out into the current and watched it being quickly swallowed by the fast-moving river. She looked about her; she was scared. She had been in the jungle many times, but never on her own and never at a point that felt like the end of the world. Everyone dying, everything changing. Nothing would ever be the same. She was frightened to continue but a nagging voice in her head said she must. Something inside her urged her forward – if she had been meant to die, it would have happened already, and she desperately wanted to find Mann.

She got out her map and compass and checked the coordinates that Mo had given her. Alak had given a pretty accurate description of their whereabouts when he had spoken to Mo. She had no need to take the detour to the old refinery as they had done before. Now she could follow the river and take a more direct route towards Gee's village and hopefully she would find Mann on the way. Another half a day should see her there.

She would give it till mid-afternoon. If she didn't find any trace of Mann by then, then she would turn back.

In the early afternoon, just as the sun began to make its way westward, she came across a place that had been a campsite. It had been used for a few days. It was definitely theirs; Run Run's bag was there, Alak's radio. Sue went over to see if it worked. It didn't. There were the remnants of a fire. Several people had recently hung their hammocks here but now there was no one left, just their footprints. A monkey carrying its young stared down at her.

Sue looked down towards the river. She wondered if Mann's body had gone the same way as Louis's. All around her she felt a sense of dread. She would speed along the way back and hope that Saw and his men did not find her first.

98

Mo smashed the rum bottle.

'There will be no more drinking now.' She had just finished listening on the radio. 'That bastard Boon Nam is near. I heard him talking on the radio. He is tracking Saw Wah Say. He is going to kill the hostages. We must decide what will be best. We are not enough of us to attack both of them. We cannot take on two armies. We will track Boon Nam and trust in others to take care of Saw and recover whoever is left of the hostages. We will hope to give them one last chance. We will have our day of glory, huh, Phara?'

Mo turned back to look at Phara. Phara's eyes said it all, her lip quivering as she nodded, unable to answer. Mo sniffed, wiped her nose with the back of her hand, and looked out on the swirling river that was taking away her daughter's ashes. Now they circled and swirled as they met with Alak's and joined. Mo shouted across the wide river, her voice breaking.

'Listen to me, spirit of the river. I give you my only daughter, Run Run. You keep her safe and you give her all she needs and . . .' She bowed her head for a few seconds, her shoulders heaved, then she looked up again and spoke, quieter this time. 'You tell her to marry her love in the peaceful wash of your moonlit banks. Tell her to be joined forever with Alak. Look after her, river spirit.'

As the plumes of ashes entwined and were swallowed by the rushing water, Mo turned away from the river.

'Phara . . . call the women together. We go to war.'

99

Saw tied a rope around Jake's neck and pulled him on. Jake's legs stumbled, weak from the exertion and the beating he had taken from Saw. His head pounded and he could not lift his eyes without his vision splitting. He longed to look back at Anna but he could not. He felt useless. He hadn't managed to protect Lucas. His best friend was gone, dead, and so were Silke and Thomas. Jake did not understand. Why had he kept him and Anna alive? What did Saw want from them? Wherever they were headed, thought Jake, this was the end of the road.

It was well into the next afternoon when they reached the river. Saw left them hidden in the jungle whilst he sent his men to capture a boat. Saw's men threw the fisherman overboard, along with his catch, and dragged Jake and Anna on board. They pushed off from the jetty and began their journey to Mae Sot.

Jake watched Saw as he stood at the helm, his eyes always looking, his ears always listening like the animal he was, attuned to the jungle. He watched the flashes of gunfire light up the sky. His men sat pensive, quiet as the water lapped against the side of the boat and the engine droned. Saw's men listened to the boom of mortar attacks and the rattle of automatic gunfire and they looked furtively from one another and to Saw.

Anna and Jake glanced at one another and both knew what the other was thinking. For the first time in two weeks, they could hear the sound of someone fighting. It must be on their behalf, they thought, and so maybe there was hope. They smiled at one another. Maybe there was still hope for them.

100

Brigitte carried on walking all day, pulling down branches from overhead to eat their leaves as she went. Occasionally her trunk came back to investigate Mann. By late afternoon, the sound of fighting drew nearer. The tranquil air was peppered with the rattle and pop of automatic gunfire and the boom of mortars exploding and echoing through the hills. Plumes of smoke rose from the dense teak forests.

'We are one more day from the river now, my friend.'

Mann looked up through the gaps in the canopy overhead.

'Why are we headed east?'

'We must avoid the fighting, we must travel around it. We will hit the river further upstream but it cannot be helped. Mo is busy with the mortars I gave her; we will be caught in it if we are not careful.'

He tapped Brigitte with his cane. She broke into a rolling trot. Mann's body was still struggling to cope with soaring temperatures and endless muscle pain and fatigue. Now they seemed to be deep into jungle and far away from the river and Mann felt a sense of foreboding.

'Do you think it is definitely Mo fighting?' he asked.

'Yes. I do. Mo is a brave woman. She is also a fearless fighter. She will seek revenge for her daughter's death. She will keep Boon Nam busy whilst we try and catch up with the young people. He must be trying to head up to the mountains. He won't escape Mo, she knows every path in these jungles and her women are fearless. I pity him when they catch him.'

101

It was late evening when Saw's boat pulled up along-side the bank, a quarter of a mile before the bridge. In the distance Jake could see the braziers that lined the start of the bridge and the market. He heard the throng of people doing business.

Handsome dragged Anna and Jake along the rough bank as they scrambled up along the edge of the river towards the market. It was eleven p.m., the night just beginning in Mae Sot. The lights of the market reached them as they entered the outskirts of Mae Sot. A few wary eyes watched the troop pass but none stopped their dealings to comment. Mae Sot had seen every type of creature in human form passing through, selling each other's souls under cover of night. Saw, his wolf-pack and his two white-faced hostages were just a few more.

102

Magda peeked around the corner of the blind to see who was banging on the door of the PIC. Dorothy was standing outside, looking very upset. Magda let her in and locked the door behind her. Dorothy's face was flushed with anger.

'I saw the light on and knew it would be you,' she blurted. 'I was looking for you. I want you to come over to the NAP offices. I have something to show you. I cannot believe that Katrien has caused so much misery. It's all coming out now. We are under an official investigation. It appears that the money from all those people who have been giving so generously over the past two years has been going straight into her own bank account. She's been buying drugs from her friends in Burma to pass on to all those scumbag dealers here.' Dorothy suddenly stopped and looked around at the mess all over the floor where Magda had been sorting out the boxes of old papers.

'Oh God! What has happened here? Another break-in?

'No, Alfie's asked me to look into all of Deming's affairs.

He thinks we have something that they want. Something that is connected to Jake and to Burma. I am trying to find anything that might help.'

Magda looked so exhausted and distraught by it all, Dorothy's eyes filled with concern.

'Come on. I'll help you.' Dorothy slipped off her jacket and put it over the back of a chair. 'Bring me the papers; I'll sit here at the desk.'

'Do you remember a company called the Golden Orchid?'

Dorothy nodded. 'Deming got most of his merchandise from there.'

'What merchandise?'

Dorothy hesitated and then shrugged. 'I have no doubt that he made his money in a dubious way but the invoices all read the same – locally-sourced artefacts for export.'

'What did that mean?'

Dorothy sighed. 'He said it was handicrafts, locally-made toys, souvenirs, jewellery, that kind of thing.'

'You didn't believe it?'

'Yes, to a certain extent, but I only saw a small amount of merchandise arrive. There was a massive difference between the value of that and the amount of cash that Deming always had. He bought this place for you with cash. He bought the flat with cash. Plus, at that time, Amsterdam was full of heroin and Chinese businessmen – the two things went together.'

Magda shook her head and closed her eyes for a few seconds.

'I can hardly believe how bad this all gets. The more I find out, the less I like the man I thought I loved.'

Dorothy reached over and squeezed Magda's hand.

'But the main point of this story is that Deming changed. I always suspected it was after he met you. He gave away a lot of his money to charities like drug rehabilitation units.'

Magda pulled out the photo of Deming with the dark-skinned Asian man.

'I found this photo amongst the papers. Do you know the man in the picture, Dorothy?'

'I haven't seen him for years. He was involved in the Golden Orchid. His name is Gee.'

'Who was he?'

'He was an ex-addict that Deming liked. Deming handed over his share of the Golden Orchid to him and helped him with ideas for advancing the handicrafts. He set him up in a shop here. It's in Chinatown – Gee's cousins run it.'

'So that was the end of Deming's involvement with the Golden Orchid?'

'Yes, as far as I know. Of course, he still owned all the land and the buildings that were registered to the company.' Dorothy paused and looked up at Magda. 'You do know that, don't you?' Magda shook her head. 'Well, that was one of the last things I did for Deming. I liaised with the solicitor when Deming had the land transferred into the boys' names. Jake and Johnny Mann must still own all the two thousand acres of land in Burma.'

103

Mo's eyes were bright and burning with an unearthly sweat of exhaustion and of satisfaction as she approached Boon Nam. They had fought solidly for twelve hours and now just a handful of Boon Nam's army remained. She stood over him as she watched him being tied to a tree by Phara and the others.

'Boon Nam, every soldier deserves to die an honourable death.' He looked at her in the dusk, his eyes defiant. He was ready for death. She pulled his trousers down and held his penis in her hand and began to work it. Boon Nam became semi-hard. Just at the point that his eyes began to take on a new look, a hopeful look, that, despite the terrible predicament he found himself in, he might just be about to get laid, Mo smiled at him.

'But you are no soldier; you are a murderer of women and children and a rapist . . .' She got her knife and sliced it right through at the base of the shaft. Boon Nam screamed in agony as his body convulsed in pain and shock.

'Bring me a cooking pot, girls,' Mo shouted. 'Meat's

on the menu tonight.' She looked him in the eyes. Boon Nam's face contorted with agony as he fought against the pain. 'Let your death be without dignity and let your spirit roam forever.'

104

Shrimp caught a domestic flight up from Phuket to the small airstrip two hours outside Mae Sot. Then he caught a taxi to Mae Sot and checked into Mary's before walking the few doors up to King's bar. 'You have a bag for me?'

Eric was reading a magazine and listening to 'Stairway to Heaven' on the juke box. He stopped and looked up as Shrimp approached him. He did not seem fazed by Shrimp's battered face – a mixture of fresh swellings on old bruises. He studied him and smiled.

'My name is Li,' said Shrimp. 'Johnny Mann left something for me.'

'Ah yes,' Eric replied. He disappeared out the back and came back carrying a bag. 'Your friend said you would come for it and he said you would pay me well for looking after it.'

'Of course. He is a good judge of character.' Shrimp smiled to himself. If Eric had known what was in it, he would never have held out for the two hundred US dollars. As he was leaving the bar Eric called after him.

'Where is your friend?'

Shrimp turned in the doorway.

'On his way back.'

'And you, are you staying here long?'

'Just passing through.'

Eric nodded.

'The whole world passes through Mae Sot. It is like a Stairway to Heaven is it not?' he nodded towards the juke box and grinned. The music changed. AC DC came on. 'Or maybe it's a Highway to Hell,' said Shrimp as he left.

Shrimp went back to Mary's to wait. He rang Ng.

'NAP's prints are all over some big deception cases in Patong. They've been making money-brokering deals between local corrupt officials and foreign investors.'

'Yes. We know. Alfie's found the evidence in her emails.'

'Keep it all for me, Ng. I intend to help these people.'

'I will. Katrien's been doing the deals and pocketing the money. She's been using it to bring in large drug shipments. She's been trying to buy her way into the big league in the world drug trade.'

'What do you want me to do, now?'

'We dare not risk Katrien finding out Mann has back-up; she may decide it's not worth the risk of getting caught. Stay where you are till we know what's happened to Mann.'

'How was he the last time you spoke?'

Ng paused. 'He was very sick. If he doesn't make it, if something has happened to Mann, then we have to hope she will contact you through Magda or Alfie. She is not going to want to say goodbye to that money.

She will want it, whoever she gets it from, and that might well be you.'

'I'm not giving up on Mann, Ng.'

'I know, but you might have to.'

Shrimp hung up and texted Mann again

I'm here, Boss. Have the goods, awaiting instructions, Shrimp.

105

As soon as Alfie got the call from Ng, he went back to the shop in Chinatown. He knew he was out on a limb – he should have applied for a search warrant – but if he did, he knew the shop would be emptied before the warrant was issued. Ng had said there was a link between Deming and the Golden Orchid and Burma. Right now that felt as good a link to getting Jake home as Alfie had had so far. He wasn't about to let it slip through his fingers.

Alfie went into the shop opposite to watch discreetly. A young designer had taken advantage of the space and low rent; Alfie was standing in the doorway of a young woman's passion for plastic baby dolls and rubber handbags. He watched the activity opposite. He saw the same man as last time, the owner, hovering just inside the doorway and watching Alfie. Alfie paid for the bag he had bought for Magda and looked tentatively around as he crossed the road. The ache in his side reminded him that he was still strapped up from the wound and the stitches were not due out for a few more days. But the panic he felt in his lungs and his heart told him he had to risk it – they didn't have a few more days. They had waited too long to act as it was. At least these people would realise he was a problem that wasn't going to go away, if nothing else.

As he reached the shop doorway, he flashed the owner a big broad grin and the man nodded, looking puzzled, and stepped aside for Alfie to enter. Inside, there were three men, swarthy, tricky-looking types, sitting on boxes that looked like newly arrived stock. They were drinking small shots of strong coffee. The owner closed the door behind Alfie.

'This is the policeman I told you about,' he said. The men stopped drinking coffee and stood up with knives in their hands.

106

'She is in so much trouble, and that dirty little receptionist as well. She's been helping Katrien to cook the books.' Magda and Dorothy sat in Katrien's empty NAP office and Dorothy opened a drawer hidden on the underside of the desk. 'She thinks I don't know where she hides things but she forgets how long I have been here. This is what I wanted to show you.' She pulled out a folder about the history of NAP. She turned the plastic sleeves until she found what she was looking for – an article about the missionary couple who had rescued Katrien from Burma when her village had been destroyed.

Magda took the article out and opened it out fully. Dorothy explained.

'When the couple tried to legally adopt her they ran into problems. She had a relative who wanted her back. The couple insisted that she had been living with them for three years and she should stay. They even went back to Burma to try and sort it out. In the end, the relative was outvoted and the girl was allowed to stay with the missionaries in Amsterdam. But it was the beginning of the trouble for them. She spent a lot of time out there. I suppose it was only natural . . . he was her brother. But the story doesn't end there.' She dug deeper into the drawer and pulled out a packet of old photos. She handed them to Magda.

These were photos taken when Katrien's village was destroyed and she was rescued. 'There she is . . . see?' Dorothy pointed to a small child in the arms of her rescuer.

'I see.'

'But do you see who's holding her?'

Magda peered closely and recognised him.

'It's Deming.'

107

'We are here.' Gee pointed with his cane into the distance. Mann could see nothing but blackness ahead. 'Gee has delivered you to a safe place. I know the fishermen here. We will be back in Mae Sot by morning. And then – where will we go?'

Mann thought back to his vision of Daniel and the monk on the shore and shook his head. 'All I know is "We are what we think. What we think we become."'

'Of course!' exclaimed Gee. 'That is the *exact* translation.'

'Of what?'

'You saw the Buddha outside my lock-up. The inscription above it. You asked me what was on it and I tried to translate for you. That was what was on it. That is the saying – "what we think, we become".'

Mann felt charged with adrenalin. Now he had the answer to the riddle.

They reached the jetty. Brigitte gave them a final nose with her trunk before heading back towards the forest and freedom. Mann knelt down on the jetty and splashed his face with the river water. The eels came

413

up to investigate. He trailed his hand in the water and they swam between his fingers.

It was nearly midnight. Gee whistled in the evening air. From the bushes came a whistle in reply and a man appeared. Gee negotiated with him and a boat was made ready. Within a few minutes they were on board and making their way downstream.

'Rest, my friend,' said Gee. Mann put his legs up and stretched out on the seat that ran the length of the boat. Mann dozed. His sleep was interrupted by a tug on the arm from Gee. Mann sat up to see what Gee was pointing excitedly at. The fisherman was steering towards a small jetty. Mann looked and saw a sight he never thought he would – Sue was waiting for a boat.

108

Sue opened her backpack and took out her medical kit. She tore open the sealed packet containing the diluted quinine salts and gave it to Mann. He drank down the liquid.

'What's that?' She had begun preparing a hypodermic.

'It's just a shot of vitamins; help you recover your strength.'

'No, thanks. No shots. By the time we land I will have all the strength I need.'

Sue looked put out for a second and then she slid over to Mann with a mischievous look in her eyes.

'You'll need to keep your stamina up. I have lots of arduous work in store for you.'

'As nice as that sounds, Sue, it's not going to happen any time soon. First, I intend to find Saw Wah Say and kill him and whoever gets in my way. I am going to make sure he feels the pain he's caused. For every time he's hurt one of those kids, I am going to hurt him a thousand fold. And, at the end, I am going to watch him die. There will be no ransom for him. He has left it too late to bargain with me now.'

Mann got out his mobile phone and turned it on. It searched for a network and then buzzed into life.

109

Riley eased his bottom to the side of the hospital bed and reached for the crutches. Outside he saw his taxi arrive. The headlights shone through the window into the ward. He took out the gun from beneath his pillow and tucked it into his trousers. He was heavily bandaged up. His right foot had been saved but very badly cut and two of his toes had had to be amputated. He knew it was a tall order to expect it to take his weight. He had cut down on the morphine for the last two days. He needed to stay sharp. He had a job to do and it wasn't over yet. The headlights stayed on. The taxi knew to wait for him. He put the crutches in place and gradually adjusted his weight onto his right foot. With a growl of pain and a head rush he stood and it took all he could muster to stop himself falling back down onto the bed. He wavered, grabbed on to the bedside locker for support and then took a few deep breaths to try and beat the pain that threatened to split his throbbing foot and burst the stitches on his amputated leg as the blood rushed down. Already there was a bright red patch appearing on the stump. Riley pulled his trouser leg down over it and made his way towards the door.

110

Saw pushed Anna and Jake down the unlit lane at the back of the market and through the lock-up doors into the damp, dark room. Handsome locked the door behind them and lit a lamp and placed it on a table just inside the door. Saw pushed Jake and Anna into chairs opposite one another across the table, and then he refastened the piece of material that acted as a curtain at the window. He went over to one of the boxes stacked in the corner of the room and broke it open. He pulled out a bottle of rum and went back to sit at the table with Anna and Jake. He didn't speak for several minutes as he drank the rum and watched them both. His eyes glinted in the light of the lamp. His chin ran with rum. Jake had never seen him look so menacing as he did now.

'Do you know this place?' Saw's eyes hardened as he looked at Jake. Jake shook his head. 'I came here with the master of the refinery.' He looked around at the walls of the lock-up. 'We sat at this table and drank rum and we talked about things that would come.' Jake listened. Anna looked full of fear as her eyes searched

Saw's face. 'I brought you to this place because someone is coming here; someone I have waited a long time for and then . . .' He leaned towards Jake and breathed into his face '. . . then I will have my revenge.'

Weasel came behind Jake's chair, held on to Jake's shoulders and pretended to be fucking him like a dog. Handsome howled. Saw drank deeply from the rum. He wiped his mouth and looked from Jake to Anna and then he reached over and stroked her hair. She turned away. He grabbed her around the neck and pulled her to him. He kissed her, his mouth wide, his teeth chewing her face, he covered her face in saliva, and then he twisted her face towards Jake.

'This is your last night, boy. It will be a long night; the longest night of your life. By the time morning comes, you will beg me to end it. I will have my revenge and I will kill you. And your bitch.' Anna's eyes were shut tight and she began to cry. 'You will watch me take her many times.'

Anna screamed as her chair was dragged out from beneath her.

111

Katrien had had too much methamphetamine. She was hyperventilating now. Her heart raced. She was feeling claustrophobic and panicky in the hot stuffy room. She looked at herself in the small mirror that she used for cutting lines on: her mascara was down her cheeks, her face was blotchy. She threw the mirror down on the bed as her phone bleeped; she had a message. She read it and started to laugh and couldn't stop. This was it. This was what she had worked for. She re-read the message. She couldn't believe it: all her dreams were coming true. She went back into the bathroom, redid her makeup, and smiled smugly into the mirror. She was a clever girl. Even if she had misjudged things slightly and had to leave Amsterdam prematurely, it would all work out tonight. Then she stopped and smiled at her reflection.

I wonder if anyone has found my leaving present yet?

112

Shrimp waited in Mary's till the message came and then, at four in the morning, the money stowed safely in his backpack, he got on a scooter and drove down to Friendship Bridge. The night was nearly over now, the last few shipments were being loaded onto lorries and heading into Thailand. Tired dealers were at the last of their energy, nervous and jittery, and sweating with exhaustion and adrenalin.

Shrimp knew what he had to do. He parked his scooter and slipped around to the back of the market.

113

'We are here at Mae Sot, my friend,' said Gee.

'Moor the boat under the bridge, Gee,' said Mann.

'And then what?' asked Sue as they stepped up onto the bank. 'What do you want us to do?'

'Head back to King's bar. I'll find you there afterwards.' She was reluctant to leave him. 'Go with Gee. I'll be all right.' Mann didn't have time to explain.

Mann made sure that he wasn't followed and then he went to find Shrimp. He had a hard time spotting him. He had camouflaged himself well – he looked like every other dubious type in Mae Sot, hot and dirty with a dash of colour. It also helped that his face looked like he'd been run over and then beaten up.

'What the hell happened to you?'

'Hello, boss. I had a lesson in Thai hospitality.'

'Hope you returned the compliment.'

'Sure did. What about you, you better?'

'I'm okay.'

'What's the score, boss?'

'You hold on to the money and I go in alone. When I need you I will call. Stay close but stay hidden.'

'I've checked it out, you were right – they're in a lock-up around the side of the market. I heard maybe five or six voices. How are you going to do it?'

'I am not sure yet. But, if it comes to it, I will exchange myself for the boy.'

114

Alfie automatically took a step backwards, but his way was blocked by the owner of the shop. The first of the men, knife in hand, took a step towards him. But just as Alfie thought he was about to be stabbed for a second time, the man held out his other hand in a gesture of friendship. 'Please join us,' he said. Alfie watched the men slice through the rest of the boxes as he drank his coffee. He set his cup down next to the box of carved teak elephants.

'Nice elephants.'

'I told you, we did nothing wrong. You looked at our papers? All okay? You check up on my cousin Gee? He's a good man. He helps his family many times. Now, take some pearls for your girlfriend.'

Alfie thanked him, accepted the pearls, and then he cycled over to Katrien's. He had an urge to see if she had really gone for good.

Alfie opened Katrien's door and punched in the alarm. He heard voices, muffled. It was like a bad porn movie was playing. And, from his place in the hall he could look into the lounge. The curtains were drawn;

the room was dark except for light from the PC monitor. There was the smell of stale perfume, of sex, rancid wine and there was something else, a sweet, rotten smell of meat thrown into a bin and forgotten.

Alfie walked into the lounge. He could see the back of the monitor and the edge of the chair in front of it and he saw a pale leg, with its knee jutting outwards. The inside of the leg covered in brown dried blood. Beneath the chair was a pool of congealed blood, vivid against the white carpet. He moved slowly to the right and around. As he came from behind the monitor he saw the contorted face of a young woman, blindfolded. Across her mouth was a gag, her hands were tied to a harness that looped around her neck and strapped between her legs. Between her legs was the dildo that Alfie had seen Katrien wearing. The girl was dead. It was the young receptionist from NAP.

115

Saw rested his bloodied hands on the table as he leant across Anna's naked body.

Then he looked straight into Jake's eyes.

'Are you ready yet, boy?'

Jake nodded, mutely. He had reached the bottom of hell and now there was nowhere left to go. He looked at Anna. Her blonde hair was matted with dark blood and her head twisted unnaturally to the side. Through misting eyes she seemed to be watching the dawn as it filtered through the rank air and began its trespass into the long night.

Saw smiled as he turned his head and spat a glob of sticky black phlegm onto the dirt floor beside the table. Saw had faced death many times. He enjoyed watching others die. He looked down and breathed in the mist of atomised blood and death from Anna. It caught in the back of his throat, he could taste it. He could taste her. Then a shaft of light hit him in the eyes and he turned his head towards the window. The corner of the makeshift curtain had dropped and the sun was beginning to rise. He knew that the game was coming to its end now.

Saw's men moved in around Jake like jittery wolves waiting to finish off their prey. Their chests were bare, rank with stale sweat, sticky and thick with smeared blood. Their breath was heavy with stale liquor. Saw had given them a night to remember. Now there was one thing left to do. They edged closer and looked back and forth from Saw to the boy, waiting.

As Jake looked at Anna, he felt a terrible calm. He glanced up at the hovering men, waiting for his death like vultures, and then he stared hard at Saw's face. Jake stopped crying. A boy he might be called but he would end his life as a man. He reached out and touched Anna's cold hand. In the morning light her skin was grey and he knew she was gone. But her screams still rang in his ears. He didn't want to hear them any more.

'Yes,' Jake said. 'I am ready.'

116

Katrien checked the room and made sure she hadn't left anything behind. She wouldn't be coming back, that was for sure. She was about to start her new life. She was nervous and excited. She couldn't afford for anything to go wrong now. But, when she was the ringmaster in a circus full of unpredictable animals, she wouldn't be happy until she was holding the money in her hands and long gone.

She checked her phone and smiled, reassured, no message from the Big Man, Boon Nam must have got away. She'd be joining him soon enough then they could really kick start their business partnership.

She texted Mann.

Wait near the main entrance to the market for my instructions. Bring the money

She closed her phone, picked up her bag and left the room. The taxi was waiting for her. It dropped her at the far side of the market. From there she made her way furtively, through the side entrance and onto the lane than ran alongside it and came to a standstill outside the lock-up. She looked at the Buddha beside the door, read the inscription and sneered. She knocked lightly on the lock-up door and Weasel opened it a fraction for her to enter. She stood just inside the entrance, hands on hips, and looked around at Saw's men and at Jake and Anna and she hissed at him:

'Where are the other kids?'

Jake stared at her as if she had come from another world. She belonged to a different life. He knew her, and yet he didn't know how, until he realised that it was the woman from NAP. It was the woman who had interviewed him about going away. But she hardly seemed to notice him or the hell that he was in. She barely glanced in his direction. She seemed more annoyed than shocked by what she saw. 'Is this all that's left?' She looked around the room and then looked at Anna. 'Fucking hell, Saw. Couldn't you control these animals just once?'

Handsome came up behind her and held on to her hips and rubbed against her as he licked her neck. She pushed him off. 'Get your fucking hands off me. You stink.'

She glared at Saw. 'We'll be lucky to get anything now.' She looked nervously towards the door and then back at Saw. 'At least the boy is still alive. He's the only one who really matters. At least I have fulfilled my side of the bargain.'

'Is he here?'

'Yes. He's waiting for me to text him. And he is bringing the money.'

'I don't care about the money.'

'Fine. You have your fucking revenge and I will keep

430

the money. I will be starting a new life in the hills, growing opium, getting rich, whilst you are dead and gone. But that's your choice. I have put two years of planning into this, Saw, I am not about to blow it.'

'They both die here, tonight.'

'Whatever . . . but I won't be hanging around. As soon as he gets here with the money, I am going. You can catch up with me if you're still alive. I will be meeting Boon Nam in the hills.'

'Where are the deeds to the land? Did you get them?'

'Forget that. We have to take what we have and run. We don't need it.'

'But I want what was promised. All my life I have waited to get back what was mine. And now here we are, in the very place where Deming promised me it.'

'You seem to forget, Deming ruined my life too. He took me away from my home. He put me to live with some weird couple who never really loved me.'

'When the opium lords warred and our village was destroyed Deming took you. I was your brother, they should have given you to me, but they did not listen. Deming had money, they listened to him. He gave you to the missionaries.'

'They hated me. They left me nothing in their will.'

For a minute Saw's anger flashed dark and brooding across his face and then he grinned at Katrien. 'Perhaps they didn't like you because they knew you were going to kill them.' Saw grinned and offered her a swig of his rum. Weasel giggled.

She pushed the bottle away. 'I didn't do it.'

'You made someone else do it, the way you always

do, hey, little sister?' Saw stepped close to her and held her chin up to his face. 'So beautiful, so evil.'

Her eyes were as cold as his. She pushed him away. Saw made another move to touch her. Weasel was still giggling. He turned towards Handsome and the giggle turned into a noise in his throat as if he had swallowed something that got caught, lodged, something that hurt like hell and had stopped him breathing. His eyes opened wide in panic as he twisted his long neck to turn and see what had hit him and then his throat opened like a shark bite and a bubbling plume of blood jetted out several feet. Mann burst through the window.

117

Magda followed Dorothy back along the office corridor.

'Yes, she was from the Lisu tribe. They live in the hills, they're the opium farmers. She was rescued by Deming when her village was destroyed, caught up in some local drug wars.'

'Do you think he was involved in those drug wars?' asked Magda, dreading the answer.

Dorothy shrugged and shook her head.

'Who knows? Maybe. But I seriously think he thought he was doing the best thing bringing her over here. He gave her to a missionary couple. They had just returned from working in Africa. They were a nice couple, bit strict, they lived very simply. It was a terrible tragedy when they were killed in the fire.'

They stopped halfway along the corridor just by the *orphans of the conflict* photo.

'No one knows who started it?' asked Magda.

'No. They left all their money to the church. You would have thought they would have left it to their other child.'

'What other child?'

'They had a child of their own before they adopted Katrien. That's what I wanted to show you in this photo.' Dorothy put on her glasses and scrutinised the photo. 'Look, here is Katrien standing beside the missionary couple. Here are the survivors from the attack and can you see there is a child hiding there, just behind the man's leg, you see?'

Magda moved closer to the photo. 'The child looks blonde,' she said, surprised.

'Yes. She was a beautiful little girl. Her name was Sue.'

118

Shrimp moved around the market and kept out of sight but never far from the lock-up. He kept his phone on vibrate only and held it tightly in the palm of his hand. He could not afford to miss Mann's call. He was sure he would need him. He had no trouble blending in, no one gave his Oriental looks or his battered face a second glance, unlike the woman he spied from the corner of his eye. She was blonde, a plait down her back. She was an incongruous sight moving furtively amongst the dark and the dreadful of a Mae Sot night. Shrimp watched her as she came into the market from the lock-up lane. She seemed to be hovering like him . . . He waited until she had passed him and was out of sight, hidden amongst the stalls, before he slipped out onto the lane where she had come from.

A man lay on the ground, moaning in agony. Shrimp knelt beside him and looked at his injuries. He was badly hurt from a single stab wound just below the ribs.

He clutched at Shrimp's arm.

'My name is Gee.'

Shrimp recognised the name. Here was the only man trading under the Golden Orchid. He knew enough about him to make him wary, but he had to help him.

'I will carry you out of here,' said Shrimp.

'No, no . . . leave me. There is no time. Are you a friend of Johnny Mann's?' Shrimp nodded. 'Good, my friend. So am I. His father, Deming, was my friend; he was very good to me when I was young. He gave me a chance when no one else would. I told him I would repay him one day and I have been looking after Johnny. But I cannot help him any more. I was about to go in when she stabbed me.'

'Was she blonde?'

'Ah ha, you have seen her. Sue her name is; be careful, my friend, she is mad. She will kill again. Quick now, he needs your help. I have heard them fighting, the window is smashed, Johnny is inside.' He clutched his chest as he whispered. 'There is a door at the back of the lock-up. Here is the key.'

119

Two of Saw's men turned to look as Mann smashed through the window and fired five, six-inch hardened steel throwing spikes out of his right hand. Their feather tips pierced the air in a volley of red as they found their marks and the men were blinded by the needle tips as they pierced the eyeball. They didn't see the seven four-inch flying stars that followed the spikes. One cut Weasel's jugular, the others mortally wounded the blinded men. A star embedded in one man's throat. He drowned as his lungs filled with his own blood. Another had a star cut deep into his temple and one stuck in his chest. One man was left wounded but alive. Handsome was unhurt, he had used the dying Weasel as a human shield.

Mann rolled across the dirt floor and came to a stop opposite the table. He saw Jake petrified, thin, his eyes huge with fear, sat in a chair opposite the dead body of Anna. There was a gun at his head. Mann rose slowly, his hands raised, his back to the wall. He looked at Jake, and he felt an instant bond. It was like looking in the mirror. Mann's emotions took him back to when he was eighteen. Took him back to his father's execution. Mann's temper roared inside him as his heart broke to see his brother so abused. He looked at the man holding the gun and he knew it must be Saw Wah Say. He was a wild man, his eyes alight with blood lust and madness. He feared nothing . . .

Jake stared at Mann; he knew that he must know him, but he didn't know how until Saw said his name.

'Johnny Mann. I have waited many years to come to this moment. To have all Deming's sons here in one room. It is a pity your brother Daniel died before I could kill him.'

Jake stared at Mann, trying to take it all in. Katrien crawled out from under the table where she had been hiding. She stood and glared at Mann.

'I told you to wait. Now give me the fucking money.'

'You don't get it till the boy is safe.' Katrien was fuming as she turned to Saw. 'Let him go. Let's get the money and leave,' she hissed.

Saw didn't answer her. He didn't take his eyes from Mann. They grinned at one another. Mann felt his anger settle into a white heat. Nothing would stop him now. Saw would never leave the room alive.

'I am not finished here,' said Saw.

'Yes you are. I didn't do all this work to have you fucking blow it, now let him go.'

Saw kept his eyes on Mann as he reached across and hit Katrien full in the face. She yelped in pain and surprise as she was knocked sideways.

'I am your sister. Show me some respect,' she said, clutching her face and looking at the blood on her hand.

'You are my bitch. Shut up or I will kill you.'

Saw turned his attention back to Mann.

'You stole something from me, you and this boy . . .' He tightened his grip on Jake and dug the gun hard into his temple. 'I want it back. Deming promised me land, he promised me wealth.'

'Deming is dead. His promises died with him,' said Mann.

'No, the sins of our fathers must be paid for.'

'We have paid enough. Let the boy go or you will die here in this room.'

Saw laughed, 'Big words.'

'Let the boy go and we will settle this, you and me.' Mann could see out of the corner of his eye that Handsome was on the move, coming up behind him, and the other man was working his way around the side. But then they stopped. Someone was standing in the doorway. Sue stared around the room as if she didn't understand how she got there or why she was there. She shook her head and looked down at her hand. She was holding a dagger. It was shaped like a crucifix and still dripping with Gee's blood.

'It's all right. It will all be okay.' Katrien said softly when she saw her. 'Don't come in here, my love.' At the sound of Katrien's voice Sue seemed to come awake. She looked at Saw and at Katrien's face.

She looked puzzled. 'Did Saw hurt you?'

Katrien shook her head emphatically as she quickly wiped the blood away. 'No, no, he didn't mean to. I'm all right.'

Sue stared coldly at Saw. 'What's happening, Saw?

We did all this so that we could be together. We are one family: you, me and Katrien.'

Saw looked at her with contempt. 'You are not family. Katrien has tricked you all along. She has used you. You will never mean anything to me or to her. She got you to kill your parents. She used you to get close to Mann. She doesn't love you or anyone else. She is incapable of love. Her heart is twisted even more than mine.'

Sue's face took on a pained look of confusion as she shook her head and her eyes filled with tears.

'Don't listen to him, my love,' Katrien said. 'I love you. He is lying. He—' Saw struck her again, harder than the first time, and she lost her balance and gave a cry of pain as she landed hard on the dirt floor.

Sue let out a roar of anger as she flew forward and lunged her dagger at Saw. But she never made it. Handsome's blade came singing through the air. Sue stood for a minute swaying, staring at the knife as it protruded from her sternum, and then she looked up at Katrien and at Saw and shook her head, a look of complete bewilderment in her eyes as she fell to the floor dying. Katrien crawled forward to hold her for a few seconds as she died and then she crawled back and clung to Saw's leg.

'Please, Saw. I am your sister. It will be just us. We can be happy. We can have everything. Please . . . please . . .'

Irritated, he tried to shake her off but he couldn't.

Shrimp eased himself through the back door and stood behind Handsome. Shrimp knew he would get only one chance to kill Handsome and the other man. He edged closer.

Katrien was crying.

'No, Saw, don't forsake me again. You let them take me when I was a child. I cried for weeks. I missed you.' Saw tried to ignore her but it was a noise he remembered from his distant childhood. The cry of a baby who belonged to him, who needed him. He could not ignore it, its pitch, its tone was designed to penetrate his concentration. And it did. The sound of Katrien's plaintive cries distracted Saw for two seconds, only two seconds. But two seconds was all it took for Mann to reach inside his shirt, extract the Death Star from its leather pouch, lower his stance, raise and level his arm and send it flying, curving through the air like a boomerang and then coming down to cut Saw's spine in two. Delilah flashed from her hiding place inside Mann's palm and she darted straight and powerful and thumped into Saw's heart. At that second, Shrimp rolled forward into the room to face Handsome and shot him through the heart and the other man through the head.

Saw's body juddered as he took his last breath. He lost control of the gun and his hand turned away from Jake's head. He looked down at Katrien clinging to his leg and staring up at him and his fingers contracted in a death grip. He fired one shot straight between Katrien's eyes.

120

'Sue?'

Mann turned and saw Riley standing in the doorway looking very sick and on his crutches. 'I'm sorry, Riley, she's dead.' Riley looked about to collapse. He leant on the door frame for support.

'I tried to find her in time. She was very sick. She was a schizophrenic. She needed her medication but she hadn't been taking it. Katrien told her not to. She was easy to manipulate then.' Mann could see that he was bleeding from his amputated stump.

'There was nothing you could have done, Riley. Katrien had been planning this a long time. Let's get you back to the hospital.'

'Gee's outside. Sue stabbed him. We need to get him to hospital fast.'

'I'll do it.' Shrimp went outside to look after Gee.

Mann walked over to Jake and knelt down beside him. Jake stared into his eyes and shook his head, he couldn't speak. He looked across at Anna and his eyes filled. He looked back at Mann. Mann nodded and smiled sadly.

'We will wait here with Anna until we can make arrangements for her.' Mann stood. Jake looked up at him in panic as if he were about to leave him. Mann put his arm around Jake's shoulders. 'Don't worry. I'm not going anywhere, not until I get you home.'

121

Mo was waiting for them, dressed all in black, a rifle over the crook of her arm.

'Thank you for agreeing to see us.' Mann greeted her as the boatman steered towards the jetty. 'I wanted my brother to meet one of the greatest soldiers in the longest civil war in history, and to thank her.'

The boat came to a stop. Mo nodded and smiled as she held up her hand.

'I am not alone,' she said, glancing to her right. Mann looked at the dense undergrowth. A shadowy figure was lurking there. Someone stepped out.

'Wassup, dude.'

Jake nearly fell out of the boat with the shock of seeing Lucas.

He looked at his friend, pale, sick, but very much alive.

'I found him near to death.' Mo squeezed Lucas's shoulders. 'He needs feeding up, but he will live.'

Lucas and Jake hugged whilst Mann shook Mo's hand.

'I hope we meet again one day, Mo.'

She shook her head. 'There is nothing left of my village.'

'I am sorry, Mo. Where will you go?'

She shrugged and turned her eyes to the distant hills. 'Somewhere. The days of the Karen are numbered, deals will be struck between the Thai government and the Burmese junta and we will be wiped out.' Mann nodded his head sadly. 'But for me, there is only one way to live and to die. "Never give up, never surrender" . . . Churchill was a good man.' She turned and disappeared into the jungle. Mann looked up and on the bank he saw Phara, waiting. She raised her hand and waved a sad farewell.

122

'You okay, Riley?' Mann had gone to visit him at the hospital. Gee was sleeping in the next bed.

Riley nodded. But his eyes said otherwise.

'I should have stopped Sue years ago. I always thought I contained it in her. She was diagnosed in her late teens.'

'She must have had some serious religious issues to have used a sharpened crucifix.'

'Yes, her paranoia was always based on religion. Something to do with her parents. She heard voices. Sometimes imaginary, other times they were real. Katrien – she could make Sue do anything. I am sorry I didn't speak out sooner, I might have saved Louis, and the murdered soldier at Mo's camp. She liked to flirt and turn men on, but she killed them when they tried to touch her. But I loved her, she listened to me – most of the time. When did you suspect she was involved?'

'When I met with Hillary at Mary's. She told me it was Sue who told her not to pick the kids up from the camp that day. I knew you were over-protective – I figured you were covering for Sue, but I didn't know the rest of it.'

Riley lay back exhausted.

'Will you be okay?' asked Mann.

'The refugees need me more than ever. We have to rebuild and we won't be getting any more money for a while.'

There was a knock on the door. Shrimp came in.

'Hey, boss. I wanted to see you before I go. What do you want me to do with this?' Shrimp held the case with the two million dollars in his hand.

'Give it to Riley here. He'll put it to good use.'

For a moment Mann thought Riley was going to cry. But instead he reached over and shook Mann's hand.

'I'm grateful, mate. Really grateful.' Mann could see his resolve returning.

'Shrimp and I are going now, but we'll see you next time we're in Thailand.'

'Uhh . . . boss. That's what I wanted to say. I'm going back down to Phuket. I have loads of leave owed to me and I am going to help a few friends in need of my legal expertise.'

'Would that be Summer?'

'Summer, June and July.'

'Sounds like some girls I used to know,' said Gee, opening his eyes and grinning sleepily. It was the first time Mann had seen him without his hat. He was as bald as a baby.

'Glad to have you back with us, Gee.' Mann went to sit on his bed. 'You're a man of many secrets. Shrimp told me you felt indebted to Deming.'

He nodded. 'I have been waiting for my chance to

447

repay my debt. I knew you would come when your brother was kidnapped. I told my cousins in the Chinese dragon shop to watch over Magda. They told me they had seen you at Casa Roso. Then I made sure to be in Chiang Mai for when you arrived.'

'He must have meant a lot to you.'

'Yes, Deming was my friend. I didn't tell you before because I felt I could serve you best if you didn't know my history. The past is not always welcome in the present.'

'How did you know him?'

'Deming gave me hope when I had none. I was nothing. He gave me the Golden Orchid so that I could take over for him. We stopped heroin production and moved back into village crafts. He gave me the lock-up at Mae Sot. He kept the refinery and the land. He said it would never be used for anything but destruction. It was a place of ghosts and he said, in years to come his sons would decide its fate.'

'Whatever you feel you owed Deming it is definitely repaid now.'

Gee nodded his head thoughtfully. 'Ah ha. I agree. But I will never stop being grateful.' He looked at Mann curiously. 'I know you have learned much that you did not want to know about your father on this journey. I understand your mistrust but in one thing you can believe – your father tried to change. He tried to make amends for his bad ways. It was Deming who wrote the inscription on the Buddha outside the lock-up. *We are what we think. What we think, we become.*

'He tried to become someone better.'

123

Mann sat in King's bar and ordered a vodka. He played with the phone in his hand and stared at the screen. He finally rang Ng.

'Tell me it straight.'

'Okay, Genghis . . . Your father was one of a syndicate, the Golden Orchid. They had business concerns in Burma and Thailand. They traded in teak, artefacts, toys, anything . . .'

'And opium.'

'Yes, and opium. Deming handled the distribution at the Amsterdam end. He was responsible for getting it out to the rest of Europe.'

'Who else was in the syndicate?'

'The only one left alive is Split-lip Lok. He said that when the books started not adding up and the money dried up they realised what he'd done. He'd been giving the money away, turning the company back to selling locally-made produce: toys, baskets, you know the kind of thing. Split-lip said something happened to Deming in Amsterdam. That's when it all changed.'

'Shit, Ng. Who the hell was he? I feel sick to my stomach when I think of my father.'

Ng paused at the other end of the phone. 'He was a Hong Kong businessman who got in too deep. Getting out cost him his life. He was naïve.'

'He was a triad,' said Mann. 'Once a triad always a triad. He should have known that. No one leaves a society. They killed him because he went against orders. They killed him because he tried to get out.'

Mann closed his phone, finished his drink, and asked Eric to call him a cab. He had one last place to go.

124

Mann took off his shoes and entered the temple in the grounds of the Enlightenment Centre. The monk smiled at him as he entered and greeted him with a small bow of the head. Mann bowed low.

'I have come to say thank you.' The monk studied Mann and smiled.

'You have come far on your journey.'

'Yes.'

'Walk with me.' The monk got slowly up from his seat and walked out of the temple. Mann followed. The sun beat down on them, the sky was azure blue.

'Remember, Johnny Mann.' The monk turned to him and smiled. 'Holding on to anger is like holding on to a hot coal – you are the one who is burned.'

The old woman was there again, with the baskets of birds. She stepped into Mann's path and held up a basket with a dusty sparrow, flapping its wings in distress.

Mann looked at her and nodded. She opened the cage and the bird flew up and away into the cloudless sky.

'Free bird, free soul.'

125

'How is she?'

Mann waited with Alfie in the kitchen as Jake went into the bedroom to see his mum. He had been in there for over an hour.

'She has hung on just long enough. It was as if the minute she knew he was safe, she let go. She has only a few days left now.'

'I'm sorry, Alfie.'

Alfie took a deep breath and nodded. His eyes were red-rimmed. His shoulders rose and fell as he began to cry and then he stopped himself. He stood and went to the window to look out. The trees had all come into blossom on the street outside.

Jake appeared in the doorway. His face was stained with tears.

'Mum wants to see you, Johnny.'

Mann gave Jake a hug as he passed him.

Magda was in her bed. She had lost a lot of weight. Her cheeks were hollowed, her eyes sunken and dark.

She smiled at him. He sat beside her on the bed.

'Thank you, Johnny. Are you okay?' He had a lump

in his throat and couldn't answer. Her face was ashen. The silk scarf around her head was pale blue like her eyes. They seemed to reflect a sky in some distant world. He nodded and tried a smile. She wasn't buying it. She put her hand on his. 'This has been so difficult for you, I know. To find out so many things about your father, a lot of them not good. I understand how you must feel. I have felt it too. I have thought about it over and over. Who was Deming? Who was he really? I wanted to make sense of it before I die.' She thought for a few seconds before continuing. 'I realised that I only knew a part of him. But that part was good. And maybe you can't ask to know everything about everyone. You can't and you shouldn't. Everyone needs their secrets. Do you think you will be able to forgive him?'

Mann looked down as he thought about the answer and he shook his head.

'I just don't know, Magda. I despise triads with every bone in my body. To find that Deming was one, albeit one who tried to change, it's going to take time for me to get my head around it.'

'Please try for Jake's sake and for mine.'

He nodded and looked into her eyes, cloudy as the early morning mist veiling a blue summer's day. 'The one thing I am certain about, Magda, is that Deming loved you. You are the reason why he wanted to change. You and the boys were the reason why he wanted to stop being a triad.'

'And the reason he was killed?'

Mann shrugged. 'It was his choice, Magda, he played with fire and he got burned. But then we wouldn't be sat here now if he hadn't, would we?' He smiled at her concerned face. 'And I am very glad to have known you and proud to have Jake as my brother.'

She squeezed his hand and she sighed and her eyes went to the open window; the scent of spring was in the air.

'I am so scared of dying, Johnny.'

He shook his head. He fought hard to stay in control of his emotions. He took a deep breath and took her hand in both of his as he smiled at her.

'Let me tell you something, Magda. When I was dying in the jungle I had a dream. I saw Daniel in that dream. He came to bring me back to the living. He wanted to show me that he was content, he was happy. He will be watching and waiting for you. Don't be scared.'

Magda turned away as a tear trickled from the corner of her eye and she listened to the sound of children playing on the street below. Then she turned back and smiled.

'Thank you, Johnny.'

Mann got up to leave. He leaned forward and kissed her forehead as he whispered: 'Bye, Magda.'

Magda looked up at him, her eyes swimming with tears. 'Jake's going to need you when I'm gone, Johnny.'

Mann nodded and swallowed hard.

'And I will always be there for him, Magda; he's my brother.'

454

Read on for an exclusive extract of Lee Weeks's new novel coming in 2010

She made him hard in the elevator. She stood in front of him and rubbed her pert bottom up against his crotch. He loved the way she had turned from a shy schoolgirl into a rampant sex goddess in a blink.

He felt his excitement surge. What was it about having sex with strangers? He had a wife at home, nice house, nice car, he was happy. The kids, Ben and Belinda, would be at school now, different time zone, different world. He snapped that side of his mind shut. He mustn't think of that now. He was here, in this lift, waiting to reach the eighteenth floor and his hotel room, waiting to have sex with a girl he'd met in the hotel bar. This was his world. Here on one more business trip. Here where no one knew him. He liked to think it enriched his marriage. He liked to think of himself as clever for leading two lives. His wife would never know, no one would. How could they on the opposite side of the world? Tonight he was in Hong Kong, tomorrow he would be in China. Wednesday he would be in Sydney and then Singapore on the way home to the UK. He pulled her to him and made sure she felt his hard cock pressing against her. She giggled again. The Asian women liked to giggle like school girls, tottering along on the balls of their small feet. The Asian women did as they were told.

The girl felt his heat, it was making her head itch and the wig was becoming uncomfortable. She kept her eyes down. She knew where the camera was. She couldn't risk anyone seeing her face. She reached her hand behind and squeezed his cock lightly, through the fabric of his trousers. She smiled to herself as she felt its wide girth. That would be the last thing she would cut from his dying body.

What's next?

Tell us the name of an author you love

Lee Weeks | Go ▶

and we'll find your next great book.

book army

www.bookarmy.com